Dear Audrey,

Best!

Kevin hoho

GOLGOTHA

THE THORNBEARER CHRONICLES

KEVIN LOBO

TUNDRA
WOLF
PUBLICATIONS

First published 2017
Canada

Library and Archives Canada Cataloguing in Publication

Lobo, Kevin, 1966-, author
    Golgotha / Kevin Lobo.

(The thornbearer chronicles ; book 1)
Issued in print and electronic formats.
ISBN 978-0-9865053-5-5 (hardcover).--ISBN 978-0-9865053-6-2 (softcover).--
ISBN 978-0-9865053-7-9 (PDF)

    I. Title.

PS8623.O2G65 2016   **C813'.6**   **C2017-900088-8**
                                                    C2017-900089-6

TUNDRA WOLF PUBLICATIONS

5 LANARK AVENUE TORONTO,

ONTARIO M6C 2B2

Publisher: Tundra Wolf Publications

www.tundrawolfpublications.com

lobokev@gmail.com

For Daddy,

With gratitude and affection,

for the gift of my life,

and my faith.

Acknowledgements

The author gratefully acknowledges the following persons for their help, suggestions, edits, criticism, review and support in the production of this book.

Stanley Shen

Gavin Barrett

Amelia Mckechnie

Author's note

I am a dreamer – always dreaming of fantasy battles between heaven and hell - good and evil. To have seen my Lord and Saviour, Jesus Christ, walk this earth in person, 2000 years ago, is my ultimate fantasy. That will not happen; so I created this fictional work and linked up Good Friday, that greatest day in the history of the earth, to our current world.

On this journey you'll meet Daniel, Amanda, the mad-preaching man, the hooded figure, Fr. Brian, Yokatherine, Officer Terri, Officer Clare, the Romans and the Pharisees, and many others. All of these characters were born out of that fantasy in my head.

Thus far they exist only in my dream world, and at the end of the book, hopefully, in your wild imagination too. After journeying through this tale you may really want to meet them, sorry, they don't exist in real life. I am hopeful that Hollywood will bring them to life.

If you find a resemblance to names, people, characters, businesses, locations, places, events and incidents, they are either the products of my imagination or used in a fictitious manner. Any resemblance to actual persons, living or dead, or actual events is purely coincidental.

You will find some explicit language. It's just a true-to-life representation of the way the world speaks today. This book is recommended for those 16 years old and over.

TABLE OF CONTENTS

The Thornbearers

The foreboding Gethsemane hours

The 6th - 9th hours, Hell's battle

Easter

The

Thornbearers

I

Daniel

"They've killed him – They've killed him – They've crucified my Lord." The high-pitched scream burst its way through the closing double glass doors. Daniel looked around stunned – his hair stood on end. Strangely, no one else reacted.

"Repent – your sins killed him." The shriek turned into a loud sobbing wail. A gust of wind held back the outer glass doors for a second longer before the auto hinge slammed it shut. Daniel caught the faint ending of another cry before the din of the busy Tim Hortons drowned out the brief moment of disturbance – "....the Lord is coming."

The words still echoed in his ears like a haunting scream from another world. Daniel swung around on the tall circular stool. "What the...," he muttered looking around surprised at the crammed coffee shop that stretched deep within. There seemed to be a million people in there – laughing and chatting. "Whatever happened to the good old, 'where are the people?'" thought he muttered. As a new immigrant, that peculiar sight always crossed his mind when he looked at the empty Canadian streets.

"Weird, where could it have come from?" he wondered staring silently into his cup again. "The cry came through the door, stupid!" a light bulb went off in his head. Daniel stared out through the glass panes. The bright March midday Toronto winter sunshine was misleading – it was cold, bitterly cold – thanks to the frigid Arctic winds.

"Damn Old-Man-Winter," he sighed.

"Yes, damn Old-Man-Winter," a heavily accented female voice whispered in his ear. It seemed too close. "East European," he thought. A garishly dressed lady in bright orange pants, a golden yellow shirt buttoned down with a jazzy black bra sticking out was pushing her way through.

"Lord help me," he pleaded as she thrust herself into that last seat between him and the wall. He reached out to warn her about the little iPad wielding kid that nearly got smashed into the wall against her rear that extended nearly a mile out.

"Stupid kids," she cursed as the kid fled, "don't buy anything – simply hang out for nothing."

"It's for the free Wi-Fi," Daniel answered using all his will power to look straight into her face. The breasts exploded in his face – the jazzy golden jewelry flashing their way down the ravine that Daniel blinked against. It tested all of Daniel's resilience not to look straight down her bosom. Aghast, he turned away. "…lead us not into temptation, but deliver us from…." the prayer was never completed.

"Oh sweetie, you can look down," she laughed, bending over generously, "see, your cup is empty – can I get you another – or whatever it is you need today…" she left the sentence unsaid with a wink. Her hand slid down Daniel's back in the smoothest of caresses.

"Why me, Lord?" he prayed silently again, "surely not on this the holiest of days." The tension, the throbbing, and the pounding heart erupted again. This time he was a little surer of its source as the dark hooded man passed once more. That strange, evil, foreboding had haunted him all night. The man's head was bowed, yet Daniel felt a gaze pierce him. Panic seized him and he held his chest as if his heart would explode any minute. "I have to talk to Dr. Fisher," he swore, "or just pray, pray and pray."

"You said something, darling?" she reached out and gently placed her left hand around his shoulders as her right hand casually dropped into his lap. He froze as the firm mass of her breast bored into him.

"My God, not her breast – not today, Lord," his mind screamed as her mobile rang. "Britney *bitch* – scream and shout," the ringtone wailed. The cell phone got her busy and Daniel sighed in relief.

"An early Lent – over so soon – and this of all the things on Good Friday, damn it," Daniel muttered angrily.

"Ya – damn it. Why did Lent have to come so early this year too?" a hot coffee breath hissed in his left ear, "seriously – nearly a month early." The weight of a heavy muscular arm crashing onto his left shoulder nearly broke it. "Gotcha!" the coffee breath hissed – this time in his right ear. A guttural laugh – thrilled at its silly old trick of having got him to turn the wrong way.

"Marco!" Daniel feigned a happy surprise, "how nice to see you."

"Ya – nice to see you too, my friend," Marco leaned close, in a near hug. Daniel looked away fast – nearly throwing up. Somewhere from deep within the old man's stomach, the pungent odor of garlic hit him in the face.

"You know, Marco, Dracula would come nowhere close to you," Daniel muttered sarcastically; feeling remorseful instantly for the comment.

"Totally agree, brother, I pray a lot," the old man answered, oblivious of the sarcasm. Daniel froze. Marco was pushing his way to the end of the bar stools that looked out onto the street. There was just one seat between him and the wall – occupied by the garish lady. Marco was headed for it. The panic in his head shot up in a near explosion. A fight this close – it was the last thing he needed.

"Wanna sit in my lap, ya?" the woman in the seat exploded – nearly slapping Marco as his big beefy arm fell in her lap. The heavy East European accent let out a litany of profanities. A drop of sweat trickled down Daniel's brow.

The throbbing started again. "Darn," he muttered, again finding the source of the sudden panic that had sent his heart once again into a wild thudding that threatened to explode in his chest. Suddenly he was not so sure about the source as a strange dark shadow blanked him out. Was he passing out or was it – and then he saw the mysterious dark hooded figure turn and walk away hurriedly.

"The lap would be great, big girl – if it wasn't Good Friday today," Marco's grin stretched from ear to ear.

"Bloody hypocrite – here take this," the woman screamed and grabbed Marco's arm thrusting it into the unending chasm of her bosom.

"Oh glorious rack," Marco took off in glee before catching himself, "curse you, woman," he screamed, reluctantly pulling his hand away.

Daniel was about to grab his empty cup and run when Marco and the woman broke into delirious laughter, hugging wildly. "She's a hot one – this big girl here," Marco muttered suddenly lowering his voice and cautiously glancing back at the busy interior of the Tim Hortons.

"Silvana is in there, you know," Daniel teased. Marco froze at the mention of his wife.

"Nooo – ah – you had me there. She's in church today – won't leave till she's shed every tear," he said relaxing a bit.

"Obviously, praying for your rotten soul," Daniel teased.

"Gotta go, darlings," the colorful woman suddenly purred and got up – pushing her way out, as a shiny black Mercedes pulled up outside the coffee shop. Smack, the kiss on Marco's cheek echoed leaving a heavy, dark imprint of a bright lipstick. Daniel pressed forward hard into the little shelf-like table against the outer glass to avoid another brush from the breasts. "You give this baby my number, darling."

She winked at Marco hugging Daniel from the back. The door opened and once more the voice burst in.

"Repent, the Lord's hour is at hand."

"Darn, not again," Daniel groaned as the voice from outside shocked him back from the messy conversation with Marco and the woman. The din got louder inside. Daniel turned back and looked. The narrow coffee shop stretched a long way inside. Little circular tables lined the café on one side and little booth like tables and benches on the other side. All were crammed. A little wave from one of the tables made Daniel gulp. The little circular table near the counter was jammed with teens from the parish. "Nathan, Ethan, Kimberly --," he waved back hesitantly – had they seen that little episode with the whore? "Whoops! Sorry, My Lord – didn't mean to judge her." The kids waved back.

"Nice kids," Marco burped loudly not bothering to cover his mouth.

"Yup – great kids – always ready to do collections, readings, cleaning --,"

"Do you know they serve the Sunday masses as well?"

"I know, but what were you doing back in church on Sunday? Saturday liturgy not enough for you?" Daniel asked.

The old man blushed, "I like the women at the Sunday Masses – truly beautiful – Saturday is too sleepy."

"You dirty, old dog." Daniel laughed this time at the old man, nearly slapping him back, till more of the garlic breath hit him in the face. "And you plan to lend a shoulder to the Pieta for the procession this evening?" Daniel chided.

The old man's face fell, "I'm a good man you know."

"I know," Daniel replied turning back to the kids. Two more joined them – Filipinos. "I like them," he thought to himself remembering the hundreds of teens that

passed through his hands in the Confirmation classes at the
parish, "future Catholic adults," he smiled proudly. The
newcomers, girls, happily squeezed onto the laps of the boys
– something said in Tagalog got them roaring with laughter.

"Would you like some more coffee, old man?"
Daniel offered, finally deciding that a refill would not break
his fasting resolution. The aroma of the donuts, scones,
Danishes and toasted bagels swirling in the air, was
tempting. The one hot chocolate was all he had had that
day. A second one to pass the time would be great as every
possible baked delicacy did a tempting dance in his head.
Someone waved from the line.

"My friend, Daniel, Ola! A coffee for you, amigo?"
a voice called from the line that stretched just past the
circular tables. Daniel strained – the Latino voice sounded
familiar. "Darn, if only I could remember the names." The
bright sunshine outside faded from his brain as the dull
interior came into focus.

"Gabriel," the name suddenly popped into his head,
"sure Gabe, make it a hot chocolate, please – but I'll --,"

"No, you gonna stay right there, amigo – my treat."
Daniel nodded and turned back. A heavy rattling of tongues
took over from where Gabriel left off. Daniel closed his
eyes and soaked in the sounds. The heavily accented Spanish
from the Latino tongues touched a sweet cord somewhere
inside.

"It's like their talk is poetry," he remembered telling
Michelle almost regretting the words as they lay in bed one
day. It had messed things up instantly after a most beautiful
morning.

"So, you've been eyeing those Latino women?"

"Latinas!" he corrected teasingly. Michelle's color
went a deeper red. Daniel knew the time for messing around
was over. "For God's sake no – I was talking about all
Latinos and the way they speak."

"And what about the women?"

"Woman or women? Oh, my beautiful, jealous wife. They are my hardest praying friends with the deepest faith. But, I get it; it's because of one woman, Arianna, hmmm?"

"Ya! She always wears bikinis tops under see through shirts and makes sure she always sits in the front of us." Michelle muttered angrily lifting herself onto an elbow no more thrilled with her own nakedness – pulling the sheets over.

"Just her, how about my friends Maria and Lucia, always with a scarf and always praying for everyone." He realized it wasn't working. "You look so good when you are angry," he said brushing back her thick black hair.

"Don't change the subject," she slapped his hand away.

"Someone is jealous."

"Don't you dare."

"Ok, we'll changes places, and how about you do that for me – in Punta Cana only – polka dotted bikini top under a white --," he teased till they had both fallen back laughing.

"A hot chocolate for the senor," Gabriel's hand shot through. Daniel pulled himself out of his thoughts with half a smile. "The senor remembers something good?"

"No Gabe, just a passing thought. I have to pay --,"

"Don't even think about it – your roof ok, senor?"

"Perfect Gabe – you did the best job ever."

"Gracias," the Colombian beamed, "you're a good man, senor."

"No, he isn't," Marco teased from the other side.

"Amigo, there were chilled bottles of water and pop every hour last summer when we worked on his roof," Gabriel said to Marco patting Daniel on the shoulder.

"It was the least I could do on a hot day like that. I don't know how you even managed to stay up there on those hot shingles."

"Hot shingles – do you know, senor, a day later I worked on a rich white lady's roof – she nearly called the cops on us because we took a long break."

"Cops?"

"Si – she threatened to report us as unlicensed aliens – asked to see our passport or SIN card."

"Toasted bagel with cream cheese – toasted bagel with cream cheese," the girl shouted from the counter.

"Coming," Gabriel yelled and ran to the counter.

"Nice man," Daniel said and turned back as a large group of old men burst in. "What's up with this place today," Daniel asked, "it is as if they can't withstand the austerity and silence of one holy day," he said.

"These are coming from the Spanish service," Marco answered. Daniel recognized some of the faces from his church down the street. "I guess when we're not praying, we're here drinking coffee," Marco laughed raising his cup.

"The crown of thorns tore into his skull – oh the pain," the voice burst in again just before the door closed.

Daniel looked outside, suddenly wanting to get away from the coffee shop. The laughter and celebration seemed to desecrate the sanctity of the day. His feet had been aching. He had been on his feet since 5 am that morning. Cleaning, decorating and mopping up the church hall. Daniel felt the multitude of languages hit his ear and looked out at the busy intersection – Dufferin and Eglinton.

"It's got to be one of the busiest intersections in Toronto," he said thoughtfully.

"It is," another crisp voice joined in.

"Hello, Sebastian."

"Daniel," the pure British-accented, Anglo-Saxon voice almost seemed alien in that place. Sebastian seemed to catch on. "Busy intersection, busy coffee shop, busy ethnicity," he laughed.

"Do you read minds?"

"No, but I sensed what startled you about my voice."

"Coming from choir practice?"

"No, just a prayer service," Sebastian answered, pulling off his dull, gray, muskrat, fur hat. A thick, ugly and shaggy mop of salt-and-pepper hair seemed an extension of the hat itself. Daniel was tempted to ask if a beaver lived in there. Sebastian was busy, vigorously ironing out the knots and shaking loose his damped down hair making everyone pull their coffee as far as they could. He wished Sebastian would put back the hat.

"He's just a rich, bland, middle-aged guy," Daniel remembered describing Sebastian to Michelle.

"Seriously – and – you're spicy?"

"Exotic. Kidding. No really, he seems to want to do all of the cool things in the church, except that, well, it just does not fit. Someday he'll find a gold digger, looking for a 'just-can't-land-a-gal-rich-guy'. They'll get married – win, win."

"So judgmental. Go for Confession," Michelle scolded.

"Sorry," Daniel replied with a laugh. He knew the middle-aged, devout man was single. He generally hung out with the prayer groups, Bible study groups, attended every single retreat, sponsored coffee for the various choirs and dabbled in a few instruments – yet never seemed to fit in anywhere.

"Would be nice to get a franchise like this," Daniel wished as he looked at the lineup. The old Spaniard gang had gotten into an argument right in the middle of the shop. "Not today," Daniel prayed. A woman with a stroller was pushing her way through – the old men hardly noticed or bothered.

"Why the *fuck* don't you leave the way clear?" the woman swore. Silence fell on the coffee shop – like a rapt audience waiting for the start of the next round. Everyone seemed to have been waiting for some sort of action to take a break from the chattering. Expectant faces waited eagerly as if the gladiators were about to draw their swords.

"You show them whose boss, miss," someone egged on the lady.

"Go Papa!" others shouted. It was just short of cheering on the old men and the woman in a real fight. The old men glared. "Stupid white trash," an older meaner looking man with a ponytail from the gang shouted as the men moved aside reluctantly. Daniel jumped off his stool. It suddenly seemed the perfect getaway. The woman was abusive – the men taunted back – the kids enjoyed the show gratefully. He reached the glass door just as the woman's stroller got there. The stroller had been well covered for the cold. Daniel looked through the transparent plastic cover and saw a sleeping, little bundle. "If only it was Christmas," he thought. He pulled open the door as the walker and then the woman passed through.

"Thanks, sweetie," she said with a tap on his arm. Daniel choked as the pungent odor of cigarettes followed the lady outside. Daniel was about to step out behind her when a throng came rushing through.

"Hi Daniel!" the girl at the head of the line beamed.

"Hello Fatima!" he wished the lanky Eritrean girl, continuing to hold the door.

"Repent, repent…" the voice was screaming outside.

"Oh, Hello. What time be Good Friday Mass in afternoon?" the mother with the fully wrapped headscarf and African-accented, broken English asked.

"Beautiful," he thought as a bright row of white teeth smiled from the round African face. "2.30 pm, and, it's not Mass, it's the reading of the --,"

"The crown of thorns tore into his skull – oh the pain," the voice was crying in agony – it was Jamaican.

"Oh, you were saying," the mother reached out gently held his chin and turned his face back to her. Embarrassed at her touch – he muttered.

"Sorry, it's just the reading of the Liturgy."

"Help the Lord. The burden of my sins," the voice outside wailed louder than ever. The woman's hand reached out again.

"Mom!" Fatima shouted. "Sorry about that, Daniel," she apologized for the mother in her spotless Canadian accent.

"No problem. Sorry I keep getting distracted by that voice out there," Daniel mumbled.

"Oh, he be madman," the mother laughed, "he be there for years – preaching – talking about fighting the devil."

"Really – how long have you been in Canada?"

"Oh, many 15 years since come – Fatima 13 now – she be born here," the mother answered proudly.

"Nice – I've been here just 10 years," Daniel added.

"Oh, really, and you be manage all that stuff in church!"

"Ah well, I come from an English-speaking country and a very Catholic background too," said Daniel.

"Oh, be India, right?" the mother asked curiously.

"Yes."

"But aren't be all Hindoooos live there."

"Yes, nearly 80% Hindus and many other religions too," he answered back, "but we Catholics blend in like yeast in the dough or like sugar in a cup of milk – enriching and sweetening everyone around us."

"Nice. Oh, is my Fatima be a good student?"

"Outstanding!" he lied, glaring at the African-Canadian girl with the braided hair and bright beads. They had stuck in his brain from the first moment – she was a talker. The teacher – a young university student volunteer had threatened to walk out if Fatima wasn't silenced. "We'll see you at church in the afternoon," he excused himself.

"Oh, see you. Oh, you be usher, ya?"

"Yes, Ma'am," he replied.

"Call me Miriam – and – save me seat on the last bench," the mother added with a big smile.

"MOM!" Fatima screamed, "gosh, she can be, like, so embarrassing." Daniel thought Fatima's face would burst in anger and embarrassment.

"Don't worry," he laughed remembering how he was no different with his mom. "Mom," it struck him suddenly, "guess you're with Jesus......"

"Jesus, my Lord Jesus. They crucified you, they killed you," the voice was in a mournful melancholic agony now. The heavy Jamaican accent was interrupted only by its own groans and moans that interlaced the shouts. Daniel involuntarily lets the door go. It flew in the face of a rather stern-faced, disciplinarian-like, old woman.

"It's almost as if he's feeling the pain," Daniel whispered with checked emotion.

"He's a sham. He'll be here for a free coffee and donut as soon as he has everyone's attention," the Tim Hortons girl in the brown pants, peach shirt, and hair net laughed gently holding his elbow as if to calm him. The old lady had dropped her shopping trolley in the passage between the two glass doors. Two teens were helping her. One held the door open and the other bent down to lift the handle up to her.

"Now don't you dare steal my cookies," the old woman shouted at the embarrassed kids. The girl continued to hold Daniel's hand. A naughty wink from Marco caught Daniel's eye.

"You seem to make the women want to touch you."

"Shut up, Marco," he barked as the girl moved on.

Daniel looked out hoping to catch a glimpse of the man. Instead, the dark shadow of the hooded man hovered all over the place. The Tim Hortons was on the southeast side – on Eglinton. An equally busy McDonald's adjacent to it was followed by a busy Esso gas station on the western corner. Traffic inevitably piled up at the intersection as both, the north-south and east-west bound TTC buses dropped and picked up their loads. Daniel moved to the wall near Marco and tried to look out as a bright red and white bus went east, blocking his vision. The old lady was finally through. The teen was about to let go off the door when Daniel heard the heavy thuds of fists on a chest – the dreadful sound hurt. The man was violently pounding his own chest. The panic was back – his head throbbed and his heart broke off into a dramatic beat.

"You've got the perfect pressure and pulse," the nurse at the Canadian Red Cross blood donation clinic always told him. "Not true today," he groaned, "help me, Jesus," he begged. Another thud of a fist on a body caught his attention as a high-pitched wail followed. Another westbound TTC bus pulled up on the opposite side – the beep-beep sound indicating the bus was lowering down. Daniel craned his neck trying to scan the busy intersection. People moved in droves in all directions. A group of young girls stopped outside the glass to finish off their delirious laughter.

"Beautiful," Marco intoned again.

"They're still kids for God's sake, Marco," he glared. He liked that tone of his voice – it had come from the many years of dealing with the students and their parents.

"Bossy," Michelle would tell him. The girls looked like they had just walked out of a rock concert.

"I bet they miss the glitzy malls, all closed today," Sebastian gently opined, "poor kids. No values and no substance."

"Youth, these days – bah," Marco grumbled. Daniel felt a tinge of sadness but dismissed the thoughts quickly – the voice had filled his mind. It was calling.

"Is that you, Lord?" the thought came almost naturally and Daniel gasped.

"The voice is definitely Jamaican," he mused.

"True," the two men next to him confirmed.

"And definitely a grownup's – a real man's voice."

"Again true," the two men hummed.

"Then, where the heck is he?" A smirk filled the space from behind them. A hot, tea breath glided through. Daniel turned, "William!" A bow and a nod as the old Chinese man smiled.

"You're looking for the Lord in the wrong place, young friend," William laughed. Marco joined in. Sebastian smiled. Daniel waited. "Down there," the old Chinese man pointed as the pretty, young girls disappeared, "is temptation – the Lord is up there," he said pointing a little higher up.

"No, no, up there," Marco boomed raising his hands to the skies.

"No!" this time it was a firm answer as the half-bent Chinese man straightened up – hand extended forward – slightly above his line of sight. Daniel looked straight ahead. The north-east corner was filling up quickly with people waiting for the next bus. Strollers, shopping carts, cell phones, headphones, jackets, parkas, boots, cigarettes and a multitude of colored faces filled his vision. He half turned back to see William Ng put a scarf around his neck. The hat looked rather British. Newspaper rolls stuck out from under his arms. "Crossword," Daniel asked, "no, let me guess, Sudoku?"

"All of that, my young friend, and the news too," the frail Chinese voice said, "but it's Good Friday – don't look for the Lord down there – a little higher – remember he came down but just to the cross and lifted us up there."

"Mr. William Ng --,"

"I know, I know – look across, that is no madman."

Daniel looked again, following Mr. Ng's hand closely. A retaining stone wall bordered the raised ground of a Christian church on the north-east corner opposite them. The well-dressed ladies that wandered out from there usually mingled with the crowds at the bus stop, distributing pamphlets and trying to talk them into coming into the church for a while. "I admire your evangelical spirit," he told one, many years ago, waiting to board a bus with a heavy sack of groceries on his back. Daniel pushed aside the thought and was about to start another scan when the tall figure on the wall – about 6 feet above the ground stood plainly in his sight. Daniel stared – and the man stared back – across the street – through the glass windows – straight into his soul.

"The Lord's hour is at hand!" the man proclaimed.

Daniel didn't need an open door. The words were coming through clearly like the sound of a little meditative waterfall in a silent church. Daniel's spirit rose above the din of the busy coffee shop. The man was tall, very tall. His dark skin shone in the daylight. His hair was a massive mop of unkempt hair. The bony face was striking and fierce. His long hands wove big loopy patterns in the air as he gesticulated wildly. He reminded Daniel of the tall, lanky and fearsome West Indian fast bowlers that ripped through the batting line-ups around the world when cricketing countries played them.

The man was shabby. A tattered, camouflaged winter coat came down to the knees. The pants were torn. Daniel couldn't tell if there were indeed any pants there or just some ragged robe that hung down below the hemline of the coat. A pair of torn leather boots covered the dancing feet. The feet moved all the time. Daniel wondered how the man didn't topple over – standing, jumping, pacing on that narrow ledge with the steep, grassy slope behind him. The hands were bare as was the head – no mitts – no hat. Daniel felt a chill sweep his own body. The forecast had called for frigid temperatures, -20C with wind chills of -35C. There was a gentle breeze – more of a brisk wind – whatever – he knew there was a severe wind-chill out there. The man should have been severely frostbitten by now. Another figure outside caught his attention,

"China man wants your attention, sir," a female voice sang out next to him.

"Not nice, Rebecca," he scolded the teen from the Confirmation class and looked out at Mr. Ng. Mr. Ng bowed and turned back to the man on the wall. For an instant, their eyes met and Mr. Ng walked on. A sudden wave of panic began to engulf Daniel again. He looked at his watch hurriedly. Was he late to be somewhere? "Calm down, calm down," he told himself closing his eyes and placing his hand on his chest in a bid to calm himself. Instead, the heavy thumping of his heart sent him into a well of panic again. Opening his eyes in desperation Daniel looked out and the horrifying image of a man in a dark hooded garb swept across the bus stop. The preaching man on the wall seemed to stop his screaming as a wild fury swept across his face. His eyes searched out the dark hooded man but the figure had disappeared. Something deep within warned Daniel there was more to the figure than he could fathom; a kind of connection between the hooded man and the stranger on the wall. It was almost as if in answer, the preaching man's voice on the wall screeched a warning, "Repent, repent; dark are the ways of the fallen angel – an evil that my Lord conquered."

Daniel ran to the door and yanked it open – desperation creeping in. A long line of people streaming in blocked him again. On the other side the man had gone wild – wilder – "Oh Lord, Oh Lord – it hurts!" he heard the painful yell. Daniel began to push his way through the narrow passage in between the double doors. Time was flying by and he suddenly felt like a prisoner in the coffee shop. It was nearly half an hour since he had been trying to make his escape from there.

"Easy, dude," a young white male scolded. Daniel stared back. "Eminem," his mind labeled the person, "sorry," he said to the young man for his folly again. The man and his friends smiled and moved aside. The voice outside was screaming now – ecstatically, "The Lord is here; heaven is at hand." The coffee shop laughed.

"Now be a good lad and take the madman a coffee, will you?" a group of seniors teased from the other glass panel.

Daniel pushed his way through as the man jumped off the wall. Daniel was nearly out of the outer door, when the drone of engines picked up. The signal had turned green, the traffic was moving and the man was running south, across the east-west traffic.

"Help the Lord, Help the Lord – the Romans are shoving the thorns deeper," the voice cried, as it got closer. Brakes slammed and horns blared as the man danced across the moving traffic. Another horn blared angrily, as the man screamed – "One in the skull – Oh Lord – did that thorn go straight into your skull?" The man danced two more steps past the westbound traffic – into the eastbound lanes coming through the signal.

A speeding pickup truck suddenly burst ahead. The bonnet of the truck struck, lifting the man's tall body into the air – suspended – as if in a still shot. Daniel saw the cab strike the horizontally, suspended body a second time. The squishing of tires shocked Daniel. It should have been a screeching of brakes-locked wheels. Someone was intentionally slamming down on the accelerator. He saw the driver's face. It was filled with a wild frenzy, eyes bulging with murder, swearing, and cursing. The driver yanked the steering wheel to pull away. The turning truck hurled the body towards the sidewalk. The car following the truck braked hard as the truck spun around trying to speed away on the icy road. It was too late. The cars rear-ended into a continuous line with massive metallic thuds; the slippery conditions taking away the slightest chance of stopping. Horns blared and screams rent the air as two of the cars flipped over onto the westbound lanes causing another long pile up on the other side as well. In the blink of an eye, a dozen cars on either side lay crushed in an unending chain.

Thud, thud, crash – the sound was surreal – Daniel was back in the demolition derby as the sound of cars slamming into each other filled the air. Horns blared. Horrid screams rent the air as one of the cars flipped over and crushed the little TTC bus shelter.

"Oh *shit*!" someone yelled as the man's body came flying through the air and landed on the sidewalk outside the Tim Hortons. Daniel tried desperately to dismiss the sound of that crashing body on concrete – it stuck – he knew it would haunt him forever. The coffee shop erupted with a cacophony of voices. The men rushed out, the women screamed and Marco swore. Daniel was back in the packed commuter trains in Mumbai during rush hour – the crowd was carrying him out.

The preaching man lay groaning on his back in a pool of blood. In the blink of an eye, the busy intersection was a mess and had already filled up with traffic. Daniel was sure the wails of approaching sirens would begin soon as people reached for their phones. "Better be fast," he thought. A leap over the little iron rail and he was kneeling next to the man. The sound of the bone cracking on concrete still rang in his ear.

A sudden swishing sound behind him startled him. Turning around Daniel stared into a black figure and nearly fell back in fright. Another scan – it wasn't the dark hooded man. Instead, Daniel gasped in amazement at the slender figure shooting them with a large camera. Their eyes met and Daniel felt his body erupt in a wild frenzy as the stunningly beautiful face stared back at him. Deep within, that face framed itself in his heart, or mind, or soul, he could not tell. A word, a feeling, an emotion – something seemed to find its way to his tongue but the man on the ground groaned in pain and Daniel turned back to the man on the ground.

The teary red eyes bulged open as if they were fighting to be freed from their sockets. The shabby and ragged man strangely smelled sweet – fragrant. Daniel lifted his hand from the sidewalk where it had come to rest next to the man – it came away sticky and wet – and red. The man miraculously leaped up again. The crowd fell back. "To the Lord's house," the man shouted and ran east. A bunch of wild teens emerged from the McDonald's next door and instantly took on the fallen man with their taunting shouts. Daniel felt his temper rise but something else caught his attention.

"What the – die you cursed one?" he heard an eerie scream and knew instantly the haunting voice that echoed through the crowd somehow seemed to belong to the evil he had sensed emanating from the dark hooded man. A wild chaos filled the intersection – it looked like a picture perfect Hollywood doomsday thriller scene.

Daniel ran after the man – and then a light bulb
went on – the Lord's house – his own church was a bare
200 meters east on Eglinton. The man had been struck and
flung, across two lanes of traffic, onto the sidewalk. There
was no way he could run – but the man sprinted. He was
huge – his strides large – a dying man with some unknown
surge of heavenly energy to get to the Lord's house – he ran
faster. Daniel followed. Large red blotches left a trail behind
the bleeding man. The shabby high-rise, the vegetable-
strewn grocery market, and the Maria Shuka Library, all
blazed past Daniel as if he were in a speeding car. The
crowd followed. They crossed the shabby little strip mall.
The man tripped over a pile of large black garbage bags. He
nearly hit the ground, but managed to pull himself back up.
Just when Daniel thought the man would collapse, he stood
up straight, as if powered by some super energy and carried
on.

"Darn," Daniel cursed, wondering if that large pile
of garbage came from the bars and restaurants around
where beer-guzzling patrons hung out on the patios. The
stumbling stranger reached the foot of the west side
concrete steps leading up to the church and collapsed. 15
seconds later Daniel reached the large frame of the man
lying face down. The head was turned to the right – the eyes
were shut.

Daniel felt drawn to the man by an unknown
power. Something about their destinies being tied together
seemed to dawn somewhere deep in his thoughts.

"Just one more time – rise up, brother," he called
and nearly felt silly as the crowd began to huddle around.

"Stupid man is dead," someone called from the
crowd.

"Right after all that mess he created," another
added.

Daniel bent low over the man. "This is not the end – this a new beginning," he heard the faint words slip out of his mind, or was it for real, he could not tell. To his shock, the man stirred.

"My end – your beginning," a faint voice whispered. He tried to rise but the futility of the attempt seemed evident. Daniel noticed another desperate gasp and the man collapsed again.

"Hello 9-1-1," Daniel heard the voice of the nearest man that followed them, "what – yes – he is down – what – yes a pickup truck – what – blood – yes – lots – a whole trail."

Daniel shut out the voice and knelt beside the fallen man gently helping him turn over. A peaceful repose filled the man. The bulging eyes lay back – deep in their sockets. Daniel had never seen an African man this close – the shut eyelids were dark, glistening with sweat, the smooth shade of the skin was startling – as if a delicate eyeshade had been painted across.

Reluctantly Daniel reached out his left hand and raised the head that rested on the concrete. The touch of the damp fuzzy hair felt strange. Daniel pushed his hand deeper under the head gently lifting it. A painful groan escaped the closed mouth that had fallen silent. Daniel felt his hand wet – the head was soaked in blood. He slid his knee underneath the raised head like a pillow. The man groaned louder and sprang wide awake. The lips moved again in silent prayer. Daniel's right hand reached out and the man grabbed it in a firm, crunching grip. Daniel was sure a bone or two was about to be crushed with the strength of the grip.

The crowd had closed in as fierce yells all around filled the air. "Give him some space – give him some air," a voice commanded. It was the voice on the phone calling 9-1-1. Daniel was grateful for that voice. "Roberto – The General", his mind prompted, with a laugh. He knew that voice – the man ushered the 9.30 am Mass in strict military style. Michelle had named him, "The General." Daniel was grateful at the sound of that voice.

"Hold on, brother," he heard an unfamiliar voice escape his lips once again as the man spluttered and coughed up some blood.

"Jesus, Jesus – Oh Lord, how did you bear such pain?" the man cried.

"Easy, brother," Daniel instructed gently again, "stay silent – help in on the way."

The man stopped and opened his eyes wide. It was the same pair of eyes that had looked at him from across the street. The staring eyes looked beyond Daniel as a dark, deathly shadow fell over them. The man's bloody hand rose from the sidewalk in desperation and fell back.

"My brother in Christ, you are the one, I have to give it to you."

"Give me what?"

"For over 2000 years we have carried on the Lord's mission."

"We all have."

"No, my brother, you and I, we are part of the chosen ones," the man gasped. The words escaped his mouth like jets of hot lava spewing out of an erupting volcano. Daniel felt the powerful spirit of the man begin to engulf him. They seemed cocooned from the noisy crowd around them.

"We carry on the Lord's mission – straight from Calvary."

"We all do – take it easy now," Daniel tried to calm the man. Instead, he felt overpowered by a deep mystical spirit. The man's face lit up as if he was looking into a raging flame.

"From Calvary, the Lord gave us his mission, literally, to be a thorn in the side of evil. To never let it forget that the Lord died for our sins. That sin and death were conquered."

The man choked and spurted jets of hot blood. Daniel felt it in his face but did not flinch. The blood seemed to burn its way into his skin. There was a fire in it that grew like a burst of energy and filled his being.

The man continued. "For, as long as there is evil, the thorns that pierced his head will be a thorn in the side of the evil one."

Their eyes met. Daniel felt like he was in a hallowed presence. They were in a distant time and place – in a universe where everything came to a standstill. The sun darkened, the moon stood but like a faint shadow, the planets stopped and the stars looked down to bear testimony. Somewhere deep within, some scripture from the book of revelations about angels, dragons and demons played in the back of Daniel's mind, except that, it seemed real.

"The universe stopped that day, my friend," the man filled in, "the universe stopped to bear testimony to its master who was slain on the cross that day."

Suddenly Daniel knew – the time and the place. He felt like an insignificant speck of dust. Before him loomed a massive tower of energy that reached the heavens above. It stretched deep into the bowels of the earth and pierced the soul of evil. Daniel shivered as doubts racked his mind. The man seemed to understand.

"You will learn in time," he smiled in pain, "for now I give you this to carry."

The man struggled to raise himself – nothing moved. Daniel sensed the man was close to death. His body burned in pain yet his face was enchanted. The man made one last effort.

"Have to give you the Lord's…." he started.

The hand rose ever so slightly and fell back again.
The eyes stared and the voice seemed to scream but nothing
came forth. The body convulsed wildly once more. Daniel
stole a glance backwards and felt a scary, evil force try to
engulf them. The hooded man was reaching out for
something. To the other side, the ever-snapping shutter of
the black clad photographer seemed to be going nonstop.

"Never – Never – will you have it," the man on the
ground screamed and Daniel felt the evil one back away.

Daniel bent down further as the man's eyes closed
and the lips chanted furiously. Daniel tried to make out the
words on the lips but became aware of an intense mind-
numbing pain that shot through his own left hand.
Surprised he looked down – his left palm was still under the
man's head. His denims had taken on a dark color and the
ground below was red – a little pool of blood. Daniel tried
to adjust his hand under the man's head but a million
electric shocks bolted their way to his brain. He nearly
passed out with the pain.

The man opened his eyes and smiled looking up
into Daniel's face. Daniel tried again. Panic seized him as he
realized something had pierced his palm. Something from
the man's head had attached his hand to the man's head. He
tried to wriggle it free and the pain was back as he felt his
body drenched in a strange mixture of sweat and fragrance.

The man let out one more groan, "Take me home,
my Lord – let me die with you today." He tried to sit up and
a jet of blood from one of his slit wrists shot out. It struck a
clean, white Good Friday shirt.

"It's over for me," the man said looking up
ecstatically into Daniel's eyes, "it's yours now to carry."
Daniel shivered nearly beginning to feel he knew. The man
smiled and turned his head, "Just one thorn from the crown
that bored its way into the Lord's head."

Daniel felt the life quietly ease out of the man – and his own. His own crippled hand failed to hold the head. He was in shock – a daze locking him up. The man's head toppled to the left and fell back onto the sidewalk. Sirens wailed – brakes screeched. "He's here, he's here," Daniel heard Roberto shouting. He fell back and landed against one of the giant concrete planters. The hard, pimpled grains of rock embedded in the planter's sides felt soothing. He looked down fearfully at his left hand – it was shut – a little lightly – a loose fist. He felt the muscles in his palm straining as if they had been slashed causing the wrist to close up in a painful death curve. Daniel reached over with his right hand and forcefully opened out the little finger, fearful as if it would break away. It opened, and Daniel breathed a little easy. The other fingers followed painfully, each like brittle, frozen sticks protesting the opening motion. Gentle spasms began to rack his body, his left hand shivered violently as torrents of sweat poured out. Steadying it with his right hand, Daniel looked in the center of the palm. A black, pointed object protruded from the center of his palm. Daniel felt it gently with his right index finger. He swirled as he felt himself swept away in a wild vortex. "My Lord, My Lord," his mind chanted furiously shivering with pain. The base of a single, large, black thorn jutted out from the center of his palm – it was ugly – it reminded him of the base of the horns on Satan's skull.

The skin had darkened around it. Daniel turned his hand over. A painful prick confirmed what he thought would be the on the other side. A bright, red haze filled Daniel's vision and he blanked out swimming in an ocean of blood, his vision blurred.

Daniel opened his hazy eyes – he seemed to be standing apart from the crowd. Confusion reigned. From every street around Daniel could see the emergency vehicles speeding in. Strangely the wailing sirens seemed silent –

everything was silent – the world moved slowly – as if in slow motion. A paramedic gently rolled him over.

"I'm fine," Daniel heard his voice answer, hiding his fist behind his back. He looked over at the screaming, preaching stranger. A peaceful gaze filled the dead face – "ecstatic actually," he corrected himself. The lips rested in a gentle smile as if he were still alive. The paramedics shook their heads, putting away their stethoscopes. They lifted him onto the stretcher and began to cover him up.

"Please, just one more minute," Daniel begged – he had to ask one final question.

"He's gone, friend," the paramedic with the wild pink dyed hair intoned back in a mechanical voice. Daniel rolled forward on to his knee and lowered his face close to the man just as the lady photographer in black did the same. A gentle fragrance from the dead man filled his senses just as a wild passion from his nearness to the young photographer made his body erupt. Daniel hoped the man would open his eyes one more time. Strangely, he was sure the lady wanted the same. The dead man didn't open his eyes – he didn't need to. Daniel knew deep inside what he carried embedded in his palm – a thorn – from the crown of thorns the Romans had rammed on to the Lord's head.

He felt the evil presence of the hooded man nearby yelling in anger. "Someone will pay," the voice pierced through the crowd. It was a low, hollow sound, like the rumble of an earthquake that had traveled beneath the ground.

The foreboding Gethsemane hours

II

Amanda

❧

A single beam of moonlight shone through the narrow gap in the broken blinds. Neither the brightness of its silver radiance, nor the angle of its reflection, seemed to have changed in the last ten minutes. It entered the room on the east side, through the single broken shaft of the aluminum blinds, traveled across the untidy desk piled with binders, crossed the little gap, barely enough for someone to slip their legs through, to the single bed where it finally ended its journey.

The darkness of the rest of the tiny room lay undisturbed by the bright, silvery glow that preferred to reflect on its set path. The bed on which it landed was the only spot where the light reflected off the sweat-drenched white half vest that the single occupant of the bed wore. The breasts underneath the soggy, white vest heaved back and forth in a rapid breathing motion. Each gust of the heavy breath made the sweat pour out of the body that lay drenched.

Somewhere under the pile of clothes stripped off at the foot of the bed, an iPhone chimed the hour – 2 little beeps – 2 am. The 2 am moon was completing its journey across the earth. Another 2-3 hours, and it would have safely gone to its rest after its journey across the weary western skies. For the occupant of the bed, a mental note recorded the 339th night of the 2 am rising – a weary torment for the unknown, wild power that sought to burst forth.

"*Bitch*," she cursed herself. "May I sleep now, Mr. Moon?" she asked aloud in the darkness. She could have screamed – not a soul would have stirred – there was no one in that deserted wing of the crumbling old brick building on Nelson Street off downtown Toronto. It helped. "Just talk out aloud," the shrink had said and that is what she had begun to do. She turned over facing the beam as a faint niggle of some muscle in her arched back complained. It had been sore ever since – from the many hours hunched over her Nikon, in the frigid temperatures, up in a lonely cabin in North Bay.

"Capture the bear – natural – as it breaks through that fence – SLR only – no flash," was the mission the man had given her. "A 1000 dollars a night for as long as you can stick it out there – 10,000 for the real shot if you get it." Amanda had stared at the man as she devoured the second of the Big Macs on the upper floor of the crowded McDonald's in Eaton Centre. It was a strange request that had followed an equally strange invite to meet in a burger joint in a crowded mall. Hundreds walked through that mall daily. The McDonald's was standing room only – most of the time.

"Dude, I could spend the rest of my life there and earn a 1000 bucks a night," Amanda challenged the man as she devoured the second Big Mac.

"For sure, miss. Trust me, a week and you'll flee – no one survives up there." That was when she thought beyond the money but the man seemed normal enough.

"You're not a wacko who'll come up – rape and enslave me, or hang me by the boobs for some strange sexual pleasure, or, will you?" Amanda retorted in her typical rebellious grunt that scared most normal men. The man sat stoic.

"Tell the cops your location and details – tell your friends – whatever. It will be just you, the lonely cottage up in the mountains, rations and a single hunting rifle to keep you company."

"A rifle?"

"Yes, a full, high-powered Winchester and enough ammo to hunt down an army."

"Dude, you expecting robbers or vampires?"

"Nope, just you and the bear – maybe some deer but alone up there the feel of the rifle butt and the cold gun metal is the most comforting thought."

Amanda downed the 2 burgers, large fries, golden hash browns, 2 apple pies and the hot chocolate in a single go. A free meal for a broke photographer didn't come too often.

"More coffee – sorry, hot chocolate?" the man offered. A big loud involuntary burp to which her hand reached up rather late was all that she managed in response. The little kiddies at the adjoining table clapped and burped in response. Amanda wished she could go over and smack them – and the mother. The woman had got on her nerves from the moment the noisy family had walked in.

"Let her listen," the man added casually sensing her thoughts. The woman unabashedly eavesdropped on every word of their conversation. "You do know how to shoot, do you?" he said aloud, drawing back her attention and scaring away the nosey woman. Amanda shook her head fearfully. The dread in her face was answer enough. "No worries – you'll learn," he said.

That first conversation played over and over again in Amanda's head each night since. She turned over in her dilapidated, little, moonlit bed under the steps – tucked in the corner of her little one room den if it could be called one. Someone had sealed off the narrow passage next to, and under the steps, added a ceiling, thrown in a tiny washroom at the end and let people like her, struggling through life, beg for it. "Stop," her mind screamed as she sought to reach for that picture that had nearly given her an orgasm. The moment of that shutter snapping rapidly, was glued in her brain forever. It's where she had lost her sleep.

"One more try, Mr. Moon," Amanda said as some faint recollection of the shutter snapping rapidly gave her a high, "one more try – to sleep."

Amanda turned and felt the damp bed and groaned in disgust. Its dampness brought out the sweat that had soaked through in the days since returning from the haunting mountain. In disgust, she peeled off the damp T-Shirt, flung it and felt the cool of the bed envelope her chest. The darkness of the corner under the steps helped as the faint stink of some beer spilled long ago crawled through the little, round, boulder cushion Bob had left her. "*Arse'ole*," she cursed and fell asleep as the thought of fleeing from her agonizing waking hours and the exhaustion of another sleepless night consumed her body.

Amanda was deep in slumber land when a distant howl of wolves in the wild tried to burst forth in her subconscious memory. It was always back to that night – the bear had come and gone – a decoy, but it was the wolves that had surrounded the cottage for a whole week. They had slowly encircled the lonely cottage high in the mountains. Like watchdogs left behind by the bear, they sat around – all day and all night. After a week, their long mournful howls to the moon, the constant gnashing of their teeth on the wood finally got to her. She had picked up the rifle not knowing a thing about it. It was in that moment she felt the memory of a long, forgotten instance resurface. Chucking the rifle, she had marched out – blood splattering everything, was all that she remembered, whose, she did not know. That was as far as her subconscious mind allowed her to go.

The next morning, the sound of a Jeep had come crashing through the side path. A few more meters and the Jeep would have gone over the edge crashing hundreds of feet below. It did not. The man knew the mountains well. She sensed his arrival had been well timed. "A week," he had said.

It was a long time since then. The whirring was back and Amanda jumped out of her bed. Her grandmother's old alarm clock under the bed was creating a racket. It had been designed, a full 50 years ago, to rattle ever so loudly that no one could possibly sleep through it.

"Morning already?" Amanda gazed through eyes that barely opened beyond a slit. On the other side, she could see the first glows of the dawn begin to light up the world. The little, metal, alarm clock fell from her hands and angrily burst into another loud, ringing racket. "Good morning, grandma," Amanda called out, completing her ritual, before finally getting the push button down firmly. "Oh grandma," she sighed remembering the warm cozy days in the country house away from her perpetually depressed mother.

"Another day to be defeated," she sighed and swung out of bed craving for something to put in her mouth – a coffee would be a luxury. Her own nakedness startled her as a cold shiver enveloped her body – how had she finally fallen asleep? The 2 am memory was too vivid.

The stained bathrobe came off the little radiator under the table by the window. The sneezes would come soon – Amanda waited, letting the warmth of the gown envelop her. The decade old, bunny slippers came on as Amanda hustled over to the window.

The blinds still worked. Bent and disfigured all along their length, a decade later the little aluminum plates responded with surprising agility to the pull of the cord. The massive construction site next to her old 5-storey Torontonian structure had grown rapidly. Barely 50 feet away, she had spent an entire day snapping the artful

structure as if it was the next big scoop for the Toronto Star
or the centerpiece for the Art Gallery of Ontario.

"How soon before they take ours down, old man?"
she would always ask the old janitor at the foot of the steps.
He would shake his head sadly and say, "I hope I'm gone by
then, miss."

Something felt strange. Despite the dull glow of the
dawn, the construction site was silent — they were early birds
usually. The long boom of the tower crane directly over her
building was still. "Not a Sunday for sure," she told herself,
"not another rotten Sunday to lie indoors in my hell and rot,
hungry." Something was different about the day. Odd
feelings of happiness and sadness engulfed her in turns. An
odd whim drove her to try and to squeeze open the old
copper latch in the stuck up wooden window with peeling
paint. It had been shut all winter. There was no way it was
going to budge.

Amanda was about to give up on it when another
wave of excitement and happiness engulfed her.
"Crackpot," she chided herself as she brought down the
heavy cardboard album on to the little unyielding latch. It
budged and the window swung open. "Coffee," she
squealed, "lovely, hot and roasted." Amanda thought she
was imagining it. No whiff of fresh hot coffee on a frigid
winter morning ever drifted by her little dump of a living
place. "Oh grandma," she sighed as another wave of sadness
engulfed her.

The memory of brilliantly, brewed coffee with fresh
hot sconces, laden with butter, handpicked berries, and
fresh baked apple pie lit her being. Life with grandma on the
farm was heaven. She had lost it a long time ago. She
wondered when the next man would share her dirty little
dump and the dilapidated little bed and get her some coffee,
in bed, from the Coffee Time on the corner of Nelson and
John. Her stomach growled in hunger. A twitch and then a

near spasm – she knew it was the craving of an empty stomach. She didn't even dare to reach up to the little shelf above the window. The cheap, Dollarama cookie tins were empty – long finished.

"Oh grandma," Amanda sighed again and fell back onto her bed as the desolation of her broke and empty life hit her. "No money, no friends, no job and no future – congrats, darling!" Amanda wished herself sarcastically and closed her eyes as her stomach cramped from hunger. "Cry and let it out," her doctor had said and so Amanda decided to try and weep for the moment.

She would have spent her morning that way had it not been for a knock a few moments later, and the smell of the hot coffee that was to once again change her life. The innocuous little knock nearly went unnoticed. Hundreds of rats ran through the old brick building at all hours.

"Some of them, darn jeepers, are as big as cats, miss, you watch out for them," the old janitor always warned. Another little knock and Amanda jumped out of her bed, shaking in fear, or was it excitement? A visitor? No one came up there – no one knocked. The second hesitant step towards the door brought the smell of the freshly brewed coffee. Whoever was bringing it had climbed up on the fire escape below her window. By the third step, Amanda was sprinting as the smell of the hot coffee penetrated her shoddy, little place.

"A take-five hot chocolate, a take-five hot coffee, hot scones with butter, apple pies and a dozen assorted donuts – pretty warm still," the hooded man announced through the door that Amanda had flung open. She stared.

"Man, did you just peek into my head?" she blurted.

"Not sure – but no fresh berries to pick around here, miss," he answered teasingly.

She expected it was probably Bob, back from another tour of duty in Afghanistan or Iraq – tired and desperate for any kind of sex. He could not manage it anywhere else. He took what he got despite the abuse she heaped on him – it was better than nothing. Instead, the cold hard eyes of the man under the hood smiled mockingly. She stared – the hat he wore in the McDonald's had seemed a lot more appealing.

"I could leave if you don't --," the hooded man reminded her of his presence as she stared. Silently Amanda grabbed the packages and stormed off to her little table. It was the McDonald's all over again.

The man seemed content to wait – watching her intently. The lips curved up slightly at the edges of his mouth. He pulled the only chair in the room away from the sunlight bursting through the open blinds and sat down. Amanda glanced again. The eyes felt eerie. At the McDonald's meeting, she thought again – he had seemed pretty normal.

"You wouldn't happen to be a Sith Lord?" she mumbled through a mouth full of the donut as she smeared the entire contents of a little butter capsule onto a scone with a plastic knife. "Red-eyed, Star-Wars Sith Lord?" she mumbled uneasily.

"Maybe," he laughed.

"You seem to be in a nice mood."

"I am - planned a few events for this special day."

"What's special about this day?"

"It's Friday!"

"Ah TGIF!"

"Close – as in a TGIGF."

"And what might that extra G be?" she asked feeling more normal at the regular conversation.

"G, as in Good."

"Good? Good, Good, Good as in …" Amanda thought for a moment over the acronym. "What's good about a Good Fri --," she barely finished her sentence and stopped. "OMG – it's Good Friday – as in the day --,"

"Never mind," the man cut her off angrily, "I need some good shots – still using that old camera of yours?"

Amanda felt her blood boil. The Nikon D2XS was her life, her passion and her future. "It's the best professional --,"

Amanda never finished her sentence as the bags in the hooded man's hand came out of his cape. Three big, glossy, white bags. Two steps and the bags were gently settled on her bed. "It's the latest Nikon, D4S."

The nearness of the man startled her. She stole a glance at him and looked away quickly. His unflinching gaze was fixed on her. Yet, she felt no fear. In that old desolate building with just a robe over her – Amanda quickly abandoned the thought. A distant memory of being a little child running out of the shower into a warm embrace, and the comfortable feeling of a hot towel, seemed to spring from somewhere. She dismissed the thought; there had never been a father in her life.

The hooded man stood a full two feet above her. As quickly as he had stepped forward, he stepped back into the shadows, away from the sunlight through her little window. Amanda was almost about to step away herself, when his shadow flipped past her bed. It was there for an instant – enough for her to see the little, black spikes shoot out from all over the shadow of the man's body.

Amanda froze – she had seen those spikes – somewhere, everywhere. They were in her pictures, all of them, from the mountain. Suddenly, like a sledgehammer crashing through a massive floor of concrete, it burst forth on her – there was a connection. The man seemed pleased. She was sure he meant her to make that connection.

"Dufferin and Eglinton – 7.30 am – start as soon as you can," he ordered with a steely glare from the door.

"I suppose the camera needs to be --,"

"It's yours."

"But I guess I'll still be --,"

"There's 10,000 in the bag and an outfit. Be a nice girl and bring me back what I need." There was a threat in the voice. He needed it – she had been commanded – there were no "ifs."

Amanda trembled as she heard his steps fade away in the wooden passage. The dirty, white, sweat-drenched vest from the night before still lay on the floor. With it, a night full of bad memories came flashing back until the aroma of the hot chocolate drew her back. In a flash, her world had changed again. She felt the three bags – they felt surreal – as if they had appeared there by magic. She screamed in delight. From another day of nothingness, her life had erupted again. A gulp of the hot chocolate and she was diving into the packet. The 10,000 came away with a yelp of delight. The feel of money felt good – her last pennies were long gone. The Salvation Army Soup Kitchen at Sherburne and Queen, and the Covenant House at Gerrard, had been her only options for a meal. The clothes and shoes she chucked aside, diving greedily into the camera bags.

The loser was gone and the passionate photographer was out. The bathrobe had long fallen away as the brand new Nikon D4S was unraveled. "Holy *Shit*," she whistled as the long lens emerged from its packing. "AF-S 80-400mm f/4.5-5.6 G ED VR Telephoto Zoom Lens," Amanda read the box and gasped. Like an expert at work, she fixed the long, telephoto lens on the Nikon. The construction site magically came into her room, as did the Paramount Theatre a little further away, at the corner of Richmond and John. Amanda changed shutter speeds and turned on the 15FS. Like magic, the Nikon responded with ease clicking the 15 rapid frames. A sudden burst of adrenaline with a brand new strap hanging across her naked breasts made her wish she was at the other end of the camera. One desperately hungry and broken day she had even considered the ever-open job offer at the Hooters at John and Nelson. An innate feeling of being born to rule put paid to that offer. On a whim, she strapped on the broad lens belt over her naked body and a feeling of power swept over her.

Amanda looked down at her body. At 22, a brunette, with a sleek mop of thick, long hair that she let Bob hang on to once, in the heat of their passion; a figure that made the rich businessmen that frequented the high end bars around her dump, tumble over, literally, and a face that her grandmother would call raunchy, she wondered how she could be single. Amanda felt a surge of new energy sweep over her body as she plugged in the battery chargers preparing for the day ahead.

"Welcome back, baby," she squealed and ran into her shower, "he'll get what he wants, and me is a winner!" Amanda had a long wait before the hot water reached the shower. She turned around and stared at the little vanity. The sunken eyes reminded her of the many hungry and depressed nights she had spent. Somewhere deep within a voice reminded her to be sad. "No way, *bitch*," Amanda scorned as the hot water finally enveloped her excited body. Something seemed to align. Until now, nothing had been right about her life anyway.

An hour later, the young woman that walked off the last flight of steps, could have been mistaken for a movie star – stepping out of a limo, onto the red carpet for the Oscars at the Dolby theater. Amanda's black hair was combed down, dried and straightened, as much as she could manage. A dark lipstick and mascara, and the deep, blood red eye shadow, was shocking. The dark, black lipstick magnified the red. Black and red – something in the man's appearance had inspired that look for the day – an all-black and red day. The low-cut, black blouse over the long, black, woolen, figure-hugging skirt, finished with tall, knee-high, black leather boots – all from the bags the hooded man had left her were a perfect fit. He had given her a new lease on life and she would get him the picture he needed.

Amanda dumped two shiny Nikon bags at the door. The old man smiled. Rain, shine or snow – he was always there. The old man and his sleeping bag lived by that door. Four leftover donuts, two scones and a couple of cups of coffee, brought a big, toothy grin. She knew he starved just as much as she did.

"Morning, miss – may an old man say how stunning you look!"

It startled her, "Thank you!"

He opened the bags, "Didn't see these in your hands last night, miss. Where'd they come from?"

"The hooded man."

"Really, which one?"

"The one that probably left a short while ago."

"Been here every minute, miss. No man came nor left."

Amanda thought for a second. The depressing feelings fought to gain ground. "You're not allowed to be happy or carefree," she reminded herself. Her mind searched for a reason to sink back into its depression again, as if it was all an illusion.

Amanda drew out the brand new Nikon D4S and felt its ridged sides. It had been hard trying to put away her old Nikon D2XS – she had slung it on for old times' sake. It was a brand new morning – a brand new start. She had to banish the loser with all its feelings and attachments.

"We can do it, Amanda," she told herself.

Drawing up the D4S, she looked into the cragged face of the old man – set it to rapid speed and pressed the trigger. The sexual feeling was back.

"Tell me again, Pa – how do I look?" The creases of age on the man's face made a delicate mosaic in her lens – click, click, click, click, click, click, click, click, click, click.

The man stared – "Pa – Bless you, child."

Amanda waited – the man's emotional voice creaked through a choked throat. She tossed him a few $20 bills.

"Get yourself a nice beer and some grub."

"You look lovely, child – what will you shoot today?"

"Life and death," Amanda answered not knowing where her mind had picked that answer. She tightened her scarf and pulled on the black, sleek leather jacket the packet had held. She did not care where the hooded man had come from or disappeared to – she had a picture to shoot.

III

Trisha

"You've not said much today."

"Hmmm…."

"And you've not touched the donut either."

"Hmmm…."

"It's your favorite – Honey Cruller."

"Hmmm…."

"Please, say something."

Trisha did not mumble her answer this time. She simply snuggled deeper into Ezekiel, her head barely reaching his chin. She liked it that way. Barely 16 and half way through high school, she always wanted a tall boyfriend. At 6 feet and a couple of inches, that still seemed to be increasing, Ezekiel 17, had easily swept her off her feet. Being on the football, rugby and basketball teams were bonuses. It had not been a slam-dunk though. With a big mop of golden hair, sky blue eyes and an angelic face, Trisha was the one on top of every boy's list. Their matchup though, was a given. When it happened, every other teen, boy and girl, simply shrugged, accepted defeat and carried on their pursuit for some other.

"A bagel maybe?" Ezekiel tried again.

She simply shook her head. Her wavy blond hair enjoying the soft feel of his chin. She broke away suddenly and felt his chin with her hands. It was smooth – as smooth as hers was. She giggled and then burst out laughing.

"It will come, I mean grow, dammit," he protested.

"Soon, ya think?" she asked trying hard to control the giggle threatening to break out.

"Yeah – very soon and then you'll complain how rough it is."

Trisha burst out laughing nearly knocking over the hot coffee in front of her. Though a year younger, she looked older than he did despite their height difference and his massive build.

"Thank goodness God designed us to mature faster than you bums," she teased again, "maybe that's why I --," she trailed off thoughtfully and fell silent again before finishing her sentence. The mournful looked returned.

Ezekiel squeezed her tight. Her sadness seemed to permeate his being. The closer she snuck in, the sadder he felt. A long, helpless sigh escaped his lips. "Ah well," he kissed her on the head, burrowing through the big mop of hair and idly stared out.

The neon lights in the coffee shop looked dull compared to the bright sunshine that radiated through the big glass panes that covered the front of the coffee shop. People streamed in and out of the busy coffee shop. It was a busy place. Ezekiel was thankful for the quietness that pervaded the back of the coffee shop. The little table in the dark corner kept them safe from the prying eyes of the tons of people who would probably recognize them.

Ezekiel longed for the action of Trisha's bedroom. The thought of her doll-covered, pink bed suddenly had his heart pondering – racing. He stirred within.

"Your place?" he asked with a mischievous grin.

"My place is jammed," Trisha retorted angrily, "my dad's work buddies are camped all over the house."

"Doesn't your mom object?"

"They're both equally bad – there's stale food and smoke everywhere. It's supposedly some religious day."

"Good Friday," Ezekiel corrected.

"Whatever – and the liquor bottles are half downed already."

"Maybe you can try to --,"

"Don't even go there," she snapped.

"But they're the nicest people," he tried. He knew she loved them despite her earlier protest.

"Simply because they let us hang out in my room with the door shut?"

"Yes," he blushed and knew it was a mistake.

She tore away from him angrily. "Maybe if they were stricter with a little more morals, or, like, just plain damn strict, this would not have happened." Ezekiel felt defeated again.

"Damn, if only I could go back to before that," she sighed.

"You enjoyed it!"

"That's the sad part."

"Then why grumble?"

"You, dumb idiot," there was venom in her tone now, "our worlds are going to explode and that's all what you can think of?" she burst forth at him. The granny with the little infant in the walker jumped with a start at Trisha's outburst.

"Sorry," Trisha apologized, "hope I didn't disturb the baby."

"No worries, sweetie – he sleeps all the time. A good feed is all he needs," the granny replied.

"Grandchild?" Trisha asked innocently, instantly regretting the question, "sorry, I didn't mean to pry."

"Oh, no worries, child. I am only the nanny; the poor mother is working."

"But today is a holiday."

The nanny laughed – "People still have to eat and make a living, my dear."

"Poor mother, she must miss her child," Trisha said suddenly feeling a pang of sympathy for the working mother. It surprised her. She hated babies or anything to do with them. Feeling bad for others in that way was not her style.

"May I hold him — only if he is awake, you know," Trisha said suddenly wondering where in the world that thought had come from.

"What the --," she heard Ezekiel blurt out behind her.

"For sure — sweetheart but you'll have to ask the mother," the nanny replied.

"It's ok — I don't need to," Trisha tried to wriggle out.

"Why don't you ask the mother yourself?" the nanny said with a big smile.

"Where is the mother?"

"About 10 feet away," the nanny said and laughed. She turned and pointed to the counter. The bright light from outside shone on the old nanny's face. It seemed to reflect off her face. There was an angelic look about her.

Trisha pretended to look towards the counter. There were 4-5 women behind the counter. The line was long and the women behind the counter moved quickly to clear the orders.

"The blonde at the cash register now," the old lady interrupted Trisha's thought.

"It's ok, nanny," Trisha said turning melancholic again and withdrawing physically to her own seat.

"Call me Yokatherine," the nanny said.

"I'm Trisha."

Trisha suddenly reached out — drawn to the lady.

"I must leave you my number," the lady said as she dug into her purse, missing Trisha's outreach. Trisha sighed in relief. The nanny was still fumbling. Her white hair was tied back in a tight ponytail that fell to her side as she bent into her purse. Despite its bright white color, it was gorgeous and regal.

Trisha felt a strange longing for the lady again. "The mother I never had," somewhere in her mind that chilling thought burst forth. Stunned, she sucked deeply and nearly choked. She loved her mother despite the perpetual smell of smoke, and foul language that hung around her all the time.

"Here you go, Trisha," the lady finally looked up. Trisha had expected some kind of a card but a crumpled piece of paper nearly rolled up was held out to her.

She looked into Trisha's face and smiled, "If you need a babysitter, or a nanny, or help."

"We're kids, Yokatherine," Trisha recoiled, feeling guilty at the cover-up or the lie – she couldn't tell.

"I know, sweetheart," the nanny smiled purposedly. She reached out her arms and Trisha fell into them as if it was the most natural thing to do. A gentle peace enveloped her. She let go reluctantly – fearful to look into the lady's face. It was almost as if the lady would look within and see what lay there.

The lady stood up suddenly, "I must be going now – the world is about to change and I must be there to help save it." Trisha had the most amused look on her face.

"I hope I can see you again when you're, like, done saving the world," Trisha smiled feeling natural again – a bit of her nasty self was back.

"You will, my dear – don't lose it," she said pointing to the crumpled piece of paper.

The lady pushed the stroller gently and guided it between the tables as Trisha looked on after her. The baby's mother at the counter stepped out. The apron and hat were gone. An envelope changed hands and the lady left.

Trisha expected the lady to turn back and wave — she didn't — yet Trisha felt strangely cared for by the old woman walking away.

"Who was she?" Ezekiel interrupted her thoughts.

"An angel," Trisha whispered silently and sat back resting against Ezekiel. Surprisingly she felt an anger grow within her and moved away from Ezekiel.

"Maybe if she had been my mother, this would not have happened," she said and closed her eyes as an unknown giddiness enveloped her. She swayed and then fully slumped into Ezekiel. He smiled, barely knowing what was happening to the young girl in his arms.

The peace of the Tim Hortons was suddenly shattered as the sound of a series of large crashes outside echoed through. There was a commotion as people rushed out to more crashes and screams.

Ezekiel saw the crowd in the coffee shop rush out. He rose from his seat as well, instinctively, but Trisha was hanging on to him for support. Her nails dug into the skin of his forearms.

She stirred finally.

"What's all that noise about?" Trisha asked.

"Some stupid accident outside — everyone's gone out — yeah!" He was suddenly grateful for that. The nearly deserted coffee shop gave them some more of the privacy they had longed for all morning. Ezekiel tried to draw Trisha's lips to his but she brushed him away.

Ezekiel looked out at the chaos. Every now and then, the wild wailing of sirens filled the coffee shop as people came in and went out. It was more frequent regardless of the fact that most of the people had left to satisfy their curiosity at the chaos unfolding outside. Despite the bright sunlight and the flashing lights, a strange dark shadow seemed to dart everywhere. He remembered the day — Good Friday. A pang of guilt enveloped him. It was barely

3 years since his sacrament of Confirmation and he felt
totally detached from the church. "You're an adult and you
can decide for yourself," his dad declared one day trying to
be a modern dad. The weekly Masses had withered to
Sunday Masses which then withered down to the odd feast
day Mass.

The sight of Daniel had brought all those memories
roaring back. "I know once you are done with this
sacrament most of you will stand here at the altar next when
you want to say 'I do!'" He had laughed and so had his
parents, rather impressed and suddenly alert to that fact.
"However, I'd rather you would come back day after day
and become even more fervent Catholics," Daniel had
continued. Ezekiel thought of that time – grade 8 – he and
his buddies thought they were big – seniors – until high
school hit them.

"You are standing at the crossroads of life," he
remembered Daniel belting out – flipping through a dozen
slides on a glitzy power point. The soft music, the troubled
teens, the praying teens and the beautiful pasture with a
church somewhere in the distance on the slope – the slides
had stayed with him somehow.

"Come away and rest for a while, my yoke is easy
and my burden light," Ezekiel remembered that quiet
afternoon – life was simple then.

He had seen Daniel walk in. A half-raised hand had
barely been noticed from the coffee line. The noisy teens at
the table – 3 years his junior had done all the hellos and he
had seen Daniel respond with a reminder – he always did.

"Don't you all forget the procession this evening."

"Should we all be, like, serious? Like, not smile and
stuff?" they teased back.

"No," the cool demeanor barely blinked, "keep
smiling, especially today, God loves you."

"You know him?" Trisha had suddenly asked. Her eyes had not left Daniel since he had walked in. She was still staring at Daniel when Ezekiel answered angrily. "Yup – I know the guy."

"How?"

"Ran the Confirmation program in my parish."

"What's that?"

"A religious thing – like coming of age – like becoming a Catholic adult – like, why do you ask?"

"Nothing – just curious – must have been nice though. I wish I had been a part of something like that."

"Really, why?" Ezekiel felt a pang of guilt. Trisha smiled and winked, "you'll understand some day."

The door swung open and a hooded man came through. A strange silence followed him despite the noise outside. Ezekiel remembered noticing the hooded man all over the place outside. He calmly stood in the line but Ezekiel felt the hooded man's eyes bore into him and then onto Trisha's stomach.

"Hey, kid – I know you." The old man startled him. Ezekiel remembered seeing the old man talk to Daniel earlier. He nodded to the old man hoping he would go away. Trisha still lay slumped heavily against him – awake now. Her sadness had been troubling – he himself seemed to casually dismiss the storm that was about to turn their lives upside down. He knew it would, but until then he wanted to enjoy her love.

"Didn't you always serve Mass and do the collections?" The insistent old man was still there.

"Go away," Ezekiel's mind screamed. He knew the old man had nothing to do and was just looking for some idle chatter.

"Right," Ezekiel nodded trying to turn away.

"Ah, now I remember – you were with Daniel – right?" the old man smiled a false smile.

"Yup."

"You good kids."

"Hmmm --,"

"Are you serving Mass today?" the old man persisted.

"No," Ezekiel answered angrily.

The hooded man had reached the counter. He seemed to be part of the conversation even though he was some distance away.

"That your girlfriend?" The old man kept on nosily.

Ezekiel felt his hold slip. He was about to leap at the old man but the hooded man's eyes seem to have locked on to the old man.

"I must talk to Daniel – shouldn't let you kids drop away from the church so easily, huh?" Ezekiel felt a deep pang of guilt fill his soul. The old man was about to sit down and continue his lecture when he became aware of the deathly stare on him. A shiver racked the old man's body, he half looked up, saw the hooded man stare at him and fled.

The hooded figure now stared openly at Ezekiel and Trisha. Ezekiel felt a disconcerting unease fill him. His empty stomach seemed to want to throw up despite nothing being in there. His normally steady fingers holding the Iced Cappuccino felt wet – they shivered involuntarily as the figure approached.

"The church guy," Trisha suddenly jumped out of her sleep, "Daniel, that's his name right?"

"Right."

"Where is he?"

"Gone."

"Then let's go find him – talk to him," she pleaded.

"Why?"

"He looks young enough and yet you told me he seemed to impress the parents a lot."

"But what can he do?"

"I am sure he can do something – seemed impressive – like, if he could handle a 130 plus like you, then I'm sure there is something he can do for us."

"I don't think so," Ezekiel felt an unknown rage rise within. He had never ever been angry at Trisha, no matter what.

"Ok, suit yourself – I'll go talk to him."

"You won't do any such thing!" Ezekiel felt himself lose control. They moved away from each other – their eyes locked in a fierce stare. Ezekiel felt the hooded man settle into the table next to theirs. A quick glance – the man seemed least bothered as he stared into the screen of an iPhone.

"I don't understand you," Trisha was suddenly mellow. "We can't hide this much longer, Ezekiel," she said pointing to her stomach, "it's going to explode soon – every single one around us is going to know – Oh my God – school," Trisha shrieked, "can you even imagine the sight, or just the news about it?"

Ezekiel closed his eyes and slumped back into his chair. "Those church people will have only one thing to say."

"But, seriously, you can't be thinking otherwise."

"For God's sake, Trisha, you're just 16, I'm 17. This can't be our future – there is only one way."

"No," Trisha screamed and burst into tears, "I hope you – the stupid church-goer is not thinking, like, what I think you're thinking."

"It is the only way, Trisha."

"Not for me."

"Think for a minute, sweetheart – you know what's happened."

He saw Trisha step away from him and knew in that instant he had lost her. He felt like a coward, a namesake Christian. Trisha had never been in a church – it was the way her parents had raised her. An unknown look filled her face – it was distant look – a look of a stranger. He knew he had been shut out.

"No one knows more than me what's happened, Ezekiel – I'm pregnant."

She turned and walked away slowly. He wanted to run after her but remained slumped. The hooded man's eyes followed Trisha. Ezekiel was suddenly scared for her. Was it the chaos outside that unnerved him or was it the presence of the hooded man? The chaos seemed to come from the hooded man next to him. A police cruiser was parked on the sidewalk. Its flashing lights cast bright colored flashes in the coffee shop as they spun. The bright flashes inside the dull neon-lit coffee shop, cast a depressing shadow in his mind. Trisha went through the doors and turned right barely conscious of the tragedy unfolding all around. Ezekiel sensed where she was headed. The hooded man's bony fingers were drumming the small coffee table softly. Ezekiel felt hypnotized. It was as if the hooded man was spinning a strange web around them.

"There's an easy solution," the hooded man said ever so softly.

"Excuse me!"

"You'll need this," the hooded man continued without bothering to repeat. Ezekiel knew his defense had been dismissed. He looked at the hooded man's face. Under the hood, the face was barely noticeable. The eyes seemed like fiery red slits with a strange scaly face.

"Just think of me and I'll come around to help – or – just go here – they'll know what to do – quiet and discreet."

Ezekiel stared at the card. It was a plain white card with a name and an address. He read it and nearly laughed. It read – LIFE MEDICAL SERVICES. Ezekiel looked at the hooded man in surprise and recoiled once again as the strange eyes stared back at him, unflinching.

"There is a number at the back – call them – they're good, quiet and discreet."

"What can they do?"

"Ah! Men," the hooded man blurted in a loud baritone voice standing up. "Your girlfriend needs an abortion my friend and... I need that sacrifice." Ezekiel did not catch the whole sentence but the word sacrifice rang in his ear like a death roll from a retreating drum.

"Abortion," he blurted out as the reality and the truth of the solution that had so easily formed in his mind was laid out before him.

The hooded man was already at the door. He hesitated and stepped back in. Ezekiel saw the white haired nanny pass by towards the church. The hooded man waited and then went out – turning right. Ezekiel stood up and followed with wobbly feet.

IV

Terri

"A coffee and a donut, please."

"And what type of a donut will it be today, offi-cerrrrr," the woman behind the counter purred teasingly – her body following in a slow sensual motion along with her words.

"A Maple Dip, please."

"This one, sir?" the waitress said pointing to a golden, maple syrup coated donut – her eyes never leaving the cop's on the other side of the counter.

"Yup – the one with the hole – I hate the one with the creamy filling."

"Watching our weight – are we, officer?" A wink with a seductive whistle followed the rather personal comment.

"Not really – just love to stick my finger through it and nibble all around." The police officer replied teasingly moving his lips in a delicate pincer action.

"Now, now, are we being naughty, officer?"

"Ah! Dear Katy – just as attractive at 60 – what were you like at 20?" He finally gave in with a laugh. At 50, the boyish laugh made him look half his age.

"A delightful bunny – if you please, young man," she said, thoughtfully admiring the big burly cop across the counter. Her mind drifted for a second before the sound of the tissue paper making contact with the delicate donut drew her attention back to the job at hand. Eyes fixed on the cash register, Katy rang the transaction through.

"Just a dollar for you, young man," she said quoting the discounted price for the man in the blue uniform. He held out a 5-dollar bill. She was tempted to waive it off knowing that he would drop part of the change in the tip box, strategically placed next to the cash register.

"You don't have to – you know that – putting your lives on the line daily for us is tip enough, officer."

Officer Terri McKusky smiled. He knew what he would do – those little coins in tips in Canada, across the Atlantic, decades ago had given his family back home in Ireland a new life. It was the story his grandfather told him at every family meal. The old man was more of a father to Terri than his own dad. Terri had sworn on the old man's deathbed that he would always carry on that tradition. A loonie clattered to the base of the little glass jar. Terri smiled – raised his empty hand in half a salute to the lady, picked up his coffee and donut and marched out. The conversation was still ringing in his ears as half a smile played on his lips. Katy always touched his heart.

"It's the chemistry, silly!" his partner, Officer Clare, would tell him.

"Ah, cruel life; she would have made a hell of a lover."

"Dream on Blondie1 – I wonder what Mrs. McKusky would make of that comment?"

Terri never answered. He knew the beautiful Clare always drew his wife into those delicate conversations intentionally. It worried him lately.

"Life has a strange way of repeating itself," Terri told people around him all the time. The conversations with Katy seemed to always crop up with a hint of Deja vu in them. "It's as if I am reliving those moments and words."

"Life is just a plain old sequence of events, Blondie1," Clare would tell him, "stop the dream act – life is a *bitch* – events after events – nothing more."

"Not so Blondie2 – not so – someday you will see."

Terri was nearly at the door of the coffee shop when the cruiser's buzzer horn blared followed by the fierce blasting of the foghorn. It brought him crashing out of his dreamy world. Officer Clare already had the blue and red lights spinning. She was his junior and never touched the lights with him not there. Terri ran. The donut would soon be lost in the action. He rammed it in, in a single go, licking his fingers as he reached the driver's door. She had reached across the center stack and swung open his door – it had to be critical he thought as his heart started thumping. Strange, he thought, after all those years in the force it normally didn't happen. "It sure doesn't look good – Blondie2," he said stuffing the coffee in the little pod and strapping himself in.

"Not good, boss, Dufferin and Eglinton, level 5 alert."

"Level 5!" Terri whistled softly in surprise – glanced in the mirror – flipped on the rest of the sirens and swung out with a squeal of tires.

"Fill me in," he said to Clare eyes fixed on the road as they sped up north on Dufferin. The hilly road made him choke on the last of his donut. A side glance and Clare had the coffee nearly up to his lips. "My love," he nearly blurted out and gulped before sighing inwardly at his near miss. They knew each other inside out and looked after each other – the personal expressions never figured in. It was early morning – a public holiday and he didn't expect any traffic.

"They're scrambling every cruiser and ambulance in the area – sounds bad."

"Shooting?" Terri asked as matter of fact, expecting the worst.

"Maybe. Only confirmed part – a major pile up and some other strange stuff as well."

"Dammit – and this was supposed to have been a quiet Good Friday morning."

"It was quiet last night Blondie1 – something had to happen this morning – the law of averages, duh!"

"See even in that statement you sound fatalistic – there is a plan for this world," Terri quipped; proud of his calm thinking mind despite the mad scramble. Yet somewhere deep within a nagging feeling was beginning to upset him.

Clare did not turn to give Terri her usual skeptical look nor did she answer. Instead, for the first time, Terri's words began to ring in her ears with an element of reality. "Bloody hell," she exclaimed angrily drawing herself out of her momentary lapse as the radio crackled. Over the years, they had learned to filter out the regular chatter on the radio and tune into events around them or meant for them.

"Team-Blondie come in."

"Team-Blondie here," Terri answered hoping newer details were to be added. He hated walking into a crime scene with little information.

"2 dozen cars reported piled up at Dufferin and Eglinton both ways – 3 teams and 3 Ambulances dispatched."

"Roger."

"Head east to Glenholme Avenue."

"Eglinton and Glenholme?"

"Roger that."

He was about to ask for further details when it struck him. "That's the church!"

"Right on."

"Details?"

"Man down – crowds – panic calls."

"Ok, we're headed there."

"Detour – Dufferin and Keywest – over and out," the dispatcher signed out.

Terri swung the cruiser east at the last minute onto Keywest Avenue and nearly drove straight into a parked car. Swerving at the last minute, Terri hit the sidewalk, got one wheel on it and raced ahead. The chaos up ahead was already evident. Traffic was already backing up on the northbound Dufferin. The last minute swerve sent his coffee spilling through the air hole in the lid – Clare did not react. He half turned in surprise before looking ahead again. They had turned east and the morning sun was coming in straight through the front windshield. Terri caught the light bounce off Clare's bright beach blonde hair.

"Miss Blonde," he teased before turning on the wail to caution the traffic up ahead, slowing a bit, and swinging left on the northbound Northcliffe Boulevard. The wheel hit the extended curb before the cruiser came bouncing back onto the road. Again, Terri noticed Clare's silence with surprise. She had not reacted to his blondie tease either.

"Blondie team," – they were the first words he had said to her on shaking her hand nearly 10 years to the day. It was tough to tell whether his or Clare's beach blonde hair was brighter. They made an attractive pair and the name stuck. As the senior officer, he claimed Blondie1 and she happily accepted Blondie2.

"Ah well! At least we'll be past the blonde jokes quickly," she consoled herself.

Over the years they had turned out to be a super-efficient team and had been left alone as the legendary, Team-Blondie. They hit Glenholme from the south. A short 100-meter drive lay ahead to the church. "Strange day – I've got a bad feeling," Clare suddenly blurted out.

"Team-Blondie," the radio crackled again as if in answer to Clare's comment. "Man down in front of the church – multiple car pile-ups at Dufferin – possible gunshots – a riot at Timmy's – over and out."

"Gloom and Doom," Clare repeated, "again, a bad feeling about this --,"

Terri reached over and squeezed her shoulder reassuringly, "Always by your side, Blondie2." She patted his hand once and then looked away. Over the years, they had responded to hundreds of such calls. Their thick skins hardly elicited a reaction after the first year or so. Clare's reaction surprised him. He was the dreamer – she was the realist. The church came into view but the road was blocked. Terri turned on the piercer. People seemed to be pouring out from everywhere and running to Eglinton up ahead. Terri pulled on to the sidewalk near the clergy parking – jumping out, they ran. Their right hands instinctively reached for their guns as the left hands reached for the radio activate button.

"Team-Blondie on site," Terri radioed in.

The scene was a mess. The crowds surprised Terri.

"Never seen crowds like this come pouring out in all our years together."

"Looks more like a riot in an overpopulated Asian city," Clare answered. Their long partnership had turned into an implicit understanding of each other's thoughts. Clare knew it had saved their lives on many an occasion.

"Around the steps, officer," a man shouted as Clare ran left onto Eglinton. Terri instinctively turned and looked the other way – his sharp eyesight and cop instinct scanning the scene around. Every piece of open space seemed to be occupied by people. Terri was about to head to where Clare was when a dark shadow caught his attention. It was there for an instant and then vanished. Surprised, he turned back and scanned the crowd – something had definitely caught his attention. Whatever it was – it was gone. He turned and was about to join Clare when the dark shadow flipped past him again. Shaking his head in disbelief, Terri reached Clare when the presence of the ambulance loomed over him. Ordinarily, he would have noticed it from a mile away.

"Man down here – 2 paramedics on site – shots reported up ahead," Clare gave him a quick appraisal. Terri looked at the tall ragged black man on the stretcher. He was dead. The paramedic was rising from the ground as the other pulled the stretcher out.

"Male, 50ish, dead on arrival, blunt force trauma," the paramedic monotonously updated Terri. "Apparent accident I guess, thanks."

"Man down at Eglinton West," the radio crackled again in Terri and Clare's ears. The paramedics seemed to have new instructions as well.

"One victim dead in front of church – repeat – confirmed dead," Terri added when the full weight of his sentence hit him. The scene had been chaotic – the fleeting black shadow had awakened the strange haunting fear in him in the brief instant it had passed him. "Church," the words rang aloud in Terri's ears. He turned slowly and looked at the quiet brick structure rise high in front of him. He had wanted to be in there all day – this day – it had not worked out. Terri's hat came off in his hand out of respect as his hand rose to sign himself with the Sign of the Cross. Something peaceful was drawing him in – something strangely evil outside was awakening the deadly ghosts that had begun to surface in his mind again. The chaos seemed to emanate from his fears. Startled he reached for his gun but Clare was already a few steps ahead.

"Permission to investigate situation up ahead, Blondie1?" Clare asked.

"Granted. Full radio contact. I'll cover the right flank."

"Noted," Clare half saluted and ran. He saw her petite shapely figure run ahead – the bright, blonde Reverse-French-Braid hung out and Terri's mind reached out for it.

He was drawing her to him – alone in a shower – their naked bodies drenched. He imagined her turning around to him and clasping him closely as their wet bodies met face to face. The petite figure was endowed with large shapely breasts – after 10 years together – Terri knew that outline well.

A scream in the distance drowned out the cacophony of noises that filled the street and Terri was out of his little fantasy world. Sweat poured out from under his hat despite the mercury hovering way below zero that day. A second passed and Terri nearly squeezed the trigger as he realized he had been fiercely gripping his pistol. "Noooooooo," his mind screamed. They were both married – happily – with children. They had been professionals – down to the core and life was perfect – at least until a year ago.

Terri glanced up at the church, a silent, "sorry," escaped his lips and the panic demons in his head did a wild dance.

"Clare," he pressed the send button, "come in, Blondie2."

"Blondie2 reporting."

"All well? Heard a scream."

"There are a million screams out here – will report back soon – out." Terri breathed a sigh of relief.

"My Clare is safe," he heard the words in his mind before a fierce curse in his mind shocked him. Terri took his hand off the hilt of his gun before glancing down again. The tall dead black man was being carried away. There was a stunningly beautiful photographer dressed more for a formal ball than for a crazy day he thought. There was another man down – on his knees. Terri was sure the man had been attending to the dead man. The kneeling man had a shocked look on his face as he rolled back on his bottom –

hands held closely in his lap. He knew the man was injured in some way.

Terri knelt down, pulled back the zipper of the body bag and studied the face of the dead man. "DOA," the paramedic blurted without emotion. Terri looked at the dead man's face again. The peaceful look surprised him – the man could have been asleep. Terri looked up and saw the people crowded around. Suddenly, like a fierce deathblow – another face stared at him from between the hundreds of faces that surrounded him. Terri felt his stomach churn. It was as if his fears, temptations, and worries all erupted in that one instant.

The sound of the two gunshots that followed seemed a logical blast to what was erupting inside him.

"Blondie1, come in."

"Blondie1 here."

"Gunman on the loose – reported sighting of one gunman – two shots fired – man on the ground – dead."

"Roger that, Blondie2."

"Need immediate backup, boss."

"Coming up!"

His own lack of urgency surprised him. Clare was on the go. She had skirted past the relatively safe situation in front of the church and already seemed to have a hold on the situation ahead while he felt like a wimp dealing with the unknown ghosts in his head.

"I need a bloody shrink."

"Or the peace that only the Lord can give." Terri looked up surprised. An old woman with a marble-like face, angelic smile, and long white hair was holding his hand and raising him up. "Come to me all ye who are heavily laden and I will give you rest." Terri felt the old woman's words flow down his body like a soothing lotion. "One day at a time, officer – for now, duty calls, hurry to your partner before it is too late!" the woman said and disappeared.

Terri smiled after her. He felt a quiet peace fill his soul. His palms still felt the touch of her hand. He looked down at the dead man's helper. He lay slumped against the planter. Terri knelt down and looked into the face. The man was an Indian — brown faced — with an expression that spelt turmoil. It was as if Terri was looking in a mirror. He reached out his hand and tapped the shoulder. The face that looked up seemed to relax a little. Terri had the strange sensation of having disturbed a quiet personal moment.

"Are you ok, sir?"

"I'm ok, officer."

Terri felt his heart twitch a bit. "Are you injured?"

"No," the man lied. They both seemed to know that.

"Your hand?"

"Just a little cut, sir — nothing that a Band-Aid at home won't take care of."

Terri smiled for the first time. "Ok, I must go — you didn't happen to know the man who just died?"

"No, sir — wish I had — I am so sure he was a special one — chosen by God."

Terri stared at the man for a second and reached out his hand.

"The Lord takes care of those whom he loves," the man whispered taking Terri's hand.

"I know," Terri replied.

"Sometimes that can mean suffering too."

Terri stood up confused. The peace that the old woman had left him was gone. Terri knew it would not last. He had spent countless nights lying awake imagining every possible disaster and disgrace coming his way — the end was always the same. He was fired. A disgraced ex-copper, separated and lost from his wife and kids.

"Help me, Lord," he had prayed suffering from those nights of anguish. Tired he would fall asleep. His first thoughts when he rose were always the same tormenting ones. "But I have never crossed the line – never, ever – he would reason in his mind – never, ever have I even touched her with anything in my mind in our long years together." He imagined himself explaining to a jury in the deadly little basement hall where they held their enquiries.

Terri pulled himself out of his thoughts again. The dark hooded shadow as he now knew it was all over the place. It was almost as it floated from group to group, always leaving more chaos behind. Terri felt the evil from that shadow.

"It's the day of the Lord – Satan will not rest," the man on the ground said wincing in pain part way through his words. Terri felt something stir deep within and knew something was about to go drastically wrong.

"Move – get going – go home if you have no business here," he shouted in his cop voice. It boomed and echoed and the crowd took an involuntary step back. Terri pressed the 'send' button and instead heard Clare's words go through to the dispatcher.

"Confirmed, one gunman in the crowd. Confirmed, one man on the ground. Confirmed, gunman missing. Over and out."

Terri ran. His place was by his partner's side. The first step felt strange. It was as if something was blocking him – holding him back. Terri took a second, hesitant step when he heard two clear gunshots. Like firecrackers – the sound of the gunfire stuck. Terri's ghosts broke loose in his head threatening to explode.

"Can't be good," he muttered reaching for the radio.

"Come in, Blondie2."

Instead, Clare's voice was replaced by a series of thuds. He was sure her radio had fallen off – hit the ground. "Just a bump from someone," he told himself expecting

Clare to come back online anytime, she did not. Terri felt his feet wobble. "Not her, Lord, not now," he prayed. One more step and he thought he would fall. His heart sank as the voice faded away and the static crackled. It was his worst fears coming true. He had left his junior to run right into harm's way, all alone. He was before his police union and the jury again – "You failed a fellow officer – fired," he heard the fatal words.

Terri punched the talk button for Clare's radio. It buzzed back and forth. He buzzed again – in panic – sprinting towards the sound of the gunshots as he saw a stampede breakout in the opposite direction.

"Blondie2 – come in."

"Blondie2 here – goodbye, my love." Terri heard the fading words loud and clear. Stunned, he stopped dead in his tracks. Clare had said it finally. In that instant he knew, it was the last thing she would ever say.

"My Clare," Terri screamed hardly bothered now to hide his feelings. "She's ok, I'm just dreaming." He felt his face wet – tears. He was crying as he ran, fully aware that a mocking, hooded, dark, shadowy stranger ran next to him.

"Go to your Clare," the figure mocked and disappeared.

V

Fr. Brian

"Brian, Brian, cryin, cryin," Giuseppe teased. At 15, he was the eldest of 9 kids and 3 times the size of his tiny 7th sibling Brian. "Oh, he's no brain, that Brian, he just a drying drain," Paolo joined in. Paolo was second, all of 14, born barely a year after Giuseppe but nearly the same in size. The teasing carried on as the others joined in. Brian ran and hid behind the life-sized, stuffed bear. The family of 11 lived on the sprawling farm, deep in the countryside way off, of what was to become the main highway 400 that connected Toronto to Barrie and the rest of Northern Ontario.

The Giordano family had just finished dinner in the largest of the hay-covered buildings that was the family residence. In the dark shadows, as dusk fell, a cluster of buildings lit up against the dark backdrop of the farm. The next largest building, some way off, and discreetly built on the other side of the massive grain hopper, housed the transient workers. Other smaller buildings, housed the families of the permanent farm hands. The chimneys were busy from the fires that burned in the wood stoves. Winter was on its way out, and the warmer embrace of spring enveloped the farm as nature gave birth to new life.

The first seedlings were springing to life and Francesco and Margherita watched with pride in the falling, dusk shadows. "See, my love, we made it," Francesco said to his wife of 16 years. He said it to her every evening.

"I know – we still have some ways to go but we'll see it through," she answered as always. The simple farming couple repeated those lines to each other daily. It was more than just a pledge of their love. Barely a month into their newly wedded life in the vineyards of Turin, an urgent cable from Francesco's brother, Luigi, in Toronto, had turned their lives upside down. "You need to take the first possible ship." There was no explanation – just the money to begin the journey. There was no reason not to go and begin a new life in the land of plenty.

"The ships sails in 3 days, love," a young Francesco said to Margherita. "I go where you go – I am not staying behind alone." "Just the words I wanted to hear," the young groom said to his bride. "It still means that there will be no one to look after your parents," Francesco warned again with the confidence that his beautiful bride was ready to leave with him.

"God will take care of them, Francesco – you go and get things ready for our voyage." "It's a 2-day journey to Sicily by road – we have but a day to pack." "Then so be it," said Margherita pledging her support.

The 2-month voyage had lasted 3 months due to severe showers, frigid temperatures, stormy seas, and ice floes. The young man and woman that stepped off the boat in Toronto, 3 months later, looked as if they had been freed from a concentration camp. Weakened, bundled in layers of clothing, cold ravaged hands, skin sticking to their bones and a drawn blank look. In stark contrast, Luigi, there to greet his elder brother and his bride, looked cheerful, hale and hearty, and rich. His slick suit, shiny leather shoes, shoulder to ankle overcoat, costly hat and a cigar hanging off the edge of his mouth painted a different picture.

"Brother," was the only word exchanged between the two men as they hugged and the tears flowed. Two weeks later, Francesco's recovered frame challenged Luigi's westernized personality. The couple recovered quickly in Luigi's large home. One night as they sat by the fire, Luigi finally broke the news to Francesco and Margherita. "I'm sorry, brother, but your home is far north from here. It will be a tough start, but you'll make it." The brothers had discussed it many times at the local Italian pizzeria down the street. "You always wanted to be a farmer so when I saw this giant piece of land up for grabs I just bought it." "But I can never pay you for it, Luigi – I have nothing." "I want nothing – just the two of you to be happy." "And how will we survive up there with our little English and no knowledge of the land?" "Don't worry brother," Luigi assured them, "I will always be there for you."

Francesco had told the story many times to his children. The cold, frigid wasteland had turned into a marshy land as they headed into their first spring. Their living quarters was a small log cabin, generously stocked by Luigi. Giuseppe was born that very first year. Each year, with each new kid, the Giordano family's fortunes grew. They toiled, morning to night. In the long, cold winters, they turned to breeding their livestock. The barns on the farm multiplied and soon Francesco was hiring workers to help keep up with the farm.

Francesco looked with love on his farm as the last of the setting sun sank below the horizon. The screams of the children below filled the house. Suddenly it was a shriek – "Papa, Papa, Brian is nowhere to be found." It was Maria, their third born and a second mother to her siblings. Brian was turning out to be their favorite child and his absence sent alarm bells ringing through Maria's head.

Brian was indeed missing from the sprawling living room of the farmhouse. Blinded by rage, and hurt with the incessant teasing, he had slipped out of the front doors. Someone had forgotten to lock the two massive wooden doors that Francesco had built and installed himself.

The little boy knew his way around the farm well – just that it was dark now and he had never been out alone this late. Francesco's orders were strict. "Only the men venture out at night – armed. Kids and ladies are to be out only when accompanied by the men when there are festivities." It was an ironclad rule – Grizzlies, Coyotes, Bobcats, Lynx, Cougars and a variety of wildlife wandered through.

Brian crossed a long row of smaller houses along the broad dirt road that was the main artery of the farm. The smell of food and the sounds of laughter drifted from them. It angered him even more. He walked faster to get past the family houses. The first barn housed the cattle, the second the sheep and goats, the third the chickens – Brian lost count in the dark. The smell from each locked shed, stretching long into the distance, told him what each one was. A short while later Brian stopped. The sun had fully set and the darkness was complete. There were no lights around. The men that patrolled the farm at night, carried their own lamps, mounted on tall sticks, stuck into the stirrups on the horses. "The horses!" Brian suddenly exclaimed. He knew what the longest and biggest last shed was. The horses were his love and his father had promised him a pony of his own, from the next lot to be born – not to be sold – not to be worked on the farm.

Brian rushed to the shed and stopped uneasily. An uncomfortable feeling engulfed him. It was not the fear of the night, or the darkness, anymore. It was an eerie feeling he got when the scary dreams came at night. "Everything appears in a fog and I see floating creatures," he would confide in Loretta, his favorite elder sister. "Just dreams, Brian – you know, you and me read so much – it's just our imaginations creating those images at night." "But there is something real about those dreams, Loretta." "Dreams are not real." "These are," Brian would say, "I know it because I am fully awake."

Brian was fully awake now and the landscape was
changing. He knew the dreams were coming alive. Loud
noises emerged from the barn. "Strange," he thought to
himself, "it's all supposed to be silent." If Brian had any
doubt, then the wild neighing of the horses proved it. "My
ponies are in danger," he declared and ran, feeling like his
fearless father. Just like the impregnable door of his house,
the massive barn doors seemed slightly ajar. A thin beam of
light filtered through. "Someone checking on the horses,"
Brian thought feeling reassured but the door surprised him.
It was barely open, a slit, but the chain outside was in place,
securely. A long metal rod that served as the lock to hold
the chain in place was still there.

Brian pulled out the iron rod, reached out to open
the door, when it swung open with a blast, tossing him aside
on the bales of hay. It was a lucky accident as his beloved
horses bolted out in a wild stampede – all 60 of them.

Brian rose from the hay as the light that had
emerged from the barn, vanished. Had he imagined it? Brian
walked into the barn. The long center aisle running down
the length of the stable was empty, as were the stalls on
either side. Someone had obviously opened the stalls. Brian
began walking to the other end. He knew what lay there – a
little, bright, green platform, bordered by a bright, white
picket fence. Brian hated that spot. "The brightness of the
little, white picket fence is cruel, papa!" he would complain
to his dad. "Oh, you little one, we've got to make a tough
cookie out of you." Francesco always answered with a little
laugh. "But how can you sell away the horses, Papa? They
are our family," he would protest, as each horse was
displayed on the platform, bidden on, and sold. It was a sad
spot for Brian, and tonight, in the dark, it seemed alive.

Brian ran – had someone brought back a horse?
The gloom in his heart lifted momentarily, and then filled
his soul with an intense darkness. The picket fence seemed

to change colors, black and then white, and then black again. Brian realized something was on the platform, alive. It was a living being; with arms and legs, like long thick serpents that looked more like tree trunks. Each part seemed alive in itself, as was the main body of the creature that twirled.

"Can we see the devil?" Brian remembered asking Sr. Rosa at the Sunday Catechism class. "No Brian, we can't?" "But is he real, Sr. Rosa?" "Yes, he is." "Then --," "That's enough, Brian," the strict Sr. Rosa stopped him, "If you think you see the devil, just make the sign of the cross, and pray to Jesus."

Brian's little body stood frigid and cold. Shivers racked his body, and his hair stood on end. "Make the Sign of the Cross, quickly," Sr. Rosa was screaming in his ears but his hands hung paralyzed by his side. It was a long time before Brian's hands rose up. He saw the creature jump back and yell in the loudest ear shattering death scream. Brian crossed himself again, loudly, "In the name of the Father, the Son and the Holy Spirit, Amen." The creature melted away, he thought so. It enveloped the white picket fence, as its molten mass flowed over, towards the door from where Brian always saw the last of his favorite horses. The door opened and the black mass rose to take the form of a man. "Uncle Luigi?" Brian thought the figure resembled his uncle, only bigger. Shiny, dark hair, silk suit, polished shoes. The figure waited by the door – pulled out a cigar, and struck a match. "Is that you, Uncle Luigi?" Brian asked again. The figure turned and stared. It had a long, sharp face, a thin mustache and red eyes. It stared at Brian once more, grabbed a hat from the rack and then vanished into the darkness.

The thundering sounds of the hooves from the fleeing horses, matched the sounds of the boots that were bursting forth from the chaos that was enveloping the

Giordano household. Francesco emerged first, his loaded muzzleloader in hand as he hammered in the powder and the charge. His hand reached to the side and pulled the hanging bugle. Two blasts later, every door on the farm was bursting open as the men ran out. Half-buttoned coats and hastily drawn guns accompanied the men. The bigger youth carried lanterns and clubs – soon the farm was alive with frantic calls.

Another blast of the bugle, and the ragtag force fell silent. "Brian, my little Brian is missing," Francesco's tear-choked voice came forth. The little army scattered instantly - they knew the drill. In teams, they scattered in all directions, north, south, east and west. Only Francesco stood still, not knowing where he would go. A second later, he knew, as the strong hands of Margherita pushed him towards the stables. "The horses, Francesco, the horses ran, Brian loves the horses, something has happened there."

Francesco ran, accompanied by the dogs, barking wildly. Half way through to the stables, the dogs whimpered and turned back. It was the first sign that told Francesco that it was something more than just a wild animal. Margherita was right behind him. "Keep going," she said, gently nudging him forward. Francesco moved his gun to his left hand, as Margherita moved the lamp to her right. Hand in hand, the couple ran. The stable door was ajar, wide open. Francesco pulled up his gun and aimed ahead, as Margherita held up the lamp. The stable was empty. Far in the distance, at the other end, something moved and Francesco aimed. "Stop – No, don't shoot," Margherita howled and ran ahead, putting herself between the gun that nearly went off, and the moving object at the other end. She beat Francesco to the other end as a small voice greeted her, "Mamma – it's me, Brian – you needn't worry, I scared the devil away." She grabbed her son and then fainted. When the 3 were found, Francesco was stupefied, with shock – he simply held his son in a tight embrace, and stared.

* * *

Fr. Brian sat back from his keyboard as the chills swept through his body. 39 years later the feeling was the same. He could remember every little detail, vividly. The visions grew after that encounter. In the darkness of the rectory, Fr. Brian leaned back heavily into his hole-ridden, leather office chair. The two pages he had typed, was his first attempt, at what, he was not sure. He rubbed his aching eyes. The darkness created strange images in his brain, as he looked away from the glare of the bright, little IKEA lamp that sat on the old mahogany desk. He felt the desk lovingly. It was probably one of the first pieces of furniture moved into the rectory. He let his eyes get accustomed to the darkness, and on an impulse, hit the little light switch. "Gotcha!" he squealed with kiddish delight, as his hand slid down the cable and found the little switch, half way to the plug. It had taken him weeks to master that little trick. It meant the end of randomly jabbing at the wire, and looking for the switch, endlessly. Now in his tired state, the little distraction helped.

The darkness felt good. The dull glow of the laptop screen seemed gentle, and then it suddenly went duller. "That's the power save option," his mind heard the words repeated. Somewhere, some technical tip from Daniel was jumping in his head. He shook his head as the little voice became louder, then a scream, "save, save, save – hit it as many times as you can," Daniel's voice screamed in his head.

"Omigosh!" Fr. Brian yelped and jumped forward. He had lost too many of his sermons until that little tip had been drilled into his head by the techie parishioner.

The screen caught his attention again as the blue squiggly line on the Microsoft-Word software warned him of an extra space. Clicking the touchpad in the dark, he hit delete and looked on his little writing with surprise. He was not sure why he was doing it. He knew he was only delaying the eventual dread he hoped to avoid. "One more time," he told himself and started to read again.

*   *   *

St. Thomas Aquinas – a brief history
"Long before the asphalt roads, concrete sidewalks, traffic signals, pizza joints, sports bars or the tiny one room apartments that rested above them, lined Eglinton Avenue West, a very different landscape defined this part of Toronto.

A simple two-way mud road ran from the center of the city around Yonge Street, into the nothingness of the West. Like a lonely road in the middle of nowhere, Eglinton Avenue stretched miles to the west – half of what was to become Toronto decades later. Lush green farmlands stretched into the distance on both sides. Crops and fruits were eagerly harvested in the short summer months. For the rest of the year, Eglinton was a dirty brown artery flanked by pristine, snow covered, endless stretches of empty land.

In time, a few houses began to dot the sides. Picket fences sprang up on the turns. A muddy, bumpy intersection defined the spot where Oakwood Avenue ran south. A little further west, a small chapel catered to the needs of the Catholics that lived around. Most walked, some rode their horses, while the others came in horse-drawn carts. That was in the early 1900s until the archdiocese decided that the growing Catholic population needed a befitting church. Soon, a beautiful brick structure sprang up. It was massive – someone had thought far ahead, rather optimistically, and correctly. A generous rectory was added to the adjoining southern side, which housed the altar. To the mostly Italian immigrants, the first parishioners, an entrance right on Eglinton, became a symbolic blessing – an invitation to pray. And thus was born the parish of St. Thomas Aquinas."

*   *   *

Fr. Brian hit the save button, shut the file and slammed down the laptop lid.

"There you go, Daniel, happy?" he joked in the dark. He had no idea why he had even pulled down that massive log of the church's history, and tried to compile it into two pages.

"On a holy night like this – go to sleep, Brian – you need to be fresh for the Lord's important day," he chided himself.

Strange thoughts nagged him. He sat back in the darkness and looked at the bright red numbers on the timer at the other end of his office that opened into the secretary's office. The 2:00 am numbers startled him. It had been an extraordinarily busy Maundy Thursday. He had been on his feet since 4 am that morning. At 10 pm, when the Maundy Thursday service ended, and the faithful departed in silence, sleep was the first thing that came screaming into his mind. The Blessed Sacrament would be exposed for adoration for the next few hours. There were enough committee members around to take care of things – he could grab an hour or two of sleep.

It did not happen – never did. At 1 am, the last parishioner left and Fr. Brian gratefully locked the main doors. He had no energy to do his daily walk all around to all the doors – front and back and side and below. There had been enough break-ins already, despite all the security.

"Take care of your house this night, dear Lord," he prayed.

Instead, a last look outside the office window on to Glenholme Avenue, made the haunting memories come racing back. The dark hooded figure was there for an instant, in the shadows on the other side, and then it vanished. Fr. Brian did not need to look again. His spiritual mind had already unraveled the dark figure. There had been too much of it lately.

Standing in the shadows of the blinds, he went back to the window knowing fully well the figure would be gone. It was the least he could do to keep away from the picture in the book that drew him like a magnet. The giant history book lay untouched since his one brief glance through it 3 years ago, when he took over the parish. It was the black and white picture of Dufferin and Eglinton, probably taken on a rainy day, which had brought his childhood nightmare come screaming back. Back then, he had stared at it for the longest time ever and then passed out.

"Tonight I face it, finally," he declared as he pulled down the book. There was a scary past he had to confront.

"A brief history," is what he promised himself. It was a perfect thought that would keep him moving through the album, rather than run straight to the little black and white picture, and stare at it endlessly. Despite his best efforts, it happened exactly that way.

"Mamma," the words sprang out instantly from his lips trying to find a distraction. Mamma Margherita, Papa Francesco, his 5 brothers, 3 sisters and he had come a long way from the tough farming days up in the cold stretches of Northern Ontario. "It's a steal, Francesco," Brian would always picture his dad imitating Uncle Luigi. Now he forced himself to keep thinking of the farm details, other than the terror that drew him.

"But why did Uncle Luigi want you to come so far out into the wilderness, away from the city?" Loretta always questioned. There was no answer.

"We tried to sell the farm once, and move into the city when we had enough money," Mamma Margherita chimed in, "we could have run a successful bakery, and be in the heart of the city."

"That would have been so nice," the kids wished

"But Uncle Luigi never let us move – he wanted us here – on the farm."

Brian always wondered about that statement and the vision that had changed his life forever.

Fr. Brian smiled in the dark as the beautiful nostalgic memories came flooding through. By the time, he, their 8th child was born; Francesco and Margherita had turned the deserted marshland into a sprawling farm, laden with livestock. Brian did not face the challenges of his elder brothers and sisters.

Brian remembered the chaos that followed that evil night, in vivid detail. The sound of the thundering hooves, the scared neighing, the blasts of the bugle, and the shouts of the farm hands – Brian had followed the events outside the barn, closely. The calls, the shrieks, the shouts and the warning shots as someone approached the stable. "Careful – could be a grizzly in there." "Or a Lynx." "Don't shoot!"

A few more thundering shots from the farm hands around had echoed through. His dad, the bravest, was first through the barn door – gun pointed straight ahead. That scene would haunt Francesco all his life, thinking of the moment, he had nearly pulled the trigger on his little 5-year-old. The chaos had quickly settled down. The horses were corralled back in and Brian had stayed tightly wrapped in his father's arms.

A caning followed. Both the elder boys had taken two lashes on their bottoms, two on their hands and scampered to bed. Finally, it was just Brian, his father, and mother by the fire. "Next time they go after you, bambino, you tell me." "Yes, papa." "There won't be a next time," Brian remembered his mother's words distinctly as she gathered him into her arms, and asked the question he had been so dreading. "What happened out there, my son?"

Brian knew that life on the farm would never be the same again. Uncle Luigi had rushed in with Fr. Camilo the next day, and every inch of the land had been blessed. "But I saw it – clearly – like a dark squirming serpent – bathed in silver light and then it turned into ...." Brian repeated for the umpteenth time, staring hard into Uncle Luigi's face and catching a queer stare back. "Was it really Uncle Luigi out there that night – a creature like the devil himself, or was it just an illusion?" The question haunted him all his life.

"Was it a snake?"

"No, but its many arms and legs seemed like serpents, coiling around."

"So it wasn't a snake."

"No, but there was a body with all the snakes on it."

"It's just a child's imagination," Francesco dismissed the boy again.

"You can deny it all you want, Francesco," the priest had finally concluded, "but the boy's vivid descriptions are no imagination."

Margherita's words sealed the truth of the events that occurred that night, "Besides, how do you explain 60 horses freed from their stalls, and bolting into the night, in fear?"

Fr. Brian closed his eyes and thought back to that conversation. The priest was leaving. He stood by the big wooden door of their farmhouse, with Luigi, Francesco, and Margherita. "The boy is born with a gift, with God's grace Francesco," Fr. Camilio was saying. "What gift – that's no gift," a still dejected Francesco was protesting. "A gift to see and banish demons, just like our Lord." The comparison to the Lord brought a smile to the parent's faces for the first time. "Do you think my Brian will be a priest like you, padre?" "Mothers know best, and are always right." Fr. Camilio's hushed words could barely conceal the excitement. Brian knew that in that instant, his mother's words had sown the seed of his vocation.

Life on the farm changed dramatically after that night. No one ventured out alone in the nights – even the patrols were done in pairs. The men wore large, wooden crosses, and prayed, as they checked on the many barns and sheds throughout the night. A week later, Brian was sent off to live with Fr. Camilio, and study in the city. The priest took the little boy under his wings. By the time Brian finished school, he was already known as Padre Brian – priest-to-be son of proud parents.

Brian's visions got only more rampant. He did not need to see visions to know evil abounded. He saw it in various forms. Fr. Camilio kept his knowledge of the boy's visions a secret. Soon the boy and the priest developed their own coded signals. A simple name scribbled with a cross across meant that Brian was warning the priest of a certain parishioner that needed help, with an exorcism. Brian hated those. Each vision came with a deeper anguished prayer for the gift to be taken away. It only got stronger.

* * *

Fr. Brian gently closed the history book in the dark and held it close to his chest. Pushing back his chair gently, he walked back to the window on the east side. A gentle moonlight bathed Glenholme Avenue. Huge banks of ice from the harsh winter, covered large chunks of the road. The sloping hedge, running down on either side of the steps, was bare of leaves. The thick layer of snow covering it, flowed down along with the hedge, like a mini ski run. Fr. Brian's vision continued on to the road, and then across. He had seen the 2-storey houses on the other side, thousands of times, but something drew him that night. He started his scan again at the sidewalk and moved his eyes up further. The picket fence came into view, and then, as his vision was about to move on further, something exploded in his brain. The picket fence – it was flashing across his sight. There was another picket fence somewhere, far away, at the end of a stable, with a little platform, where the horses were displayed to the potential buyers. Instead, something else was wrapping itself in large coils.

A single drop of sweat broke free and rolled down from Fr. Brian's temple, and then, a million pores sprang open. His heart broke into a furious beat, and the big history book slipped from his hands and crashed to the floor. Fr. Brian knew he was passing out. He was a little boy, standing transfixed at the evil vision, displaying itself at the end of the stable. The creature at the other end, looked at the boy with a million eyes, and melted away over the fence, into the cigar smoking, red-eyed figure. The bright, white picket fence turned white again as the stranger disappeared.

Fr. Brian, fallen on the floor, felt the carpeted floor all around him. His glasses had fallen away, and so had the book. It was dark. His BlackBerry's flashlight app, that is what he needed. He had to find the phone. He felt around gently, hoping not to smash his glasses. Instead, the green blinking LED of the phone got his attention. "Thank you, Jesus," he exclaimed, and reached out for the BlackBerry, as the LED turned red. On his third attempt, he got the password right. "The shortcut key – remember that Father," Daniel was telling him as he helped him set up the new BlackBerry, just a few weeks ago. "In an emergency, you don't want to be scrolling across screens and hunting for an app – instead a single push of this side button, and you will have all the light you need." Silently, Fr. Brian thanked his techie guide and pushed the button. The bright flash of the BlackBerry's camera, turned into a bright, silver beam.

The book lay upside down where it had fallen from his hands, open, like a tent. Some of the pages and newspaper cuttings had fallen out. The book needed fixing. Then he saw it, almost as if it had been pulled out and laid perfectly across for him to see. Fr. Brian's shivering hand brought the light of the BlackBerry down on the photograph. It was the Dufferin and Eglinton intersection. He lifted it gently. There were no buildings, stores, petrol pump, nor the Shoppers Drug Mart. No McDonald's nor Tim Hortons either. No bus stops nor traffic lights. Instead, the intersection looked like it could have been on his dad's farm. Two simple intersecting mud roads – lined by white picket fences. He nearly threw the wretched picture away but held it for a second longer. "There's nothing here," he told himself, "just a picket fence like the one in the stable, like the millions all over Canada, like the…"

Fr. Brian knew he was rambling – loudly – trying to calm himself. This time he rolled over properly on to his bottoms and freed his left hand from supporting him. The photograph came closer and the bright silver light poured onto the picture. An instant later, he knew it was not his regular vision that was looking at the picture. He shut the BlackBerry light – the moment was here, and he was going to face it. The darkness of the rectory returned, but Fr. Brian's vision gazed deep into the past in that picture.

"Dufferin and Eglinton," – his thoughts blared – he had long mastered the art of simply soaking in all the words, the visions threw at him. Those were not to be argued, or debated with. The photograph had been clicked from the south side. The view was of an intersection on a higher ground – Dufferin climbed up a short hill. In the short distance ahead, the picket fences at the intersection came

into view. A single horse drawn buggy rolled across to the
East. A moment later, another followed, overtaking it, its
two horses doing a better job. It was raining – pouring – the
ground was soggy. The wheels of the buggy churned slowly
in the muck until both had crossed the intersection. A small
group of men in full-length mackintoshes and wooden
handled umbrellas walked across. There was a funny noise –
an old horn and a clattering car rolled by. "A Ford, one of
the first," he knew.

Fr. Brian knew he was looking back in time. A short
while later the intersection was empty – yet a strange
presence filled it. There was good and there was evil. To the
north-east side something moved behind the white picket
fence, it rose and fell. It reminded Fr. Brian of Jesus carrying
his cross to Calvary. Surprisingly he could picture the crown
of thorns on Jesus' head. It seemed fresh. A thorn from the
crown of thorns broke away and pierced the figure behind
the fence. It rose and fell again – another figure was
crushing it – an evil one. It was about to land one final fatal
blow but a crowd swarmed across. They were carrying a
large cross, and were dressed in all white. A long line of
carriages crossed the intersection and then it went blank.

The dark night stretched on. A fine beam of
moonlight was beginning to come through the eastern
window. Fr. Brian did not know how long he sat on the
floor, bathed in his sweat and thoughts. In answer, the tall
pendulum clock sitting on the floor shattered the night with
3 gongs – 3 am. The vision was gone.

Fr. Brian switched on the flashlight app on the
BlackBerry once more and stared at the picture. The evil
that had been at his farm had been at the intersection many
decades ago. He knew the vision was from a Good Friday,
from the procession that had passed across in his vision. He
turned the picture over in the light of the BlackBerry. The

date read April 21, 1916 – Good Friday. The picture had been clicked on a Good Friday, a hundred years ago.

The vision, the picture, the revelation and finally the presence of the mysterious shadow outside his window – Fr. Brian something was building up. He crossed himself with the Sign of the Cross. It was already Good Friday –the dark forces of evil had their own plans. The challenge had been delivered – he would be ready.

Fr. Brian lifted himself off the floor feeling divinely invigorated now that he understood. It would be 4 am soon – time for his morning vespers and the preparations for a busy Good Friday, sleep would have to wait for another night. He replaced the loose contents into the book gently and left it on the table – it needed fixing. He walked back to the window and looked out one last time. Not a soul stirred. He looked deeper and he knew a strange dark shadow looked back at him from somewhere in the dark.

"I'll be ready for you," Fr. Brian whispered as he turned and walked up to his room.

"On a hill far away, stood an old rugged Cross," sang Fr. Brian as he stepped into the shower.

"On that same hill today – evil will win and this land will fall," the figure murmured and stepped out of the shadows. "A 100 years back and 100s' of years' back, I failed – today I will destroy that thorn and claim this land."

"I will cling to that old rugged cross," Fr. Brian sang letting the hot water take him racing back to the cozy warm baths on the farm in big wooden barrels, "and exchange it someday for a crown," he sang.

"A crown definitely, priest," the dark figure murmured not too far away, "a crown of thorns – a thorn – I will destroy and claim this land."

"Not so fast – Mr. Evil – not so fast," Fr. Brian said aloud, stepping out of the shower, strangely sure he had rebutted an evil call. Something was flashing again in his mind. The LED on his BlackBerry had gone red when he was sitting on the floor.

"Who would text me at 3 am in the morning?" he wondered and went looking for the BlackBerry. He never got to it as the craving for a dark roast, waiting to be brewed; and the long day ahead, brought him racing over to the pantry.

"A cup of coffee is what I need," he sang as he reached for the shiny golden packet.

VI

The Cabbie

"A hand with those bags, madam?" the old cabbie asked.

"No," she answered in the faintest of tones fumbling with the assortment of bags and equipment she carried as she reached for the cab door. He reached across to the back door from his seat, nearly horizontal and yanked the latch, half pushing the door open. She nodded in acknowledgment as the cabbie gasped. The young woman was stunning – deadly pale, white, dark hair, dark makeup, and a body-hugging black leather jacket. The deep blood red eye shadow, the only color on her, seemed like a stroke of a callous red brush on a black and white painting.

He turned again to stare at the darkness of her black lipstick when her jacket came off. He nearly fell over as his eyes fell on the top of her breasts above the low dress – white curves that stunned the eyes against the black landscape that encased them. The black top flowed on seamlessly from where her jet-black hair left off. He regretted the stale smell of his cab as if it was a desecration of her heavenly perfume. The face never looked up – "Princess!" – he called in his mind, confused at the wild feelings flowing through his brain.

At seven in the morning, he was used to driving home the ones with smeared makeup, disheveled hair and vomit smelling dresses. The ones that went home with a violated look on their faces. He was their shoulder to cry on – their confidant and confessor, as they vented out the horrible regrets of the night gone by. This one was sharp, immaculate and cold.

As assortment of black gadget bags and holster cases tumbled from her hands on to the back seat when he noticed the 2 large cameras around her neck – the lenses seemed to stretch out a mile.

"Those are some cameras you have there, madam," he tried in his friendliest tone, rather confident of his charms and his ice-breaking skills. She did not look up.

"I'm one of the 'point-and-shoot' kind of guys you know, ha, huh," he tried again with a little self-depreciating laugh. He was by now, totally hypnotized by her looks. Her gaze never lifted as she did a quick check of her bags.

"That's truly some cool stuff you got there, miss. Where are we going today?" he tried a collective noun, getting a little friendlier. Her face lifted slowly. Her eyelids flipped up once, like a switch arming a deadly missile.

"Eglinton and Dufferin." The deadly, clear, low, harsh voice with a stare, lashed him like a whip. The stare stayed focused – icy and sharp – there was to be no senseless, casual conversation. He gulped, choking as if his words had turned into a rock that had come stuck in his throat. Turning around he fumbled with the ignition and swore as the already running engine screeched in protest. A strange fear gripped him.

"And make it quick," she whispered, gently this time. He suddenly felt as if he was back home in Mumbai. The rich and the powerful commanded – the poor and the lowly obeyed, as per a rigid social structure controlled only by one's power and wealth. He sensed a bit of softness in her voice, and looked in the mirror. A hint of pity danced fleetingly across her face, and all at once, it was gone.

"Double the fare, if you get me there before 7.30," the cold voice whispered.

"Yes, madam," he whimpered like a chastised puppy being treated to a consoling pat. The taxi moved in silence except for the sounds of shutters clicking, lenses changing and zippers opening and closing. The cabbie brushed away a drop of sweat. It was freezing outside — the heating made it toasty warm inside — he was confused and decided to let it go. They crossed Queen and John and headed north. A few more turns through some older back lanes, past Spadina Avenue, then Bathurst Street and with a final right turn they were on Dufferin Street. He tried to beat an amber at Bloor, but screeched to a halt as the signal turned red. Fear gripped him — she did not seem to care.

"A few more signals and we should be there, madam," he dared — quietly. He did not expect an answer — did not get one. A cautious glance in the rearview mirror told him she was lost in some distant purposeful thought. Dufferin was empty, except for the odd car and the north-southbound TTC buses. He sped, not knowing whether it was the offer of the double fare, or just the thrill he felt at her presence.

"The gas station on the right," she ordered like a GPS suddenly waking up with instructions. He complied; veering sharply to the right just in time as the Esso station at Eglinton came up on them, rather suddenly.

"Is this ok, miss?" he asked pulling over, hoping to hear her voice one more time. He felt a deep longing for her. It was the end of their journey. Sadly, he wished he could drive her a little longer. Instead, he heard the door open. The bags — he suddenly remembered — he could help her with those. She was out of the taxi, all packed up, before he could reach for his door. The broad, black waist belt held and an assortment of pouches, holsters, and equipment. The bigger camera hung around her neck — the smaller one hung over her right shoulder.

He hit the auto button and had the front passenger window glass sliding down in a hurry. He still had to check the meter, "Delay her, delay," his soul pleaded. A crisp plastic 100-dollar bill sailed through the opening window. By the time he made contact with the floating bill, and looked up, she had turned away. Her slender back — and a patch of white skin exposed through a circular cut in her dress, had him sucking through his teeth as a wave of wild sexual arousal gripped him. "Point and shoot," he cursed, slapping the steering wheel in anger. He had never owned one — if only he had one now.

He bowed to her disappearing back in reverence. "In my world — you'd be a queen, madam," he called after her as the feel of the 100-dollar bill made him sigh with pleasure.

*   *   *

Amanda waited until the cab pulled away. The intersection was busy — bathed in golden sunlight. A cold gust sent a shiver through her body as she pulled on the leather jacket the hooded man had brought her. After the stale warmth of the taxi, she breathed in deeply and sensed a wild day ahead — it seemed to flush the rustiness out of her body. She put the lens to her eye and a strange darkness filled it. Puzzled she put it down. "It's work time, Amanda," she told herself and looked again in the lens. Like a thundering flash, her world came alive — frames, images, and voices all around came crashing through her scanning lens. She looked for the hooded man, as thoughts of the eerie bear, high in the mountains, flashed across her mind. She thought she felt his presence nearby, but he was nowhere to be seen.

"Yieeeeeeeeeeeeee!"

A high-pitched scream shocked her quiet world nearly making her fall in fright. Heart pounding, she turned drawing up the Nikon instinctively – ready to shoot. A tall, shabby Jamaican passed her. A few steps later he turned back to her, threw his hands up to the sky, and screamed again. She thought she heard the word 'Lord' in the garbled monologue that followed as his presence filled the lens. Shutter snapping wildly, her hands tightened around the camera, as the man's words began to flood her mind. Her heart burst with the connection of the sight and the words of her subject – this was her day.

"My Lord, My Lord," she heard him say and went shutter happy, capturing him in her lens and filling her soul with some religious discourse he was preaching. He was reaching out to her.

"Ok Amanda – this is your day," she egged herself on, "make it your best."

The Nikon shot like a furious automatic weapon. Her hands moved on the large zoom. Click, Click, Click the camera went. She was tempted to put it down, and scan the first prints when she felt the man look into her soul.

"God loves you, sister," the big man said in the gentlest of tones. She aimed directly into his face, just a foot away now. It was tender, and then in a flash, his expression changed. From a soft look of pity, to one of horror, and finally rage.

"Wretched are you – wretched and damned – oh daughter of the evil one."

She did not react. The shutter hammered away endlessly, as she captured each emotion on his face. This was her passion, with a crazy live subject to boot – it thrilled her. His face was right in the lens. Gasping, she put down the camera – strangely unafraid of his presence, towering over her – just inches away.

"Repent, daughter – you serve Satan."

She burst out laughing – an involuntary laugh that burst forth with the sheer shock of what he had just said.

"Even Satan does not come into my wretched life," she said a little sadly, remembering the reality of her life. His dark red eyes scanned her in silence. She was tempted to close her eyes in prayer – strange sensation – she had never done it.

She sensed her hooded sponsor close in rapidly. The Jamaican seemed to sense it too. He turned and ran back towards the intersection where he was originally headed. The camera went up again. Click, click, click it went, her left hand rapidly adjusting the lenses. The hand slid forward to the aperture and she zoomed in on his head.

It was dark with his thick, shaggy and matted African hair. On the third shot, she hesitated, and then zoomed in a little further as he reached the signal and stopped. There was a duller color filling the screen – red – another shot later she figured it was blood. His head was bleeding as if it was the most normal thing happening on his body. She zoomed right in and shot again – the blood seemed to go splat, and fill her screen. He had run across the intersection. The camera stayed focused and then it fell on a face that should have given her comfort. Her sponsor was there across the road – a cold face hidden behind the crowd at the bus stop. A cold hard look into the camera from beyond. The gaze did not remain as she walked up. A victorious sensation pervaded her entire being. "I'm back, Baby," she gushed to herself, when she noticed her sponsor turn and vanish from her lens.

A little further up, a bunch of teens were walking south on Dufferin, approaching Eglinton, slowly and noisily. Another black figure filled her lens – it seemed to fill her being with a sense of calm despite its anxious wait at the signal. Puzzled she looked directly – a priest. She saw a panicked look on his chiseled handsome face and shot furiously. He seemed to be struggling internally, with something – like a whiff of some delicious stew it came to her. Another great shoot, she wondered.

She saw him struggle externally as well; his fumbling hands trying to draw out the BlackBerry from its holster. She felt the vibration through her lens, and knew some deadly news awaited the priest. Her irritation finally got the better of her, chiding him, as she saw him react to her feminine presence. "Score1," she cheered herself for the briefest of instants. The priest stopped suddenly in the center of Dufferin – concern written all across his face. His gaze fell on the hooded man who had just skirted deftly past the preaching man. She felt a powerful force flow between the 3 men. It clashed, forcing her to put the camera down, as if it had snared a heavy load.

The hooded man was walking towards the teens. Amanda zoomed in – they were an assorted bunch – white, black, yellow and brown – 13 to 14 years in age, she estimated. Their boisterous voices filled the square, as each tried to cuss louder than the other. The priest looked on in worry – looked at his watch, hesitant. Her mind looked furiously for a connection – there was one – just like the bear it eluded her.

"What the *fuck*, man," said Shamar, the black kid, "lost everything last night. Dude here shot me up mean and hard." Amanda's shutter went into a frenzy.

"Like a Bozo," James, the white kid added.

"And if that wasn't enough – the sucker got chewed up by the Nazi zombies."

"Even the f-ing helicopter couldn't help with its rapid fire," Danny, the Portuguese kid said with a forced laugh, "f-ing Nikolai – you should have chosen a f-ing marine, dude."

"Yeah, shooting up zombie *arses* with an M16."

"And grenades – blowing their brains out," the others added as they went along.

"Personally, I'd love the Beretta M9 – single-action – double action," Dylan, the Filipino kid added. Amanda paused – sensing something from the Filipino kid – her sponsor had stepped aside. The kid was his target. She shot a single frame, and felt the connection.

"Yeah – put one in his brain first," James added, pointing to Shamar.

The black kid jumped on James' back trying to bring him to the ground. They rolled on to Dufferin as a car screeched to a halt – inches away from crushing the boys. The driver stared in shock – a horrified look on his face, white knuckles gripping the steering. He turned around slowly, surveying the near pile up he had caused on the northbound traffic. Horns blared and drivers screamed at him, to move on, unaware of the boys he had nearly crushed to death.

Amanda had learned her lesson a long time ago – mixing emotions and feelings, meant losing the perfect shot. Her last shot caught the two kids in mid-air, falling in the path of the speeding Honda. Her finger froze for the briefest of instances.

The kids took their time to get up – unfazed. Danny jumped on Shamar this time. The traffic waited. The driver's rage spiked – he was about to get out, when he saw the menacing baseball bats the kids carried, like clubs. He drove on quietly, shaking his head. The teens laughed, screaming after him, "*Fuck* you, dude," Jaime, the brown kid yelled after the driver, and they burst out laughing again.

"Man, I want to shoot something," Dylan suddenly declared, "one clean shot through the head."

"Hormones," Amanda thought, "immature teens."

"Here shoot this nut, Dylan," said James shoving Danny before the raised hand. A scuffle broke out again.

"Enough," Shamar screamed, "I'm hungry, Bro."

"McDonald's," said someone and they all laughed breaking off into a run. Jaime reached the north-east corner of the intersection, first. The others followed in a wild scramble just as the tall, shaggy Jamaican crossed over.

"Repent, the Lord is coming," he pleaded going down on one knee. They laughed in his face. "And you must be the prophet, who?" Fabrizio, the Italian kid teased. The man seemed oblivious. In two quick steps, he climbed on to the tall retaining wall. The kids watched in wonder.

"Blood," one of them screamed, pointing to the sidewalk, "has Dylan already shot someone?" another tanned skin kid asked with a mocking laugh. They looked at the retaining wall – the shaggy Jamaican had left a trail of dark blood.

"Dylan is a murderer," they laughed.

"Not yet," Dylan shouted from way behind accompanied by the hooded man where he had fallen back, "not yet!"

Amanda debated – the group, or the lone Filipino kid with whom her sponsor had picked up a conversation. Click – Click – Click she went as a chilling sensation gripped her. "Darn, that's a kid, dude," she muttered as she saw the hooded man laugh while showing the shocked kid a real pistol. "Focus," her mind screamed and she shot another few.

An icy chill sent her digging for the e-tipped North Face gloves she had pleasantly discovered in the bags. The chill was from the conversation. She looked into the lens again.

"Very well then," her hooded sponsor was telling the Filipino kid, "Call of Duty – Ghosts, it is, but I bet you're a chicken when it comes to pulling the trigger for real."

"Oh man, you can count on it – anyone."

"How about a cop then – and what's the name?"

"Awesome – let's shoot a cop," the kid boasted, "and the name's Dylan."

Amanda reached the signal and hesitated. A little concrete island held the signal post. Standing against it, she looked around through the lens. The boys were headed over to the McDonald's, next to the Esso gas station. Dylan followed them like a ghost – a dark shadow filled his path. Click – a dark shadow pervaded the kid's picture. She scanned a little further – the Tim Hortons next to the McDonald's seemed a busy place as a regular stream of people walked in and out. Her mind wandered back briefly to the way her day had begun – the aroma of hot coffee wafting up her desolate life. "Focus," her mind screamed.

A youngish, brown man caught her eye. He hesitated for a second, outside the Tim Hortons, turning in her direction. She zoomed in and gasped before the shadow filled up her frame. He sized her up in a quick instant as Amanda felt her heart flutter, "Score:1-1," she counted. Funny, she had not felt that sensation in a long time. "Like never, sister," her heart corrected. She shot rapidly, overpowered by a bursting impulse. For the briefest of seconds, everything melted away in Amanda's life – the camera, the money and the pain of her miserable existence.

"Hey," her soul beckoned him, "wait!" He vanished into the coffee shop. Something odd struck her. The dark shadow in her frame had not appeared since shooting the bear, but then, she had not done anything significant either way.

A little red light lit up on her screen, and then vanished. "Low battery warning – this soon," she grumbled aloud, reaching for the spare.

"Mine's charged, beautiful," a male voice said.

"Charged and ready," another added.

They laughed on either side of her. Amanda felt her rage flame up – just as with the cabbie, she seemed to sense a power erupt within – a power that made her feel she could strike them down. Another interruption took care of that.

"Excuse me, please," a regal old lady with a stroller was trying to pass through.

"Sorry," Amanda exclaimed regretfully and moved aside. The woman stopped.

"Trouble, my dear?" she said to Amanda, staring down the two men. They were gone in an instant. "No worries I could have taken care of that myself – may I," she asked lifting the camera. The woman did not answer, but suddenly stared into Amanda's face.

"Ah, my dear," she finally exclaimed, "another one to protect and care for."

"I don't understand," Amanda answered, feeling a strong power from the lady engulf her.

"You won't, my dear, not yet, but I'll be there," and with that, the woman walked on. Amanda's camera followed the lady. The thick, long, white hair hung on her back in a neat ponytail. Click – Click – Click. A heavenly, white glow filled the lens. She felt dark within, pushed away by the radiance from the woman.

"They've killed him – They've killed him – They've crucified my Lord," the shaggy, bleeding man was screaming from the top of the retaining wall on the other side. On a whim, she put down the D4S and grabbed her old D2XS.

"Hello, sweetheart," she patted the camera and shot, wondering about the shadow. On the third shot, it crept in, like a silent dark smoke, and began to spread across the frame. Amanda shot furiously – changed cameras – it was the same.

Men and women in white passed by – prayer books in hand. The little children followed with their donuts and chocolate milk. She shot a large group of old men – they seemed European – Spaniards, she thought. They walked slowly into the Tim Hortons. That is where the action was, she figured. A shiny silver Mercedes pulled up outside the busy coffee shop. The fat, garishly dressed lady came out and jumped in. Amanda's camera followed – and then her hand stayed – it was an insipid shot, and the black shadow didn't show up either. She let it go and thought she heard the hooded man say, "Well done." Startled she looked around. No one, but the white haired old lady seemed near.

"A nice hot chocolate, your favorite, my dear," the white-haired lady smiled holding out a tall extra-large Tim Hortons cup, "I doubled the cup, a bit too hot to hold, even on a cold day."

"What the – how did you --," Amanda stammered.

"And you'd better zip up that jacket, my dear – it's going to be a long day out here in the cold." The lady's voice was tender, yet firm, and Amanda obeyed. She liked that feeling – someone had mothered, and cared for her.

"Thank you," Amanda looked up but the lady was already walking back east rapidly. She reached the Tim Hortons, paused for a second, and then went in.

"They killed him," the preaching man on the wall was screaming again. She saw the hooded man eye a teen couple, walking into Tim Hortons. A flurry of shots went off as the shock of the situation made her squeeze the button. The hooded man eyed the wavy, blond haired young girl with a delicious grin.

"What does he want of them?" Amanda wondered. He saw the old lady approach, and moved on quickly.

The preaching man on the wall was getting desperate as he screamed, "Oh help, help the Lord, oh the pain for my sins."

The warmth of the hot chocolate cup felt good. For the first time, Amanda put her camera down. Wild theories flooded her mind. The bear, the wolves, the darkened and locked memory, the preaching man, the priest, the wild teens, the white-haired old woman and the sad blonde teenage girl. And then, there was her, Amanda. She took another sip and the extra sweetness of the drink filled her. She loved her hot chocolate extra sweet, always adding an extra sachet or two of sugar.

How did the white haired old lady know? Who was she? What did she want to protect Amanda from? And then the thought hit her hard as she heard another loud lamentation from across the road. "Repent, repent...."

"Daughter of the evil one," the preaching man had called her. Somewhere deep within something rang true. Suddenly, like a thunderbolt, it struck her – the voices, the feelings, the inexplicable colors in her camera, but above all the power that always seemed to want to burst through. It was no imagination – it wasn't human. It had become second nature to her, yet, it was unnatural.

"Who am I?" she moaned and looked around for the hooded man.

VII

A Good Friday, 100 years' back

No one knew when Dufferin, a small road, first came into existence in the insignificant, unwritten pages of history. A simple mud road that climbed, sometimes gently and sometimes steeply, winding its way up north from Lake Ontario, through the city of Toronto. A short distance from its origin by the lake, it crossed the then significant King and Queen streets and disappeared into seeming wilderness. Dense forests broke open to gentle meadows, bordered by bright country fences that provided a dash of white during the summer months. For the rest of the year, the snow camouflaged everything in its white embrace – the country fences included.

Dufferin, a little mud road that the electric tramcars or the emerging petrol locomotives never used. Literally owned by horse riders, and their carriages, it traveled north until another insignificant muddy intersection with Eglinton, let it pass on to the wild North beyond, where lakes and forests existed side by side in an endless magnificent landscape.

That North would someday become home to a young Italian immigrant and his bride, some of which we have read and we will read a lot more over the course of these chapters. However, in a time not so long ago – which would precisely be called a century, the road, Dufferin, as we know it, awoke one morning to a sight not very wintery. On a sunny yet brittle Palm Sunday morning in April, the normal snow covered Dufferin stood out as a distinct brown path. The frozen ground, rendered frigid by the frost, had lost its snowcap, thanks to a sudden winter thaw. Unseasonal showers aided the melting process until Old-Man-Winter decided that the reprieve the humans had enjoyed was enough. And so, that Maundy Thursday, a Nor'easter dumped a few feet of snow. That night, the frost returned, the temperatures crashed to tens below zero and the humans groaned in protest, yet, grateful for the little relief that had come their way.

On that cold, brittle Good Friday morning, 100 years ago, a sharp-eyed gentleman of a rather serious disposition rode up north on a tall, black thoroughbred. His dark garments, a long, black winter coat – formerly an unfortunate bear, covered a stately black winter suit. Tall riding boots stuck out of the stirrup. The leather of the saddle still smelled of the fresh polish over which someone had slaved for long hours. A tall, black hat held on tightly despite the stiff, northerly breeze that came off the lake. Black leather gloves extended out of the long hands that held the reins with gentle ease. They were rarely used; the horse and its master understood each other intimately. The man rode up north, alone that frozen winter morning. The clippety-clop of the hooves wasn't the only sound shattering the sanctity of the morning. The man and his horse rode amid a pack of howling bloodhounds. The pack of 20-30, howled, grunted and remained ever alert to the scents that wafted across their extremely sharp nostrils. It was not the season for the foxes, or the hunts yet, but then they were used to other wilder hunts that normal hunting folks didn't take part in.

A faint whiff of a hot body, the stale smell of a badger, far in the distance caught their attention, and the dogs went into a wild frenzy. Howling and yelping, they turned to the rider, their natural wild instinct beckoning them to break into a run into the countryside to tear apart some unfortunate winter beast of the white lands. The man simply rode on, eyes glued to something way beyond what the human eye could see. The dogs were in a frenzy, enough to tear apart one of their own; one that would be the first to bleed from an angry bite of one of its mates. Then suddenly, with a sudden move of the arm, the leather-gloved arm drew out a whip and cracked it in the air and the bloodhounds broke over the fence in a wild, frenzied charge across the countryside. Soft hooves flew over the snowbound countryside as ravenous, panting snouts and ultra-sharp nostrils picked up the trail. Just moments before the carnage, the family of badgers realized that death was just a second away. Violently engulfed and ripped apart, the soft, furry bodies disappeared into the jaws of death before they took the first step of their escape.

The man waited – silent and still. The dogs would return, primed and bloody. He needed them thirsty for more blood. It was a day to shed blood – he liked that thought. From the Son of God, to the smallest, meekest creature on God's earth – this was the day. He laughed at the thought – a low, grunting burst that made the horse rear its head and stir a little.

The man was after blood – not any – he needed to shed blood and end the continuity of another that had flowed from the Son of Man – the Son of God. A day he remembered well. A vein throbbed in his forehead and his grip tightened on the reins. 2000 times he and his ancestors had tried it – 2000 times it had eluded them. Little pieces of a tree – a mere locust bush – long bristles – thorns that had done their job brutally at the hands of the Roman soldiers. It was to be his day of victory – it had become the seed of his continuous defeat.

His anger burst forth and a soul-piercing scream burst high into the skies above. This was the thorn, from that crown, that he wanted destroyed first – this was the thorn, which had caused him untold agony. The whip cracked fiercely as the evil cry sent waves of terror through the land. It caught the frolicking, satiated dogs playfully chasing the largest of the pack who held the last of the body of a mutilated badger. The dogs broke into a run, fearful of the whip and reached the man a few minutes' later, standing and panting silently around the horse. The leader of the pack, a large black and tan, full-coated beast rose on his back paws as a sharp steel sword slashed across and sliced through the Badger. Unfortunately, it was not a human as the man and the dogs were normally used to.

The dripping sword was wiped on a fresh silk handkerchief and returned to its scabbard at the side of the horse. "Animal or human, it's a start, lads," he called, "now for the real one." The bloodhounds wagged their tails and barked at his voice. The horse neighed in anticipation, waiting to break into a fierce gallop at the energy that was bursting through its veins. The man reached into a side pouch and fed the horse a handful of sugar.

"I need that blood – I need that thorn," the man yelled and the troop burst forth in a wild sprint. The countryside trembled and little animals borrowed deeper still in their burrows – a deathly fear making them forsake any thoughts of venturing out for any vegetation that would be still exposed from the thaw just passed.

The fierce cry from the man was felt far and wide. It echoed across the continents, across time and across the hearts of men and women who fought against the evil the man represented. The horse and the dogs were in a wild charge up north, until a peasant was the first unfortunate soul to cross their path. Delighted to see some sign of life, the poor man halted his little carriage and doffed his hat.

"A pretty, little conversation I will have," he exclaimed ready to exchange a word or two and enjoy his day of rest from working on the barn. The sight of the dogs and the tall stately gentleman made him hesitate as an unknown fear gripped his heart. The thundering troop approached at a fierce speed. The peasant froze, almost statue-like as if he had cast his eyes on Medusa herself. The troop halted, surrounding the man like a large beast toying with its prey.

"And a very good morning to you, kindly sir," the poor man cowered in fear.

The dogs circled the man with gnashing teeth waiting for a command from their master.

"And what would a good man like you be doing out on an evil day like this?"

"Why it is but the holiest of holy days, good sir."

The simple man missed the growl that passed through the pack and the restless tapping of the hooves. Most of all his bowed head missed the rage that lit up the rider's face.

"And why would this day be holy, my man?"

The poor man looked up in shock, suddenly troubled.

"Surely you test me, noble sir. It's a sin even to doubt or joke about the day." The thought hit him a little late and he quickly crossed himself, remembering his confession a few days ago, in preparation for the holy week. Another shock rippled through the wild troop now bursting with an evil rage.

"You haven't answered me, my man, why would you consider this day holy?"

"It is, as you would know, noble sir, that this is the holy day, when the Lord was crucified."

An angry scream rent the air.

"I know that, you dumb man. I have known it for 2000 years. It was supposed to end that day with his death."

"It was the start, sir," the peasant answered suddenly emboldened, "it was the day my lord gave his life for me. To wash away my sins."

"No, No, No," the man on the horse bellowed nearly lurching out of his saddle, "I will quell it yet."

It made no sense to the poor man. Yet his poor humble soul grasped something profound in that instance.

"You are but a breath away from joining that man on the cross."

"Oh no, good sir, that would be a sacrilege to imagine me up there next to my lord on a cross."

"Then how would you like your end to come about?" the man on the horse asked in a cold ruthless rage.

"If it pleased my Lord, sir, I would choose to be a new Barabbas who chooses death and lets my Lord be pardoned," the peasant answered.

From being one crack of the whip away, from setting the dogs on the peasant, the man laughed. A sudden amused laugh.

"Well you'd better be on your way, my man, you speak well despite your poor state."

"The preaching of that Holy Friar, sir, that's where I learned my faith. Though I thought for a minute you were going to kill me, sir."

"And why would you think that?"

"Just a feeling, sir."

"It's not you that I seek. It's another that I go for."

"On this day, sir?"

"Yes. Only on this day, for only on this day would that which I seek be open to my quest."

"Be it an object, or be it a soul?"

"The life and the soul of the man that bears the --,"

"I think I know who it is that you seek, sir?"

"Don't you go tempting fate, peasant, I would --,"

"The holy friar at the intersection that preaches and heals and exhorts --,"

A fierce crack of the whip ended the conversation. The glaring eyes would have burned their way through the peasant's body, instead, the troop charged leaving the peasant feeling like the victor.

* * *

A fierce crack startled Fr. Brian out of his vision, just as he waited to see the picket fenced intersection from the photograph, from 100 years ago, emerge in the rider's sight. A head peeped through the side door. Two strong hands partially lifted the door and swung it enough for the man to squeeze through.

"My bad – darn that stuck door, padre," Francesco cursed entering from the side door, "jams up all the time. Gentleness doesn't work – first a crack, then a hard push and then it swings – sorry." The man kept mumbling – confused at the dazed look on the priest's face. Was it anger, irritation or just plain surprise?

"And a very good morning to you too, Francesco," Fr. Brian said with a shrug and a smile, "really, would you start this holy day with swearing and complaining?"

Francesco, nearly 80, blushed like an altar boy as he crossed the marble altar, bowed deeply to the empty tabernacle, and sat in the pew, next to Fr. Brian. The fresh fragrance emerging from the priest caught his nose.

"A shower, padre – early before dawn?"

"Only way to stay awake, Francesco," Fr. Brian answered, closing his eyes and hoping to go back to the vision that had taken him back 100 years to the existence of the evil man, even then. A man – a friar – that bore the....... unfortunately, the vision was gone.

"But, I saw you here well past midnight, padre."

"Ah – but it is a special night, my friend. The Agony of Our Lord, I decided to share it with him."

"Like a sleepless night?"

"You can say that, Francesco."

Fr. Brian opened his Missal, and jumped to the Psalm of the day. It was Psalm 22,

"My God, my God, why have you forsaken me?" Something there had triggered his dream. The little, white picket fence, that he had waited to see emerging in the man's eyes, as he cracked his whip in rage, had not appeared. "The preaching friar," the peasant had sworn. Fr. Brian had nearly seen it in the man's eyes – yet it was gone now. He remembered the creature on the white fence in the barn instead.

"A Good Friday, 100 years back – and then there's today – and the man is restless," he thought out aloud, "if only my faith was strong enough to see --,"

"Your faith is our guide, padre – it is strong – you know that."

"If you only knew the struggles of a priest – say would you know anyone around here, well past their 100?"

Francesco stared and then smiled. "Sometimes you can be so strange, padre!"

"Strange as in mad, Francesco?" Fr. Brian teased back.

"No, No," Francesco gulped, crossing himself as if he had committed a grave sin, "strange, as in how deep, or where your thinking goes, or as in --,"

"It's ok, Francesco, I understand, but you will look out for me, won't you?"

"Oh for sure, padre."

"Coffee then, Francesco?"

"Oh for sure, padre."

The two men bowed to the Altar of Repose and moved to the sacristy. A stained glass door in the sacristy led

to the priest's quarters. The priest's huge bundle of keys
jingled as he pulled apart a master key and opened the
stained glass door.

The two men were soon joined by another noisy
bunch coming in from the rectory. The bright light hanging
low, revealed puffed, sleepy faces, pulled out of bed rather
early.

"Good Morning, Daniel."

"Good Morning, Father Brian."

Fr. Brian was about to walk on, when something in
Daniel's face caught his attention.

"Not sleeping well are we, my friend?"

"Not really, Father. It's just that – ah well, never
mind."

"No, no, tell me," the priest insisted.

"You might call me crazy, and take me off all those
ministries you trust me with."

Fr. Brian looked at the man before him – a dull,
dark sensation filled his soul and somewhere deep within he
knew what the man before him was alluding to.

"You might be surprised, Daniel, at how really crazy
our real worlds are, or how close they are to --,"

"To the dark and evil side?"

The priest stood dumbstruck, another piece in the
puzzle.

"You must let me help you – the powers of God's
light are strong, and protect us, but the powers of darkness
are not to be messed with," Fr. Brian warned.

"Somewhere in the depths of the night, I stood by
my window and saw a darkness sweep down. Actually, as I
drove home last night, after the adoration, it was as if we
were heading into some sort of a battle."

"A battle, Daniel?"

"Yes, Father – a sort of a reckoning – as if something or someone wanted to settle an old score, a big one."

The priest felt his blood grow cold, leaving chills, that drained all the way down his body. He wanted to get Daniel away from the rest and share their experiences in detail.

"Maybe the Lord has an answer for me after all," he whispered quietly.

"Coffee for everyone then?" Francesco interrupted, "come on, someone else is here early," he said trying to hold out a hot carafe of coffee – the aroma swirled through the air.

"I'll take care of that," Jojo shouted through the kitchen door. Fr. Brian felt thrilled. It helped distract him from something deadly that was brewing out there.

"Be back in a minute, folks – don't forget we're fasting today – don't raid the fridge."

"Aww, you had to come out with that before I could remember to remember, padre," Francesco grinned sheepishly backing away from the refrigerator.

Fr. Brian reached his office and looked out of the little office window, the city was quiet and peaceful. Not a soul stirred. "The calm before the storm – stand by me, my Lord," he prayed, wondering where that thought had come from. The premonition of something catastrophic happening that day, was growing in his mind. Daniel's intuition was no flash in the pan. His mind wandered to his first days in the parish. The man had struck him with his presence as an usher, at the back of the church. There was a warmth and genuine welcome in his handshake. Two quick chats with the older ladies, and he was convinced he had found the dynamic coordinator he wanted in a place, to lead the hot-blooded grade 8s' in their Confirmation program.

Francesco laughed his usual loud laugh in the back of the rectory. It shattered the peaceful silence and brought Fr. Brian out of his thoughts, yet again – something was gnawing at the back of his mind. He heard the team move to the church and followed them quietly. They were busy discussing plans and splitting up the tasks at hand. He tiptoed from the west side of the church and settled into one of the rear pews, watching the team from the back of the dark church. They were rechecking all the purple cloth draped statues. Extra chairs needed to be laid out. The hall in the basement needed cleaning for the large numbers that would descend on it through the day, especially after the evening Good Friday procession. The gnawing was back.

"And how's technology treating you today, Fr. Brian?" Daniel startled him emerging in the dark, from the usher's room at the back of the church. Something was beginning to click in his head – he stayed silent.

"Remember to save, and remember to charge that BlackBerry, especially since we've set the default profile to vibrate," the chatty techie lectured as he walked away.

"The BlackBerry – darn it – oops – that's it," Fr. Brian swore, looked around as he covered his mouth and ran. The LED was blinking red when he last saw it, early that morning, after the encounter with the dark figure in the shadows. "Me and my cup of Jo," he muttered under his breath as he ran. Fr. Brian's path to his room was littered with interruptions along the way – none of which he could say no to.

"Please, please, padre," old Nonna Maria stepped decisively in his path, "please a 2-minute confession."

"Now, Maria – but we did organize a special evening for confessions and --,"

"I know, padre. I did go to that sexy, young Italian priest who heard confessions in English, and Italian," she said winking at him mischievously.

"Nonnaaaaaa!"

"I know, padre," the old woman grinned taking his hand, "now you know why I need a confession, especially on Good Friday."

Fr. Brian shrugged and started walking to the back of the church. Nonna's confession lasted all of 15 minutes as she debated a moral issue that she thought was a sin. In fact, another 3 arrived, making him go back inside each time he tried to exit the confessional. Fr. Brian did not make it to his BlackBerry for another hour. The crew had finished their clean up and decorations. The tables in the hall below had been laid out with fresh plastic tablecloths for the hundreds of hungry ones that would descend there in the evening.

When he finally walked into his room, the feeling in his stomach was sickening. The BlackBerry was still on the floor, outside the shower – it was still flashing its red LED incessantly. He pressed the unlock button on top of the phone and saw that the battery was close to dying. Hurriedly, he logged into the device, making his way across the screen using the little touch pad. His sweaty fingers did everything wrong, and instead of scrolling across to the text messages icon, his finger moved the cursor up so that when he moved his finger right, he was right inside the games, right back inside the chess app, desperately asking if they could continue the game.

"Easy, Brian," he spoke to himself taking a deep breath, "calm down."

Wiping his hands on his pants, Fr. Brian maneuvered his way slowly down to the text message screen. "Way to go, Brian, maybe the side shortcut key was better suited for this," he told himself, thrilled at the very rare and brilliant technical idea that had emerged in his head. "Beat that, Daniel," he called and clicked on the text messages. There were 3 messages. He read each of them – one at a time. Shock, anger at himself and then sorrow engulfed him as he slumped to the floor. 3 messages from 3 different people – how could he have missed them?

The first was from his elder sister, Maria. She had left her family to come over and spend Holy-Week looking after their parents, now living close to the church. One of their rental homes was vacant and they could be close to Brian for the Holy-Week services. His mother's health was poor and she had absolutely refused to see a doctor. The sisters had shared the weeks in between them but only Maria, the eldest daughter, could slowly work her way through that stubborn head that rested on Margherita's shoulders.

"COME HOME SOON – MAMMA'S HEALTH FADING FAST." He scrolled over the message and it said, "Received 4 hours ago." Fr. Brian muttered to himself.

The second message was from a person that sent a shiver down his spine. "It just can't be," he told himself, "he does not even have my number."

"BE READY FOR ME LATER LITTLE NEPHEW – OR SHOULD I SAY – YOUR HOLINESS."

Fr. Brian scrolled in shock over the message. "Received 2 hours ago." There was only one person in the world who spoke to him with that sarcasm and disdain. The third message made his hand shudder. The number showed as unknown – a protected number. The reply option did not appear, and a strange set of characters appeared where a name should have been. Fr. Brian tried to make sense of them – there was a pattern – not that he would ever figure it out.

"2000 YEARS LATER – THIS IS THE DAY I WILL WIN – READY FOR DEATH, PRIEST?"

Fr. Brian scrolled over the message. His mind told him what his heart had already perceived, and believed, the moment he saw that message. The face of the dark hooded man flashed across his face.

"Received 1 hour ago." Fr. Brian did not need to
look at his watch, or think back. It was probably right in the
middle of his vision of the man on the horse. Fr. Brian's
hand went into an involuntary shiver. He reached out with
his left hand and stopped the shaking. The BlackBerry
display had gone dark after the lack of activity on his part.
He pressed a button out of habit to make the screen come
alive. Unfortunately, he held the button too long – a
shortcut. "Darn," he muttered furiously at himself. The
shortcut was dialing out to someone. With shivering hands,
he hit the end button. A few tries later, he was close to
smashing the BlackBerry in anger – it finally responded and
he breathed a sigh of relief.

"Oh my, dear Lord," Fr. Brian sighed, "if only I
could get one thing right."

He suddenly realized he was on the floor, unsure of
whether he had fallen or sunk to the floor. Mamma
Margherita, that's who he had to get to first. Maria never
texted or used her phone beyond the minimum phone call
to say she was arriving, or to order him home, for a meal,
that she had cooked specially for him. An urgent text meant
that things were bad.

He was about the rise from the floor when he felt a
deathly chill in the room. A shiver swept his body as the
presence of someone or something in the room began to
take shape in his mind. The first rays of the morning sun
were far away still, but the dull glow of the dawn formed the
silhouette of a figure sitting in the window. The fedora was
unmistakable, as was the thin figure. The suit appeared
distinctly baggy and out of date with the latest fashion of the
day, but there was no mistaking the figure that had sent him
the second of his texts.

"Uncle Luigi," Fr. Brian laughed as something else
fell into place in his head, "I should have known."

"Known it, or know it, my dear nephew?"

"You can twist the words as you like, Uncle Luigi, but it all makes sense now."

"Well, nephew, the signs were there – you kids should have seen it coming."

Confused, Fr. Brian looked at the man.

"What are you talking about?"

"Your mother, child."

"Oh," Fr. Brian said, surprised.

"And what is it that you were going after, priest?"

"Your sudden appearance here today, in my room of all the places – your text – your suspicious figure all those years ago – the appearance of the dark stranger – and above all you here, in these early hours of a Good Friday morning. Uncle Luigi – it all makes sense today."

"You had better rush over to your mother, child, because whatever you are saying, makes no sense to me."

"You know it does, Uncle Luigi. You go and tell your evil master that I am ready – the Lord will walk with me today, like the pillar of fire that led Moses and the Israelites in the Sinai desert."

The
3rd
hour

VIII

Abaeze and Abayomi

"$33.99, miss," the bud tender calculated and punched in the cash register. The 5-dollar bills went in. "Your change, miss," he smiled, handing the young woman a loonie.

"Just a dollar? And my penny – that goes into your tip jar, does it?" she remarked sarcastically.

"Wake up, miss – the penny is no more – scrapped," he added as an afterthought.

She walked away silently. Abaeze smiled at the thought of all the change he did not have to return, thanks to the scrapping of the penny. He wondered if she even understood that as she was doped first thing in the morning. The stink of the weed from her clothes reeked of some spurious strain.

"Counting your pennies?" Abayomi, his wife teased from the recreational side of the marijuana dispensary.

"Bloody nuisance it was anyway – see I told you, voting for the conservatives was a good thing," he laughed back. "Lower taxes and my hard earned money stays with me. BTW, that woman should be on a *sativa*, she looks the very incarnation of an *indica*," he sighed, wondering how easily he could trap her in bed, high on a joint.

A regular stream of patients streamed in and out of the little dispensary – higher traffic than normal; it pleased the couple. Public holidays generally came with a deceptive lull outside, and big business inside.

"Quiet, yet busy," said Abaeze, owner of the bustling medicinal marijuana dispensary, on the southwest corner of Dufferin and Eglinton.

"Just the way it should be. Here's to a busy register," whispered Abayomi as she rearranged the bongs and the pot pipes. She passed him a half-smoked pot pipe, from the secret smoking room they maintained behind the long, sliding, glass jewelry, display case. It held dozens of mason jars containing samples of a plethora of pot strains. A morning treat for the hardworking African couple who had converted their addiction into a successful business.

A bevy of excited ladies marched in. "Some Durban Poison, please," one woman shrieked. "And some Agent Orange for me, tonight – we're blowing it all out."

Abaeze smiled and hit the register, as Abayomi began preparing the order.

"I'm Gabriela, and I like your shop," the first one said.

"Not a shop, or a store, beautiful Gabriela," Abaeze corrected, "it's a dispensary, and, you are my patients, not customers. How about some Golden Goat for my lovely patients as well? Absolutely rare and fresh batch," he finished off, desperately making a mental note of the woman's name.

"Yup – throw it in," answered another giggling excitedly, "why not – make that for 50 dollars, please."

"Mexicans," Abaeze thought happily.

"All *Sativa* for my lovely patients, no *Indica*. And some bonus edibles for my beautiful queens," Abaeze rubbed his eyes – popping out at the deep cleavage on display as Gabriela innocently bent over, studying the samples on the counter.

"Pot Brownies – on the house," he said, handing out a Ziploc bag that Abayomi reluctantly tossed over. The cash register opened with a clink.

"Colombians," Abayomi chimed in sarcastically as she watched her middle-aged, pot bellied, balding husband eye the attractive ladies walking out.

"Brazilians probably," Abaeze blushed, caught in the act – he had no excuse. Luckily for him, a PTSD suffering veteran walked in, "the usual, and double that order, man."

"74.99 worth of Goat Dawg coming up, sir," he said, quickly taking the 100-dollar bill from the wobbly man across the counter.

"I wish public holidays, came even more often," Abaeze said, "never had a brisker morning," he added, quickly taking a gulp from the bong that his wife had passed on to him.

"Strange one, that," he said suddenly, pointing out to a lady in black, visible through the dark, film covered glass window, that looked out on Dufferin. He had been searching for the group of women that had just left. Instead, his heart raced at the sight of the one across the street.

"Keeping a good lookout today, are we?" Abayomi's stern face betrayed the anger creeping into her face.

"Look at those cameras," Abaeze tried to distract Abayomi as he turned his attention to a bunch of college students that had just entered.

"What would one want to shoot with all that gear on a mundane intersection like this?" Abayomi wondered, as she got ready to follow the group. Young people meant trouble – either Abaeze or Abayomi always followed them around the dispensary, keeping a watchful eye. These turned out to be the quiet ones.

"For the ADD," one added nervously, "exams coming up." The couple laughed. They could sense the first timers from the scared faces, as the overpowering smell of the marijuana enveloped them.

"Never know, must be from some big daily, hope she gets the dispensary in one of her shots," Abaeze added thoughtfully.

"I could ask," offered Abayomi suddenly fascinated with the woman across the street. "That's how I'd like to be if someone offered me a new life, or a complete makeover."

"Makeover – keep dreaming," teased Abaeze.

"Seriously, look at her clothes, her hair, her looks, her body – I bet she's powerful too – and lost," Abayomi finished, wanting to go across and talk to the woman. "Nothing ever happens at this intersection – except of course the crowd."

"And the madman, " Abaeze added.

"Yup, he seems rather animated today."

"As long as he stays put on that side."

"Oh, check this out," Abayomi shrieked with delight, "that's the young handsome priest, they say he's charismatic, and a real charmer too." She looked out dreamily; blissfully ignoring the jealous rage openly evident on her husband's face.

"Looks pretty troubled to me. He could do with a smile, at the very least," Abaeze tried to bring down the object of his wife's adoration.

"What do you mean? He's a priest on Good Friday – he's got to be serious."

Abaeze burst out laughing. "What a ridiculous thought – lame argument."

"Ah, I wish he'd drop in here, just once – out of curiosity," Abayomi continued dreamily.

"Say, do you remember that old Jamaican man?" Abaeze asked suddenly, "the one that we thought was long overdue for the grave."

"What's wrong with you, Abaeze – that is such mean talk," Abayomi scolded, "he was a devout man, and a kind gentleman who spoke like an Englishman."

"That's because he was a butler, just a butler, in the British army."

"Whatever," Abayomi argued back, "he was a kind soul, who fought many wars — was old — yet so dignified."

"Still, just a butler."

"So, what about him?" Abayomi reminded her husband.

"Didn't he have all those stories about Good Friday, and all those strange events and occurrences?" Abaeze said.

"True," Abayomi sighed, "I miss all those ghost stories grandpa used to tell under the giant boɗarlaa-hi tree, in our village square back home at night, under the starry sky, as we roasted corn, huddling together as the roars of the big game on the adjoining reserve, sent chills down our spines."

"Ya, but these were no ghost stories," Abaeze corrected, "the old gent really believed that their devil --,"

"Satan!"

"Yes, that one — was at work here, in this place, this square — especially on Good Fridays."

"Ah well, at least it's comforting to know that the gorgeous priest is around if something were to happen," Abayomi retorted, getting even with her husband for his roving eye, as a frightful shiver rippled through her body.

* * *

Fr. Brian indeed carried a rather serious look on his face. To anyone who knew him better, it was more than just serious. The visit from Uncle Luigi that morning, out of the blue, had sent his world into a spin. Uncle Luigi emerging out of nowhere, on a day that dawned with what promised to be the most tragic news about his mother, troubled him. His old suspicions of the strange man that had surfaced out of the creature in the stable, in that horrid vision in the barn,

seemed to gain more strength over the years. The dark
hooded man had become inordinately busy. It troubled him,
strengthening the theory even further in his mind. Were
Uncle Luigi and the hooded man the same person?

"And a very good morning to you too," Fr. Brian
said absent-mindedly to someone and kept on walking.
"Sorry," it came out almost instantly as he turned back to
apologize for the impersonal response. The person had
passed on, heading in the opposite direction. Relieved, he
was about to turn and head back west, when the woman in
black caught his eye.

Was it a flash from the large camera, or a strange,
furious clicking of the shutter or something else – he knew
not but something sinister seemed to engulf him and then
bounce away. He gave the lady another look, and felt her
watch him intently through her lens. He was about to look
again when another troubling sensation swept over him – a
scream followed, and he turned the other way.

"Repent, repent, the lord died for our sins." He
smiled at the sight of the preacher on the wall – the
Jamaican had warned him many a time of some great
apocalypse nearly upon them. Behind the crazy man that
shrieked out doomsday warnings from the wall, was a
friend, who never ceased to stop Fr. Brian dead in his tracks
to alert him to the impending end of the world.

"You dismiss me, reverend, but the signs are
everywhere. It is coming soon, reverend, real soon, man.
Satan is here, in our midst, and is about to unleash a war."
Fr. Brian suddenly felt edgy at the thought. He had tried,
but could never ever find the signs that were supposedly out
in the open according to the big man. The previous night's
vision of the dark figure suddenly came alive in his mind.

"Just like the woman in black," his mind prompted
from somewhere. She was nearly reaching him – the camera
had not stopped clicking. He felt a gripping energy flow

from her. Curious, he was about to look again, when a succession of events took him crashing back to the depressing realities unfolding around him. The walk signal was about to turn green when an explosion of sounds hit him.

A violent screech of brakes, shattered his thoughts. The cars heading north had come to a screeching halt.

"Get the hell off the signal, man," a driver midway through the intersection yelled at the car in front of him. The driver in front promptly honked back, and a hand with the middle finger stuck up, shot out of the window. The driver next to Fr. Brian reversed hurriedly to get back south of the signal, nearly crashing into the car behind him, causing another angry blast of horns. Fr. Brian covered his ears. People stared north at something happening just past the northbound signal.

"Blasted punks," a tall man next to Fr. Brian cursed as he gauged the scene a little further up north, "nearly caused a pileup."

"Good for nothing teens," another added in, shaking his head vigorously from side to side.

"Seem ok," the first man added, watching the boys rise from the road.

"Wish one of them had really got a good slam."

"And let the poor driver go through hell – cops – insurance – lawyers – sued," the first man argued back.

"Ah! That's jaywalking – besides the cops would love to nail one of those young punks," the other said.

"Now, now, that's not a good thing to say, my brothers," Fr. Brian intervened, "remember we were all hot blooded at that age."

"You don't know this group, priest," added the first one, taking in the sight of Fr. Brian's roman collar.

"And what about them?" Fr. Brian asked curiously.

"They are a mean bunch – those – see those baseball bats in their hands – they won't hesitate to use them on some poor soul."

"Bad teens – maybe you should do something to correct the blokes now, before they turn into full-time thugs," the second man added and they carried on.

"Teens," Fr. Brian thought caringly, "the Lord knows – we need so much more help in his vineyard – those young souls need a guide."

He debated for a second going up to the boys as the traffic slowly came back to life and limped on. He looked again, and yet another time the shock of the sight hit him. Dumbstruck, he stared ahead. The faces of each of the young slowly began to form a name in his head.

"James, Danny, Dylan – oh my good Lord." His sadness turned to anger as he looked up north to see a familiar group of his parishioners acting every bit as wild and menacing, as the two men had described them earlier. Their demeanor worried him.

He was determined to head to them when a fierce buzzing of his BlackBerry brought him to a standstill. The BlackBerry went silent for a minute and began to vibrate again, furiously – continuously. Someone was not happy with just a text or one call. He was fumbling with the BlackBerry in the holster when a fierce snapping of a lens right next to him, startled him. He loved that sound – the long swishing of those powerful lenses as a succession of slides fell into place, followed by a final stamp – as if a real masterpiece had been captured each time by those mighty cameras.

"Gently, priest. Calmly and a little gently," a deep, sensuous female voice intoned. There was a hint of irritation in her voice as she saw him struggle with that simple task.

"Masterpiece!" the word suddenly popped in Fr. Brian's head again. Stunned, he gulped, realizing he had said it out aloud, "the camera I mean."

The woman's eyes remained serious, not entertaining the priest's remark at all. He laughed quietly to himself, blushing like a little boy.

Up north, a scream from the preaching man filled the intersection. "The moment is at hand, repent."

The camera was busy again and Fr. Brian sighed with relief. "Some professional," he thought. The moment of relief was but transitory. Once again, a fierce blast of something dark and evil hit him. The woman had crossed over to the little island that separated the free right turn lane from Dufferin to Eglinton.

He followed her camera. It was pointed at the bus stop across Eglinton. Faces of all kinds filled the crammed space around it. He knew something in that little crowd there, had caught the woman's attention. That same something, was gnawing for his attention as well. A white face, a fat face, an old face, a black face, a kid's face, a smiling face — all seemed normal. He scanned again and like a silent clue, camouflaged in a vast painting, he saw it. Tucked in quietly behind the crowded bus shelter, the face stared out at him. Cold and ruthless — Fr. Brian felt the evil hit him from across the street. A smirk and a smile as the dark hooded man looked directly at him. He felt his feet wobble a bit as the dark hooded figure quietly began to weave his way through the crowd. The preaching man stopped in mid-scream and looked down, but the hooded figure with the nimble agility of a gymnast had already ducked and hidden in the crowd.

It startled Fr. Brian. He looked furiously for the hooded figure but a TTC bus pulled in just then. "Move, move," his mind implored. Fr. Brian tried to see the people getting on the bus. At long last, the signal changed and the

bus was ready to move but the right lane next to the
Shoppers Drug Mart was blocked. The bus driver waited to
merge but was cut off by a speeding car.

."Now, now," Fr. Brian muttered with baited breath
as the intersection cleared. He looked about furiously as the
rapid snapping of the camera filled his ear. The dark figure
of the woman, the snapping of the shutters, and whatever
was evil in that place, seemed to find a connection in his
head. He followed in the direction of her lens and for the
umpteenth time that morning, his heart pounded as he held
his head in disbelief.

Walking up towards the rowdy boys was the hooded
figure of the man that had been the sign of everything evil
that could befall them. He saw the evil figure duck and skip,
trying to avoid the gaze of the tall Jamaican tracking him.
Suddenly, things seemed to fall in place. A faint light of
worry that threatened to mushroom into an evil of great
proportions, came to life. For a start, he knew the teens
were in some grave danger. He hesitated for a second when
the thought of his dying mother fell like a heavy anvil on his
head. What if this was the end – his final chance to see her
alive, one more time? Maria's message had said it plain and
clear.

Shaking his head at the dilemma that engulfed him,
he was about to walk on towards his mother, when the
powerful burst of a deadly, evil presence, hammered him
like the blast of a bomb. There was something mean and
evil that gripped the intersection. Bits and pieces of a
complicated jigsaw puzzle swirled in his head. The hooded
man seemed to be showing something to one of the boys
left behind. He knew it well – he had worked with the cops
in problem neighborhoods, to know what a gun looked like.

"I'll be home soon, mamma – wait for me," he
prayed hoping to sprint across the road towards the last kid
when the BlackBerry buzzed again. The westbound signal

changed and Fr. Brian felt himself walking back west. Half way through the signal, he fumbled again with the BlackBerry. It vibrated one last time – it was Maria.

"Hello, Maria!"

"Brian, she didn't --," and the line went dead.

"Hello – Hello – Maria – you there?"

He screamed trying to squeeze every possible button to coax the phone to come alive again. Nothing happened – he hit it once more – the same result. It was dead. Close to smashing the BlackBerry in frustration, he closed his eyes and muttered a prayer for patience and strength.

"Come on, Brian – nice and slow now," he told himself and tried once more. The screen came to life briefly – just for an instant for him to see that dark red outline of a dying battery and then it faded away. A deathly hollow and dark feeling swept through his body. Two more steps and the full weight of what the message could mean, hit him.

"It can't be – It can't be," the priest chanted frantically. His ministry had been to console and heal – be a shoulder to cry on. He had stood around death and helped families prepare their departed ones for their final journey. The late night calls, the last sacraments – he had been a rock of support for grieving families. Suddenly, he stood in the middle of the road, exposed, a mere mortal – a man.

* * *

Across the street, Abayomi followed the priest's back and forth movement continuously. She saw him with the dark clothed, photo snapping woman and felt a tinge of jealousy.

"They would make a great pair, and make beautiful children," she mused in her mind. "Do they know each other – that beautiful woman and the handsome priest?"

"Lord – how I'd love one chance to do something for him," she wished silently in her mind, suddenly aware of the stink of the weed in her clothes.

Abayomi saw the priest begin to cross the street – her heart pounded. The woman and then this man – something was drawing her out to that intersection. Abaeze was busy with a long line of seniors. The priest would have to pass close to the shop entrance. Abayomi could hear the chattering voice of her husband as he busily totaled and chatted up the customers.

"That strain is perfect for all those side effects of your husband's chemo, Ma." Abayomi checked Abaeze's bustle at the counter.

"And of course that Magic Rice Krispie treat is a perfect gift to pamper yourself with. Go slow though, they take a bit of time to kick in but can last all of 5 to 6 hours." A big toothy grin lit his face. Abayomi couldn't tell if it was for the money coming his way, or for the wild and pretty party type white lady next in line.

Abayomi slipped out of the shop pulling the door gently behind her. It felt like a strange world out there. Shorn of the warm comfort, overpowering smell and narrow space of the shop, she felt frozen and exposed. She had hardly closed the door when a powerful gust of wind slammed the intersection from the north. Abayomi shivered – it felt eerie – as if she was in a scary movie. In her excitement to get to the priest, she had forgotten to grab her jacket from the back room. The priest was half way through the signal when she saw the wind slam him again. Already wobbly, he stumbled a bit. His tall frame seemed to shake a little – he staggered forward a few more steps as the

BlackBerry fell out of his hand and onto the road – he followed soon enough.

On the third step from the center of the crosswalk she saw him collapse in a heap. Abayomi jumped forward to hold him. Her tiny frame was no match for the tall, broad frame of the priest. They fell backwards. Someone held her from the back and lowered her to the ground with the priest in her arms. He was out – cold. She saw his immaculate face resting on her shoulder – he had fallen into a deep sleep. "Weird," she wondered, "could he be under a spell?"

She tried desperately to lift him up while rising again. The wind ensured they stayed that way. It was an angry wind that decided to add a loud howl to its power. Abayomi swore it sounded like the big game – a large, angry wild animal in a dark forest announcing the start an evil attack by the demons. Another wild gust caught the priest's hat and sent it flying.

* * *

The hooded man watched in glee. The evil wind he had drawn from the farm, way north on Dufferin, found its mark almost as if it remembered the little teen who had seen the vision and survived. The priest's arrival was not what he had planned – certain powers were beyond him. Life and death, they still belonged to the almighty – he could only intervene in his own dark and nefarious ways. The scene before him was God-sent – he laughed at the thought. The fragility of the priest's mind gave him new ideas. He watched Amanda capture the scenes. "Brilliant – a true opposite of why I hated your mother – a weakling. Amanda, ah, well you carry my genes," he thought.

The frail priest was falling into a trance – induced by a situation he had only joked about – weakened by the negativity of life that the wind swept in.

* * *

"Oh mamma, don't worry I'll wear my best possible suit, smile and rejoice, as I send you off on your last journey to our Lord," Fr. Brian would tease his mother in her moments of self-pity.

It was a joke then – not anymore – he told himself as the full weight of the news hit him. Another step and he was halfway across the street, when his feet buckled under him. The last thing he remembered was a middle-aged African face looking into his face. He was resting on her shoulder as she tried to revive him.

* * *

The hooded man clapped with delight. It was time for the final showdown. The bearer of the thorn was exactly where he wanted him to be – a mad man ready to be cast unto death, and the thorn claimed for its final destruction. He saw the long lens swing away from the chaos that surrounded the fallen priest. The mad man was reaching a feverish pitch. The evil wind blowing south was nearly at its peak. He was ready.

IX

Dylan

The preaching man atop the tall retaining wall screamed out one final, passionate prayer. He sensed the attack that had originated from the hooded man.

"Lord, be my strength," he bellowed and held on a little more to his precarious perch. "Perhaps there is one more soul I can save for you, My Lord," he prayed from his worldly pulpit. He saw the second deadly evil gust take down the priest. "No, no, be strong brother," he called out aloud.

"Lord be --," he was about to yell out again when his upward raised face caught a majestic vision through the skies. A glorious vision of paradise that he had waited for all his life. The dark clouds parted, and a brilliant white light shone onto him. Were those angels he wondered – they were. Singing glorious praises of the Lord, they reached out to him. His hard life of sacrifice was nearly done. His heavenly reward, his place among God's angels was but a few moments away. The vision left him blissfully stunned, paradise at last.

"Oh Lord, how my soul longs for thee," he gushed happily as his soul yearned for that final entry into paradise. With death just moments away, it was time to hand over the thorn. Suddenly, it struck him, "I know not the soul, the chosen one who will carry thy thorn, my Lord. Who have thou chosen for this glorious privilege, a heavenly burden no human with ordinary strength could carry."

"It is your hour, Lord, your holy thorn, your glory – guide me," he smiled ecstatically knowing his battle with evil – the weight of what he had carried for decades was about to end. His heart was bursting with joy but for the moment there was one final battle he had to win for the Lord, one final battle against the forces of the Anti-Christ.

"To lay down my life with thee on this holy day, Lord," he prayed, "I am so blessed." He looked at the hooded man anxiously. If he could get to him, all the evil that was to befall mankind that day, could be prevented. The hooded man seemed to be everywhere, across the street, at the Tim Hortons, outside the church, catching up to the teens – everywhere. There was a battle to be fought. For the moment, the only one who could help him, the priest, was struck down.

"Rise, oh priest," he cast a prayer across the intersection, "rise, for the Lord needs your steady hands and your strong faith." A sudden thought of the priest being the next Thornbearer crossed his mind but his heart knew it wasn't. The white haired lady flashed across his mind. "Sister," he called out, feeling her soul nearby and felt her strength, but it wasn't her either.

At that moment, just like the vision of heaven, a curious, brown face looked back at him from across the street, unaware of what lay ahead. He peered into that soul – his words and eyes reaching out like a silent anointment.

"Oh bless the Lord, my soul," he wept with joy.

The Thornbearer's mind worked furiously. The fallen priest, the wayward teens, the dark haired girl – only then it dawned on him – they were baits, pawns, to be sacrificed in evil's lust to get the thorn. The slight distraction of the vision cost him his balance. A clap from the hooded man brought forth another deadly evil gust that sent him tumbling from the wall. The impact of the fall ricocheted through his body. Its impact vibrated through the thorn in his head sending severe jabs of pain through his brain. He had to get to the priest somehow. The intersection seemed to turn dark in his mind – a swathe of red glowed over it.

"You evil hooded one, a mass killing or just me? Who are you after? Lord, be my strength," he chanted closing his eyes and sprinted through the signal, across Eglinton, to the south side. Those giant strides would have taken him across easily but the hooded man's hypnotic gaze flickered a bit. It was almost as if at each stage his prey were offering themselves to be sacrificed. The hooded man snorted in glee – he would not need the teen to shoot after all.

A powerful pickup truck was first off the eastbound signal from the west side of Dufferin. The clean-shaven – tattooed – Mad Max like driver pulled on a cigarette racing across the signal. The hooded man looked beneath and smiled. The man was a ready accomplice – his horrendous life and deeds made him a fertile ground. An evil possession flowed from the hooded man's eyes, through the man. A nod and their union was complete. The hooded man pressed down his foot and the driver slammed on the pedal.

"*Fuck* off the road, you *arse'ole*," the driver yelled as the truck leaped forward with the sudden surge of power through its axles. With the roaring power of the massive 8-cylinder engine, the driver took the powerfully built truck into the body of the Thornbearer.

* * *

"It's my day," the hooded man screamed, clapping with fierce delight. The priest was down, the Thornbearer battered and the thorn just a few steps away, "Mine, mine, mine," he chanted. With a wave of his hands, he swiped in another burst of the evil wind to keep things chaotic. The wind answered and the hooded man moved towards the

fallen Thornbearer, his eyes glowing red with evil
anticipation. Time stood still as Satan sensed a victory after
centuries of waiting.

"Now, now, now," the hooded man hissed with
glee. With each hiss – fear, dread, panic and gloom filled the
hearts of those around. All around the world, in the hearts
of holy men and women, a dread crept in. Some prayed
harder, unaware of what was to unfold – yet deeply
distressed at the thought of some deadly evil that was to be
unleashed somewhere on God's earth.

A few steps and he would be on to the preaching
man who had been flung across the road. He heard the
shutter snapping rapidly not too far away and knew Amanda
had unknowingly channeled her evil powers, capturing the
mad man in midair, and accentuating his fall.

He was a step away when the Thornbearer stirred.
"No, you should be crushed – dead," he screeched as the
first shards of doubt hit him. He felt the full despair and
defeat that had hounded his ancestors since that first Good
Friday. "Die," he yelled, wild and angry, as he had done over
the years. The yell was lost in the blaring of horns. He saw
the Thornbearer begin to rise as the crowd spilled over from
all sides.

Furious, he stomped his foot and felt the weight of
the evil he was dispersing, slam everyone around. An engine
burst into flames and people yelled, expecting an explosion.
"The fires of hell shall rage upon you," he cursed at the
sight. He needed a few more of those. Another car erupted
causing a blast – some fell, some shivered and some grinned
with evil delight as the evil that the hooded man dispensed,
found a home. Some of it bounced back. To his dismay, he
saw the priest rising. He sensed the powerful burst of energy
the Thornbearer had sent the priest's way. The power and
purity of that energy surprised him. If the Thornbearer was
indeed that powerful, and pure, then taking the thorn would

be no easy task. Just getting close enough to someone so
pure would be the greatest challenge. Furious, the hooded
man looked to the skies and bellowed in anger. The clouds
darkened even further. A dreaded gloom and darkness crept
over the intersection that until a short while back had been
bathed in golden sunshine. It was time for something more
drastic.

"A sacrifice for you, my master," the hooded man
prayed. He shivered at the thought of failing his own master
— Satan. He had to slay someone.

"Blood," he swore in grunts, "blood — need lots
more of it." He felt the chilly feel of the pistol butt in his
hand and remembered the teens.

"Dylan! Where are you?" he called as the first wails
of the approaching sirens filled the cold and darkish
intersection. It was happening too fast and defeat seemed
imminent yet again. In the meantime, he needed a cover
from the cops.

"Riot — a riot is what I need," he sang with an evil
twisted mouth, "come forth, ye earthly souls," and the
crowds poured out.

*   *   *

Nearby, Amanda felt a shiver sweep down her body.
It wasn't the cold — she was sure of that. The sudden gusty
wind had a familiar feeling — it was the cabin in the
mountains all over again. A dark force was flowing.
Strangely, she felt it from within — like a dark magic she was
controlling it. The final yell from the preaching man caught
her by surprise. She raised her camera to shoot just as he fell
over. Frame by frame she captured his fall in still shots
feeling she had controlled it with an imaginary magic wand
from afar. She hit the shutter release once more and saw the
man land awkwardly. She felt the shove that had sent him

down from the wall and watched a dark shadow fade away. A few seconds later, his body landed close to her feet – dispatched across the signal by a truck. She shot rapidly. A dark shadow was filling her lens. With each passing shot, the pictures were turning darker. The thrill of the morning was gone. Evil was enveloping the intersection – it emerged from her employer, and from her.

"Just keep shooting, daughter," the hooded man's voice whispered in her ear. She obeyed quietly, too stunned at the way she had been addressed. For the first time, she felt the connection. The dark shadows, the dark frames – the evil seemed to be pouring out of her, her camera.

Pensively, Amanda shot once more as the preaching man began to rise. She turned her camera to the hooded man opposite the coffee shop, but he busily moved on. She caught his mouth through her lens as he yelled, "Riot." Amanda's joy and thrill turned to despair and fear as the crowds poured out from all corners. Gaping, she looked around letting her finger on the shutter release of the large camera do all the shooting.

In the midst of the chaos that seemed to get darker by the minute, someone or something was sending a wild excitement through her body. Something was making her heart beat faster. Confused, Amanda looked around. A million people seemed to have poured out on to that little stretch of Eglinton. Yet, somewhere she felt a presence draw her.

"Wake up, girl," she chastised herself but the warm feeling stayed. She looked behind – a most matter of fact glance and then she saw him. A wild, erotic surge swept her body, her breasts threatening to burst through as the brown man emerged from the Tim Hortons.

It was him – the same one from before – she didn't debate it. Their eyes met for the briefest of moments as he leaped over the iron rail in front of the Tim Hortons. She felt his eyes pore deep within her. The bitter cold around her vanished as she felt a warm glow of love envelope her. A long, distant, happy memory filled her with a wild, simple, abounding joy. She was a happy little girl again, cared for, pampered, loved and treasured. She suddenly did not feel alone anymore.

"Stop it, *bitch*," she yelled aloud this time as the word, 'love', rang furious alarm bells in her head. Amanda knew she had to catch up to the man before she lost him again. There was life in her suddenly. She let the camera hang, adjusted her dress and ran her fingers through her hair. The action seemed almost erotic – seductive. She did it again – more for the relief it gave her cold, aching head. She let her fingertips massage her frozen scalp. She had been busy shooting for the past hour and had totally forgotten herself. She put her hand on her stomach and knew deep within a wild hunger for the man had overtaken the moment. She imagined a long day, over. She was falling into his strong yet tender arms. His fingers tips were massaging her scalp as his other hand gently rubbed her hungry stomach. There was a hot meal cooked with love, waiting for her.

"Focus, *bitch* --," she nearly yelled out aloud when the strangest of sensations played a sweet melody through her ravaged brain. She stared long and hard at the brown man and felt a deep longing to be held by him – to be close to him. She took her first step in his direction and felt the evil in her fade away, when the preaching man shockingly got up and ran. The brown man sprinted behind and the crowd followed. The intersection was about to erupt with something again and she was ready to capture it.

Gripping her cameras, Amanda ran. Two steps later, she fell. Someone, or something, had tripped her. A stab of pain shot through her foot. She was about to hit the sidewalk headlong when the thought of her Nikons smashing in first, hit her. A last minute roll and surprisingly she found herself sitting perfectly balanced on her bottoms. Some unknown energy had gripped and steadied her. She looked up and saw the hooded man pass her as he approached one of the teens from the wild gang. Their conversation was lost in the din of the crowd, but what Amanda saw in the split of a second, left her stunned.

$*$ $*$ $*$

Across the signal, Abayomi saw the priest open his eyes as if rudely awakened from a deep sleep. Wild emotions gripped her – most of all panic.

"Abaeze, Abaeze," she screamed, "someone, anyone – help – the priest is dying – call 911."

"Calling 911," someone answered.

"No, please don't, I'm ok," the priest suddenly opened his eyes. Embarrassed, he tried to stand up but stumbled right back onto Abayomi. The sound of cars smashing into each other and the blaring horns made him jump up again. A series of thuds followed as engines burst with deafening blasts, sending glass crashing all around. Wild screams were filling the air. People were yelling and screaming. The woman gently held him up straight. He saw the worry in her face.

"Just a bit of --,"

"It's ok, reverend. Please come into the dispensary for a minute and steady yourself," the African lady pleaded.

"I'm fine, and I don't want to mess up that doctor's dispensary."

"That's quite alright, reverend. It's my disp – er – shop."

"What happened here?" the priest asked her horrified, surveying the damage around. He stood up

shakily. His hand was still gripping her shoulder firmly.
"Looks like a scene straight out of a doomsday movie."

"That madman caused a massive pileup, reverend."

"Madman — but this looks like a war zone," he said trying to make sense of the destruction and noise around.

"The stupid mad man ran across the street at the peak of traffic and got knocked down by a truck. Everything else that followed was just a terrible chain reaction."

"Oh my Good Lord!" the priest exclaimed as his mind registered what was happening.

Abayomi saw the color drain from the priest's face. She held him tightly thinking he was going to faint again — a deep longing in her wished he would. She wanted to keep on holding that angelic hunk of a man.

"Don't worry, reverend, he probably needs the devil to come and take him down."

Fr. Brian stared at her quietly, standing on his own for the first time.

"It is the devil that is taking him down, my sister, he needs help and I am going to be there. Thank you for helping me."

"I am always there in that shop, reverend, please do drop in sometimes — it's a small humble little business."

"Why — thank you, sister — I most certainly will. God bless you and those strong arms." He hugged her, turned around and ran shakily towards the crowd.

* * *

The hooded man saw the gang of teens emerge from the McDonald's. Their wild demeanor had cooled off a bit — the food and the warmth had had a soothing effect. Their emergence on the sidewalk coincided perfectly with the rising of the Thornbearer.

"Oh – Oh, it's the prophet," Shamar yelled seeing the Thornbearer began to rise from the sidewalk.

"Stop! You, idiot," James screamed at Shamar, quickly grasping the situation. Blood seemed to be pouring out from all over the man's body. "Stop, you dumbass, the man is probably broken and crushed inside."

"Let's chase the crushed man," Shamar yelled.

"Let's stone him a little more," Danny added, "it's our own modern day passion play."

"He looks pretty busted to me," Jaime added to the chorus of shouting voices and the teens ran after the Thornbearer.

*   *   *

Dylan emerged last, a few minutes later – oblivious of the chaos that had unfolded outside. His face was a mixture of sorrow and pain, nearly on the verge of tears. Externally he put on a brave face, having rehearsed a line or two that would mask the storm erupting inside him. The line had been carefully picked. It would preserve his macho standing in the gang, and mask the wild emotions burning inside him. It was the furious buzzing of his Samsung that had driven him to the washroom. He had dared not pull out the large screen phone in the company of the boys. He would have been kicked out of the gang for answering his mother's call. The large screen of the Galaxy S7 would have given it all away.

Internally, he was sure it was his mother. Only she called continuously until he picked the line. Initial anger at the persistent call turned to worry, and then to remorse, as he remembered her toiling at work on that holy day. She worked at a small Falafel joint, 7 days a week, for a meager pay and a mean dictator of a boss.

"I'm so sorry you have to work today, mama," he had said to her as she left early that morning. On an impulse, he had jumped out of bed and hugged her. He knew it would end up being the best part of her day.

"One day you make lots of money, my son, so that this poor mother of yours won't have to slave like this — even on a Good Friday." The words early that morning melted his soul.

The number had definitely turned out to be his mother's — the male voice not so. "Your mother has been injured in an accident," it informed.

"But, she was ok this morning," Dylan stuttered back in shock — his mind unwilling to accept what he was hearing.

"That's right, this happened a short while back."

"Is she ok now?"

"Now don't you worry, son. First, tell me how old are you and what is your name?" patiently the voice on the other end of the line said in the most soothing of tones.

"I don't give a rat's *arse* about my name and age, you twit — just tell me about my mother," Dylan yelled into the phone.

The deep voice on the other side stayed calm. "Ok kid, now it's time to get a little more patient so that I can guide you to where your mother is."

"I don't give a --," Dylan was about to break off into another abusive rant when the words made sense, "ok — give it to me quick."

"That's better," the voice at the other end encouraged.

"Get on with it, man," Dylan screamed again.

"Princess Margaret Hospital, son," the deep male voice said, losing some of its patience.

"Is she er, ok, sir?" Suddenly, Dylan's voice was a plea.

"Just a few cuts and bruises, a bit shaken up but don't worry she will be fine. They're running a few quick checks and getting some X-rays just to ensure she doesn't go home with broken bones."

"Thank you!"

"Now you must go home and await her arrival, son, she will need you. Is there a dad, or any other elder in the house?"

"Yes, my dad is home," Dylan blurted out, feeling the relief in the voice at the end of the line as well as his own.

"Well, you stay there with your dad and an ambulance should bring your mom home soon."

The visit to the McDonalds washroom had ensured Dylan had missed all the action outside. The utter chaos made his jaw drop open. He saw the preaching man run towards the church followed by the crowd. He was glad to have been left out. It was the perfect getaway without having to inform the unruly group. If he ran north on Dufferin, and then took Livingstone, running parallel to Eglinton, heading east, he would make it home safely without bumping into the gang. Relieved, Dylan leaped over the little metal rail.

"Hopewell, not Livingstone," he decided, "perfect, quiet street – mama, I'm coming."

The leap over the rail was perfect. Dylan had done it a hundred times with his friends, without spilling a drop of his Coke. He could probably have done it blindfolded and known where he had landed except that this time he bumped into a robed figure.

The impact sent Dylan bouncing back into the metal rail. The robed hands of the figure reached out, grabbed, and steadied him. A pungent, burning odor emanated from the robes. It reminded Dylan of the sharp smell left behind by the matchsticks that his mother used to light the candles for the Rosary, or was it something from the chemistry lab?

"Sulphur," Miss Wang, his science teacher was saying in his head.

"Oops sorry, sir – thank you, sir," Dylan blurted out and turned to run but the figure held on. The sudden jerky movements against the strong hands that held him, sent stabs of pain through Dylan's shoulders. The grip was vice-like. Somewhere deep within he felt himself cry. It wasn't from the pain that shot through his shoulders. The grip was sending a dark and depressing feeling through him. The sadness of some long past memory was swirling in his head, like a bad dream from which he had just woken up.

"Mom," he cried out in fear, but no words came out. A prisoner like feeling had taken hold of him – bound up amidst the chaos and din that was playing out all around him. From the dark abyss that he seemed to be falling into, Dylan looked up slowly. Every bone in his body screamed at him not to – he sensed who it was.

"Hello, Dylan," the baritone voice intoned in a half singing, half-mocking voice.

"Hello, sir – please let me go – I have an emergency."

"Ah – a chicken even before we speak," the hooded man teased.

Dylan burst into tears. The dread was becoming unbearable. He was caught, in a dark, evil castle – escape was but a few feet away as the giant doors were closing forever. The bright, beautiful world outside seemed to be shutting out, and the damp and dark castle was overpowering him. A silent rage overtook him. The recent conversation on the phone brought his anger bursting out.

"Get your rotten hands off me, you jerk," he yelled.

"Anger – I like that, Dylan. Your anger and this weapon will make you the dreaded commando we spoke

about," the hooded man said silently pressing a gun into
Dylan's hands.

The lifeless feel of the cold gun sent a shiver
through Dylan's body. His hands nearly collapsed with its
weight.

"Careful now, son – we don't want to drop that."

"But, I don't want this," Dylan cried.

"Now, let's see who's the man?" the hooded man
said, letting go off Dylan's shoulders. "Look, the enemy
escapes," the hooded man said, pointing to the preaching
man running towards the church.

"The mad man? Enemy?"

"Ah – huh. Not a mad man – he is the enemy
running away with our secrets – a spy. You have to take him
down, soldier."

Dylan stood frozen as the hooded man slowly
backed away and disappeared. Every muscle in Dylan's body
screamed at him to drop the gun and run away just as he
had planned.

"So be it, mama, I'm coming," Dylan closed his eyes
and prayed, but the feel of the gun grew on him by the
second. Suddenly, there were 2 shots fired in the near
distance. "The spy was attacking," thought Dylan, he had to
defend his base. The prayer in his heart melted away as his
hands slowly firmed themselves on the butt of the gun. He
pushed his thumb and like a pro, flicked off the safety catch
even without looking.

Dylan still had one last chance to drop the gun and
run away as the Samsung buzzed again in his pocket. He
was sure this time it was his dad. Dylan would have bet his
last dollar his fragile dad was crying on having heard the
news about his wife. He needed Dylan.

Dylan tried to reach into his right pocket for the
phone but his hand was occupied with the heavy gun. He
made a feeble attempt to transfer it to his left hand when

the phone fell silent. Dylan hesitated, and then stopped as the gun began to feel like an extension of his hand – he didn't want to let go. He felt its power. *"Pussy,"* he heard Shamar call him. He felt a desperate urge to lift the gun, aim for Shamar and squeeze the trigger. He looked up and saw the battlefield in chaos.

"Time to kick some *arse*," the bra clad animation of his game host said in a sexy voice.

"Time to do some shooting," Dylan decided. He was the brave commando, about to storm the old Nazi castle, full of German zombies.

"Come in, soldier," a baritone voice was urging him on, in his head, "enemy at 3'O'clock." The mad man was nearly reaching the church. Dylan thought of his poor, slogging mother once more and then burst out crying. He could not tell what the tears were for, or about. He simply remembered sticking the gun in his belt under his winter jacket and running towards the crowds – he was a soldier – duty called.

X

Clare

The final words of her conversation with Terri, in the cruiser, played over and over in Clare's mind. She remembered his firm hand gently squeezing her shoulder. She had loved, nay, longed for that amazingly protective touch. All along the ride speeding into that emergency, their senses focused on the disaster awaiting them, she felt his heart reach out to her in some unknown way. After all those years in the private space of their cruiser, facing life and death, they understood each other better than two spouses did. Whether it was breaking up a deadly fight in a dark alley in the dead of the night, or responding to 911 calls for little kids having swallowed a little toy, or watching each other's back, when gangs indiscriminately opened fire on their cruiser – they had been through it all together. Terri didn't have to say it – Clare sensed it – love, affection – except that every pore in her body rejected it with disgust. It would be a betrayal of the worst kind. She enjoyed working with Terri for that very reason. Two cops, innately one, yet never threatened or attached by any personal relationship.

At the church, she welcomed the chaos. It was what made her adrenalin shoot to the skies. Seizing her chance, she had broken away. A few steps away was when she felt something wicked happening.

"Trust that instinct, officer," Terri, a few years her senior had taught her at the start, "your life, your survival depends on it."

"But how do I --,"

"Exactly the point, officer," he had screamed, cutting her off, "shut that very first doubt – believe that instinct."

The instinct was kicking a wild storm in her heart now, with each step she took into the crowds. The crowds seemed berserk – rabid – as if awaiting an evil command to begin a rampage.

"It's as if they're zombies controlled by some --," she muttered to her side and stopped in surprise realizing that Terri wasn't next to her. She felt alone – lonely.

* * *

A little further down, west of Clare, Amanda sat on the concrete sidewalk still shaken. Her relief was more at the survival of her cameras, rather than the break from the fall. She tried to rise but her awkward position hardly let her move. Two cigarette-puffing old men nearly tripped over her.

"Go home, miss – no place for a hottie – this," the first old man admonished, looking greedily at her.

"Delicious," said the other.

Amanda felt her fury rise. She stared back hard and saw their lustful looks change to timid ones, and then to fear. They fled as if she had let loose a bag of vipers on them. Surprised, she tried to rise in one quick swing, with a roll onto her side and straight onto her feet. It did not work. The cameras made it awkward. She was about to try again when a hand reached out. Amanda stared, surprised, it was the pretty teen whom her sponsor had eyed wickedly. The giant mop of wavy blond hair was distinct. There was warmth in the blue eyes looking down at her.

Amanda did the strangest thing in her dictionary.

"Hold these for me please, honey," she said handing the cameras to the teen. The weight of the cameras surprised the teen. Her hands fumbled a little with the two straps but held on tight. Amanda rocked onto her back, rolled forward, and stood up in a single swoop, grabbing on to the teen.

"Thank you, Hun," she said and tossed the camera belts back around her neck when something in the teen's eyes caught her attention. She stole a glance east and did not see the preaching man. His head was not sticking out above the crowd. Nor was the crowd moving or chasing him.

"I'm Amanda," she said holding out her hand.

The teen took it gratefully – almost grabbing it.

"Trisha," she replied in fascination, "and you're so beautiful, and so talented, powerful probably," she said pointing in awe at the cameras.

Amanda felt her heart stir – something in the teen's blue, admiring eyes caught her attention. "Not as angelically beautiful as you, honey. I'd trade anything for those blue eyes and golden hair."

To her shock, the teen went glum. "Inside that head with golden hair and blue eyes, is a slut," she shouted and burst out crying. Amanda felt the crowd stirring near the church – something was happening there. She let the cameras hang for a bit, the clicking could wait. She sensed something of herself in the teen.

"Darling, at your age even I thought a few missteps were bad, wait till you --,"

"I'm 16, and pregnant!" the teen blurted out.

Amanda had known the teen for as little as a minute or two but in that instant, something in herself bonded to the teen. The full impact of what the teen had blurted out sank in slowly. She saw the blue and red lights of an ambulance flashing near the church – she had to go. Trisha understood.

"Let's go – I know you need to do your thing."
They turned and ran towards the church. The crowd seemed
to have multiplied even more.

"Like, where the heck did all these people come
from?" Trisha remarked as they weaved their way through
the crowd. It was impossible to run. They were barely
making it through the people scattered all over.

"Where are you headed, Trisha?" Amanda asked,
pushing her way through some erratically chattering men.

"To find a guy named Daniel – might be able to
help."

"And you expect to find this Daniel guy in this
crowd?"

"A brownie – ran after the mad man – shouldn't be
that hard."

Amanda hesitated, stopped and turned to Trisha.
The wild stirring within her was back.

"Describe this brownie, your Daniel."

"Well, not my Daniel," Trisha blushed, "but an
Indian guy – youngish. Taught some religious stuff to my
good-for-nothing boyfriend. I know it's not much of a
description."

It was Amanda's turn to gawk. All her instincts
about that day had been true. Strange patterns seem to
form, right down to a pretty teen now accompanying her.
Their warmth towards each other seemed worth a lifetime,
and on top of it all, there was the brown guy who seemed to
have a magnetic effect on her. Her sponsor, the preaching
man, the priest, Trisha, the brown guy – they all seemed to
be part of some complex web.

They had gone ahead a little when Amanda saw the
bunch of teens the hooded man had targeted earlier. They
seemed to have gone wilder. Their boisterous voices rose
above the crowd. Amanda saw the black kid jump up. It
seemed like their earlier mischief.

Amanda was back to her professional self – eyes glued to the camera, fingers snapping, regardless of the dark shadows dancing across her lens. Two soft hands held her waist and led her through the crowd. The touch was gentle yet firm – she liked that hold. No one had held her like that or cared for her in a very long time. She sensed Trisha had naturally taken on the role of her guide.

The black kid jumped again. This time the flashing light from the ambulance reflected off his dark face. Red and then blue. The split second was enough for Amanda to shoot two frames before the dark shadows turned red and vanished. It was only then that her mind registered what she had seen – the teen's face was frozen. His eyes dilated wide with fear. He half rose again and then for another time that day, blood filled Amanda's lens. Amanda shot once more, gripped suddenly by a nagging feeling as if she had pulled a trigger. A wild scream pierced the wild cacophony of sounds that filled the area.

"Yieeeeeeeeee!"

* * *

Clare's radio buzzed instantly. "Heard a scream, Blondie2."

"Dear old Terri – sharp as ever," she laughed in relief when the thought of Terri struck her like a massive wrecking ball. Did she feel the same way about him after all these years? Perhaps her extreme disgust at the situation was her own defense mechanism against showing her feelings.

"There are a million screams out here, Blondie1 – will report back soon – out," she told him and sensed his relief – perhaps she liked his protective presence. The scream came again. That was when she noted the difference.

* * *

A little further west, Dylan gripped the gun as if his life depended on it. He was back in his game – hiding behind the bombed out wall of the armory, on the abandoned Russian base. He hit the A button on his SX7 controller. His view changed to an aerial one.

Dylan hit the B button. The static came on instantly. "Come in, Gold Finger," he whispered into the headset as he reloaded. There were two clicks in answer. Gold Finger hung up. The other click was the sound of an empty magazine. He felt his waist, the ammo belt was empty too – he needed to get to the armory.

Dylan hit the X button. The map lit up in his visor. To his immediate right were the large silos that had held the ICBMs. To his left lay the covered hangars from where the fighter jets launched out, as they came to the end of the underground runway. He had to watch out for that. The last time he had taken his eyes off the automatic hydraulic doors – he had been sprayed by a blast from a Spetsnaz's Kalashnikov. Those special operations Russians got him each time. Up ahead were the railway tracks with the specially designed rail cars to launch a variety of missiles on the go. Rusty and deserted, they still held a menacing look. The steely silence of the base was total.

"Ammo – dammit – I need ammo."

"You have 20,000 gold points," the bra clad sensual voice of the game operator popped up in the right corner of the screen. Dylan hit the right joystick and the flashing stopped. Dylan reloaded and blew a kiss to the purple lipstick and dark eyes.

"A date sometime, *bitch*?" he shouted. He liked her. "This summer for sure," he swooned thinking of the Toronto women in summer. He loved the cold, static, English accent of the operator as if it were from another dimension. He imagined wrestling her. She was a 9th degree

Black Belt – British Special forces who would most likely
take him down in a second with her little finger. He loved
the thought of himself trapped under her, looking into the
steely eyes of the cold-blooded killer as she debated whether
to rape him or kill him.

A scream from somewhere nearby startled him. He
awoke from his daze. He was running towards the church.
The gun in his hand was real – fully loaded. It was the first
time he was holding it physically, but he had done it enough
times on his game controller to know exactly how it worked.

Dylan was itching to fire off a round. He had to feel
the thrill of the kickback. He stopped and set it to single fire
mode. The crowd was dense. His own hands were unsteady
– sweaty and shivering – both from excitement and fear.
Dylan hopped over a fallen man and landed just in time to
see his group in front. They had come to a stop. The laugh
from Shamar brought him further back to reality. He
remembered the buzzing phone, and his fear of being seen
answering his mom's call. Dylan's fierce, warrior gaze
changed to his usual meek and tame one. The group had
seen the awkward jump.

"What kept you back there, Mr. Sissy?" Shamar
scolded.

"Washroom," Dylan answered hesitantly.

"Oh! Baby went to pee," Danny teased. Dylan felt
his fury rise.

"Hey! Did you see the sissy boy jump?" Shamar
continued. Dylan felt his grip tighten on the butt of the
Glock. He had tucked the gun held hand under the jacket.

"Give the guy a break," Jamie tried. He was the only
friend Dylan could count on. Shamar wasn't about to let go.

"Hey look at this – this is how the sissy jumps."
Shamar jumped a silly, wimpish jump. The group laughed.
Dylan felt his thumb reach in and release the safety catch.
James clapped as Shamar was about to jump again.

"Stop!" – the scream that erupted from Dylan was full of desperation and anger. "Don't push me anymore – I am this far from shooting you down," he yelled, holding up his left index finger with the thumb pressed hard against it.

"Oh – Oh – the boy has a scream too," Shamar yelled and jumped again.

It was the exact instant Dylan drew the Glock from under his jacket. The slide was drawn back. Shamar saw it as he reached the top of his jump. He landed unsteadily. An apology ready to flow from his lip – the sight of a real weapon too much to bear in the hands of an angry and bullied kid. There was no time to raise his hands, or surrender, or apologize. The first bullet struck him in the stomach throwing his frail body back a few feet. Dylan and Shamar's eyes met for an instant. Each radiated an equal amount of shock and surprise.

Shamar raised his hand in defense as he saw the Glock follow him to the ground. It was too late as a second bullet shattered his femur. Shamar died instantly from the massive blot of pain that exploded in his body.

*   *   *

A beautiful, golden sunshine had welcomed Terri and Clare racing into the disaster that was unfolding. It was now replaced by a dark shadow that blanketed the earth. The odor, the very air reeked of some stench – death. Clare felt the gloom creep into her soul as her mind prompted for some rational reason to dispel it. That was when the sound of the shots reached her.

"Bam – Bam."

After all those years in the force, the sound still surprised her – like a firecracker – easily ignored. Instinctively, she looked for the source. It seemed close, too close, a little west – the direction she was headed in.

A short sprint brought her to the man on the ground. He had been hit in the stomach and leg. Blood drenched – the man lay motionless. She knelt and felt his pulse – dead – she concluded. She looked again and realized it was a boy – a young, black male. She had made it to the scene in a few seconds, the gunman had to be close. She had to take him down fast before he went after someone else. A crumbling cement planter lay loosely rolled over. Clare hopped on to it for a better view – gun outstretched, she scanned the immediate area for a fleeing figure. There was no sign of the gunman. Then again, she reasoned, with the massive crowds around, any one of them could be the gunman.

"Anyone see the gunman?" she yelled, her voice blasting the frenzied crowd like a stun grenade. Silence fell, no one answered. "Come on, somebody's seen something – speak – before somebody else gets hurt." The people around her simply stared. "Bloody zombies for sure," she cursed in her mind.

She hopped down and a dark, hooded figure smiled at her. His calm demeanor and strange garb made her dismiss him at first. "Lunatic," she muttered. No one could be calmly standing or smiling in that situation. He could have been standing on the deck of the sinking Titanic with a Pina Colada in his hand. The people nearest to him stared in shock, some began to run away but no one moved to help the fallen man. A middle-aged woman – scarf and all, was shivering violently in shock at what had played out before her.

The hooded man gazed intently at Clare. "Dammit," she muttered uncomfortably. There was something disconcerting about the man. Clare was used to men lowering their eyes in fear or self-doubt from the stare of her cop eyes. This man seemed to look right through her. She felt him play with her mind.

Could he be the gunman? Clare's eyes and gun followed him closely as he very calmly stepped to the side. He wasn't the gunman – hidden behind the dark mass of the hooded man, was a boy. Clare swore he could have been no more than 14 or 15 years old. He stood standstill, as if in shock. The gun in his hand held ready, as if looking for his next victim. She saw the semi-automatic Glock 9 in his hand and knew she could be his next victim in the blink of an eye.

"Drop the gun," Clare screamed, drawing her gun level, ready to shoot. "Drop it now," – Terri was back in her head – "keep pounding," – he was telling her. Clare took a step forward menacingly. She was about to scream again but her police voice did the trick as she saw the boy hesitate. 10 years earlier, she had practiced it at the academy. It always worked – it did today. People scattered in panic at the sight of the drawn weapon. A split second distraction at some movement on her right, caused her to turn quickly – was there a second gunman aiming at her? She needed Terri by her side more than ever. He was supposed to be covering that right flank. Instinctively her hand hit the radio.

"Gunman on the loose, Blondie1 – armed kid with automatic – two shots fired – man on the ground."

"Roger that, Blondie2."

"Need immediate backup, boss," she yelled to Terri wondering why he was not already by her side at the sound of the shots.

"Got it," he replied but he seemed distant. The sharp, rasping cop voice was missing – so was the sense of urgency.

*   *   *

The two shots that brought down Shamar seemed frozen in the Amanda's camera. Trisha's hand tightened around Amanda's waist – her nails dug into Amanda's

stomach. The black teen disappeared from the lens. A
dreadful silence – shock, thought Amanda – filled the road
before terrified screams replaced the brief, silent moment.
The stunned silence vaporized instantly as panic seized the
crowd again.

Amanda saw the crowd part in fear. At the end of
the path, opened up by the parting crowd, stood the hooded
man – his back to Amanda and Trisha. They ran ahead
hesitantly. Their arrival was greeted by a cop, coming from
the other side of the hooded man. The cop was a lady –
petite, attractive, fierce – gun drawn. Amanda's senses were
in frenzy as she shot away at a military pace. She saw the
cop advance slowly, gun drawn – shouting, calling for
something. The cop had taken a few steps, when Amanda
saw the hooded man step aside. Amanda's heart was
beating furiously – she expected something to happen. Her
lens captured the teen who had been camouflaged against
the black robe of the hooded man. She had seen him
speaking to the hooded man earlier. She caught sight of the
gun in the teen's hand and cursed silently under her breath.
She zoomed in on the teen – capturing as much as she
could.

"Dylan," Trisha's choked voice gasped.

"You know the gunman?"

"Yeah, just a teen, junior to me, how the hell could
he have shot Shamar – Oh my God – Shamar – Shamar
shot?"

Amanda turned and saw a horrified look fill the
teen's face. She was in total shock.

"You know those guys?"

"Yes, my juniors – still in grade 9 – it can't be."

Amanda stood speechless. Slowly she lifted the
camera to her eye. A stab of pain shot through her heart.
The boy Dylan had shot Shamar – she was sure of that.

"And they were friends?"

"Yaaaa," a shocked whisper escaped the teen's mouth, "how could he, and with a gun – they never had one within a million miles of them."

Trisha's voice was choking up with emotion. "There's Dylan aiming again," Trisha was screaming again, "OMG and he's going for the cop."

Amanda's camera panned left and froze. The hooded man was drawing the cop's attention to her right – away from the teen. The teen was raising his gun. The cop stood still – nearly hypnotized by the hooded man. Amanda screamed, trying to warn the cop but nothing came out of her mouth. The camera stayed focused, steady, just below her eye, her finger as if on auto pilot snapping away.

To her right, Amanda heard Trisha whisper frantically, hoarsely, "Don't Dylan – don't do it – stop."

The girl and the woman turned to each other for the briefest of glances and then turned back in time to see Dylan's gun held out. At the end of his tightly outstretched arms, the gun was aimed firmly at the cop.

* * *

Dylan stared at the weapon that had just brought down his friend Shamar. He felt nothing other than the clicking of the trigger. His hands were frozen. He didn't remember any kickback, or the jolt he had so longed to feel. He imagined himself a tough lad with no after effects. This felt strange. There was no time to think. He has seen the cop headed his way. He had briefly seen her in the distance as the group had accosted him. On the second shot, he saw her break into a run towards him.

"Run, run," his mind screamed but his numbed body stood paralyzed. He could see no more movements from Shamar – Dylan knew Shamar was dead. The others had bolted in fear. He heard the cop scream for the killer.

She had not seen him. He was still too numb, when he saw the cop emerge, as did the hooded man. Dylan felt a cold, dark cloak engulf him. The safety was off. Dylan had no idea what was happening but moments later, he was exposed again. The cop had her side to Dylan. His eyes caught the eyes of the hooded man.

The purple lipstick of the operator changed to a deep red one. Her voice wasn't sexy anymore. It was a deep baritone one, hammering away in his head, "Shoot, Dylan, shoot – shoot the cop." Dylan slowly raised his gun. He felt cold and emotionless. The sounds around him had vanished. He could see the people but not hear them. They moved all around him, but to him, they appeared like ghostly figures floating past. There were hundreds of them. He recognized some of them. His hand was fully raised – stretched out. The cop lay squarely in his sight. Dylan knew he was about to shoot the cop.

"No – No," his mind screamed.

He looked back and saw Trisha and a lady in black with a large camera. "Darn," he thought, Trisha his senior from a while back. She knew him well. The entire school was in love with the blonde beauty. He caught sight of her lips – "Dylan, don't." She had seen the gun in his hand.

Dylan's attention turned back to the cop. Instead, his eyes locked in with that of the hooded man. His hand tightened around the butt of the gun. The silence in his mind was chilling. People around him screamed but something dark and strange shut them out. He screamed but something inside choked him. Dylan's world turned dark and cold. He saw a shot strike the cop. It racked her petite frame – shook her up. She was still turning. Dylan saw the gun in her hand. She was an instant away from firing back. Through his haze, Dylan saw a second shot strike the cop.

The gun in Dylan's hand felt cold and lifeless. He had just shot two people. The shivering was gone and along with it all the feelings in his body.

Amanda and Trisha heard two shots, watching in horror, the sounds numbed from their horrified minds, as the scene played out in silence in their minds.

The cop staggered as the first bullet hit her. Her delicate frame wobbled. A look of painful surprise filled her face. The cop in her – still alert, reacting sharply – started to turn left to where the shot had come from. She was halfway through her turn when the second shot caught her squarely in the chest.

Clare never finished her turn. Her body fell in a twisting action. The gun fell from her hand. The impact of the two bullets – like a million sledgehammers driving through her body disappeared a second later.

Clare knew death was but a moment away. A few precious breaths before it was all over. Her world spun. A bright dazzling light was filling her eyes as her brain pumped furiously with all its might to cling on to the last shreds of life.

From some distant land, she heard Terri call, "Blondie2 – come in…." a last loving thought of him stirred some herculean effort inside her. She had to tell him. Her hand hit the button on her radio one last time.

"Oh Terri, you trained me well, my love," she thought. She managed one last message to her partner.

"Blondie2 here – Goodbye, my love."

Clare was looking down upon the world. She felt no more sensation in her body. A dark figure had grasped and lowered her gently to the ground, breaking her fall. The peaceful face of a man in a roman collar – was signing her.

"In the name of the Father, and of the Son, and of Holy Spirit, Amen."

Clare never finished her final sign of the cross – the priest held her hand and finished it for her. Clare was dead before the priest fully laid her down on the pavement.

XI

Lynx

Greta stood on the 15th-floor balcony of her seniors' home on Eglinton. At nearly 250 feet above the ground, her balcony on the northwest corner of the 20th floor was a privileged possession. It was one of the most sought after L-shaped balconies that faced two directions. Up north, it faced Eglinton. Its view stretching far beyond to the ever busy Highway 401 and beyond. To the west, it followed Eglinton snaking its way through the busy city. The summer evening sunsets were the crowning glory across the sprawling building tops, interlaced with vast green patches. However, at the peak of winter, the narrow 2-feet broad passage was a dead, frigid, no-go zone. For Greta, it was her very own personal oasis – illegal and treacherous, but a safe smoking zone.

Greta's smoking jacket – she loved that term – took her back to her hey days. She loved to travel – long voyages in luxury. With her Sophia Loren looks and easy style, picking up lonely rich old men came easy. She dreamed of meeting her own Steve McQueen someday, it never happened. She still had her smoking jacket; that, and her tall rubber boots were her best allies out there on the balcony. Everything else was layered white with snow. The boots helped push the snow aside leaving her just enough place to stand.

"Now don't you be caught smoking inside the building again, lady," the tough supervisor had warned her when she moved in. That was nearly 20 years ago. Then, at

55, she was a young retiree with a generous pension, and a well-invested income. She still considered herself a hot prized catch. The Jews that came in their designer suits and luxury cars to the synagogue next door never ever acknowledged her existence.

"Too prayerful or too devoted to their wives in haute couture dresses," she reasoned. The building supervisor ignored her, "Hey Superman!" advances, as did the cops down the street and the merry old check out guard at Walmart. Even the forever frozen crossing guard, looked sternly away. Weeks turned to months, to years; Greta eventually gave up. Most of the other residents were too old to think of romance. She had grudgingly accepted the single life. Hairdressers, bingo, shopping and of course her smoking despite the doctor's warning – that was her life now.

"Smoking – ah well that's what I'm married to," she claimed. No one stepped out on those adjoining balconies in the freezing months, leaving Greta to enjoy the rare privilege of stepping out on to her own balcony to smoke anytime, unseen and undetected.

The sound of the first siren that Good Friday morning barely caught her attention. She was mildly curious. Was it an ambulance for her own building? "Slipped in the bathroom again did we, Barry?" she joked aloud to herself about the oldest resident and laughed. The siren carried on. A few minutes later she heard another distant one, and then another. This morning the sirens wailed with a particular mournful feeling – there was a desperation in them, she thought.

Her cigarette was nearly done, when the sounds picked up from all sides. Greta looked left and saw a commotion further west. Her heart throbbed with excitement. "Some action, my dear," she told herself.

Anything was welcome compared to the bored silence of her room in the home. Greta reached for another cigarette.

"Another one, darling?" she exulted suddenly, "how nice — another game of bridge, darlings?" she spoke, drifting to a time long past. A deadly gust of wind was the only answer. The wailing of the sirens was even louder now. Curious, she peeped over to the left and froze in shock. A little further west, Eglinton was a riot. Hundreds seemed to have poured out onto the street.

"Toronto — really?" she wondered out aloud.

Emergency vehicle lights flashed everywhere. Greta puffed on her cigarette furiously, suddenly wondering if the combined sounds would penetrate the sealed windows and draw the odd curious soul outside. Another deadly gust of icy cold wind told her no one would. She pulled her jacket tighter around her body when the sound of the first shots reached her. There was no mistaking that sound — she had hunted enough to know it.

From somewhere down below she thought she smelt coffee. It was indeed — people had poured out of the Coffee Time with their hot coffees and newspaper — curious, just like her at the action unfolding further west. It was enough to add weight to the sudden urge that was building up inside her.

"Some more cigarettes, a coffee, and some interesting news — let's go, darling," Greta said loudly and charged back indoors to dress up.

* * *

Down below, fire engines, fire Marshalls, ambulances and a dozen more police cruisers raced in from all directions. The combined decibel level of all the sirens, howlers, piercers and foghorns punctured the sacred indoors of the homes all along the path of the incoming emergency vehicles.

For the 911 switchboard operators, the incoming lines blazed furiously. On the 50th call, Ret. Captain Barnaby McIntyre saw the red beacon in the center of the busy room begin to start turning, as it flashed red all across the room.

"Level 5 alert, sir," the sergeant blurted out from the door with a hurried salute. "13th cruiser just dispatched, sir."

"I got it, for now, sergeant – but keep the score going for me, will ya?"

"Very well, sir."

The sergeant saluted and left. Captain Barnaby did not need that reminder. As an ex-army officer with all those years spent in the blazing heat of Afghanistan, there was never a time to relax on the job. When the suicide bombers blew themselves to bits they generally took down another dozen with them. Captain Barnaby's team were the first emergency responders that sealed off the disaster site, just in case a secondary bomb went off on those rushing to the site.

Captain Barnaby followed each call diligently. No 9-1-1 call was too trivial, too disconnected, or too irrelevant to merit attention. Someone out there was in trouble. By the time, the second cruiser was being dispatched to the same location he had already zeroed in on the source of the originating calls. Before the sergeant left his desk, Captain Barnaby had already referred to his procedure manual. The police commissioner's number on the secure line was already being punched in.

The conversation was short and crisp. There was a boss and a subordinate – it did not matter to Captain Barnaby. He respected the rank but crisis called for experienced hands, straight out of a real war.

"I wasn't informing you, sir. I am stating that the Dufferin and Eglinton mess needs a high level ramp up."

"And what makes you think that, officer?"

"Level 5 alert, sir – in a few minutes we'll be pulling every damn cruiser we have on patrol anywhere in the city, and if I were you – sir – I'd haul myself there right now."

"Anything else you got, officer before I haul you to your union."

"Yes, sir – one officer down – shot – want some more – sir?" Silence followed as Captain Barnaby waited patiently. He understood human dynamics well – this was time for shockingly rude talk. The commissioner would respond appropriately soon – he was sure of that.

"Anything else you've already done, officer?"

"Yes, I've already got word to the new SWAT team – awaiting your signal, of course. We need them there now, sir, not after --,"

"Very well, officer," Captain Barnaby knew the conversation was over, "keep me posted, directly." The commissioner was gone. The good old calm, cold and direct army voice did the trick.

* * *

Further south the SWAT team was busy scrambling together.

"A minute to departure," the leader's cold metallic voice called as he jammed in his Colt M1911 .45 ACP into the side holster. His left hand held the MP5A3 submachine gun. A second later, he was charging out to the roaring engine of a massive Mine Resistant Ambush Protected vehicle or MRAP as the commandoes called it.

"Report," he yelled jumping inside the MRAP. The dark interior of the van, lit by a series of tiny LED lamps in the roof displayed a center rack that held all kinds of displays. The armored behemoth weighed a massive 16-ton with a V-shaped hull to deflect the IEDs that had taken precious American and Canadian lives in Afghanistan. Beloved by the commandoes, marines and soldiers who scribbled grateful notes of thanks, the massive metal giants were packed with sophisticated computer technology. This particular one had a rather significant 'Lynx', scribbled on the hull next to a nasty IED shrapnel mark.

"On alert, Team-Alpha," one of the heavily armed and helmeted commando on the left yelled out, "6 men strapped and ready to roll, Lynx."

"On alert, Team-Sigma," another dark clothed commando in similar uniform yelled out, "6 men strapped and ready to roll, Lynx."

The leader, Lynx, had reached the interior front end of the MRAP. Unconventional, and as secret as the team was, so were their names. There were no titles or real names – just codes. Two pounding fists on the metal center door from Lynx sent the MRAP shooting out of its hi-tech, deep, basement lair sending tremors through the building. A series of doors opened and closed, rattling endlessly as the giant engine reverberated. The MARP took a sharp left and shot out of the ramp after the seventh door, straight on to the intersection of Oxley St and Charlotte St. The road had been cleared. Two cruisers with their lights flashing, had already closed off the lane at both ends.

Up ahead, the sight of the emerging van sent another cruiser shooting out of its position on the sidewalk. The SWAT team was on its way.

"6 minutes to arrival," the static filled, deep voice of an operator filled the silent space. Lynx hit a row of switches and a blast of communications filled the van as the screens on the sides lit up with a ton of data. He looked intently and then hit a brightly, flashing orange button.

"Commissioner Ford on the line, sir," a voice echoed.

"Alpha and Sigma ready for action, commissioner."

"Gentlemen – 23 cars piled up – a man dead, maybe more – possibly an officer shot – missing gunman – and hundreds of disoriented folks on the street," the husky voice on the other end said.

"Gunman or gunmen, commissioner?" Lynx asked sliding out the magazine of his M4 5.56mm Carbine and shoving it back in, trying to soothe the adrenalin pumping in his veins already. He felt the surge of energy sweep the van. Somewhere, a vein throbbed on a forehead and another hand tightened around the hilt of the Benchmade's 970 knife on the outer side of the right leg clamp. Just like the Samurai's love for his sword, Lynx had a special affection for the blade. "Skill and perfection of the highest order," he would declare to his team, challenging them to take down a suspect with a single strike to a critical spot with little or no blood.

"Hang in there, gentlemen, we may --,"

"4 minutes to arrival," the static voice interrupted the expectant silence left behind by the sudden pause from the commissioner.

"Gentlemen, 1 officer possibly dead – another fatality – possibly dead – shot – and 6 shots possibly discharged from an unknown weapon – man on the ground ready to report," another pause from the commissioner – "patch him in."

"Blondie1 reporting in – all units on full alert – Blondie2 shot – dead," the voice choked off – it came back a second later. "Gunman possibly young – boy maybe – look for dark hooded man – riot dispersal mode – out."

"2 minutes to arrival --,"

"Explain the shots, Blondie1," Lynx spoke calmly.
Blondie1 was gone.

"That's one of our most experienced officer on the ground..." the commissioner tried to fill in.

The leader grabbed a metal handle in the roof in his crouched position as the vehicle hit a bump and then turned sharply. He hit another switch and a series of monitors behind him came to life.

"Need a unit by the church – need a unit by the Eg-Duff intersection --,"

"More shots heard west – Blondie1 out."

The leader raised a finger – 1 – Team-Alpha had the church. 2 fingers in the direction of the Team-Sigma. Silently Agent X2A, the youngest on Team-Sigma exulted with a firm, "Yes!" that's where the action was. A chance to hunt down the actual gunman seemed the only action available. After months of training, and inaction, away from the real battlefields worldwide, a real situation had finally arrived.

"Gunman, possibly 14, oriental. Polka dotted bandana – black denim jacket – last seen opposite library – convenience store – Blondie1 out."

Lynx surveyed his men in the final seconds before arrival. Each handpicked – each with a distinct record of his own – he knew each one well. At a minimum height of 6 feet 6 inches the arrival of the team – all in black had the most dramatic effect of all. The men had been primed to be protectors or killers, as the situation demanded. Their lives signed away a long time ago. To be a human shield was a given. The Kevlar vest protecting their upper bodies was the only protection between an assassin's bullet and the victim they swore to protect with their lives. They knew it would never come to that. Each man had been trained to fire back in a 100th of a second – each man knew how to kill, whether with the automatic or silently with the specially ordered all black blades or with as little as a pin.

"This is your day, gentlemen – the battle lies ahead – make me proud!"

"Sir, yes, sir," the men shouted back feeling more like the US Army rangers they had served with secretly in the deserts of Afghanistan.

The leader smiled internally. He had picked the word 'battle' intentionally. The response was perfect. He wanted his men in war mode. The enemy was the Taliban – the deadliest of them all. It did not matter if it wasn't the alleys of IED laden Kabul. He wanted his men to picture the worst killers – Taliban men that carried their lives on their sleeves, and continued firing with half their guts hanging out of their bodies.

The static voice interrupted the high adrenalin pumping bodies waiting to burst forth the last time.

"Small detour gentlemen – all access blocked to the destination."

The scowl on Lynx's face appeared for the briefest of instants as a firm jab lit up the monitors again.

"Location coordinates?" he barked knowing fully well where they were.

"50 meters to Dufferin and Eglinton."

"Change of plans, gentlemen – stop and roll. Doors."

* * *

50 meters south on Dufferin, the old cabbie stubbed out his 3rd cigarette and reached for the cold coffee mug through the open window of the driver's door. He stood by his parked taxi in the little bay off Dufferin. It had been a queer morning. His thoughts still lay on the hauntingly, beautiful passenger he had driven up north. Intrigued and fascinated, he had driven up and down Dufferin till his obsession drew him back, close to where he

had dropped her off. At first, it was an idle fascination as he drove away. It became a determined curiosity to see her again by the first loop. Seeing her on the third loop, turned his passion into a wild desire. When he finally stopped and got out, it was a wild obsession.

"Get going, you old dog," his prayerful soul ordered. Yet something wicked inside drew him to the woman. "She will come back," it prompted. He finally decided he would wait and get her.

The wait had been worth it. Something was happening back there. The cabbie heard the wild braking and the crashes from where he was, a little south. He knew enough to distinguish them clearly. He counted the cruisers racing back towards the intersection and knew his instinct had been right. His mind worried – not for the casualties, but for the woman he desired.

Like a Man-Eater-Tiger stealthily stalking its prey on the village edge, he waited. Each second her vision flashed before his eyes. Each second he pictured her delicate, shapely body under the black dress. Each second he groped himself further – until he could bear it no more. There was a fierce struggle unfolding inside him. His body was on fire as he struggled to contain the wild, sexual excitement engulfing him. Soon enough he knew he had to have that woman. Sitting inside the cab, he closed his eyes and pictured every little scene. She would be a fighter, that, he was sure of. It increased his excitement even more.

He pictured himself ripping off each piece of that black dress till he would be left with nothing but that naked white body he so craved. Suddenly, the seat in the taxi became a prison. He leaped out and ran to the back. There was a bottle of good, old Captain Morgan Rum for those long, cold nights waiting for passengers outside the busy downtown nightclubs. The first swig hit him like a ton of rocks. He choked – coughed and then opened his blurry eyes as the warmth of the rum spread in his body. The wild side in him prodded for another swig. "You need it, you old dog," he egged himself on. He liked the feeling that was turning him into an animal – ready to attack. He would wait no further. He would find her – offer to wait around – drive her back. The thought of her back in his taxi sent his mind into raptures. He knew he would get her to that secret lair he took so many of his passengers to. Today, it would be his. He pictured himself like a superman, or super animal. A sparse room – with a bed – and a beautiful woman that he would rape most violently.

He lifted the bottle for another swig when a massive, roaring, metallic grey hulk screeched to a halt meters from him. The driver braked, and spun the massive monster of a vehicle around, so that when it stopped, the northbound MRAP came to a stop, facing south. "Bless my soul," he prayed as the strange small windows on the humongous metal box, burst open.

Two heavy doors swung open at the back. Was it the rum or was it real? The old cabbie saw the men burst forth. Massive hunks of men – clad in black – armed to the teeth. He saw them break into two teams and sprint north. The rasping call from the largest of the men had the undesired effect of the old cabbie dropping the rum bottle from his hands. It crashed at his feet.

The men were gone, rapidly gaining speed as they neared the intersection. So was his wild ride. The old cabbie felt the bitter chill of the winter morning once again. He shivered as much from fear, as from the cold, as from the wild desire that had consumed him minutes back. He doubted if he should still hang around.

His answer came from the van. He thought it was straight out of a modern, science fiction movie he had taken his grandkids to. There was a transformation happening. Antennas, cameras and a variety of devices materialized on all sides. The only thing he recognized was the upward facing dish.

The sight of the dish took his vision upwards – to the skies. They were dark. He heard screams and moans, as deep, depressing feelings gripped his soul. The vision of a beautiful, white, dark clothed woman changed into an evil witch with a hundred heads popping out of her body. They stared deep into him for daring to dream of a plan so vile. He was about to beg for mercy when the pair of dark hypnotic eyes staring down became real. The driver of the van stood a foot from him. The cabbie looked way up into the cold ruthless eyes of the giant of a man. He did not remember how he got into the cab, or when he drove away. He knew he was headed home for a desperate change of messed clothes.

XII

The Mob

"Run, you idiot," a strange squeaky voice yelled in Dylan's ear. Dylan half turned around to see a thin suited man egging him to run. A strange hat, a thin mustache and an old black and white pin striped suit, that could easily have been out of an old black and white movie that his parents brought home sometimes.

"Run, boy, run," the man yelled again. Dylan still did not move. The man shoved Dylan with the gun in his hand. It was hot. Something clicked in Dylan's head and then faded away. He finally tucked his own gun under his jacket, and ran as another burly officer reached the scene. Dylan saw the cop fall to his knees near the fallen officer. His hat fell off revealing a head full of blonde hair. Dylan looked at the fallen officer. Her hat had fallen away as well. Dylan wondered if they had a connection.

Dylan was about to disappear behind a crowd, when the officer looked up. His face was in shock – pain. Their eyes met for an instant before Dylan disappeared into the crowd. He could not run – there were people everywhere. He stumbled along until he reached the Maria Shuka library.

The signal was green but there were people everywhere. A lone car tried to make its way east, trying to get out, and away, from the mess it was trapped in. Dylan saw the driver inch her way east, slowly. There was no place to move. She came upon another car, westbound, stranded at the other end of the signal. The westbound driver abandoned the car and fled in fear as the wild crowds swirled about.

The eastbound driver saw an opening and was about to barge through, when a group of men blocked her off again. She honked knowing it was her only chance of getting away. The horn blared in the faces of the men who had just stepped forward. They jumped with a start. Dylan looked into their faces and saw the shock turn to anger, and then rage. The nearest of the men raised his fist and slammed the car.

"What the *fuck* is wrong with you, *bitch*?" the man yelled.

Another man stepped forward and kicked the plastic bumper. On the second kick, the bumper broke with a crack.

The driver honked back louder – in rage – in morbid fear – in desperation to get the men away from her car. The men screamed back. In a few minutes, the car was surrounded. More men poured in from all around. Dylan saw the dark, hooded man retreat quietly with a smile.

Dylan watched horrified. Like the zombies in his game, the men wore fixated looks – hell bent on murder. He shouted at the crowd to stop. His voice barely registered. The car was being rocked on its sides – back and forth – back and forth. The men snarled like dogs. On the third attempt, the men nearly turned the car onto its side. It stayed for a while, dangling precariously on its two left wheels before crashing back on all its 4 wheels again. A piercing howl filled the air. Someone's foot had come under one of the wheels.

"Call 9-1-1," someone yelled.

"Call 9-1-1," the chant got picked up.

"Burn the *fucking* car," a deep baritone voice yelled.

"Burn the *fucking* car," the chant got picked up by the possessed crowd. Dylan caught a glimpse of the lady trapped in the car. Her face was white – masked in fear. She was middle-aged – a simple working mom he guessed – just like his own. The mob began to turn even more violent – smashing the windows and trying to reach in and open the doors.

"Fire – Fire – light the *fucking* car," the baritone voice yelled. Dylan saw someone holding a cigarette lighter to the end of a kerchief. It went up in flames.

"Throw it through the window," the baritone voice ordered.

"Throw it in, throw it in," the mob responded.

"Burn the *bitch*," the baritone voice yelled.

"Burn the *bitch*, burn the *bitch*," the mob chanted.

Dylan looked at the faces of the men. Their enraged faces looked stoned – burning with anger. He saw one of the men from his building. "Emidio," he half-uttered the name trying to remember it. He remembered the man who always ruffled his hair lovingly, and gave out the best candy at Halloween.

"Emidio," he yelled, "stop – what is wrong with you?"

The desperation in his voice carried through. The mob turned and stared at the boy – a new target. It was then that Dylan saw their faces up close – the fixated zombie faces were hell bent on murder.

"Burn the boy – Burn the car," they yelled. Some turned to him – some turned back to the car.

Dylan felt a cold surge of anger. He wasn't sure how he had shot two good people but this time he would shoot to save the woman. The gun emerged from under his coat. Dylan aimed and then remembered the safety. He fumbled. He had to shoot fast. The mob was a couple of feet from grabbing him. He looked right and saw the black clad photographer approach. She was shooting him rapidly. He looked left and saw the Daily Convenience Food Mart. It was his only escape. The crowd was about to seize him – the safety catch was still jammed when Dylan heard the eerie sound of a gun going off again. Dylan looked at the men before him fall like flies. Shocked, he turned to see where the shots had come from and caught sight of the same old-fashioned hat.

"Run, boy, run," the voice ordered again.

Dylan turned and ran into the Daily Convenience Food Mart as a final gunshot sounded. The ever open store was in the process of being hastily closed. The metal grill doors were nearly drawn and the glass doors behind them were down to a few inches.

"Shop closed," the Chinese woman yelled at him in her Chinese accent. Her voice quivered with fear and tension. Dylan kept running towards her.

"Shop closed – no open now," she yelled again.

Dylan could not stop and ran headlong into her as he threw himself in through the last few inches still left open. They both crashed onto the floor inside the shop. Dylan felt himself land on top of the woman and rolled over landing on his knees. He was about to fall back on the floor when the wild shouts of the men outside reached his ears.

"The convenience store," someone yelled, "get him."

Dylan dashed for the door. He could see the men outside approaching quickly. Heart pounding, he reached for the outer, grill door just as a hand reached in. Dylan grabbed the two metal doors, and slammed them together.

'Aiyeeee' – a scream erupted and the hand withdrew.

"Get the *fucking* kid," another voice yelled.

"Burn him in the car with the lady."

"Burn the whole *fucking* shop," another voice yelled. The crowd was getting wilder. Another pair of hands reached for the grill door and shook it up violently. In a flash, Dylan snapped the lock in place and slammed the glass door shut. The gun still lay tucked in his belt.

"The gun," his mind screamed. It could go off. With shivering hands, Dylan reached under his jacket and lifted out the gun. The safety finally came off. The cold feel of the gun sent a shiver through his body. Dylan rubbed the gun against his jacket to warm it up. It was too late. A violent sneeze erupted from him. Dylan tried to hold the gun away.

"Quick, quick, quick, you dope," his mind screamed. It was too late. Dylan had been firmly gripping the butt as he rubbed the gun against his jacket. The sneeze made him grip the gun even more firmly. As he lifted his head, he saw the gun pointed at the lady. She had taken a nasty fall and had passed out. She was slowly coming around. Her first instinct was to still reach for and close the shop doors.

"Out boy – out now – shop --," she froze as her eyes fell on the gun in Dylan's hand.

Dylan's hand was shaking violently. He sneezed again and felt his finger squeeze the trigger. He heard the click of the gun and waited for another victim to die from his gun. Instead, silence followed. The woman saw Dylan's hand squeeze the trigger and passed out again.

Surprised, he nearly laughed aloud at the comical sight. And then, it slowly dawned on him – the gun had not fired. Was it empty – had he fired off too many rounds earlier?

Curious, Dylan ejected the magazine. It slipped off smoothly. It was a dummy block. The gun had never held real ammo – he had been set up. Dylan remembered Shamar, the cop, the men outside the store – they were all dead – not by his gun – but he was the killer.

Confused, he sat on the floor and popped out the magazine once again. It was metal block meant to act as a filler. Dylan freely squeezed the trigger. He knew nothing would happen. He wondered if the gun itself was a dummy. Why had the hooded man set him up? Dylan cursed himself for having been ensnared so easily. His mind traveled back to the first shots that had brought down Shamar – no kickback – he had felt nothing. He remembered the shots that felled the cop – once again – he had aimed but the shots were not his.

"Fool – you darn fool," he cursed in despair as the gravity of the situation hit him. "Murderer," he whispered, throwing up at the sickness that welled up from deep within himself.

"Lord help me – lord help me," he prayed as violent tremors shook his body. He heard someone rattle the thick grill doors. It was followed up with more knocks – more fists on the glass doors. With each thud, Dylan shook feverishly.

"They're kicking it down – think, Dylan, think," he beseeched himself. The sudden thought of looking for an escape from another exit, was snuffed out quickly. A sad but relieving thought overtook him. "Perhaps, they will break it down – beat me to a pulp. No sad life to lead with the burden – yet found clean – with a dummy of a gun."

He smiled sadly, as the door shook more violently. "Lord, make it quick," he prayed. He imagined the irate mob bearing down on him. "It will hurt at first – then we'll pass out," he consoled himself.

The Chinese lady was coming around. Dylan debated pulling her away to a safe corner – away from the maddened crowd that would burst forth any minute. The lady opened her eyes briefly – saw the massive rattling on the doors and passed out again. "Good Lord," he laughed finally exhaling deeply. The laugh helped – somewhere in his mind a brief flicker of a happy thought passed by and Dylan felt good.

"Maybe I'll make it through," he said hugging the gun. It was his proof – his salvation – his redemption. He had to save the gun in case the crowd got through first. He had to hide it. The cops would find it later – intact with his prints and the dummy magazine. A smile broke out and his heart leaped with joy. "I am not a killer, Oh Lord, stupid, but not a killer."

The happy thought, like a magic bullet, began to churn in his mind. Dylan wondered if he had been seen. With the chaos that filled the scene, probably no one would remember. He remembered the cop that came in at the fall of the first one – their eyes had met – briefly. Trisha – "Oh my God!" – she had seen every bit of it and probably was convinced he had shot the cop. And then, he remembered the photographer. She always seemed to have her camera shooting. He was sure the cops would have enough proof from her camera to lock him up for a long time.

"And maybe not – if there are so many pictures then surely they will show a dead gun – no recoil – no smoke – no empty shells ejected."

That was when he remembered the stranger who seemed to have popped out, in black and white – from the 60s'. Who was he? Dylan looked up above the cash register and saw a small crucifix hanging just below the ceiling. A little red light flickered below the little altar.

Dylan knew what he was going to do – climbing on the counter, he slipped the gun onto the altar, back against the wall. It was enough to conceal his weapon. Dylan stepped back and stared at it for a long time. Then kneeling down he prayed.

"Forgive me, my Lord Jesus, for I have sinned."

XIII

Calvary

Daniel stared into a bright, blazing sky. The bitter, Canadian cold was replaced by a dry, searing heat. The sand colored, arid landscape stretched for miles. Small shrubs dotted the low hills providing the odd spot of color in the otherwise dusty landscape. Far in the distance, Daniel saw groves of palm – soothingly green to the heat strained eye. He was in a different time and place.

His heart did a little leap of excitement – was he on a vacation? Anything was welcome, anything that wasn't the frigid -25C concrete jungle that Toronto was. The fleeting thought was instantly replaced by a deep pounding in his heart. It was no time for a celebration. Something was happening – something solemn.

The passing moments seemed like the final seconds before the commencement of the grandest of all plays. It was the moment before the cymbals crashed with a mighty clang, and the trumpets blasted the start of the long-awaited scene.

This was no play – Daniel felt it in his heart. It was pushing him to kneel, to honor something divine; painful – yet grandiose, sad – yet victorious.

Daniel looked around. The silence was punctuated by the odd shouts of a commanding voice – a soldier's voice, followed by a massive metallic thud. A blast from the impact of a massive hammer on a nail. Before the sound had died, its echo had traveled across the hills and into the skies and the heavens. A brief shadow passed, the sunlight flickered a bit. Had the mighty sun flinched?

It had, shuddering as the most horrendous of moans, steeped in pain, traveled the land like a sonic blast from a miniature nuclear explosion – subdued – yet carrying a massive impact from a huge blast of energy. Another thud of metal on metal and another massive groan. Daniel felt the weight of a humongous blast of pain permeate his being. Someone was suffering brutally.

"Nail the feet – Nail the feet, quick, we don't have time," the commanding voice ordered again.

"The feet won't stretch, sire," the wobbly voice complained.

"Here, let me do it," a cruel voice interjected as if it was stepping into a most routine task.

"When the hands are nailed, the body normally contracts. Push back one foot against the upright, press the other – tug hard if you need to – break the bone clasp – the feet will then stretch," the man finished off as it were a regular biology lesson. Daniel shivered at the brutality of humanity. The series of metallic thuds he had heard were the sounds of a man being nailed to a cross.

Another metallic sound of a hammer on nail echoed – followed by a few more, lesser in impact. The nail was being driven home. The tired sighs of the hammer bearer mixed in with the gut-wrenching moans of the man through whose feet the nails were being driven into, filled the air.

The crowds around murmured in silence – some in protest, some in support. No voice on either side managed to gauge the impact of the extreme torture being meted out to a fellow human. The murmur from the crowd traveled a bit and then silence returned again. The universe had come to a standstill to witness the event. Time stood still as the heavens bowed in silent homage to the crucifixion of its master.

The whips lay silent on the hill. Bloodied –
discarded next to the rocks that involuntarily bore the dread
of having had to witness the horrific event unfolding before
them. The brutal spurs at the end of the lashes tried to burst
out – to silently shed the pieces of flesh that clung to them.
Pieces of flesh that had come off the body of the Son of
Man, from the vicious whipping in Pilate's courtyard and
then along the way to Calvary, and right until the time the
Son of Man finally reached his destination. There was no
victory lap for the man who had just reached the finish line.
There was no podium nor a celebration. Instead, the cross
he had carried up there, became his victory stand over
death. A cross he had dreaded as a man in the garden of
Gethsemane, yet chosen to do his father's will.

Daniel felt the silent screams echo from the lashes.
Captured forever in the throes of time – each lash eliciting a
millennium of sin and pain – silently absorbed into the body
of the Son of Man. It enraged his captors.

"Did it hurt? Scream, you dog, scream," the lash
bearer yelled in Pilate's courtyard, where the Nazarene had
just been condemned. The whip lasher was incensed that his
fiercest lash had not brought forth a cry of mercy to be
spared.

"You will beg – You will scream," he yelled in rage.
He took two steps back, stretched back his hand and
brought forth his fiercest lash yet. He swung the whip with
all his anger and might. The frail, collapsed body of the man,
now hanging from his hands, tied above his head to a pillar,
convulsed in the throes of pain – the mouth gasped in a
long cry of silent agony. The man collapsed – the leather
straps that bound his hands to the top of the stone pillar,
stretched, but held on.

"You must be the devil, you brute," the panting
whip lasher finally conceded, "even the toughest have fallen
– dead." Dropping the whip from the exhaustion of having

swung it, the whip lasher finally felt defeated – defied – his evil sense of power, broken. No human had survived the pain his whip had dealt out. Yet, silently and willingly, another frail human had conquered it.

Daniel shivered at the echoes of pain that burst forth and embedded themselves in the sandblasted walls of Pontius Pilate's palace.

"Here, let me show you how it is done," another Roman soldier jumped in. Undoing his red cape, he grabbed the whip. The furious whip lasher unwillingly let the whip be taken away from him – by another, who thought he could do better.

"Watch, my friend, and prepare to see this man finally broken," he boasted. The whipping resumed, mercifully, it was the last lash. The soldier groaned in disappointment. The thundering lash he had managed from his massive frame had not killed the insignificant Nazarene who dangled helplessly from his tied hands. His body yearned for his bruised palms to reach down and soothe his battered body – to feel the gaping wounds.

"Stop, you brutes," a centurion screamed finally, "we need the man alive – to carry the cross."

"Wait, wait," another soldier beseeched with evil glee in his face, "the Jews have another request to help torture the man." He burst out laughing.

"Insignificant wimps," the centurion complained at the delay.

The soldier whispered into the ears of the centurion, and they both burst out laughing.

"Apparently, the man claimed to be a king – they want him crowned," the soldier burst out again and the two men laughed while the other soldiers crowded around to share the joke.

Daniel felt a numbing pain sear through his body. There was an evil presence around the courtyard. It was weaving its way through the souls of the chief priests', the scribes and the Pharisees. It had done its bit. The seed had been sown – the Romans had taken it up – the result was ready.

In the corner stood a soldier. A purple cushion in his hand – the color of royalty. He grinned from ear to ear, feeling rather important. From his lowest rank, he suddenly felt stately – about to be part of an important coronation.

"Let's crown the king," the soldier shouted.

"Crown the king," the Jews and the soldiers cheered.

Daniel looked at the crown. It was an evil serpent – green and brown in color. Entwining itself deeper and deeper with each twist. Daniel stared at it – there was one serpent then another. The serpents grew and multiplied as they snaked their way around, weaving the crown with pain and suffering.

"Let's make it the most painful part, yet," the snakes cheered on, picking up the sentiments from the souls of the men around. They drew on the evil that prevailed around, drawing it in, until it burst forth from their bodies as long sharp thorns. The thorns that burst forth pierced the bodies of the other snakes encircled around. The serpents pierced, and were pierced with the evil thorns that burst forth from their bodies, until they could move no more, horribly mangled into a mesh with the thorns that pierced their bodies. They died miserably.

Daniel saw the crown – ready – cold – hard – dead – fiercely sharp, and evil. He saw the Son of Man look at the crown of thorns and welcome it. The evil of Satan would be his own undoing.

The agony in the garden long over the night before, the brutal, body ripping scourging done, Daniel saw the Son of Man ready to take on the next stage of his painful journey – the crown of thorns. He felt the weight of evil in each thorn ready to be thrown into a burning chasm of fire where it would burn and absolve the world of what had been. Each thorn, a cleansing for the massive burden of evil that the world had accrued on itself. Each thorn that would forever stand in the path of evil from conquering the world.

Daniel looked up after a very long time in silent homage. The Son of Man hung dead on the cross. The ground that had trembled with a violent earthquake a few minutes ago, was still. The skies were silent. The darkness from the eclipse of the sun, passed, and a painful sorrow engulfed the earth. The silence was complete. It was the third hour after noon. There were furious consultations going on around. The chief priests' and the Romans argued vehemently.

"The man must hang, today, tomorrow and the day after – the body must be left there, hanging, for the people must watch and learn a lesson," the Romans argued.

"It is a sacrilege – it cannot happen – it is the Sabbath tomorrow – the bodies cannot be left on the crosses." The head Pharisee argued back. The others cowered around him, lending their weight to the argument with nods and grunts from beneath their heavy white robes.

"Well, you should have thought about that before you condemned the man."

"It is the law of the land – it is sacred – the Sabbath cannot be defiled. If word spreads around there will be severe unrest in the land. It could lead to greater unrest." Another tried, hoping the scare tactic would work. It did. The centurion went back to consult with his men. Instead, he picked just one – the oldest and wisest of his advisors – a companion of many campaigns.

"Let's be done with this horrible place and be gone, sire," the old one advised, "there was nothing right about this. We did the dirty work of the evil ones – now let's wash our hands off this, as quickly as possible."

The centurion listened – glad that he had finally found support in what had burned in his heart from the first lash.

"Forgive me, King, or whoever you are. This is not of my doing. A simple soldier am I – let not my young ones, or their sons and daughter, or any of my generations, carry this curse on our heads," he prayed silently to the man who hung high above him, on the cross, in the blazing sun.

The centurion returned to the chief priests', the scribes and the Pharisees. A protest broke out instantly. The Jews were even more enraged. The centurion guessed they had discussed the fallout of not getting their way.

"You have to listen --," the chief priest broke off again into a long rant until the centurion angrily drew his sword. The complaining stopped.

"We have an understanding – but you must dispose the bodies quickly." Grudgingly, both side accepted.

They patted each other on the shoulders and parted ways – desperate not to be around the blasphemer on the cross anymore – their job done. Shrieks filled the air as the brutality and evil of humanity surfaced once again. Daniel covered his face at the gruesome sight unfolding once again in front of him.

"Come on, soldier – harder," the centurion, hollered in anger, reaching for his sword. The frightened young soldier – a lad of no more than 15, struck harder with his sword – hacking away until the knees of the both the robbers lay grotesquely broken. Splintered bone and blood spewed everywhere. The tired soldier came to the Son of Man, he hoped the man would look into his eyes once more and not hold it against him.

"I walked with you, Oh King of the Jews – I held back my whip – this I cannot. Forgive me," he whispered in his heart hoping to look into those soothing eyes once more. The eyes that had looked deep into his soul, and smiled at him, despite the agony of what was unfolding. Instead, he found the head hanging down – the eyes shut.

"The King is --,"

"Dead. The man is dead," the centurion completed the sentence, himself relieved at the thought. "Here take this and pierce him – we must do what we have to." The centurion handed the soldier a spear. Its head, bright and silver, sharp as the sharpest spear that could be.

"It's new – the least we can honor the man with."

The soldier stood confused, scared. He held the spear before the centurion lost it again.

"Just do it."

The soldiers had never seen the centurion, a veteran of many violent wars, so shaken and unsteady.

"I cannot," the young soldier held the spear and wept.

"But I can," said another and grabbed the spear, "you survived my last lash, filthy Nazarene – who wins now?" he taunted with pride, his revenge complete. He pierced the side of the Son of God hanging up there, and saw blood and water flow out. The stunned centurion knelt.

"I'm sorry," each giant of a man prayed silently, and wept, as a peaceful grace filled their souls. Somewhere deep within their souls, they knew that the man they had just crucified, had already forgiven them.

A trembling Daniel wiped his eyes and looked up. There was a woman standing close – a grieving mother – her holy presence filled the hill. The violence was over. She watched quietly as the men took down her son's body. She was about to experience the most painful moment of her motherhood, yet. They were about to lay the ravaged, dead body of her son in her arms. She wept silently, yet praised God in the silence of her heart. She felt his body in her hands, dead, limp, muddy, bruised and battered, sticky from the blood, yet the most beautiful of all creation.

Daniel bowed his head and looked no more. Instead, he felt the presence of the evil one nearby – waiting to rejoice – it never happened.

The mother looked at the closed eyes. The crown of thorns was deeply embedded in her son's flesh. Each thorn, nearly gelled in with the skin that had swelled around it, in the many hours since it had first lodged in. The skin had changed to dark shades of brown, blue and black. She felt his pain and looked up at the disciple who was to be her son.

"Let me," the disciple offered and gently drew back the crown. It did not budge. There was no easy way out.

"He is beyond pain, mother," the disciple consoled, knowing the brutality of taking off the crown was just as bad as when it had been rammed in. The skin broke – the blood matted hair tore, and slowly the evil crown left the head it had tortured. The crown of thorns came off one thorn at a time. The thorns were embedded deep into the flesh. The horror of the thorns filling the soul of the disciple with pain until the last thorn was pulled out and he could bear it no more. The disciple tossed the crown of thorns away in disgust.

The crown rolled a little – like a wheel – it wobbled a little but caught a little more speed as the hill sloped downhill. It rolled a little faster and then fell on its side, closer to Daniel. He felt a nudge and looked up – he was standing in a long line of men and women. Heads bowed – praying – they reached out with longing hearts to the crown as it came to rest a little ahead of them. The evil one reached out for it as well, unsuccessfully. Silently Daniel understood his mission.

*   *   *

Daniel felt another nudge – he toppled a little – balanced himself, but felt the nudge even more firmly. Was it the Romans? The presence was soothing and calm. Was it the disciple, or the many that stood in line before him? Startled, he opened his eyes. An angelic face looked into his eyes. It wasn't one of the women who had consoled the mother of the Son of God at the foot of the cross. He saw the quiet smiling face of a white-haired woman close to him. Her long white hair gently fell over her shoulder and onto his arm. Its touch, calm and soothing.

"Are you an angel?" he asked confused.

"No, but you are – the lucky one – not me."

Daniel smiled and rested back a bit.

The lady took his right hand and drew him forward, as two loud bangs filled the air. The din around quietened for a second, and then erupted again – the sirens wailed and Daniel felt the presence of the evil hooded man fill the air. He shivered remembering the presence from Pilate's courtyard and the hill from a long time ago. The lady smiled in acknowledgment

"Come, Thornbearer," she said extending her hand out to Daniel, "the Lord calls – we have work to do."

XIV

Daughter of the Evil One

Amanda clicked away furiously as she saw the paramedics zip up the body of the madman in the body bag. Her own desperate haste surprised her. It wasn't her usual drive to capture the moment in detail to get that elusive frame.

"Sorry," something within her blurted out to her reference to the man, as mad. His face looked peaceful, as if in a bliss. His last words to her, earlier that morning, echoed painfully in her mind. She reached out hoping to ask him one last question.

"Am I evil? Is the hooded man evil? Why did you call me the daughter of the evil one? Is he my father?"

A million questions flooded her mind, silently pouring out in a futile attempt to get a response. She was sure the man being wheeled away knew the answers to them all. She also knew it was too late.

"Wherever you are – give me an answer, holy one," her soul finished sadly.

Strangely, it was exactly the same thing she had seen the Indian man fallen on the ground do. Her hands had focused on the camera – her mind on the preaching man but the presence of the man on the floor seemed to draw her like a powerful magnet. She had seen him go into the coffee shop earlier, and later emerge to follow the preaching man to the church.

Her heart was screaming to look at him, yet a strange reluctance made her avoid the glance. It was as if

there would be no turning back from that point. She felt her
body on fire. The initial curiosity turned to a deep desire as
her body burned with a fierce yearning for him. A wild
passion enveloped her. She was even surer now about the
wild wave of happy emotions that had swept her since that
first look.

"Come on, Amanda – don't lose it, don't look," she
warned herself, shivering with wild excitement. In one final
desperate act, she tore out of her shell and devoured the
sight of the man fallen before her. He seemed crouched,
eyes sunken in pain but a fascinating glow lit up his face.
Their eyes met, locked into each other's and Amanda felt his
gaze.

She felt herself in a majestic palace of her dreams,
wrapped in satin. His touch caressing her naked body, his
hands drawing her to himself with her long dark hair as if he
possessed her completely; his eyes devouring her as she
pleaded with him in the throes of passion to take her. Her
body burned to reach out to him as she felt herself bursting
forth to be freed, to embrace an unimaginable force that
was drawing her. Suddenly the favorite Victoria Secret she
had specially picked out, seemed like a death noose that
would strangle her.

"Shoot, Amanda, shoot," the professional voice
within her was beckoning, "capture the moment."

She looked down at the camera in her hand – it was
pointed at the man's face. Her finger snapped away. She
pulled up the camera to her face and the sight of the
enchanted face filled her camera with a bright light. Her
body, as if touched by that unimaginable force – satiated –
relaxed for the briefest of seconds, before it drew her down
once more like a powerful magnet, about to stamp its
authority on an insignificant piece of metal.

Her hand reached out to the man below but
something shoved her away, violently. Startled and angry,

she turned and froze in fear. The face of the hooded man stared at her, inches away. The calm, professional face that had given her the assignment seemed a distant memory. From one enchanted heavenly face, she stared into one of pure evil. Her body recoiled as if she had been thrown from that palace, into a deep chasm, down in the valley where it burned fiercely.

"Go now, that thorn will be mine today. Go, girl – the killer boy will die soon – the woman will burn – I need your power there to make sure it happens."

Her mind and body rebelled briefly, but a deathly fear seized her. The suspicions in her mind had found an ally. The hooded man, with flaming hands, was about to burn her – leave a disfiguring mark on her spotless face for the brief transgression of forgetting her task, when a white presence gently drew her away in its safe embrace. The face smiled – Amanda remembered the super sweet hot chocolate and nearly fell away in relief in the arms of the woman, as a wild range of emotions gripped her.

"Go, flee from here, child, go far away," the woman implored, "escape, or be lost to the dark world."

Amanda left, a very confused woman. Her footsteps, as if commanded by the hooded man, headed back to where hell seemed to have erupted. People screamed and ran aimlessly in all directions. She looked for her newfound friend, Trisha, suddenly worried for the pregnant teen.

"Trisha," she called hesitantly knowing her voice would reach no one. She reached the body of the dead officer. A man – she recognized as the fumbling priest, knelt by the body. His eyes were closed – praying she assumed. Another officer cradled the dead officer in his arms. His hands held the dead officer's face pressed close to his chest. His head bowed.

Another man was looking down at the dead officer. He hesitated, looked both ways guiltily, before reaching down for the gun fallen a little distance away.

"Get away, you scum," Amanda shouted, reaching out protectively over the fallen gun. The man fell back, startled and scared. He rose slowly, a big man, realizing that he could easily overpower the petite woman who had come in his way.

"Oh – don't you even think about it," Amanda scowled, having no idea what she would do if the man were to actually attack her physically. She didn't have to worry, something in her voice seemed to have registered in the man's mind. The man saw her lower her camera and reach for her belt. Amanda meant to reach for her phone.

"No, please don't shoot me," the man wailed and bolted. She smiled in relief, hesitant to leave. The scowling face of the hooded man flashed before her eyes and she ran again, heading into what seemed certain death at the hands of a mob that was violently rocking a car.

A woman, her face ashen white in terror, looked out from the window of the car. Her bloodless, white palms reached to the glass. Amanda wasn't sure whether it was a sign of surrender, or a cry for mercy, or simply a desperate attempt to try and grip on to something to keep her from being smashed up in the rocking car.

Gathering her camera, Amanda shot, hoping that the enchanted face of the Indian man would fill her lens and light up her disappointed body again. It did not, but deep inside she felt a new spark, a longing for the next day, for a new day, for a new future, for a new beginning – away from the desperation and despair that her life had been. A beautiful joy enveloped her.

"I love that thrill," she yelled to no one in particular, "but first I've got to survive this day," she muttered suddenly scared – fearful and doubtful of what the end of that day would bring. An innate feeling, emanating from the dark memories of the log cabin, negated all hopes of that happy ending.

*   *   *

Daniel rose to his feet. The white haired lady was old, but her grip was firm as she drew him up. She let go of his arm and he wobbled a bit. His left hand ached fiercely. He tried to straighten it out but it remained locked in its curled, bent position. His folded wrist was a disaster. Blood flowed out from between the fingers of his clenched fist. Some of it had already dried and caked on his knuckles. With each jab of pain, he clenched harder and the blood flowed even more.

"We must tie it up," the lady spoke quietly, looking around cautiously. She pulled out the broad, white sash that held her dazzling white hair in a long ponytail. Daniel gasped at her regal presence. "Are you sure you're not an angel?"

"Shhh – not now, Daniel," she whispered urgently.

"You know my name!"

"From a long time. I've watched and blessed all the work you've done for our young in the parish." Her firm hands gently opened Daniel's left palm. At the sight of the thorn, she fell to her knees and touched his hand to her head in deep homage.

Her touch was soothing. The center of the palm had turned a dark maroon shade. In the center, the Lord's thorn stuck out. It took Daniel back to the serpents, and the first moments when the thorns had burst forth from their bodies. Carefully lifting her thick white hair, she rubbed away some of the clotted blood and finished tying the sash around his palm. The thick, white fabric gently covered Daniel's palm. She had delicately wrapped it around the thorn. Daniel reached into his back pocket, to draw out the thick winter mittens he had shoved in earlier in that day.

"No, Daniel," she smiled, stopping his hand, "the evil one is near – everywhere. This is literally a thorn in his flesh. It keeps him from conquering us – another step in his unending battle," she said pointing to the thorn.

"Is it the last, I mean the only one left?" he asked confused and saddened a bit.

"We don't know. Our brother, the one who passed it on to you, always believed that each and every one of these earthly symbols of our sins that touched the blood of Our Lord, are spread out all over the world. Together, he thought, they all keep the evil one at bay."

"How?"

"I don't know, Daniel, but look at it with your eyes of faith – believe that Calvary is still alive, and then everything else will simply fall into place."

"Sorry, for my doubts, sister," Daniel mumbled as a million fires suddenly burst forth in his head, "I want to fight for the Lord – literally, I mean."

"Me too, Daniel, but let's leave that to the Lord to call on us to serve him in whatever way he decides. I wanted to be a Thornbearer too; each time I thought of that I did so much penance."

"Penance?"

"Craving for the power of the thorn, Daniel, spiritual lust, to be a chosen one."

"How did you know about the thorn, sister?" Daniel asked curiously, as violent, loud shouts filled the air.

"Someday soon, Daniel, we'll share all our stories for now --," she stopped as desperate shrieks of help rent the air all around.

Daniel nodded.

"I saw the others – at Calvary."

"I am not one of the chosen, Daniel, but, I serve humbly, glad that the Lord found me worthy to be this close to the --," she gasped and stopped. Turning around sharply she stared into the face of the hooded man right behind her. The pungent odor that had been enveloping them suddenly became an overpowering presence.

Daniel looked up and saw the face of evil as his heart trembled. It was his first, close encounter with the hooded man. He nearly fell back onto the ground as the horror of that revelation struck him.

"The Thornbearer must be brave," she reminded him gently.

"Go back to your eternal damnation," she turned and scolded the hooded man.

He laughed quietly – silently. Daniel felt his power as he casually dismissed the lady. In a flash, the mocking laughter was gone, replaced by a deadly scowl. The eyes glowed red and Daniel felt the hissing of his breath – hot and sharp. Its tepid nature reminded Daniel of the beakers of hot, bubbling acid in his chemistry lab in school.

"It's finally my time, and no one will stand between me and the wretched thorn," he hissed in anger, "finally, so close, so close – today it will be mine to destroy." His black gloved hands reached out towards Daniel, as wisps of smoke burst out in anticipation of finally taking possession of the thorn that had eluded the kingdom of evil for centuries.

Daniel hesitated, wondering if he should run, protect the thorn or fight the hooded man. Instead, the lady jumped in between and wrapped herself around the hooded man.

"In Nomine Patris et Filii et Spiritus Sancti. Amen," she prayed firmly the Sign of the Cross. Her pure white self, wrapped around the epitome of evil. Daniel knew she was trying to buy him some time. She lasted but a second as her frail body crumpled to the ground at the man's touch. Daniel imagined her to be singed – her pure whiteness burned dark. The smell of burning hair and flesh confirmed what Daniel thought he imagined.

"Run," she beseeched with a dying breath as she fell, still clinging on to the robes of the evil one, "run, Daniel."

* * *

Daniel saw the path west as the only way before him. The loud bangs had come from there. The cop had gone that way a few minutes back, as had the bewitching photographer clad in black. He followed, before the hooded man could fully free himself from the white haired lady and come after him.

Daniel ran quickly not daring to look back. Every bone in his body screamed at him to turn back and fight. His spirit felt emboldened, yet something kept on drawing him west. He sidestepped a screaming woman who nearly brought him down.

"They're shooting, they're shooting, help, run," she yelled hysterically. She grabbed Daniel by the shoulders and clung on to him. "Help me, help me," she kept on yelling, hardly aware of what was happening to her.

Daniel looked into her fixated eyes. They stared at him for a second. Then stared at something behind him, rolled up backward into their sockets, and the woman fainted. Daniel had a hundredth of a second to flee, knowing what the woman had seen over his shoulder. Using the woman's body weight as she fell, he swung her around to his back in one swift move. He felt the impact of her body crashing into the evil one. It worked as Daniel briefly caught sight of the woman bringing down the hooded man. His black clothes looked tattered, with streaks of white running across his chest. The white haired lady, Daniel thought, and silently thanked her hoping she had survived the encounter.

Daniel ran. The crowd had gone crazy. People screamed everywhere. Some were running helter skelter like headless chickens. Daniel ducked from another crazy man who was running with his hands outstretched, screaming,

"It's the end of the world, the end of the world." He suddenly grasped Daniel by the shoulders. Daniel tried to duck but took the full weight of the man's body. It threw him to the side as the man fell forward. A group of hysterically screaming old men followed.

Daniel rolled to the right and came to rest behind another cement planter. About to get up and run again, he felt his brain scream a warning.

"Wait – wait – hide," he told himself. Luckily for him, the warning worked as he saw the hooded man free himself from the group of zombie-like old men and emerge staggering.

He looked right and left – stamped his foot in anger and then carried on. Daniel sensed the man had other things on his mind. Suddenly, the world seemed safer from where Daniel was, down by the planter which stood at the edge of the sidewalk.

The busy road that Eglinton was, seemed to have vanished – shut down. No cars or buses went either way. Instead, wild, crazy, screaming people ran about everywhere in the faint light of the darkening day. It suddenly struck him - it was barely mid-morning. He crawled out onto the sidewalk and crouched low hoping he would see the distinct, long, black cape of the hooded man and avoid him.

Daniel looked both ways and ran fast continuing to crouch as low as he could. His left hand throbbed even more violently with the pain. He barely managed to support his low down position with his good right hand. Another few steps and Daniel heard a loud commotion to the right. Looking right, trying to make sense of it, he hopped a few more steps and crashed into a black-clad figure kneeling on the ground.

"No – No," he yelled as the figure reached out to take his hand, "you won't get it." He ran hoping to escape one more time, but the black figure called out his name.

"Daniel!"

"No, you won't take it --,"

"Daniel! It's me," the voice screamed at him – it sounded familiar, "it's me, Father Brian."

Daniel, about to break away, stopped and looked. Fr. Brian was kneeling. There was a uniform-clad body laid out before him. Shocked, Daniel looked at the face, it was a lady. The eyes were shut, her police hat had fallen away and her bright golden hair lay sprawled in the lap of another officer.

Daniel remembered them both arriving in front of the church. The kneeling officer who cradled the dead officer's head in his lap, had spoken to him a few minutes back. The officer gently brushed aside a speck of dirt from the face of his colleague. His face was in shock – his eyes stared blankly ahead and Daniel sensed a wild revengeful hatred filling his soul.

"Evil is out in force today, Daniel, help me," Fr. Brian pleaded.

"I know, Father. Don't worry, we'll take this together," Daniel whispered back in encouragement, suddenly feeling emboldened by the presence of the priest. Was it that or was it the fact that the priest had asked him for help?

"The preaching man, he warned me of this day, we must help him, Daniel – he is our best bet – he ran that --,"

"That way," Daniel completed the statement pointing towards the church. "He's dead, Father Brian; and

so is the white haired lady. At least out of action – whoever
she is?"

From the other side of the road, they heard loud
cries of men chanting. It was a frenzied mob.

"Burn.........Kill......" someone chanted and the
crowd repeated, "Burn. Kill."

"What's happening – I don't understand?" the priest
exclaimed, "it's as if we're in the middle of a war, the
apocalypse. It's as if they're possessed."

The priest had barely finished his sentence when a
series of shots rang out. People ducked and screamed
louder. The panicked crowd went wilder. Someone tripped
violently over them.

"6 shots – that's a rampage," the officer blurted
now suddenly alert.

"Help me get her to the side, please," the officer
beseeched them lifting his dead colleague gently from under
her arms. Fr. Brian took her legs and they moved her to
safety behind the large cement planter.

"Thank you. Stay here with her, please," the cop
pleaded with a rare softness in his voice. He drew out his
gun with one hand and reached for his radio with the other.
He was already running by the time the gun came out.
Daniel saw him run to the other side of the road from
where the shots had been heard.

"Daniel – we must...." Fr. Brian started but turned
around to find no one. Daniel was gone too. Instead, the
priest looked in horror as he saw large flames leap up. The
smell of fuel filled the air. The car was on fire. He caught
sight of Daniel working his way through the crowd as it
parted. Suddenly, it dawned on him – there was something
strange about Daniel. He was walking upright, slow and
solemn, as if he had totally lost connection with the danger
and the chaos around him.

* * *

Daniel had seen the officer move the dead body of his colleague with Fr. Brian. He knew his lack of help surprised them. The volley of shots that rang out had served as a good distraction. He saw the officer leave and froze in fear as a collage of terrifying sights lit up his vision. He saw Dylan run into the convenience store. His terrified face briefly appeared in the glass door of the store and then disappeared. He seemed to be hiding from the mob that was all set to burn the car with the woman in it. He saw the hooded man standing under the streetlight, outside the bakery, like a general, overseeing the execution of his battle plans.

And then, he saw the photographer. Who was she he wondered? Their eyes had met briefly and her gaze had burned its way deep into his soul. He saw her exchange a glance with the hooded man under the lamppost and was sure there was a connection. Their eyes met, gazing, fixated as if nothing else existed around them. He felt a sudden tug, as if she was drawing him to herself with some unseen energy.

"Evil sorceress or a divine angel – whoever you are," he blurted out confused, "you're either from heaven or hell!" Daniel barely knew when he stood up and began to walk towards the woman.

* * *

Another blast of flames from the car lit up the square. "Oh my God – there is someone in that car," Fr. Brian screamed and ran toward the burning car. He stopped, suddenly remembering the dead officer lying on the ground. Ripping off his coat, he covered her and ran again.

"Oh my Good Lord – hear my prayer. What evil is this?" he prayed silently running across the crowded road. A few steps ahead, he crashed into a dark figure and fell to the ground. Enveloped by a dizzying haze, he looked up apologetically, hoping to get to the car in time to save the woman. The face of the dark figure stared back. His mind swirled as the full impact of the evil before him hit.

"Let the woman burn, priest. She must die today – as should many of the others, if I don't get what I want before this day is through."

Fr. Brian remembered the sight outside his window. He had seen evil from afar. In the darkness of the night – in the silent shadows. He had heard it in the heinous sins that people dumped on him in the confessional. Here it stood before him. Despite his undying faith, and his life of prayer, rooted deep in that faith, Fr. Brian shivered at what he saw before him.

The man grinned. He seemed to slither and slide firmly in the way of the priest. He changed colors and Fr. Brian drew back aghast. He was a child again – on his dad's farm – in the middle of the night – in the barn. A silent crawling creature slithered all over the white picket fence on the green auction deck. It slithered over the white fence and drew away in the shape of a man.

Suddenly the picket fence was no more. Instead, a dark mass of lightning struck, dead tree stumps formed an altar, an innately evil altar. There had been a sacrifice, and another – there had been many. He was to be one of them too, at the wrong end of a gun held by his father – an unintended, yet chosen offering to the evil one. A million answers about the farm, Uncle Luigi's insistence on Francesco and Maria never selling it, and his own horrid experience, finally lay bare.

A little ahead, Fr. Brian saw Uncle Luigi. His hand withdrew out of his pocket briefly and went back in again. It held a gun. Uncle Luigi smiled at him wickedly from afar and disappeared. Fr. Brian shook his head and prepared to confront the evil that stood in his way but it too vanished.

* * *

Daniel found himself switching between two worlds, one real, one mysterious. He knew he needed to help Dylan, and the woman trapped in the car. He debated in his mind where to head first. They both seemed in grave danger. At the same time, a hypnotic gaze kept drawing him back into a bubble. He was about to reach the convenience store, when another massive blast of flames rocked the car.

"The fuel tank will erupt any minute, run," he heard someone yell. The car was by now, fully engulfed in flames. Daniel fell to the ground, as did the others around the car. Desperate to reach the woman in the car, he put his left hand down to push himself up, and a million sparks of pain engulfed his body.

"Got to remember the thorn," he muttered apologetically, as a curse almost erupted in his mind – "Sorry, My Lord."

He reached out with his right hand for something to pull himself up. There was nothing, but his hand grasped something tender. A hand was drawing him up. Daniel realized it was drawing him to itself, to the person behind that arm. A million bolts of lightning shot through his body. He came up standing and looked down into the face that had stunned him over and over again that morning. It was beautiful, with dark eyes, dark disheveled hair and dark lipstick coated lips that seemed to murmur something. The red shaded eyes stared deep into his, longingly.

"It's you," he felt his voice betray him, "Angel!" His head spun, his soul drawing him away; his mind, his conscience, screaming warnings about something not right. Yet his body responded to her touch.

"Your first word to me – Angel – thank you, Daniel," she barely managed, blushing at his name on her lips for the first time, choking on the words, "I needed to know that."

"Who are you?" they shot at each other at the same time, and fell silent as they realized that the same question plagued them both.

"And – you know my name!" he whispered puzzled deeply, wondering at that strange occurrence for the second time that morning.

"I'm Amanda," she answered blushing.

They stood close. Their right hands still grasping each other firmly. They knew something was innately drawing them to each other. Like a powerful whirlpool, sucking them into its vortex – the attraction engulfed them.

"I've been looking for you for a long time," she finally broke the silence, "this is my point of no return." She was surprised he did not answer. There was confusion on his face.

Instead, Daniel drew his only good hand away from Amanda's, and gently curved it around her waist. Tenderly, he felt his palm open out and place itself gently on her back. There was no dress or fabric to hold, as his hand slid under her top. Instead, he felt the soft touch of her skin. It was startlingly warm and moist.

"Gently," his mind prompted, as if not to bruise a tender creature. It lasted but a moment as he suddenly gripped her back fiercely, and drew her to himself as a wild carnal instinct swept over him – like a wild beast devouring its prey. There was no resistance from her – instead he sensed a deep yearning in her.

Amanda's free hand reached over Daniel's shoulder, around his neck, and pulled him down to her face. For the briefest of moments, their eyes looked into each other's before they closed, and their lips locked together.

Daniel felt his world spin around dizzyingly. The din of the chaos around him was overpowering. It seemed to flow into the woman in his arms. His body screamed to merge with hers, as if they were one being. He felt her hand around his neck grip him fiercely. Her face was moist; wetting his – tears, he was sure. Their lips remained locked, as if they were breathing for each other.

"Stay here, for now, angel," he said pulling away after what seemed an eternity. He reached around her with his left hand as well, "the future, I do not know. You are like a wild fantasy I wished for, but hoped would never happen."

"Then I would choose to be your slave, sire," she whispered silently, surprised at the feelings he evoked in her.

"More like my goddess that I'd put on an altar and worship," he whispered back.

He felt her body quiver at his words, burying itself even more deeply into his. His right hand caressed her face tenderly, pressing it into his chest. Her body was soft and supple as he felt each detail of her against himself. Something hard around her waist hurt his thigh. A lens, he was sure, he had seen all the equipment hanging around her waist. He looked down on her face. Her eyes were shut. Her beauty struck him once again, making him wonder what the hooded man had to do with the fragile, angelic creature who had stormed her way into his world.

The thorn, the beautiful photographer, the hooded man, the white-haired lady – there was too much happening. He saw her open her eyes. They still clung on to each other as loud rasping commands filled the air. Daniel saw a troop of heavily armed commandoes fill the square. They looked more like a military force rather than the regular cops. They were fanning out all around Daniel and Amanda and past them. He presumed it was the presence of the woman in his arms. Their weapons remained drawn, fingers on the trigger, but their voices did the most to control the chaos around that engulfed the place.

"The car, the car," one of them yelled, "person inside," he said pointing to the car. In an instant, another donned a mask and pulled out an odd-looking bar from his waist. Daniel had the feeling the cylindrical bar would smash its way through anything.

"We must leave, my love," she urged, "there is only death here. I want a beautiful new tomorrow with you — starting now." The greeting stunned him. He hid his left hand behind his waist and held Amanda's with his right.

"Let's go, now," she pleaded, tugging him fiercely, "I could have found the one pearl I was looking for, and then lose it forever, or be lost myself." The white haired lady's words played hauntingly in Amanda's mind. Like a warning bell, they tolled, warning her of a narrow window of escape. Daniel realized Amanda had begun to cry. The calm, professional demeanor was gone.

"Agreed, but there are two people we must save," he said, "the boy in the convenience store and the lady in the car."

"Make that one," he corrected himself in relief, as he saw the commandoes smash the rear window. One of the heavily armed commandoes hooked a lever on the rear door as he and a colleague ripped the burning door out. Bravely jumping into the flaming car, they smashed the front doors out with their feet, and pulled the lady out of the burning car. Her coat was on fire but she seemed alive, choking and coughing with the smoke, but definitely alive. Instantly two other commandoes wrapped themselves around the woman dousing the fire.

"The paramedics – 100 meters south and east," one of them yelled. He seemed like the leader – a giant among giants.

"Ok, now for Dylan," Daniel called and tugged on Amanda's arm. She was tugging in the other direction. A smile broke out on their faces as they beheld each other for an instant – apart from each other.

"My friend – Trisha," Amanda said as desperation and panic squeezed into her voice. Daniel turned and looked. It was a strange sight. Fr. Brian lay partially sprawled on the road. The blonde girl, Trisha, stood pointing at the Daily Convenience Food Mart, but behind them unknown to the priest and Trisha, the hooded man was moving in like a dark, evil shadow.

"Ok – you go help the boy and I'll help Trisha," Amanda said moving away. They stood apart for a second, deeply conscious that their physical touch had broken. They stared and slammed into each other one more time for one more hug.

"You be safe, my Daniel," Amanda said again, gently caressing his cheek with a shivering hand, "a minute and no more – and then I'm never ever letting you go."

Daniel froze at the words that poured out of her soul. Everything they had experienced in the last few minutes was true. Yet, for the first minute apart from her, Daniel knew it could never be true. A guilty arrow shot through his soul, ripping him apart as he guiltily remembered Michelle.

"Oh my Lord Jesus, is this my first test and I failed. Lead me not into temptation," he prayed.

He saw her race across to help the blonde teen, ripping out the cameras and her jacket. His body still drawn to her, as he saw her delicate, sensuous figure laden with her equipment. A little opening in her black top exposed a patch

of skin – he had held her there – the mere thought of it sent
his pulse racing.

*   *   *

Fr. Brian had been watching Daniel in horror. The
black-clad photographer with the cameras seemed to be
hanging on to his arm – or rather enveloped around him. A
voice behind him startled him. It was a young girl with wild
blonde hair.

"Priest, I mean reverend, or whatever it is that
you're called, are you ok?" she said reaching out to give him
a hand.

"I'm fine, child," he lied hoping to reassure the teen,
"call me Father Brian."

"Are you the priest from that church?"

"Yes – what's your name?"

"Trisha, and you must help me – help Ezekiel – no
I mean Dylan – you know him, don't you?"

"Dylan the altar server --,"

"Yes, yes that, maybe that Dylan – the Filipino kid –
church – bandana-clad --,"

"What about him, child?"

"He shot all those people. Shamar, the cop and I'm
sure he's behind that," she said pointing to the burning car.

"No, no, you should not believe that," Fr. Brian
protested in disbelief.

"It's him – I saw it with my own eyes."

"No – trust me, child; Dylan would never --,"

"No dammit, you listen to me, NOW," Trisha
screamed. The violent rage in her voice silenced the priest.
"It's Dylan. I saw the gun in his hand. I saw him aim. I saw
the cop fall. These eyes, priest, saw it happen in front of
them."

Fr. Brian sighed as the weight and reality of Trisha's words hit him. He had seen the hooded man show Dylan the gun. He looked at his uncle in the distance and decided he would not believe what he was hearing.

"You're right, child, but strange are the deceptive ways of the evil one. Actually, it's that dark hooded man and my uncle over there; those are the men responsible for all this."

The dark hooded man materialized out of nowhere behind Trisha before Fr. Brian could finish his sentence. He seemed to grow in stature with each yell of the mob around the car. A little further on, Fr. Brian saw the flames begin to totally engulf the burning car. With each blast and boom, the fierce, evil gaze of the hooded man grew.

"Kill, kill, burn them," someone yelled and the hooded man gleamed victoriously.

"You see, priest – one way or another – this is the day – this wretched Good Friday that I will finally get that thorn."

The priest gazed in wonder having little idea what the hooded man was referring to.

"Don't worry, you will understand. The one thorn from that crown that still stands in my way, today I will have it."

"So many dead. All these riots, fires, chaos – still God will win – this is his day. It's Good Friday and --,"

"This is the police – You must go home, now." Suddenly a chorus of booming voices stilled the crowd. The voices were accompanied by the heavy stamping of boots in military fashion.

"This is the police – go home, now – you must evacuate this place immediately," the voices boomed drowning out the din around.

"Move. Move. Go."

A flare shot up in the air as if to reinforce the command and draw everyone's attention. The slight boom of the erupting flare, and its lighting of the darkened square, got everyone's attention as they stared into the sky. In the bright light it emanaed, the voices boomed out again.

"Go home, now," the commandoes boomed, scaring people more with their voices and their intimidating presence, than with the heavy weaponry they carried.

Fr. Brian studied the heavily armed, dark clothed commandoes. Their helmeted heads darted all over as the weapons in their hands followed.

"This is the police – you have been warned – go home, now." The voices seemed to work. A stillness settled on the crowd.

"You must go home, now," they continued spreading around yelling fiercely into people's faces and nudging them on. The arrival of the task force took everyone by surprise. Another flare shot up and the mobs slowly began to emerge from their dazed and hypnotic state. The commandoes shouted louder as people slowly began to return to their senses. The intersection was clearing up. There was another bang as another flare went up. The crowd shivered, looking for the nearest escape. In the fading light of the flare, Fr. Brian and Trisha caught sight of someone pointing the cops in the direction of the Daily Convenience Food Mart.

"In there, in there," another man yelled, "the gunman is hiding in there." Trisha froze. Her eyes seemed to plead with the priest.

"Dylan, Father, they're referring to Dylan, he is hiding in there. They will shoot him down, you must help him."

"So many dead," the hooded man spoke suddenly in a low tone, "another stupid kid about to die in there, and the Thornbearer with my --," he pointed to Daniel and the photographer. Once more, the sight of the two troubled Fr. Brian. In the midst of that chaos, they seemed to have found each other.

"It can't be," Fr. Brian, pleaded aloud, "I know his family – I know him."

"See, priest – the virtuous will fall, no matter how strong. She will bring the Thornbearer to me," the hooded man beamed with a sinister look on his face. Fr. Brian shook his head confused.

"Thornbearer? I don't understand. Either way, you will never win."

"I will, priest. I need those sacrifices – the baby in there, and the girl --," the hooded man spoke with a low, haunting voice pointing to Trisha's stomach as he began to spread his arms around her.

"Stop, stop," the cries took the three of them by storm. It was a distinct voice that the hooded man, the priest, and Trisha, recognized immediately.

"Amanda," Trisha was the first to react. The hooded man scowled and flew into a rage as he saw his daughter stare into his face, ready to challenge him. Fr. Brian was the last to realize what was happening.

"Leave the kid alone," Amanda yelled, ripping out the cameras and her jacket from her body. There was a fierce look in her face as she challenged him. Fr. Brian and Trisha both stepped back with a start, unaware of what the hooded man had just been about to do.

The hooded man smiled. "Truly my daughter – you will be a worthy successor as soon as we open your eyes."

"Take your evil and be gone, you evil man," Amanda yelled even louder. Her fierce voice grew, as did the angry stranger, into a massive, dark presence. Any pretense of being a simple, dark clothed human, was gone. Amanda and Trisha shivered at the presence that filled their hearts with dread. With raging red eyes that burned deep like the massive hollow of a raging volcano, the hooded man turned, looking for Daniel.

Fr. Brian knew something deadly was about to happen – as a man and as a priest – he felt helpless, powerless. All his pretenses of having prepared over the years to fight evil in any form, simply melted away. His mind wandered back to his seminary days looking for strength from scripture. He remembered the book of Joshua:

"Have I not commanded you?
Be strong and courageous.
Do not be afraid;
do not be discouraged,
for the Lord your God will be with you
wherever you go." – Joshua 1:9

XV

Satan's prisoners

Daniel watched from afar. There was an argument between the hooded man, Amanda and the priest. He saw the hooded man worriedly take stock of the presence of the commandoes. Suddenly, he turned in Daniel's direction.

"I need that thorn – now!" the vicious voice shouted above the loud, rasping shouts of the commandoes.

"You wait here another minute, you scum, and you can truly have the thorn – like a stake through your heart," Daniel retorted, unaware of the fury of his words. He had to delay things; the commandoes were gaining on the crowd. More and more cops were moving in as well. The number of uniforms began to grow. The hooded man noticed the change in the intersection as well. His cover was fading away rapidly.

"Very well then," the hooded man suddenly blurted as he saw the new, wild emotion that flowed between his daughter and the Thornbearer. It was a powerful force. It was time for a change of plans. The force, love or lust, he laughed in his heart – would bring the Thornbearer to him.

Daniel felt the hooded man's chilling words, "You want these 3 alive, then bring me the thorn – today, alone, before the evening is through."

In a giant swoop, he suddenly enveloped the helpless teen and his daughter. Trisha started to scream but the scream never left her mouth as the dark cape totally enveloped her. Amanda swung both her Nikons, but the stranger casually swiped away her feeble protest. Her black jacket flapped for a bit, and was sucked in as well.

Fr. Brian lunged forward, but all he managed to grab were the two swinging cameras. The hooded man, carrying the teen and Amanda, hidden within his massive dark embrace, easily sidestepped the priest. Two steps later, he was gone.

* * *

Daniel stood confused. A part of him screamed to go after the hooded man and try and rescue the ladies. Deep inside, a tiny voice told him it was futile. With a deep guilt that was beginning to overpower him, he prayed he would never see Amanda again; that she would fight her way, and save herself and Trisha. His gaze fell on his swollen left palm, now rigid like a stone, and a fierce pang of guilt, burnt within him. He wondered what a whole crown of those thorns, rammed into the Lord's head on a hot dusty day, would have felt like.

"My first test, and I failed miserably, My Lord. Why did you choose me – a frail human?" He almost knew the answer in his heart. Just like the fishermen from the Sea of Galilee, there was a plan for him – he had been chosen. The guilt turned to hope, and then courage, a smile and into a fierce passion for fighting for the Lord. Daniel lifted his left hand and kissed it. "Thank you, Lord – thank you for letting me partake in your suffering – I will never let you down."

Daniel looked in the direction the evil one had fled. He was long gone but Daniel felt his presence.

"We will fight another battle, evil one, soon," he swore, "for now I've got a life to save." Somewhere in the distance, he knew the words had been heard. He wondered what the man had meant by three souls. He felt the souls of the two women in an evil bondage, rapidly fading away. He sensed a fleeing taxi, as the evil one sped away bearing two gentle souls, and in another, tragic moment, there was to be another life taken. Yet again, someone was to be slain. "Jesus, please let this be the last one for the day," Daniel wished, knowing deeply even before he finished that thought, that the big battle still lay ahead. "How many more will fall today, My Lord?"

Sadly, Daniel finally turned around, "Ok, Dylan, let's see what you've been up to?"

The sight before him gave him the most melancholic feeling ever. The crowd had dispersed; a few clueless stragglers were being led away. He walked to one of the commandoes closest to him.

"Officer, the boy, the supposed gunman --,"

Daniel did not get to finish his sentence. The man with the strange, old suit interrupted their talk. His words were incoherent, his accent, strange – but his message was clear. He was pointing at the convenience store.

"The gunman, sir – the one that did all the shooting – he's in there," the man blurted out. Daniel could not help but notice the strange appearance of the man. He wore a loose, stripped ancient looking suit. His hat was straight out of a 60's movies, and the pencil thin mustache completed the villainous look.

"That's not true sir. The boy is innocent," Daniel tried to protest, but it was too late. The commando was already on his radio.

"Team-Sigma to Daily Convenience Food Mart, confirmation of gunman – repeat – gunman possibly holed up in the Daily Convenience Food Mart."

The Daily Convenience Food Mart stood surrounded by the most fearful, and heavily armed uniformed men, Daniel had ever seen in his life. The girl he had discovered with the wildest of passion was gone – probably for good. Another officer lay dead, and the teen he hoped to save, already set up for a vicious gun battle. There could be only one outcome against the highly trained commandoes. Dylan's death seemed inevitable.

Sadly, he knelt as his left hand sent a million jabs of pain through his body. He liked the feeling – he felt a closeness to the Lord. "Help me, Lord – help the boy," he prayed.

*   *   *

The battle was set. The commandoes were moving in towards the store, crouched, fingers on their triggers, eyes focused on the narrow door – ready to blast away a supposed trigger-happy gunman. Daniel noticed the suited figure move discretely behind a car parked next to the store. The striped suit hand came out for the briefest of instants – the barrel seemed longer – a silencer. A silent shot struck a commando's Kevlar vest. The commando fell back, rolled, and was up again. A volley of shots rang out from the commandoes in response as they charged towards the convenience store like rampaging elephants.

"Oh, my Uncle Luigi," Fr. Brian said as a shivering hand held Daniel's shoulder, "how much death and destruction has he caused in a single day?" Daniel and Fr. Brian fell to their knees in despair as the intersection exploded with sounds of all types. This time Daniel noticed the orderly influx. Officers, paramedics, and firefighters poured in from all sides. The two men got up as a heavy ring of cops began to circle the store and push everyone back.

"Come, Daniel, it's too late," Fr. Brian said quietly, "I'm sure the Lord has his own way of doing things."

Daniel noticed an ambulance near the fallen officer's body. The cops were moving fast in sealing off the entire area, but the news crews, photographers and media folk of every kind were pouring in from all sides, equally rapidly. A heavy thud of staccato sounds drew their attention up to the sky. The dark clouds had cleared. A single black helicopter hovered up there. Daniel could see the faint markings of a news channel on its side. Below the nose of the chopper hung a protruding, round glass ball – a pod of cameras, Daniel guessed.

"I guess we just lost Dylan."

"No one is dead if it is not the Lord's plan, Father, let's not talk about the dead --,"

"The dead. Oh My Dear Lord, Daniel," Fr. Brian suddenly gasped, grasping Daniel's left hand sending a million bolts of agony through his body, "what did you just say? No one is dead --,"

"If it is not in God's plan," Daniel murmured through his pain noticing the ashen face of the priest.

"Mamma," Fr. Brian whispered hoarsely, remembering the last, unfinished conversation with his sister. "I've got to get to my mother, Daniel – if only the Lord will let me see her alive one more time," he cried. Flinging Amanda's cameras around Daniel's neck, he ran, sprinting hard westwards in the direction the evil one had fled as well.

"She awaits you, Father," Daniel called after the priest, not sure where those words had come from. "From the pain," his soul answered. Daniel believed what his soul was telling him.

XVI

The Daily Convenience Food Mart

Daniel stood rooted to the spot where he had last seen the evil one and the priest leave. The intersection was all but clear of people. News crews jostled with the cops who kept them safely away from the crime scene. The big, bright flashes from their cameras reflected off the yellow police tape that had sprung up everywhere. A dazed straggler stood gaping at the barrage of questions the zealous reporters threw his way.

"Sir, can you tell us anything about what happened?"

"Uh!"

"Do you see the earlier shootings?" another shouted.

"What?"

"There were reports of hysteria," another prodded.

The man barely managed another grunt before the cops whisked him away.

"Any update, officer?" the press shouted.

"No, and you must leave now," the cops shouted.

An ambulance pulled up for the woman who had been rescued from the burning car. She lay on the ground, ashen, as the paramedics gently lifted her onto the stretcher. A pair of firefighters from a nearby fire truck inspected the car.

"Hard to believe someone actually got out of that inferno, alive," a firefighter commented, as he saw two of his colleagues spray the car with foam.

"Harder to believe you guys actually managed to get in there, and get the lady out," another said to the two black-clad commandoes who were receiving first aid for the big, red blotches that had sprung up on their hands. Another ambulance sped in, weaving its way past the news crews that were being pushed back by a line of the heavily armed commandoes. They covered their faces with their dark, grey shields from the popping flashes.

"Secret troops, are you?" one reporter screamed, trying to poke her recorder between the shields.

"Are you the army, or commandoes, or some special force?" another shouted as the flashes popped.

"Are you trained for terrorists – was this a terrorist attack?" another screamed in their faces, hoping to elicit a reaction. A team of regular cops moved in, forming a wall between the commandoes, and the reporters. Daniel noticed a massive, tank-like truck pull in. Its deadly presence caused even the hardened reporters to take a break and stare in awe. The commandoes were slowly retreating towards the store, covering their colleagues who were making a slow, crouched approach towards the store they had just blasted with a volley of shots. A reporter broke through the police cordon – his camera shooting continuously, but he was brought down in a matter of seconds by the cops.

"You're going to pay for that, officer," another reporter warned, "this isn't a banana republic, you know."

Daniel looked away, suddenly aware of a deep pounding in his heart. The ambulance that had just arrived was meant for the convenience store. The glass doors of the convenience store had completely shattered. The bullet-ridden and mangled metal doors, barely hung. Daniel noticed the first of the commandoes ready to smash down a piece, as the others stood alert – a hair's breath away from letting off another volley of fire.

"Oh Dear Lord – Dylan," Daniel screamed and ran towards the convenience store. The sudden dash took the first line of commandoes by surprise. Daniel felt the cold muzzle of a gun against his neck. It was one of the commandoes.

"The kid in there, officer," Daniel pleaded with the leader of commandoes, outside the convenience store door, "I know him – I can talk to him."

"Not a chance!"

"Please sir, you must believe me. He is a good kid, just a teen, a student of mine," he yelled as fiercely as he could, hoping to draw the attention of the commandoes away from the door.

"A kid that just shot at us and a dozen other people?"

"That's not true, officer. It is an illusion. There have been enough innocent folk shot today – we don't need another kid shot – that too by you, commandoes."

"Take this man out of here," the commando yelled, ready to turn, when out of the blue Daniel remembered the thorn. Was it truly a simple, humble thorn – like the Lord, ready to bend to the cruelty of the world, or was it magical? Daniel held his left hand up, as if a magical, divine force would flow through. None did, but a wild thought struck him.

"Let me just talk to him. Keep your guns aimed and ready if you will. Believe me, that kid is probably more terrified than anyone on this earth right now."

There was a seconds' hesitation and Daniel seized it. Throwing his hands in the air, Daniel darted through to the door before the commandoes could drag him back. The shop looked as if an earthquake had struck. Shelves lay overturned – shattered glass lay everywhere.

"Oh my Jesus, oh help me, my Jesus," a Chinese accented woman's crying voice wailed from a corner.

"Dylan – Dylan – It's me, Daniel – your confirmation teacher from St. Thomas Aquinas. You must come out, now."

The silence was endless, punctuated only by the rotors of the news helicopter, hovering high outside. Daniel moved into the aisles and called again.

"It's ok – no one will harm you – please come out."

There was no answer. Daniel knew the commandoes would not hold out any longer. They had already been at the receiving end of one shot. Just when it seemed all was lost, Daniel heard the faintest of voices.

"I did not shoot anyone – I had a dummy of a gun."

"Then come out."

If the commandoes had been expecting a heavily armed and dangerous teen – they were wonderfully surprised. The kid that stood at the door looked more like someone in need of a hug. With his baby face and disheveled clothes, he resembled a victim of a vicious beating, rather than a killer who had shot more than half a dozen people. It was as far as Dylan got, or as much as Daniel could do. The commandoes charged on him like fierce warriors. Daniel saw the tiny body brought face down on the concrete. His feet were shackled in a flash, as were his hands, behind his back. Two commandoes stood ready, guns aimed at Dylan's head, as another patted him down.

"Clear," shouted the commando patting down Dylan.

Daniel shook his head sadly and knelt near the boy.

"What happened, Dylan?"

"They set me up."

"Who?"

"The hooded man and the man in the ancient suit."

Daniel saw the commandoes haul Dylan to his feet. A million questions ran through his head. Reaching out with his thorn hand, he patted the boy on his head. More and

more he began to believe in the power of the thorn that had
played its part in redeeming the world of its burden of sin.

"Don't worry, the Lord knows you are innocent."

"Thank you, I am," Dylan bent forward and
whispered in Daniel's ear, "the gun they made me use held a
dummy magazine – it never fired a single round, it's on the
little altar in the shop, get it to the cops."

The commandoes handed Dylan over to the cops.
The leader of the commandoes, a large man, patted Daniel
on the shoulder.

"Well done, my man. Rather foolish, but brave of
you to march in there like that. Always better to end a
standoff like that, rather than in a hail of bullets."

"Sir, you must believe me. The gunman is still at
large. A man in an old 60's style, pinstripe suit – pencil thin
mustache and a fedora."

"The one who pointed us to the boy – you sure?"

"Positive, sir – in fact the shot that hit your man,
came not from the store, but from the right – somewhere
there," Daniel said, pointing to Locksley Avenue. The leader
took a long hard look at Daniel.

"Why do I want to believe you, it's as if --," the
battle hardened commando smiled.

"That's because I speak the truth, sir," Daniel
smiled quietly, beginning to feel a quiet communion with
the thorn. It has to be, his mind prompted – it came
touched from the very own flesh and blood of the Lord –
the Son of Man.

"And another thing, sir – the boy's gun is in there,
presumably on an altar – it's a dummy he told me – at least
with a dummy magazine that never held nor fired a single
round – he was just play acting, like a video game. I can take
you to it."

The leader ran into the store. The others had already
moved in. Daniel saw the commandoes still alert, checking

each corner of the store. He walked over to the corner where the paramedics were helping the Chinese woman. Fierce sobs racked her body as the paramedics tried to get her to relax. A group of commandoes was inspecting another corner of the shop. Daniel looked around, hoping to find the altar quickly – he was late. The leader was already at the altar, reaching up on his toes, thanks to his massive height.

"Gentlemen – the weapon," he called, lifting Dylan's Glock with a black gloved hand.

"Gangster's favorite," a commando whispered behind him.

"The magazine, sir," Daniel called, "you would know it better."

The leader beat him to it, yet again. He smiled holding what looking like a rectangular, black, metal piece that he had easily ejected from the gun.

"Blank," he said and his smile vanished, as did Daniel's.

"Like I said, sir – the real killer is out there."

"Describe him again," the leader ordered, punching his radio. "Lynx to Alpha – Lynx to Sigma – gunman still at large – repeat gunman still at large – look for a ..."

Daniel lost the rest of it as the commandoes scrambled once more. They were back in a war mode again. Daniel felt the tension spread like wildfire to the commandoes, and the cops outside. If only he could point the men in the direction of the assassin. He tried to remember the name Fr. Brian had blurted, "Uncle Luigi? Weird!" he thought, as the reference to the relation suddenly struck him.

He ran to the side of the shop as a blast of cold air slammed him in the face. Was it a bad feeling or was it just – "An open door!" he exclaimed and walked towards it. A K-9 unit was already there. The handlers were busy, prodding the dogs around to pick up a scent as a cop barked orders into his radio. Daniel and the leader walked out, across the road.

"Didn't the man wear some kind of 60s' style – black and white suit?" the leader suddenly asked.

"That's right, sir – silk, if you ask me," Daniel answered eagerly.

"Well, here's the jackpot then," the leader pointed to a black and white kerchief on the ground. Its distinct silken shine, stood out against the dullness of the day. The dogs were on to the scarf in a moment as the handlers called out a strange message. Mission learnt, the German Shepherds shot forward, like arrows, as they picked up the scent.

"All units on alert – the gunman may have fled in a north or north-eastern direction."

The dogs were headed in a northern direction. Slowly, Daniel picked out the hidden form of the meddling 60's man with the gun, in the distance. The man was smiling victoriously, from behind a large metal bin. Daniel saw him lift his hat off, and reach in his breast pocket to wipe off his sweaty forehead. Instead, his hand came out empty. The hand dug in frantically once more, and Daniel saw Uncle Luigi look up in surprise as he heard the sound of the dogs headed his way.

"Oh my dear sweet, Lord – the irony of it all – great indeed are your ways, dear Lord," Daniel smiled, as he saw the man realize the deadly turn of events. He turned and fled.

"You must leave now, sir, this is a crime scene," a voice ordered over his back.

"Sorry, sir," Daniel apologized, and began to walk towards Eglinton. "Dylan, you lucky bum," he smiled in relief, blowing a kiss to heaven as he walked away from the store.

XVII

Ezekiel

The bright, flashing lights from the cruisers struck Daniel's eyes. He saw the reporters rush towards him, as he stepped outside the yellow tape. A reporter was in his way.

"Sir, did you see anything of the earlier riot?"

"No I didn't," Daniel evaded the question with a brisk answer and turned away, trying to free himself from the pursuing reporter as another joined the chase.

"But you must have heard, or seen something, sir?"

"Perhaps, some pictures on those awesome cameras around your neck," the second one asked, looking vaguely familiar. Daniel was sure he had seen him on TV somewhere.

"Not really," Daniel ran across Locksley. A cruiser blocked off the pursuing reporters. Daniel ducked. He was in between two parked cars, behind the bakery.

"In here, quickly," a voice called. Daniel crouched and looked around. The voice had come from a modified wooden crate with a side-opening door. "Raccoon-safe garbage storage," he smiled at the contraption.

Daniel ducked in. The smell of the garbage nearly made him throw up. He stared at the face that stared back at him in shock. "Confirmation, right?" he whispered.

"Yes, Daniel – I mean sir – if that's ok?"

"Shhhh! That's perfectly ok," Daniel covered his nose trying to shut out the smell, "of course its ok – what the heck are you doing in here?"

"I was looking for my girlfriend, when all this hell broke loose."

"Sorry to hear that – the place is clear, so most likely your girlfriend is away, at home hopefully, safe and warm," Daniel lied, hoping to make the teen feel better.

"Actually no, sir – I mean, Daniel."

"How so?"

"I saw her back there, outside the convenience store, just before the commandoes moved in." Daniel's stomach churned. The gloom returned as his left hand and head throbbed violently.

"Oh Dear Lord – I hate this feeling," for another time that day, his mind sensed what he was about to hear.

"Your girlfriend," he asked testing himself, "blonde?"

"Yes."

"Big mop of hair – teen – blue eyes?"

"Yes, sir."

"Trisha?"

"Yes, sir," the boys barely whispered in shock, "you do know her, do you – is she ok?"

"Don't worry, she'll be fine," Daniel lied. The teen fell forward and hugged Daniel.

"Do you know where she is?"

Daniel stared silently at the teen in the dark, stinky space. He had no idea where the evil one has whisked the girls off to.

"Is there something else you should be telling me?" – He heard the words escape his mouth, just like his last words to Fr. Brian.

"She's pregnant, sir," the boy blurted, and buried his face in his hands. In that instant, Daniel knew who the three souls were whom the evil one had referred to.

"Let's get out of here, quickly," Daniel said quietly, "our meeting was no chance, the Lord surely has a plan for you and me – you might be just the one we need."

"Here, put this on," Daniel said, pulling out his toque on an impulse, and giving it to the big, shivering teen – trying to reach out to him in some way.

"You didn't tell me your name."

"You don't remember, sir?"

"Heck no – I was never good with names."

"Ezekiel."

"Prophetic – let's go – quietly," Daniel whispered.

They crouched and hopped their way in between the scattered cars, towards Eglinton. A shrill whistle pierced their ears as they hopped past the last car. A cop was directing the emergency vehicles.

"Now," Daniel called and quickly stood up. Ezekiel followed. Strangely, he saw a TTC bus make its way west. It was a good sign. Maybe the cops were getting the situation under control. They jumped in, just as the surprised driver closed the door – before a swarm of reporters realized someone from the scene was getting away.

"Some bloody action that was," the driver quipped, hoping to get some fresh news from them.

"Ah well, we missed it," Daniel lied, trying to throw off the driver.

"Heard some super awesome commandoes showed up," he whistled through his teeth, "see them?"

"Not really – got caught up in church – praying – missed all the action," Daniel muttered, dropping in a handful of coins, "say, isn't it a bit too early for a TTC bus to be out on this route?"

"Not really, was stuck here, praying for my life. You lucky you got in – I can betcha' there won't be any service on this route for many hours to come." Just then, the

MRAP shot out of the convenience store parking lot like a massive tank. It was headed north, on Locksley.

"Whoa! Look at that thing, man, like a bloody battle tank," the bus driver shouted, half rising out of his seat. By the time he got over his shock, Daniel and Ezekiel were settled into the seat by the back door.

"Ok, let's hop off at Dufferin," Daniel whispered, "there's still three more lives to save."

Ezekiel stared.

"Don't worry; we'll get Trisha back, safe and sound." Daniel smiled, patting Ezekiel's back and standing up to pull the stop cord.

"Let's go – it's Dufferin. Dufferin and Eglinton – mundane, little intersection – but here is where it all began."

A numb silence filled his heart. The stranger's screams had first echoed from the wall that lay adjacent to where he had just alighted from the bus. He walked over and felt the top of the wall with his hand – reverently – as if touching the pedestal, where a saint had stood. It was sticky. Surprised, Daniel turned his palm over – it was red.

"Blood," Ezekiel observed.

"Sacred blood," Daniel added, feeling the stillness all around, despite the noise. He closed his eyes, and placed his thorn hand on the spot where the Thornbearer had stood and preached, all those years.

"Did you ever see the man who stood here all these years and preached?" Daniel asked Ezekiel.

"I did – preached about the end of the world, and the great misery to come on all mankind. I once heard him say that Satan was here, in our midst," Ezekiel answered laughing.

Daniel shook his head sadly.

"It's actually days like today that he prophesized about. Did you happen to see a dark, hooded man?"

"Actually, spoke to me, at Timmys – the one who put those evil thoughts in my head."

"About the pregnancy – the baby…."

"How can you know?" Ezekiel asked shocked.

"Because he is an incarnation of Satan," Daniel whispered quietly. Ezekiel shivered, as if someone had poured a bucket of ice down his shirt.

"You're kidding."

"Let's get to the Tim Hortons and talk – we need a plan. Our meeting was no chance; the Lord will guide us."

Daniel pulled out his handkerchief and mopped up the blood reverently. He touched the spot one last time, hoping for a connection of some sort with his predecessor. If he expected to make a connection with the Thornbearer, he was disappointed. He looked around as people were cautiously creeping out again. Police cruisers filled the square. A cop directed traffic as tow trucks scrambled in to grab whatever business they could, out of the mess. The signal was down. Daniel saw a bright red, mangled car. It lay over the center north-south signal that it had snapped in two. Yellow tape had sprung up all around it.

"Ok, hurry, hurry," the officer shouted, waving to Daniel and Ezekiel, as he sought to wave a northbound tow truck through.

"It's ok, we're going south, thank you, officer," Daniel shouted, pointing to the Tim Hortons.

They were crossing Eglinton as the tall figure of Fr. Brian hopped over the island, and on to Eglinton, from Dufferin, as the first of the southbound cars drove past slowly, trying to catch some of the action.

"Rubber-neckers – gawkers," Fr Brian called, as a big smile lit his face. "Great indeed are your works, O Lord," he sang, looking at Daniel, his hands raised to the skies, "she is alive and well – my mamma." Daniel smiled in relief. "When Maria said – "She didn't!" – she meant to say mamma didn't want to trouble me." He stopped and finally relaxed. "We have a lot of work to do, Daniel – sorry, I've been so caught in my own world."

"You're a son too, Father Brian – but it's a good start. Your Mum is safe, and so is this soul," Daniel said pointing to Ezekiel.

"And this is?"

"Ezekiel, Trisha's boyfriend," Daniel continued quickly, before Fr. Brian could say anything. "But, first some hot chocolate for me, some coffee for you gentlemen, and then, a plan to fight the devil," Daniel said, hardly believing the words that had sprung from his mouth.

"My treat," Fr. Brian chirped in happily.

The thought of Michelle, away in India, suddenly sprang into Daniel's mind. He wished he could run home and be with her – away from the chaos. The evil stranger, the beautiful Amanda, Trisha, Dylan and the Lord's thorn all flashed across his mind. He looked at his left hand, now swollen, and hard like a rock. There was no going back. Fr. Brian and Ezekiel had already gone ahead. Ezekiel was holding the door of the Tim Hortons for him.

"You go on ahead, Ezekiel, I'll join you soon – make mine a large, dark, double hot chocolate with extra sugar."

"Got it!"

Daniel stood by the spot where the Thornbearer had been thrown – tossed over like a puppet, by the rampaging truck. Large pools of blood stained the ground – now surrounded by orange markers. Yet, he had gotten up and carried on. Daniel knelt down, quietly praying and hoping for a sign from the man. He closed his eyes and thought of the moment the Lord's thorn had passed itself onto him, from the head of the stranger.

"I am ready, my Lord. Guide me. Help me," he prayed. He was about to open his eyes and walk in, when a chorus of voices from a distant vision, seemed to echo in his head. His head swirled as a divine joy flowed through his body. He was in a line again – a hallowed one. He could not see the others but felt their company, from a time long past, from Calvary. He knew not what they said, but knew he was not alone.

"Are you coming, or what?" Fr. Brian's voice called from the open door.

"Right away," Daniel answered and began to get up. He remembered not to reach down with his left hand this time. Instead, his right hand landed on to a tall Tim Hortons cup turned upside down – there were two in fact – one inside the other. Daniel gently rested the rim on the ground, and propped himself up, using the base. He ended up lifting the cups as he stood up. The aroma of the hot chocolate from the cup was still fresh. Dark black lipstick marks smeared the edges. His body instantly lit up as his soul rebelled at the carnal desires that excited his being. The minutest of doubts about who had used that cup, vanished instantly.

"I hope you're ok," he said reaching out to the beautiful woman who had invaded his life, "Amanda." It felt strange taking that name. With the wild passion, came a deep guilt – Michelle and the Lord's thorn in his hand – it was so wrong. Daniel knew it was a cross he would be carrying.

"Lead us not into temptation," he prayed again heading into the coffee shop. Unknowingly, he still carried the double cup with the dark lipstick marks, and a lustful yearning for the lips they came from.

XVIII

Yokatherine

The coffee meeting never happened. Daniel barely made it in, when his phone went off. Like an alarm, it shattered the fragile peace, and the deceptive calm of the Tim Hortons. After the chaotic events of the morning, everyone seemed on edge – staring at Daniel, as if he had set off a fire alarm.

"Sorry," Daniel grinned sheepishly, hurriedly trying to slide the talk button. Instead, the number on the phone made him look for the person who was supposedly calling.

"Hey, it's Father Brian calling," he teased.

Fr. Brian stared cynically at the first lighthearted words of the morning.

"Definitely not," he blushed, "my phone is dead."

"A dead phone eh! The caller id says a certain Father Brian – 4167 --,"

"I know, I know, my friend – but dead phones don't make calls."

"I know, that's why I've written to the Cardinal to include a little course on technology, for seminarians."

"And what would they teach, my friend," Fr. Brian asked – hands on his hips.

"For starters, how to charge one's cell phone; how to keep it charged, and ready," Daniel quipped laughing, "seriously it's the parish office – I sense it's for you."

It indeed was. Jojo yelled, even before Fr. Brian could finish his hello.

"Father Brian, the whole world is looking for you. It's getting close to the start of the Italian service."

"I'll be there soon."

"You get here now, Father. We have to rehearse for the afternoon reading of the passion before that – the readers are here and --,"

Someone grabbed the phone from her.

"Padre, it's me, Francesco. The padre from St. Clare parish says The-Way-of-the-Cross this evening might be canceled."

"Oh my Crucified Lord – no way – this year I expect 10,000 people and more."

"Really, Padre? After what happened this morning?"

"It's not over, Francesco – you tell the good priest at St. Clare I'll talk to him as soon as I get back."

"Actually, he is more devastated than you are, Padre. Apparently, it's the police commissioner that wants no more crowds, processions or trouble."

"They dare not," Fr. Brian fumed losing his cool, "it's our 5th year on the trot and --,"

"Then you'd better get here soon, Father, the mayor and the police commissioner will be here soon."

"Oh my Dear Crucified Lord, help us," Fr. Brian prayed as he dashed from the Tim Hortons, "sorry, fellas, I still owe you that coffee."

A general murmur in the line at the holdup, made Daniel step away. Tired and thirsty as he was, both the coffee and the hot chocolate had lost their allure. Ezekiel had wandered over to one of the inner benches looking around purposefully.

"Anything the matter there, kiddo?" Daniel asked curiously, suddenly liking the way he had addressed the big kid. His intuition was peaking by the minute. He was sure there was a sense of purpose to the search. Ezekiel did not answer.

"I'm sure you're looking for something there, Ezekiel."

"I am. Trisha and I sat here this morning. We saw you in the line too. I spoke about you to her…." His mind wandered at the mention of her name and he sat down. "I love her to death – don't know what we're gonna do?"

"Ok, leave that worry for another time – we're all here with you, but keep going – you were headed on to something."

"Yup – the dark hooded man. He came over here – sat opposite me, exactly where you are – seemed to know my troubles. Gave me a card – a clinic, for an abortion. That's what I was looking for."

"You're not serious about that decision, are you?"

"Not at all. It would mean losing Trisha forever. Thank goodness. I was just curious. I sat like a wimp for a while after she left. You know she came looking for you – thought you could fix all our troubles."

"No kidding!"

"I followed a little later, but dropped that card," Ezekiel paused as he caught sight of the card, at the back of the bench and swung all the way under the table to fetch it. "Come to think of it, the evil man wasn't the only one who came over."

Daniel's senses were beginning to tingle again. A throbbing sensation and a sense of worry was building in. He felt the tension return – the morning experience at the Tim Hortons was about to play, all over again.

"The old man from the church, no, actually it was the white haired lady that came over first."

"The white haired --," Daniel gasped.

"Oh my God – now it makes sense, Daniel. She sensed we needed help. Spoke of a nanny, but something more. Gave us her number too." Ezekiel was lost in his story and looked up a little late. Daniel was already running towards the door, ashen faced.

"Come on, Kiddo! I am such a fool. Oh Lord, forgive me – she saved me – literally gave her life to help me get away, and here I am debating a hot chocolate," Daniel blurted.

He shoved people aside, dashed through the door and turned east, with Ezekiel on his heels. The situation was easing up but a tense calm prevailed. Everything remained cordoned off with the yellow police tape. Tense cops patrolled, and the running duo immediately got stopped.

"Sorry, officer," Daniel apologized, as an officer stepped in their way – hand on his gun. "Just rushing to church, sir – we're late for the Good Friday service."

"Ok, church goers only. All other thoroughfare is closed. And go easy, fellas, everyone is on edge. The last thing you want is to push someone over the edge, and get shot. And stick to the path between the tapes."

"Understood," Daniel answered with a vigorous nod, and carried on with a brisk walk. To his shock, he saw trails of blood everywhere, marked by the police evidence markers. The spots where the officer and Shamar had been shot, were sealed off. A cop made them detour onto the road, while another clicked pictures from all angles. A list of who could have bled, began to form in Daniel's mind. The Thornbearer, Shamar, the cop – he stopped. It was too much to bear even though he had just reached three.

"This is where the pretty officer died," he whispered to Ezekiel, "as did Shamar. Precious lives lost!" He had unknowingly stopped in shock while remembering the fallen ones.

"We were looking for the white haired lady!" Ezekiel reminded.

"Right," Daniel mumbled and carried on. Yellow tape and an orange marker barricaded the spot where the

Thornbearer had died near the church. There were more pools of blood, from the Thornbearer, he guessed. There was no sign of the lady.

"She fell right here, trying to save me."

"If she was injured, perhaps the paramedics --,"

"No, she is here, somewhere…" Daniel suddenly swung around, feeling her presence nearby. They crossed over to the church steps, running to the top. Daniel felt his soul leading him on. There was no place large enough to conceal a human. He closed his eyes and whispered.

"Are you here, brave sister?" He sensed her close by, badly injured, but alive. A little wooden ramp for the wheel chairs, ran down along the church wall on the west side. It was a little hidden cove, in a deep, right-angled bend. He walked down slowly. There was a little gap between the ramp and the church wall at the sharp 90-degree turn. Winter had reduced the bushes in the gap down to wooden stumps, yet they were dense enough to hide a person – especially one, who was perfectly camouflaged in white. In a flash, Daniel leaped over the wooden rail.

"What are you doing here, sister? You could freeze to death," he screamed, pulling away the branches. The frigid body of the woman fell into his arms. The hooded man had meant for her to die there.

"Call 911," he screamed frantically to Ezekiel. A faint murmur from the lady reached his ear, "Don't."

She was as light as a feather. Daniel barely felt her weight as he hoisted her alone, relieved to find a sign of life.

"How did you reach there – did the hooded man do this?" Daniel peppered her with questions, as Ezekiel held open the church door. Instinctively, her hand shot out to the holy water. Daniel paused. Her fingers barely got into the little steel bowl in the carved wooden holder. They were about to move again, when her arm shot out again – her body lurched out, and both her hands reached into the water.

"In the Lord is my hope – in the Lord is my strength," her lips prayed over and over again. She began to douse herself with the holy water. Daniel felt her get heavier. Her strength was returning by the minute as the color returned to her face. She felt heavy, and Daniel nearly dropped her.

"God bless those strong arms, child, especially ones that bear the simplest, yet one of the holiest of all objects on this earth."

"The strength comes from your faith, sister," Daniel corrected.

"I felt the power of the Lord's thorn, Daniel – it is truly in the abode of one God has chosen to be his soldier."

"I don't understand or feel worthy of it, sister – even more so now. With each passing minute, I wonder what a sinful man like me is doing, bearing something that which pierced the flesh of the Lord?"

"Remember Jeremiah chapter 29 verse 11," she answered, "for I know the plans I have for you, says the Lord, plans for welfare and not for evil, to give you a future and a hope."

"I fell at the very first test, sister," Daniel said, laying her down on the last pew, in the corner of the west wing, hidden from the sight of the main door.

"The evil one seeks my life, and yours. I would rather sacrifice mine here, in the house of the Lord."

"No one else is going to die today," Daniel answered her firmly, "there have been enough deaths, but for now I need your help – to save the living."

As quickly as he could, Daniel filled her, and Ezekiel in on the developments of the morning, including the abduction of Trisha and Amanda. Ezekiel began to sob.

"Your girlfriend," she turned to a trembling Ezekiel, "she is pregnant, isn't she?" He nodded vigorously in fear before she continued. "A fetus, a little conceived child of God – there is nothing more valuable to Satan – a perfect sacrifice for his evil kingdom."

"We must hurry then," Daniel exclaimed, himself conscious of the web that seemed to have spun up in his life as well. He sensed the lady knew. Pangs of guilt tore of his heart.

"I don't know your name, sister," he tried to change the subject.

"Yokatherine – rare one, as for you," she looked at Daniel with a bowed head, "may the Lord be your strength – there will be many challenges along the way. I believe you are already on your way to discerning, and conquering the first one."

"Where do we even begin?" Daniel looked blankly, "it's a massive city."

"The Lord will guide us, but I must warn you, this conquest is not for the faint-hearted, or the ones that may be a fertile ground for the evil one," she said looking directly into Ezekiel's eyes.

"Then I will offer up my life in penance for my sin, and to save Trisha's life and my unborn child."

"Then may the Lord guide us – let's roll," she said and began to get up. They barely made it to the end of the pew, when one of the ushers passing by recognized Daniel.

"Hey bro, the press conference is about to begin downstairs. I am sure Father Brian could use your help."

"Sure, Joe," Daniel lied, unsure how he could help.

"You go on to the hall," Yokatherine told him, "we will head back to the sacristy and wait there for you."

Daniel waited until Ezekiel was out of earshot. Either Yokatherine didn't move because of her weakened state, or she seemed to know the wild conflict in Daniel's soul.

"I failed once, sister – consumed by carnal desires. I don't know what attracted me to the lady in black. I don't know what will happen to me the second time I face her, but I will not fail again."

"Like I said earlier, Daniel – you are already on your way to discerning, and conquering the first one – have faith."

"Is she evil?"

"Not until she decides to be. The evil one will work hard to use her against you. It's what you carry, is what he is after."

"If he is so powerful, he could so easily have attacked me right there."

"Not so simple, Daniel. Remember the Lord's thorn is not any piece of wood that he can pick up, and walk away. There is a reason he wants us in that place. I sense grave evil and danger await us."

"I fear not the power of evil, sister. The Lord will guide us. The Lord will go with us. The Lord will be our strength."

"Then go, Daniel, the good priest could you use your presence to boost his strength – I sense a tough test awaits him."

XIX

The Bubbly Mayor

Fr. Brian sat in a daze at the large dining table of the rectory. A wild cacophony of voices filled the room. The table for 12, held 20 chairs, drawn up from everywhere. Another 20 people stood around, babbling like defeated generals, just routed in war. They looked expectantly at Fr. Brian, the unspoken leader.

"First and foremost," he suddenly blurted out, as if waking up from another world, "we need to move to the hall, downstairs. These are private quarters, especially if the mayor is going to be followed by half of the city's reporters."

The hall was in total chaos. Fr. Brian found himself rapidly losing his cool. A few cops tried to put order, but the press had totally taken control.

"Who authorized all these cameras, microphones, and this press conference in my hall?" Fr. Brian asked, bewildered. A whole lot of shoulder shrugs, blank stares and aimless finger pointing, was all that he got.

"Can this day get any worse?" he wondered looking at the stage. There were three chairs set out. Over the years', hundreds of parishioners from the flock, had used it for various religious and non-religious activities. "A Press Conference – this is a first!" he muttered, throwing up his hands.

"Oh! I can understand that, father," the bubbly mayor smiled with a wink, "I've seen worse, in unimaginable places," he said with a false, snorting laugh. "Even in

flooded streets. You cannot stop these guys. Take a hint,"
he continued, squeezing Fr. Brian's shoulder, "play along,
and don't react. Let them feel like you're giving them all
they need, without giving away anything – get it?" he winked
again, guiding Fr. Brian to the chair on the stage. His large
frame shook as he laughed, amused at his wisdom, and the
cheap shot at the reporters, clicking away, as if the mayor
and the priest were aliens that had just landed from another
planet.

"You don't worry – I'll take care of them," the
mayor added, still flushed from his previous laugh. To his
own surprise, Fr. Brian felt at ease.

"Sorry, did I miss something?" the husky voice of
the stern commissioner barreled at them from the other end
of the table. He sat to the left of the mayor.

"Not really, commissioner," the mayor jumped in,
"you're the man with the real news, so go for it."

"As long as you don't keep interrupting, like last
week's Jane-Finch shooting update," the commissioner shot
back without the slightest hint of diplomacy. Fr. Brian
guessed there was some past history between the two.

"And please remember, in less than an hour, I have
a prayer service to conduct, so keep it short," Fr. Brian
warned.

"Oh, and there will be no procession, or whatever
you planned for the evening, Reverend!" the commissioner
shot his words at Fr. Brian, bending over behind the mayor
to make sure he made eye contact with the priest.

The two angry fists from the priest's hands that
landed on the table, rattled everything, and everyone around.
Someone had put some bottles of water on the narrow table
– they went bouncing off the table. The press took a step
forward, licking their lips – finally, there was some action.
Fr. Brian felt like fleeing from the stage. Sadly, he realized it

was his first public appearance, and he was off to a bad start.

"Careful, father, we could be live on TV already — CP24, Global and a ton of other channels," the mayor whispered. Before the commissioner could react, he swung to the flashing cameras. "Ladies and Gentlemen!" — a wink to the sweating Fr. Brian, and a whisper — "Smile!"

"Thank you, folks, for being here." Fr. Brian sensed the mayor was enjoying the spotlight. "This morning, we had an unfortunate series of events — but before we get to that, I do want to take a minute to thank the Reverend Father Brian, pastor or rather the parish priest of this wonderful parish of St. Thomas Aquinas, for hosting us at such short notice. Many of you may recall that this parish is over a 100 years old. When I was first elected, trustee, and then councilor and then --,"

"Ahem," the commissioner grunted without trying to be discreet, "can we --,"

"Sure, commissioner. Well, folks — those surely are stories for another day that I would love to tell you about this great city of ours. However, for today, as I was saying, these unfortunate series of occurrences culminated in some very tragic events."

"What can you tell us about them, Mr. Mayor," one of the front row reporters interrupted before the mayor could go off on another tangent.

"Just coming to that, Mike. Well, we believe that earlier this morning, a mad man caused a massive pile up — about 30 cars at Dufferin and Eglinton, right, commissioner?" he turned to the commissioner, but carried on before the words from the commissioner's open mouth could come forth. "As I was telling you, the pile up at the busy intersection of Dufferin and Eglinton seemed to have had a chain reaction. We believe that frayed tempers, and some rowdy citizen behavior, really cascaded into a series of shootings."

"But, Mr. Mayor, apparently there is word out there that it was a terrorist orchestrated plot which --,"

"Now, folks, let's not get ahead of ourselves --,"

"Mr. Mayor, would you let the commissioner confirm, that the heavily armed unit that came out to control the situation, was indeed a specially trained force for responding to terrorist attacks?" a brown reporter screeched defiantly. Fr. Brian noticed her make-up and flawless appearance. He wondered if she had a makeup crew that accompanied her.

"Now, Tara," the mayor tried, realizing he was slowly losing control of the situation.

"Well, let me explain a few things here," the commissioner jumped in seeing an opening, "it definitely was not any sort of terrorist activity. We do believe that it was some sort of mischief, caused by a small gang that just happened to be around and took advantage of the --,"

"But, commissioner, gangs don't simply shoot cops, or burn cars with innocents inside, or shoot crowds. This was no inter-gang warfare either, if that's what you are trying to say," said a reporter whose mic said AM some number that Fr. Brian could not catch because of the constantly moving mic.

"Well, folks, if I may," Fr. Brian found the words coming out of his mouth. The first words from the quiet, dauntingly, impressive priest had a stunning effect on the wild horde. Silence fell – the mayor turned bright red again, and a nervous itch broke out on the commissioner's chin. He had heard enough of first-hand reports from the field to know that something weird was at play. He knew the priest had seen it firsthand. The mayor tried to chaperone the priest turning over and trying to put his arm around the priest, but it was too late. Fr. Brian stood up hastily.

"My brothers and sisters. I would like my church evacuated in the next 10 minutes as it is one of the most sacred days of the Christian calendar. I have a long series of services to follow in various languages. I was there this morning, so I'll tell you what I saw. After I recount what I went through, I would respectfully ask you to leave."

"Did you see it all, reverend?" a young reporter interrupted right away. Something told Fr. Brian, she was most likely to be the first one in line, protesting for women to have unhindered access to abortion.

"Focus, Brian," he told himself, as he saw Daniel slip into the hall at the back. A quick, discreet wave. Emboldened, he carried on. "This morning, evil struck." The silence was absolute. "The supposed madman that died in the accident, was a holy man, a prophet or a street preacher, if you please. The evil which struck through various mediums of Satan this morning, as you saw from the hypnotized and terrified folks, the senseless shootings of a young man, a police officer and others, the darkened skies that --,"

"Now let me address that, since it was one of my force," the commissioner tried, but made no headway, as he was firmly ignored. Fr. Brian saw the mayor bury his large face in his hands.

"In this modern age, you may find it hard to believe, or report what I tell you, but talk to some of those that lived through it today. The darkened skies, the zombie-like hypnotized crowd that nearly burnt an innocent woman alive in her car, and the wild shooting, were attempts by the prince of darkness to shatter the day the Lord conquered sin. I do believe the gunman that fled, and another queer hooded character who seemed to orchestrate the events today, have since vanished. But, take it from a priest who came face-to-face with both these characters, and challenged them, these were pure evil characters. I apologize that I could not prevent any of those lives from being lost.

Over the next few hours, or days, as you dig through, and unearth, what occurred here today, or talk to witnesses, you will realize that it was meant to disrupt this holy day. Well, it failed. We will continue to pray and worship. We will pray in a very, special way for the lives that were lost today. I have nothing more to add ladies and gentlemen."

The silence shattered like an overheated crystal ball bursting into a million fragments. Questions flew at the priest. The mayor threw his head back, shaking it all the way from east to west. The commissioner looked furious and was ready to march off, when a single, innocuous question that flew through the din, caught everyone's attention. It was directed at Fr. Brian.

"Reverend, the hooded man who you say orchestrated this near doomsday scenario, was it Satan himself?"

Fr. Brian picked up the bottle of water that someone had put back. His dry throat ached. He was thirsty after the long morning. "Fasting day, Brian," his conscience reminded. He put down the unopened bottle, feeling stronger for it. "Lord, accept my little sacrifice," he prayed and looked up.

"When Satan decides that he has to personally orchestrate these events in our city, and our parish – it only means that we have to pray harder. Please, come and join us for The-Way-of-the-Cross, from St. Clare parish to here, this evening, at 7 pm. Thank you. Now, may I please request all of you to leave, so that we can get back to our Good Friday services."

"There will be no such public gatherings this evening," the commissioner's husky voiced boomed. "Since the good priest is not aware of the latest developments, let

me update you – the second alleged gunman was not found.
The getaway car, a taxi, was found abandoned. The few
eyewitnesses that we spoke to, mentioned a strange man
being picked up by a cab full of people. We have no more
news. Apparently, the gang that struck had a personal
vendetta. They could strike again. And so, until we have
fully reviewed the law and order situation, my order stands."

"What about the getaway taxi, commissioner? Did
any taxi company identify it as theirs?"

"We traced the taxi – privately run. The only person
who could have identified the occupants – the taxi driver, of
course, was found dead – shot – south of here, on Bathurst.
Hence, I will review afresh all plans and advise further."
With that, the commissioner put his hat on and marched
off. Fr. Brian stared after him. A sinking feeling told him
that he had messed up. "Guess I blew any little chance of
that procession happening," he muttered.

"You certainly did. Lesson number 2, Father Brian,"
the mayor whispered in the priest's ear covering his mouth
with his hand. His laughter was gone and Fr. Brian barely
caught the words, as the reporters crammed in close with
barely a few inches left. "Let's work together, and we'll
make it happen."

"Now folks, no need to be jumping to conclusions,"
the mayor took over. "Apparently, the priest and the
commissioner are at opposite ends; both right, for very
noble reasons. One well, religious and the other, just law
and order, but I do believe in this great riding, I mean this
constituency – sorry – I meant this great neighborhood, and
city, that we Torontonians can rise above such attacks."
Daniel edged in closer.

The mayor was cashing in, and doing a great job at
it. "So what do you say folks, can Torontonians be cowed
down by such senseless attacks?"

A murmur of voices echoed. People had streamed in from the streets around at the sight of the dish antennas and the camera crews. The mayor had his chance.

"So what do all you great folks think – how about, we all show up this evening – and support this great priest here, and the other parish, and show the world that Toronto is a strong city. We are brave, we cannot be defeated, and, we know how to rebound."

"Yes," the voices echoed, surprising the mayor as well.

"And, folks, let me personally assure you, and the reverend here as well, that as long as I am the mayor of this great city, we will protect the folks that practice as per the religious freedom in our great country. As your mayor, I will make it happen."

A loud cheer echoed from the nervous parishioners that had by now crammed the hall. Fr. Brian caught sight of the commissioner at the end of the hall, frozen in his tracks – he had just been overruled.

"Now, I would ask all the folks that are not joining the services here, to please accompany me outside – I will be happy to answer any further questions," the mayor continued.

Fr. Brian sat silent, head bent and marveled at the ways of the world. Someone whispered something in Italian about getting away to the sacristy and he followed in a daze. At least The-Way-of-the-Cross was back on. He felt good.

His exultation did not last long as he stood in a daze in the sacristy. He felt a deep presence – as if being watched. It was Daniel, sitting quietly in a corner on one of the benches. The altar servers, boys, and girls, were rushing around putting on their red vestments. Someone put on Fr. Brian's robes for him. He hardly had any idea whether he spoke Italian, or English, or Spanish. Everything was in place. He recalled the extra police presence all around the neighborhood.

"Hey, Dylan is missing today – is someone stepping in for him?" someone asked.

"No worries," Angela, the Altar Servers Club coordinator chimed in, "I've arranged for another kid to serve Mass in his place."

Fr. Brian sat down as the full weight of that name struck him. At the very least, he had to reach out to the boy's mother, or go talk to the commissioner.

"Oh, Dear Lord," he prayed, "I was never prepared for this."

"It's ok, Father Brian," a quiet voice comforted him. He was grateful for that voice. "Thank you, Daniel," he muttered, without lifting his head, "and to think that I upset the commissioner further, when I had such a beautiful chance to win him over, one on one, and put in a word for our young friend."

"You go and do the service, Father. I'll take care of things here. Dylan's mother is on her way, as is Juanito. With his legal skills, we'll take care of Dylan."

"Would you be my assistant parish priest?"

"Sure – as long as I don't have to be celibate," Daniel joked back. Fr. Brian suddenly stared at Daniel's face.

"Whatever happened to you, my friend? You glow, as if the Lord himself touched you."

"He did. That is another tale for the end of the day. For now --,"

"Is it something to do with what the hooded man muttered, just as he fled?"

"Yes, Father Brian."

"Oh, Dear Lord – didn't he say something about a thorn – what could he want. Is it something – please let me come and help you."

"Father Brian," the squeeze on his forearm was firm, "you go and finish the services – that's where you are needed. More importantly, we need you praying – there at the altar – that is where our strength will come from. We will go to the battle that lies ahead for us."

Fr. Brian stared at Daniel. Deep within he knew the words were serious not simply dramatized. After a long pause, he asked. "What battle do you speak of, and, who is us?"

The two men looked at each other silently. After a long pause, Daniel spoke. "Come with me, Father," he said turning and walking back into the rectory.

"Be back in a minute, dears," Fr. Brian said shakily, and followed. The rectory was silent and dark. Daniel flipped a switch. The large chandelier over the dining table lit up. A frail, pale, ghostly face stared at the priest. The lady in white looked as if she had aged a 100 years since that morning. To her left, sat a tall teen, shivering uncontrollably every few minutes.

"We've heard from the hooded man, Fr. Brian," Daniel said holding up his BlackBerry. The garbled message with the same strange font Fr. Brian had seen early that morning, stared back at him.

"Come alone – no one must know – wait for directions – bring me the thorn, or the women die." Fr. Brian nearly collapsed. Daniel did not move to help or support him.

Instead, he spoke firmly. "You must be strong from now on, Father Brian. This is what he wants," Daniel said, painfully opening out his palm. Fr. Brian's feet wobbled, yet again. Again, Daniel watched hardly bothering to help.

"This, is a real thorn, from the actual crown of thorns, that pierced our Lord's head. The preaching man, an angel, passed it on to me – as it has been done down the ages, by the Thornbearers."

"But that is impossible, Daniel!"

Daniel paused and looked at the priest's face. "The Lord is with us, Father Brian – literally. This is what pierced the head of the Lord," Daniel said with a remarkable confidence that made the priest stand up firm.

"You go pray for us, Father Brian – we 3 soldiers will go to battle."

"A battle! Then go with the words from Samuel," Fr. Brian prayed:

'For who is God but Yahweh, who is a rock but our God:

this God who girds me with strength, who makes my way free from blame,

who makes me as swift as a deer and sets me firmly on the heights,

who trains my hands for a battle my arms to bend a bow of bronze.

You give me your invincible shield, you never cease to listen to me,

you give me the strides of a giant, give me ankles that never weaken –

I pursue my enemies and exterminate them, not turning back till they are annihilated;

I strike them down, and they cannot rise, they fall, they are under my feet.

You have girded me with strength for the fight, bent down my assailants beneath me,

made my enemies retreat before me; and those who hate me I destroy."

– 2 Samuel 22: 32 - 41

The
6th – 9th hours, Hell's Battle

XX

666 Lanark Avenue

The rectory was silent again. Faint sounds of the
Italian service that had begun in the church, filtered
through. Daniel pictured the old choir singing away
furiously as they always did. The muted, melodic sounds
that flowed through made it sound like a monastery.

Daniel and Yokatherine looked at each other –
clueless. Each knew the other's thoughts. Where were they
to begin? The answer came soon enough. For the second
time in that hour, the shrill ring of the BlackBerry rattled
everyone. Yokatherine stared blankly with big, wide open
eyes. Ezekiel nearly fell out of his chair.

"What's with that thing – it seems to – like, never
mind," he mumbled.

Daniel's hand trembled as a strange fear engulfed
him. It was as if death was calling. Once he had the details
of the place they were to go to, there would be no turning
back. He let the phone ring through. He waited for a few
more seconds for the beep to indicate a voice mail had been
left. Instead, the phone rang again, promptly. Daniel
answered this time. The voice at the end of the line was
angry.

"I don't like to be stood up, or have my calls
ignored." Daniel's heart missed a beat at the deep, angry
baritone voice. He listened quietly, steeling himself to make
sure his fears and uncertainty did not show.

"I suppose you are ready to come to my castle," the
eerie voice continued. Daniel imagined an echo as if the

voice was coming from a distant realm. His mind pictured a
big gaping hole, deep in the belly of the earth, where the
fires burned, and where demons, and souls of the damned,
burned in hideous, animal form – blackened and bronzed.

"Darn," he muttered, picturing Sr. Celine, his grade
1 religion teacher, talking about the vision of Fatima that
The Virgin Mary showed Sr. Lucy. A nervous fidgeting from
Ezekiel's chair made him look up. The hooded man did not
know about Ezekiel nor Yokatherine – he hoped they would
turn out to be his secret weapons, more like his trump cards.

"Are you ready?" the voice asked.

"For what?" Daniel asked defiantly, as a dark,
gloomy veil descended on him.

"That depends if you want to die, my friend," the
cloak of darkness was getting darker. The man laughed – the
words meant exactly what they indicated – it was eerie. "All
I need is that rotten thorn."

Daniel's heart lit up at the mention of the thorn.
The energy was back, and the feeling of power returned.
Like the pillar of cloud, that never left its place ahead of the
Israelites during the day, and the pillar of fire by night, he
knew the Lord would go with them.

Suddenly emboldened, he added, "The one you've
been trying to get for the last 2000 and some years?" he
asked defiantly. The angry grunt that echoed for the briefest
of seconds, was just the reaction he was looking for. It
echoed through the phone making Yokatherine look up
sharply.

"And what about the girls?" Daniel asked defiantly,
his confidence returning. The thought of the kidnapped
women flashed across his mind. He looked at his mangled,
disfigured and discolored left hand.

"Beautiful," he sighed in his mind.

"Beautiful! You fool, it's the ugliest sight of all," the
voice at the end of the line barked. Daniel stared at the

phone, somehow his thoughts had carried through – he would have to be careful.

"Once again, are the girls ok and," Daniel needed to keep asking the questions, "where is it that you wish for us to come and destroy you?"

The man at the end of the line burst out laughing. "I could quote enough of your own scripture to you – need I say, there have been many before you. I've destroyed them all. Today will be special – two Thornbearers' in one day."

"If that's the Lord's will, just like the others, so be it. Nevertheless, don't worry, he will send along another. And, yes, today will be different – it will mark your end."

"Enough of this, you fool!" the man burst out, "I will call, be ready to drive – till then, prepare for death." The line went dead. Daniel looked at Yokatherine puzzled.

"I thought he would want us there, ASAP! After all, isn't this the one day he gets to grab it from us."

"You are learning and perceiving quickly, Daniel, but remember, the darkness is his ally. The shorter, winter days means longer evenings. It gives him more time to take us on – in his own realm. Are you sure, you are up to the task? He will be ruthless, and your faith will have to be solid as a rock."

"It is – it will be. When I see him, all I will see is the one who seeks to destroy the Kingdom of God."

"My mind tells me – it is the daughter you will see, sensuous and highly attractive. The ultimate woman a man could desire – ready to fall at your feet, and serve you in any way you desire. What man could pass that by?"

"I will not fail today. As the psalm says: The steps of a good man are ordered by the Lord... Though he falls, he shall not be utterly cast down."

"And what about this shivering friend of ours?" she said with a sympathetic smile, looking at Ezekiel. A flash of anger burst across Ezekiel's face. "I have nothing to lose, and, everything to gain, and, I have a feeling you need me. Seriously, I am beginning to get a sense of what is happening. Sounds weird – but after today, and after actually having spoken to the man, I know what you say is true."

They slipped out of the side door to the parking lot on the west side of the church, as quietly as they could. Daniel hoped no one would see them. One last time, he turned back in the direction of the altar, and bowed, as Yokatherine quietly whispered, "As it is written in the book of Deuteronomy: Hear, O Israel, you are approaching the battle against your enemies today. Do not be fainthearted. Do not be afraid, or panic, or tremble before them."

"Let's make haste and find him," Daniel swore. If he wanted secrecy – there was to be none of it. A long line of cars, their engines running, waited on the narrow drive for the few parking spots. Daniel saw angry faces inside. Someone would have to move back, for them to be able to back out. One car moved – honked for the one behind it to move. It didn't – instead, it set off a wild flurry of angry horns.

"Don't you know this parking is for the seniors – fool!" an old man screamed at Daniel.

"Then move back, you idiot," the lady in front of him screamed, "How the heck is he going to come out?"

"You move on, stupid woman," the voice swore, "when that fool comes out, I'm moving in." The argument was drowned out by another blaring of horns from the back of the impatient line.

Daniel looked intently at Yokatherine and smiled. She shrugged her shoulders with a nod, and turned to the cars. Her walk was slow and deliberate. Daniel loved that. He sensed a deep purity and strength in her. She had survived the hooded man once – she would lead them. He saw her tap on the glass of the first car – a brief one-way conversation and she moved on to the second car, leaving a sheepish face behind.

Daniel had no idea what she said but Ezekiel put it in words. "Move back or get vaporized." Daniel turned around and laughed. "She means business," Ezekiel finished off as a matter of fact. The cars were slowly beginning to back up – in dead silence. Daniel jumped in and started his car. Ezekiel hopped into the back. It was only when Yokatherine got in with a triumphant smile, that Daniel realized it would be a challenge driving with just the right hand. The narrow drive, with the very sharp turns around the church, was the very first challenge. He began to mutter a prayer, "Oh my good angel, whom God has appointed to me my guardian, enlighten and protect, direct and govern me, who has been entrusted to you by the divine mercy. Amen." Two more pairs of hands joined in signing themselves with the Sign of the Cross. Buoyed, Daniel started off.

They pulled out onto Glenholme Avenue with no idea of where they were headed. Daniel turned right and pulled into the bus bay of the school. The red brick school building was deserted. There would be no school buses honking that day, pushing him to get out, as they picked up their bus loads of kids, no teachers with clipboards with their heads hidden deep within their parkas, and most of all no parking inspectors to worry about.

"Ok," he said blankly, turning to the other two as the cold seat, and fear, sent a shiver through his body, "where to?"

His mind worked furiously. "There has to be a clue somewhere. Let's see – the hooded man fled south. The taxi was found south, on Bathurst. Just a million odd people – a few thousands of homes, in a few hundreds of streets – we should find him easily!" he said with a mocking laugh.

Yokatherine's eyes were closed – her lips moved in prayer. Ezekiel found his voice, "We have to be quick if we want to pre-empt or surprise Satan before dark."

"Before it is too late, or, before he is ready for us," Daniel added, noticing Ezekiel in the back seat, furiously going through his pockets.

"Nice, heated leather seats and my own vent – love your car," Ezekiel commented, still fidgeting. Daniel's senses were tingling. He was beginning to like the big, fidgety kid. For all his failures, he still stood tall and strong.

"Easy, kiddo – focus on something – anything that can lead us to the man," Daniel encouraged with the least hope in his heart, "probably this search is over even before it begins."

"Not really – if you would turn on your GPS then I'm pretty sure we can head out as soon as these coordinates are mapped," the voice from the back seat spoke. It was factual. Even Yokatherine opened her eyes with a start.

"If the hooded man wants fetuses as sacrifices, as you said, then I'm pretty sure we're headed to – as he said in his words …… remember the card I had lost in Tim Hortons and found again. It's where he wanted me to bring Trisha, for an abortion."

"It's where we'll find them!" Three voices said in unison.

"What better way to find a generous supply of fetuses to sacrifice for the evil one, than to open an abortion clinic," Ezekiel declared, feeling rather proud of his contribution.

"Then it sure is the lair of our evil, hooded friend," Daniel confirmed, "great job, Ezekiel."

"Exactly," Yokatherine finished off the thought as a sudden chill descended on them, "it's where Satan himself, the evil one, will be very, very active."

Daniel could scarcely believe his ears as his hand shot forward, for the GPS, mounted on the windscreen. Yokatherine signed herself with the Sign of the Cross once more and got back to her prayers.

"Here you go," Ezekiel came back to life once more trying to be modest, as a big, victorious grin burst across his face.

"Postal Code first – please," Daniel prompted.

"M6X 6Z6," Ezekiel answered.

"That's a lot of 6s'. House number?"

"666!"

"but of course," sighed Daniel.

There was a slight pause as the GPS filled in the rest. "666 Lanark Avenue," Daniel and Ezekiel read together.

"Go," they spoke in one voice, bursting with confidence as Daniel hit the green go button that was displayed.

XXI

Revenge

Officer Terri sat in a daze. His head swirled in circles. At times, he thought he was passing out. At other times, it was a wild, throbbing headache, that threatened to explode in his head. Initially, he tried to dab his head with the palm of his hand. It did not help, the back of his head felt as if someone was smacking it hard. He jumped around to see – there was no one. It caused his cap to tip over to the right. He imagined a hand reaching across the cruiser and tipping it back in place.

"Easy there, Blondie1," the voice was saying. They had braked hard after a long chase. He barely had time to respond to that softest of rare touches as he sprinted out to nab the object of their chase. He missed it now. It was gone. He wished he had taken a minute – even a few seconds to enjoy that little gesture. He shook his head violently to shake off the gloom that was setting in, perhaps it was just a bad dream he would wake up from soon.

"Ah! Clare – what did you say – that one word," his mind ran the wildest sprint to catch it one more time. He knew it would fade. The voice, for now, was crystal clear in his head – "My Love." After all those years, it was inevitable.

There was a new ache – a numbness – he felt his bottom. He was sitting on the cold, frigid sidewalk. How he landed down there, he did not know. There was no sensation as he bent right and left to ease his aching bottom.

"There you are, bro," Jeremy, an old academy buddy was saying as he reached out his hand. Terri took it. If Terri was large, Jeremy was larger. In a single yank, he had Terri on his feet. They stood face to face – two tough cops. A moment later, Terri was in the biggest bear hug ever – and then he cried.

"Easy, bro, I know how it feels." Jeremy would know – he had seen his partner die in a midnight drug bust gone wrong. Suddenly the sympathies were everywhere. Terri was visible now.

"We'll find that sucker, partner, don't you worry."

"She was a brave one – the bravest – be proud, officer – we're with you." Every blue uniform had something to say.

"I loved her – I know you did too," Terri looked at the steely, female voice.

"Sue," he was glad for that female voice, "thank God for women," his mind said. It made sense now. Terri and Sue had nearly become an all women team. It did not happen but the two were close.

"It can't be true – I don't believe it." Sue was not watering it down. "There's no bloody way this could happen, man." Sue was angry. "I mean the brightest, and the most beautiful – shot twice." Sue's hand was reaching for her gun. "Oh – the sucker – we'll settle him right, Terri. I'll spend the rest of my life in the can if needed, but that sucker will get it nice and slow – toes, knees, elbows, shoulders and then the head – if that sucker is still breathing."

"Yes – Yes – Yes," Terri finally screamed. It made sense. A crackle of the radio and Sue ran. The pats, the shoulder squeezes and the hugs continued for a long time. It was all a blur to Terri. Then it stopped, and the aches and the throbbing were back.

"I'm sorry for your loss, officer, for our loss. We'll find them and bring them to justice," the deep husky voice said. The commissioner's voice was distinct. Terri saluted.

"Easy, officer, and well done. You were great." Terri saluted once more, barely aware of his actions. "Will see you soon. A beer this evening, maybe? Got a press conference to run to."

"Yes, sir," Terri mechanically answered the commissioner and went back to his demons. He was crossing Eglinton – back to the south side, back to where she had fallen. Back to where he had failed to stand by her. Each evidence marker stared at him like multiple counts of his failures.

"I'm so sorry, love," he blurted out and dropped to his knees. The blood – it was hers. An officer stood guard around the yellow tape and the markers.

"Your pain is our pain," the unknown cop sympathized. Terri nodded. He had to get away.

"Blondie2 here – Goodbye, my love," the words echoed in his mind, again and again. Like a wimp, he had stood by the church, dealing with the stupid demons in his head while she had marched on. Back to back – it was their strategy.

"I cover your back – you cover mine – never split." It was their strategy; it had worked brilliantly. He was supposed to have been watching her back – he had failed. The throbbing started again, the guilt and then the rage – at the end, there was always the rage. It was building. How could he have not reacted faster? There had already been two shots – he should have rushed. The Indian man – he had seen him on the ground and stopped to talk.

"Damn!" he muttered – that was the delay. There had been a strange, dark shadow – it was slowly coming back. It had been there from the first moment they had rushed onto the scene. It had toyed with him – a strange presence that he could not see. Was it something the Indian man created – some crazy, oriental, hypnotic trick? Even after the blank thuds from Clare's falling radio, something had held him back.

His mind played the scene over and over again. The man had appeared again, as he and the priest had moved her body. It was all a blur. Terri sat down again trying to sort his thoughts. There was a white haired lady and an Indian man. They spoke in strangely, fatalistic tones, damn them, it didn't sound right. The white haired lady had warned him to hurry before it was too late – they had already plotted it.

"We need to get you somewhere warm and get you debriefed," the Field Marshall was saying, "commissioner says he needs some solid facts before he starts yelling about one of his being taken down." Terri nodded. He had to escape.

He turned around one more time – maybe it was all a bad dream and she would come running from the other direction. "Nailed it, Blondie1," she would say with a mocking salute. They would burst out laughing and head back to the cruiser, for a cold coffee and a laboriously detailed report. She would take stock of more broken nails, while he pieced the facts together, too busy to pay attention – if only he had.

Instead, he saw the Indian man come running and head to the church – there was a teen with him. "Damn, there had been a teen then too, maybe a gang, one arrested, rest out still…." his mind reasoned. The arrested teen had shot his Clare. The Indian man had whispered to the teen after his arrest, just before they took him away.

A plausible theory was forming in his mind. The more Terri thought – the more it made sense. This man had orchestrated it. He was sure. Terri turned in the direction the Indian man had run. Strange, he was pulling someone out of the bushes – a strange, white lady. She had either stepped out of heaven or hell. Terri was sure of that. "What the hell," he swore as he got a clearer look at the lady, "returning from hell are we?" he swore under his breath, gasping at the change in her. They glanced around and headed into the church.

"The killers – the killers," his mind screamed, "of course, obviously," Terri said as the pieces of the jigsaw puzzle fell into place in his head. "Brilliantly done," he looked towards the church door where they had disappeared, "great place to hide."

"Just give me one quick description of her killer, Terri," Tony was saying. Terri stared him in the face. There was anger, hatred – above all revenge. "Just tell me quick, man – I'll get the sucker – I'll take the blows even if they throw me in the slammer for the next 100 years."

"Thank you, brother," Terri smiled and walked on. Inside, his mind screamed, "Not so fast, Officer Tony, not so fast. The killer is mine, from the toes to the head." He played Sue's words in his mind. He alone would hunt them down.

Terri finally stood before the church. The throbbing in his head was unbearable – this time he wanted it. He wanted it to ache so bad – it would help him as he pumped them up with bullets – one at a time. There was a longing for peace in his heart when he had stood there earlier that morning – now his world had collapsed. There was a thirst for revenge.

The lady in white looked injured and weak. They would probably hide in the church till things quietened down. Just where he wanted them. Someone held out a hand – a firm one.

"Dave!"

"Terri, brother I am so sorry for your loss. I was jealous of you guys – Blondies, what a team – you knew that didn't you?"

"Yeah," Terri smiled as his mind screamed silently, "watch the door – watch the door – don't let them escape."

"We'll give her the greatest honor we can, officer – trust me, that marching funeral line is going to be so long they'll need to close the damn 401."

Terri nodded. He had to get away. Dave could talk.

"Gotta go, Dave – commissioner's waiting for a report."

"Damn right – better run. By the way, I'd love to march next to you on her final journey."

"You're the best cop ever, Dave – thanks – the spot is yours."

He had to get to the cruiser. Their cruiser was on the southeast side, near the clergy parking where they had left it

"Coffee bro?"

"No, thanks."

"Go home, buddy, shoot a whiskey and sit back, we'll come and get you. We'll miss her."

"Thanks," Terri muttered and ran. He had to get away from those consoling voices quickly. His rage threatened to explode in some other heartless emotion. His phone buzzed. It was somewhere in his breast pocket. He grabbed it.

"Sinead," he answered, startled. He had forgotten all about his wife and kids. A guilty pang shot through. He dismissed it quickly.

"You're ok, Hun? Heard the news - an officer was gunned down."

"I'm good, Hun – gotta go," he said and hung up before she asked about Clare. These were his final moments with Clare. He had peeked into the body bag just before they had wheeled her away. She could have been asleep. "Wake up," his mind had tried to order her, "it's only a dream – we've got a job to do, Blondie2."

"I'm sorry, officer," the paramedic had been very patient, "partner?"

"Yup – 10 *goddamn* years' man." He had reached out and soothingly touched her cheek. "Come back, sweetie," he had pleaded, before they took her away. He was sitting in the cruiser – the memories came screaming back. The coffee cup from the morning was still there – she had placed it in the holder for him. He reached out to her seat and broke down.

"Oh, my love – why didn't I see it before? This could have been the most beautiful part of our lives." The tears flowed, and then there were more. He reached over to her glove box and grabbed a Kleenex – pink. They always had to be pink. It was the only feminine piece of vanity she insisted on.

"Oh my God – I must remember to tell them to bury her in pink," they had discussed death, many a time. They had seen enough of it – escaped it many times and never believed it would come true.

Terri started the cruiser. Alone in there, he wanted to run out of there instantly. Her absence was killing – it left a void – she would never again occupy that seat. He was not sure how long he sat there. The warmth of the car caressed his body, dreaming, weeping he dozed off. The thought of the Indian man came screaming into his head. "Damn," he muttered waking up, "they would have escaped by now." He was about to get out when a Black Honda pulled out of the driveway at the side. It was the brown man. The Indian was escaping. Terri looked up shocked as the feel of the cold gunmetal slowly faded to the warmth of his touch. He popped out the magazine and slammed it back. It was indeed the Indian man and the white lady – and a teen.

"So bloody obvious," he yelled, "run, baby, run. I will chase you and hunt you down. How much more perfect could revenge be?" his mind relished the thought.

Instead, the car pulled over into the school bus bay. Terri pulled in quickly behind them. He saw the Indian lean forward to the GPS on the windscreen.

"A long journey – how wonderful. There has been a change of plans, my love," he spoke to the empty seat. "By the way, did I tell you how stunning you look with that beautiful beach blonde hair of yours combed tight in a Reverse French Braid?"

She smiled – nay blushed – she gushed and burst out laughing. Terri stared – it would never be. The gushing was from the black Honda as the tires spun looking for a bit of traction on the snow as they pulled out of the bus bay. They hit the road, as did Terri. They were headed somewhere – purposefully – so was he.

"Take us to a faraway, deserted spot, my evil beauties," he called out with an evil grin, "it would be so good to have you dig your own graves and then take you down, one by one."

Unknown to Daniel, Yokatherine, and Ezekiel a police cruiser followed them. Clare's loaded gun lay ready on the empty side seat. Each bullet had their name on it.

"Justice, sweet justice," Terri swore.

XXII

Into the Valley of Death

The wait seemed long and tense as Daniel finished entering the address that Ezekiel read out. The GPS search for a satellite signal on a cloudy day was laborious. Another long minute later, a purple line indicating their route appeared on the display. Daniel stared in disbelief at the proximity of their destination. It was barely 5 kilometers south; in the heart of Toronto. "In 200 meters, turn left on Vaughan," the mechanical female voice instructed. "Finally," exhaled Daniel, as the GPS found a satellite connection and charted their course.

"The devil lives right here in our backyard," he swore, "how could evil so vile hide here, in the heart of the city?" He gave up the thought with a shake of his head as Yokatherine shook her head in caution and the GPS lady ordered once again – this time more forcefully.

"Turn left on Vaughan – Turn left on Vaughan."

"Ya, ya," he muttered in irritation, drawing a quiet smile from Yokatherine who sat with her eyes closed and her lips moving in prayer. The voice had barely finished when he caught the last few words from Harold Hussein's weather report on the 680AM news channel. "So with the Polar Vortex set to hammer us violently, prepare for ultra-icy roads, do not drive, stay indoors and if you absolutely have to step outdoors, dress for a wind-chill of -30 to -35 Celsius."

"And be ready for broken bones – where the heck did that come from?" Daniel asked shocked, "there is no way Father Brian is getting his Good Friday procession with a Polar Vortex looming."

"Polar Vortex – like, what is that thing, dude?" Ezekiel asked idly from the back. An irritated look flashed across Daniel's face.

"Do you really have to use the word 'like' before every sentence? It's absolutely atrocious English."

"Dude --," Ezekiel blurted and shut up just as suddenly with a regretful face.

"Again," Daniel continued with more irritation on his face, "that's another term I hate, so please don't --,"

"My bad – am so sorry, Daniel. Didn't mean to dude you, sir," the voice from the back seat jumped in faster this time. Daniel was all ready to shoot back but the apology caught him off guard. He continued with a gentler voice.

"Again, my young friend, 'my bad', that's rubbish English." He closed his eyes for a second and sighed. "And, I am so sorry for my short temper too, didn't mean to --,"

"No really, Daniel, it was my fault - I mean it – sorry," Ezekiel said softly and reached forward and squeezed Daniel's shoulder. Daniel began to reach back with his free left hand, but dropped it back in his lap just as suddenly, as a violent spasm of pain shot through it. A look of worry spread across his face. Did he need to have it looked at medically? He dismissed the thought instantly as the word sacrilege flashed in his mind. He noticed a nod from Yokatherine. Her eyes were still closed, but somehow internally, he sensed, she had caught on to his little doubt.

"It's been a rough day, my young angels," Yokatherine's soft voice flowed into the conversation like a soft, soothing whisper. Her hand overlapped Ezekiel's before he could withdraw it from Daniel's shoulder. "Feel this bond – hold on to it," she said giving it a further squeeze. "The task ahead is one of the deadliest of missions anyone could undertake. You, Ezekiel," she said turning over further, instinctively drawing him forward, "you, we should drop off to your home right away."

"But --,"

"I know, kid. A fierce longing for your love guides you, but I sense it is more a feeling of guilt that drives you."

"Both," he burst out as if someone had drawn a painful thorn out of his soul; a burdensome sin forgiven at Confession.

"Maybe, God does have a purpose for you today – he doesn't always choose the high and mighty. And as for you, my dear," she said to Daniel bending forward further with a painful sigh, eyes staring at the side view mirror rather intently, "you, you can't even begin to imagine the cross you carry."

"A cross truly for I am --," he broke off the thought as a flashing, orange walk signal on Vaughan came on ahead of them. A large man in a large, furry coat, furiously puffing a cigarette, and dragging a little Mutt, crossed the road. He had nearly crossed over when he stopped and looked left. Daniel followed the man's eyes and curiously peeked at the cars lined up behind them. Just as suddenly, the road was clear again and they moved on. Something had caught his attention and was lost once more in the sudden change.

"Where was I?" he wondered out loud, "ah yes, me, the Thornbearer of the Lord's thorn of the Holiest of Holies – the Son of God. In just the last hour, I've been an absolute adulterer, lost my temper with this kid here and freely spoken of hate. Why would the Lord choose me?"

"Remember the fishermen and the tax collectors?" Yokatherine interrupted sternly not letting him continue.

"I like your Latina accent," he joked back, trying to ease the tension, "tax collectors eh? I wonder what the Lord would say to the CRA or the IRS if he were to walk the earth today?" Daniel said with a big grin and burst out laughing at his silly joke. His head thrown back found his eyes glancing into the rearview mirror.

"Goodness, a cop right on our tail and here I am…. never mind," he said feeling his seatbelt nervously to reassure himself. A sideward glance and he noticed Yokatherine look ahead after a long hard look into the side view mirror. She found him studying her and broke into a smile.

"You are indeed so beautiful," he said suddenly, noticing the sharp angles of her face. "And when you smile, it's as if summer has arrived in this cold, dead place. Gosh, I only wish whoever is that lucky senor that won your love is worth it, *Muchacha Bonita*."

Yokatherine's head turned a full 90 degrees with a grin, "*Muchacha Bonita* – did you learn that as a pickup line, or, did you date a Latina?" she finished with a blush. "Young man, you are too kind to an old lady." She found Daniel still waiting for her answer with half a smile.

"I found my bridegroom very early, Daniel – and pledged my life to his service - my Lord and Savior, Jesus Christ." Daniel felt embarrassed and bowed in her direction.

They drove on, but the continued presence of the cruiser on their tail, cast a shadow of a doubt. The worries took on a grimmer feeling in both their minds. The cruiser now lagged behind 2 cars that had slipped in from the south at Cherrywood Avenue. Daniel was sure it was intentional – the cop was being discrete. Daniel's worry took on a larger dimension. Suddenly the old ghosts were back as his mind searching for something more to worry about. A little warning bell seemed to be ringing at the back of his mind. He looked at Yokatherine and smiled. He began to relish the comfort and strength of her presence. Who was she, he wondered? A rugged, young-old, South American beauty he thought and smiled wondering if she would read his thoughts. He turned to her suddenly.

"And you, dear prophet, if I may call you that, Signora? Who are you, where do you come from, what drives you into this mission, what is --,"

"Enough," she smiled and opened her eyes but the AM station burst into life again with an alert. The dramatic music was well chosen for the breaking news alerts.

"A news flash – really? What else could go wrong today?" he said as the warning music ended and the news reader's voice took over. "Wonder if those newsreaders practice a special voice that goes along with those breaking news alerts?"

"Shhhh!"

"Environment Canada has issued a special weather statement due to a sudden change. Updated computer models now predict that the ice storm is slated to hit Toronto within the next hour. The storm is expected to bring in at least 5-10 centimeters of freezing rain. The city is expected to issue a statement shortly."

"Oh Dear Lord," Daniel said, "the deadliest form of it. I would rather have 3 feet of snow – I hope they have the army out there on full alert."

"Like – oh my God," Ezekiel's sleepy voice burst open again, "if those -20s' were not enough. This is like - hell freezes over – how true that would be for today! And again, like, what is this Polar Vortex thing, anyway?"

Once again, Yokatherine's soft, soothing voice slowly came alive. "So many questions – so many observations," she said in a quiet solemn tone. The other two listened in silence.

"By the way, Daniel, pull over for a minute, quickly darling," she said, now fully staring into the mirror to her right – her left hand tapping Daniel's shoulder to convey the urgency of the request. Daniel swung out instantly seeing an empty spot between two large construction bins outside an apartment building under renovation. The cars at the back were caught unawares. Brakes, horns, curses and an instinctive swerve later, the cars carried on, followed by the chasing cruiser that missed them as it swung out to overtake the lagging cars. They saw the cruiser drive up to St. Clair and stop at the red lights.

"Be a darling and turn around quickly, and safely," Yokatherine said to Daniel. Ezekiel sensed the tension in the air and sat forward abruptly. Daniel swung the car around and stepped on the accelerator hard, grimacing in pain, as he nearly hit the steering with his left hand trying to reach for the indicator.

"Recalculating – recalculating," the lady in the GPS complained unhappily as they faced northwest again, the direction they had come from. The car lurched a little and shot forward as Daniel barely managed to steer with one hand, desperately trying to work the indicators with the other bruised one. Yokatherine had other plans.

"One more time, darling, find a safe spot and pull over quickly – good – now turn off that GPS and everything else and slide down both of you."

Neither questioned her. Worry crept onto their faces as if someone was about to start shooting again. Daniel's mind had picked up a similar worry. The cruiser had been tailing them rather closely. They sat quietly for a few minutes in dead silence. The blue and white police cruiser zoomed back – its lights flashing to clear the way. Daniel caught a faint outline of the officer's face and froze. Their eyes followed the rear lights of the cruiser until the bend in Vaughan Road took them out of sight.

"That's one less worry, my dear," Yokatherine said confidently, "let's turn around and go, and, leave that lady sleeping," she said to Daniel pointing to the GPS, "I know where evil resides tonight."

"Hell, of course – the address I gave you," Ezekiel quipped in with a shiver, "that is where the devil resides."

"So many questions – so many observations on this the holiest of days," she said thoughtfully, "funny how easily you use the terms, hell, devil or worry about the -20 temps while you live in heated homes, worship in heated churches, wear down-filled jackets and drive in heated cars. Hell is where I began life – a place high in the mountains – so high nearly 5 kilometers into the skies. You'd think it was close to heaven. No, no, it was pure hell so close to the heavens. It's where people still live in abject misery, in -25 centigrade and below, with no heating or running water, in tin-roofed shanty towns."

"Is that where Yokatherine began life?" Daniel asked.

"Very true – a place where even the oxygen is so rare, you would collapse."

"Why would anyone want to live in that hell?" Ezekiel asked, "Just damn crazy."

"Gold, my young friend. Under the icy glacier, the mountains are laden with gold."

"Sounds like hell to me," Ezekiel came alive again – the story suddenly gripping him, "what else was evil there?"

"Everything – we worked long, hard hours, through tons of dirt, sifting through it with our bare hands to find the shiny metal – me, my mother and sister. My father worked the mines, carrying heavy loads of dirt out which we sifted through with our bare hands and gave the gold to the contractors."

"Did they give you a share of the gold?" Daniel peeped in the mirror at Ezekiel's constant questions – the kid was enthralled.

"A share of the gold!" Yokatherine laughed sympathetically, "they gave us nothing, not even wages."

"No wages at all?"

"In exchange for our free labor for every month, they let us work the mines for a day, for ourselves – that was ours. That was hell and then real evil came calling one day. It wasn't the hooded one but someone similar – they came to rob the *Compro Oros*, the gold buyers. The villagers burnt them alive for they claimed not even fire would consume them – it didn't. They ran down the snow and litter laden mountains, carrying the poison with them and wishing us death."

"And?" Ezekiel asked hanging on to the backrests.

"They did leave us death. My father died a few days later. He and his team that had stopped the evil ones. They went into the mines and never came out again – consumed by the *antimonio*, the toxic gas that eventually got the miners and sent them crashing into the depths of the earth. My mother followed soon after, poisoned by the white dust that filled her lungs from the years of sifting through the mountain dirt, looking for the gold. My elder sister got taken into the prostitution rings – as she took on the mantle of supporting me. That was hell." They drove in silence as a weather discussion on the AM radio caught their attention.

"How could the weather models not have seen this sudden change – or were they wrong from the start?" The mayor was asking, trying to lay the blame on someone.

"Mr. Mayor, the unexpected strong gusts of wind storms that suddenly sprang up from the north, seem to have dragged the ice storm here, faster," someone answered. Daniel shivered at the thought, his mind going back to the hooded one, the howling winds and the chaos that had erupted – Yokatherine shook her head remembering the evil that had caused it.

"Our faith must be very strong today, those were evil winds," she said quietly, "merge and carry on to Bathurst south," she said as they reached the end of Vaughan. Daniel waited for a clearing and then merged quickly. The tall, multi-storied, concrete walls and the forest above them painted a faint, gloomy picture. He wondered how long those trees had stood – what had they witnessed – "If only these trees could talk," he observed aloud.

"Tell us more about what happened afterward," Ezekiel implored, suddenly impatient at the break in the story.

"Well, the evil one wasn't satisfied – came back for me. Even in that hell, I thought God was with us. I told him I would come after him, to free the soul of my father."

"And?" Ezekiel prompted, eagerly.

"He told me I wouldn't have to – he would find me, always. And, he has – all these years later. One day a group of nuns came visiting our desolate hell in the mountains. They did not last a day and had to be taken down in the same trucks that brought them up. The climate was too harsh for them to survive even a day. One of them smuggled me out, away from the marauding pimps; to Africa, Italy and finally, here."

The slope was pushing the car faster, Daniel braked hard as they reached the Davenport signal, remembering the red light cameras that he so dreaded and feared.

"Let her roll," Yokatherine said with a sense of urgency as the lights turned amber, "left, go left, quickly," she urged. Daniel barely managed to signal and turn left as the lights turned red. An angry, honking driver waiting to turn as well followed them closely. Daniel was about to honk back but Yokatherine stopped him, pointing to the rearview mirror. As they turned left, the honking driver swung out, swore, gave them the middle finger and sped away east but Yokatherine's eyes remained on her side mirror. Daniel looked in the rearview mirror as he caught sight of a police cruiser speeding south on Bathurst. The turning driver had been a perfect cover.

Yokatherine smiled – "Everyone has a purpose to serve, my angels – even the swearing ones." They drove east on Davenport. "Sneak in here, my love," she directed and they turned on Howland going south. At the end of the lane, a dark deserted theater and a bend suddenly revealed an opening. Another turn and a railway underpass brought them onto DuPont Street. Daniel imagined something would happen under the underpass but nothing stirred. Ezekiel seemed to breathe easier. Yokatherine scanned both sides, as did Daniel. They were both looking for the cruiser. Yokatherine simply pointed left onto DuPont. Daniel drove faster, now that they were on a bigger street.

Yokatherine suddenly panicked. "Too soon, too soon," she sighed but didn't seem to stop them as she pointed to a lane turning right, "drive through slowly – don't stop – no matter what."

"For your own sakes, my angels – I hope your soul is clean and your intentions pure. I will be your strength if the Lord would let me be. Soon we will be at hell's door – but girdle up for the Lord is with us." Just as suddenly, she sat back – eyes wide open – her face focused and she prayed softly yet firmly

"The Lord is my Shepherd, there is nothing I shall want; Fresh and green are the pastures, where he gives me repose, even if I walk through the Valley of death, no evil will I fear, for you are there with your rod and your staff…."

XXIII

The Road to Hell

Daniel tried to read the faded name of the street on the small street sign. He missed it. The street was narrow and dingy. Massive mounds of ice banks, dirty and black, formed high embankments. The series of ice storms, earlier that January, followed by frigid temperatures, had ensured the ice stayed and grew in stature with each snowfall. Snow covered cars lay jammed in the little space left on both sides of the road. The houses were old and close together. Trees bent over the road from both sides, forming a canopy of sorts. With all their leaves shed for the winter, their long, winding branches cast an eerie glow. Like long, bony arms and skeletal fingers, they reached across the street to ensnare the unwanted intruder. Daniel studied the houses. "An abandoned street?"

"More like a street nobody would want to venture into," Yokatherine corrected.

"More like a street we're going to die in," Ezekiel finished off with an involuntary shiver giving Daniel a start. Curious, Daniel stepped on the brake to check on the teen in the back. The road was a smooth sheet of ice already. The inhabitants of the street had not bothered to shovel or salt it. The car ABS kicked in with a loud series of thuds as the car kept on gliding with the brake locked in.

"Gently," Yokatherine pleaded.

To Daniel's immense relief, the slope, the momentum, and the turning action, took them sliding sideways to the left – the wheels coming to a halt on a steep snow bank. They sat quietly for a minute – hearts pounding. "The Titanic just survived," Daniel remarked, hoping to ease the tension. He could see Yokatherine pretty shaken up herself. He turned the steering wheel and eased off. The ice was firm, and they set off gliding again.

Daniel looked around wondering if anyone had noticed their little slip-up – the street was as dead as a graveyard. The blackened out wooden decks, the uneven patios with sunken tiles and the snow covered dead plants, all seemed to share a gloomy feel. No one wandered outside. Every house lay unkempt. Large piles of discarded furniture filled the front yard of one of the houses to his left. The small flight of wooden steps leading up to the patio was crumbling. The house next to it competed for the amount of garbage it held. An old American car, as big as a house, crammed the narrow drive that lay in front. Daniel felt as if the car would suddenly turn itself on any minute, reverse, and smash into them – like a possessed, evil battle tank.

A gasp from Ezekiel's mouth got their attention to the right. A clowder of cats sat on a patio and every little space that the patio provided. Like a local gang of thugs that controlled the area, their heads turned slowly, following the car that had dared to drive into their serfdom. A large grey Tomcat jumped off his perch, lazily arched its back and stretched. With a deep, probing glance around, it began to walk towards the road.

"Keep moving, Hun," Yokatherine urged, softly gripping Daniel's arm. He liked that touch – it was reassuring. Her hand stayed on. He felt a shiver in her arm and sensed her fear, or nervousness, he wasn't sure which. Daniel was mesmerized with the cats and the eerie aura they seemed to produce. He got the car moving again. A massive old house loomed into view on the right. The cluster of evergreens that grew in front, and the sides, covered it well so that the house became visible through the gaps between the trees, only when one actually got in front of it. It was dull, dark and detached, rising 3-storeys high. The paint was peeling, and the empty vines of an ivy, crept all over its front. Someone had experimented with a dirty blue on the patio – it was peeled and grey now. The house was dark except for a lit window, high in the attic. Ezekiel stooped low and looked up.

"Ghostly house – looks like someone is in there," he whispered, as if not to break the tension of the hair-raising, blood-chilling aura that seemed to have permeated the car.

"Of course there is. Obviously, someone lives there, Hun, but that's not the house we seek," Yokatherine corrected.

"But that someone is watching us intently," he whispered fearfully.

"Just a bored soul with nothing to do – keep moving, Daniel."

A deadly gloom now fully possessed the car. Ezekiel pulled forward as close to them as he could. Yokatherine sensed the fear in his heart and held his hand. Daniel pushed back the shade of the sunroof and stared through at the window that Ezekiel had noticed.

"There is indeed someone there," he said in a hushed tone, "someone who seems to be staring down at us, rather intently." They reached the end of the street. There was no cross section. Unlike most other roads in Toronto, it turned left into a curve – almost a U, but carried on straight after the bend.

A castle like house stood on the bend. Its corners were shaped into towers and turrets with pointed tops. "Looks like the fortress of Sauron, straight out of a Lord of the Rings movie," Daniel remarked.

"More like Hogwarts Castle in a Harry Porter movie," Ezekiel corrected.

"True," Daniel added. A van was coming from the other side and the two negligent drivers nearly caused a head-on collision. Yokatherine did not react – her face had gone still. Ezekiel shouted the warning from the back.

"Stop!"

Daniel hit the brakes in sheer shock as the collision warning kicked up an orange storm on his front screen. The two vehicles slid and came to a stop a hairs breath away from each other. Daniel's attention had wandered back to the tall house in his rear view mirror. He reversed quickly, wheels spinning with little traction – his attention still fixated on house in the mirror. The white-knuckled driver slowly squeezed by, nodding to Daniel. There was no acknowledgement for Daniel had noticed that the light in the attic had gone off.

"Move," Yokatherine desperately yelled, "of all the places, not this spot – move, move." Daniel seemed frozen at the bend – his attention transfixed on the house. He noticed an old, bald man exit the house. He wore no coat, hat, or boots. He did not look the typical Canadian, winter-clad resident at all. A strange yellow hue covered him from head to foot.

"Strange! That's a first for me. A poncho wearing man in Toronto, in winter?"

"And," interjected Ezekiel a little less tense, "if that was the deadly street – we just exited it – weren't we supposed to look for --,"

"It's there, Ezekiel – hell can wait," Yokatherine turned sharply, "and did you say a poncho, Daniel?"

"Sounds totally weird, but yes, a poncho."

"Describe the man to me."

"Poncho Man?"

"Yes."

"Old, bald, until he put on that sombrero – fuzzy beard."

"And...."

"Fuzzy beard that seemed to connect to his side locks, that connected to his fuzzy hair over his ears, that I'm sure went around the back of his head."

"And...."

"Stocky figure --,"

"And...."

"I don't know, Yokatherine, I just had a brief --,"

"And...."

"Let's see. Dark, woolen sort of a pant. Almost looked hand woven --,"

"And...."

"Oh, my goodness – yes a blooming staff in his hand – like a shepherd out of a Biblical movie. If it wasn't for the staff, the man would probably fall right over. Strange forward limp, as if he would fall forward, rather, topple over with each step. And really, a cool, red poncho with a real intricate design."

"And...."

"Covered in an eerie, yellow hue."

Yokatherine sat back – eyes closed. "It can't be but go back, Daniel," she said, shivering violently. Daniel was sure she was goose-pimpled all over.

"What of the house?" Ezekiel asked again.

"We crossed it," Yokatherine answered irritably.

"Majestic – castle like – Harry Porter school – right?"

"Wrong, Ezekiel. Don't look for the obvious gates of hell, guarded by demons."

Daniel looked for a spot to turn but the roads were narrow. Each second of doubt pulled them further away. They reached a triangular park. A bust of someone highlighted one end. Daniel waited at the stop sign. He was about to pull out, when a bicycle came hurtling out of the park. The startled rider alighted angrily, almost falling on the icy road.

"Uhhh — a tiny Indian man in a helmet, and a business suit, with a sling bag, riding a bike on ice, on a Good Friday," Daniel half sang idly, wanting to lighten up things, "and, with a rather feminine gait." The man crossed over, giving them an angry stare. A wild, angry, swing of his hips, and he was gone. Daniel was tempted to teasingly honk after the man but a group of young girls came from the other side and got his attention. Disheveled hair, pajamas, groggy faces and shivering bodies, highlighted further by the teddy bears they carried. Ezekiel whistled. Daniel smiled. Yokatherine frowned.

"Rather grown up for pajama parties or sleepovers," Daniel remarked, "didn't know they had those in university."

"Sleepover with alcohol, pot, and sex," Yokatherine quipped back angrily. The girls took their time crossing over.

The car was finally headed back, when Daniel asked the question hanging in the air.

"The poncho man, who is he, Signora?"

Yokatherine sat in silence — her eyes focused rigidly on the road ahead. She muttered angrily, sometimes nervously in a foreign language. "Quechua, my mother tongue," she explained, absent-mindedly. Daniel sensed a nervous anticipation in her. They came around the bend — the street looked even more daunting this time.

"Where's the damn house?" Ezekiel blurted out angrily. His voice quivered. Daniel stopped, alarmed at Ezekiel's high-pitched, fearful voice. The boy was shivering violently.

"You don't have to be afraid, Ezekiel — we're all in this together," Daniel said, reassuringly turning around.

Ezekiel was not listening. Instead, Daniel found him bent over onto the floor of the car.

"The damn card – why do I always keep dropping the damn card?" he exploded angrily and sprang back up suddenly, "666, that's the damn house."

The number made Daniel turn right and scan the nearest house for a number. They were on the turn. He grumbled and drove up a bit and slammed on the brakes as Ezekiel yelled one more time, "STOP!"

Daniel's right hand quivered and his left hand throbbed viciously as if a spasm had set in. His heart beat so violently, he thought it was probably audible to the other two. Craning forward, he looked in the direction of Ezekiel's pointed hand. The big, grey tomcat from the cat riddled house, stood in the middle of the road looking at them intently. "Stupid cat – get out of the way," Daniel screamed and honked. The big cat did not flinch a bit at the loud blast.

"Needs a bloody kick off the road, that cat," Daniel swore and yanked open his door. A series of clicks followed as the remaining doors got electronically unlocked as well. Daniel ran to the front as the key-remote hooked on his pant loop beeped frantically, warning about the separation from the running car. Daniel was about to grab it when he heard another door open and slam back.

"You guys deal with the cats and the strange man while I save my Trisha from the real enemy," Ezekiel whispered hoarsely and dashed off to the right. He tripped over a long branch, crawled back, picked it up, holding it like a weapon and was gone – slipping and sliding on the ice.

"Ezekiel, stop," Daniel shouted but it was too late. Ezekiel was already headed down the drive. Daniel took a reflexive step towards Ezekiel and tumbled onto the bonnet of the car. The warm bonnet felt good for the briefest of instants, before a long, mournful cry from the cat up front made his hair stand on end. Daniel closed his eyes in fear, involuntarily. He was back home in India – a little boy tucked in bed in a long row of sleeping kids – his brothers and sisters wrapped in thick, coarse, woolen blankets on a cold winter night, in the one bedroom they all shared. Their first floor apartment overlooked the roof of a bakery where the cats brought food that they fought over all night. Like old men casting long, magic spells, the cats would fight in long, whining, eerie moans – as if in an argument – building up the pressure, until the fight broke out. The argument was on again as Daniel came back to the cold, winter day with a start.

The freezing sheets of rain were beginning to layer him and the car hood. He stood up slowly, shaking off the ice as the feverish cries, agonizingly terrifying, from hundreds of cats, filled the air. The lone tomcat stood surrounded by countless other cats, their tails in the air, upright, with the end of each tail doing a magical twist like the famous Indian rope trick. The cats were in the front of the car, next to him and behind him. Daniel turned around slowly to his left and all the way around. His mind numbed in shock as he saw a great mass of them approach from the back. A head appeared over the boot, and then another, as the cats began to ascend the car. He finally completed his 360 degree turn, coming back to face the bonnet and nearly felt his feet crumble beneath him. He thought his pounding heart had finally exploded at yet another terrifying sight before him.

The poncho man stood by Yokatherine's door. The bright colors of his shawl drew magical visions in Daniel's head. The man's rugged face was brown, creased and lined. It could have easily been carved in stone. The yellowish hue on him radiated an eerie glow.

"Who are you?" Daniel asked in awe, but the words never left his mouth. The man was bending down to Yokatherine.

"Don't touch her," Daniel screamed in his mind, trying to reach out to protect her, but his body froze, immobilized, and his left hand threatened to explode with some unknown energy.

"Yokatherine – lock your door," his mind screamed, again knowing fully well it was all happening in his head. "The second test – and I fail again," his mind was saying, "I failed you – fight, Yokatherine, fight."

He tried to see her reaction. There was no prayerful face, nor a terrified face. Instead, the face had a childlike glow that he had not seen before in their short time together. Like a little child, totally dependent on a parent, she was reaching out to him. "Are you going to carry her, *El papa*?" Daniel's mind mocked, "Huh? Are you going to do that, *grande, El papa*?" his mind screamed in frustration. In a flash, the connection struck him. A dad whom the evil one had claimed – deep into the belly of the earth.

"What if the man indeed was Yokatherine's father?" Cynically, he dismissed the thought before it even took root in his mind. Her father had vanished decades ago, thousands of miles away, deep into a mine – in a world that had no connection to this time or place. Daniel looked at his open door and saw a bunch of cats trying to work their way in. Like crabs in a bucket, each tried to work its way over the lower ones sending the bunch crashing down. Daniel slammed the door angrily, flinching for a second wondering if one of them would find its head smashed in the metal. The slow, mournful cats moved away in time. His remote broke off into another long chain of warning beeps. Daniel opened his door, jumping in, he hit the engine stop button, and was about the slam and lock the car, when a wild, blood-curling scream filled the air.

"Ezekiel," he screamed, jumping out of the car. Yokatherine was still glued to her seat, but the poncho man turned at the blood-curling scream as well. Daniel ran towards the drive, kicking the cats out of his way. He could feel his heavy, Cumberland boots with their rock-solid, metal toecap; connect with the soft bellies of the cats. He felt their bodies fly in the air with angry, warning hisses and growls. A large one, already on top of the boot, was in the process of turning around to have a go at him as he came around. The soft grip of his hand on the furry tail lasted a second, as Daniel sent it like a missile into the mass of cats all around.

A few more steps, a slip, a fall, a bump, a slide and he came to rest on all fours a few feet into the drive where Ezekiel had picked up the branch. Someone had neatly piled up the branches that he was sure had come down during the earlier ice storms. The path ahead ran into a short, dark archway with the heavily intertwined, bare stems of some runner going both ways over a wired support.

"Ezekiel," he shouted, "where are you?" There was no response but a massive rumble of falling plastic bins drew his attention to the right of the house. There was a narrow passageway on the right. Daniel charged into it, grabbing on to the vines for support – yelling out to Ezekiel. Two steps later, he stopped in shock. The dull, dark brick façade of a typical, old Toronto home ended a foot later. It was a decoy. Behind it stood a majestic, bright white, modern building. Its glass windows set in bright white, aluminum frames, blended seamlessly with the stucco walls. Daniel saw a window partially open. It was high above the ground, possibly 10 feet high. He admired Ezekiel's ingenuity and bravery. The boy had piled up the small, sturdy, plastic recycle bins over the big, grey garbage ones, and climbed into the window. A small bin hanging precariously, slid over finally, and went rolling into a brightly

painted fence. He was about to reach for it, when his eyes
fell on some plastic sacks.

A smarting of red and white colors stared out at him
from within the large, clear bags. He bent over and stared in
shock, painfully aware that each second away kept him from
reaching in, and helping the boy. The whites were plasters,
bandages, discarded aprons, facemasks and elastic gloves.
There were dashes of color on them – red – blood. Some
bandages were soaked in it. Some patients had apparently
bled a lot. Daniel slowly walked past the bags in revulsion.

"Didn't Ezekiel say some medical services?" he
reasoned in his mind, "but this is Toronto – Canada – no
way would they let stuff like that lying around in plastic
bags." He had nearly convinced himself that it was ok, when
his foot kicked a large bag sticking out on to the path.
Something was behind it. Daniel gently pressed the sack
back with his foot – it bounced back. He kicked it to the
side. It fell away revealing a long, transparent, plastic storage
bin – securely shut. Daniel bent low and looked. It
contained a series of smaller boxes. Like the plastic, take-out
deli boxes at his local Loblaws store, he expected chicken
legs to vie for his attention. Instead, there was something
else fleshy inside – a little life form. Box after box seemed
the same. Little pieces of flesh, tiny hands, legs and other
torso parts. Another bulky box looked stuffed with little
balls; little, irregular, circular, shapes – crushed mostly. He
bent over and stared harder, and thought a tiny, little face
materialized out of the mass. In a semi hypnotic state,
Daniel stared at them as his world stood still – silent and
dazed.

Somewhere along the line, he remembered falling
on to his knees as his hand hit the cobble-stoned path neatly
finished in crazy paving style. He knew it was his left hand
as he felt the wild, electric shocks from his bruised nerves

travel all over his body. It felt good to share in the pain of the Lord as the heinous sins of the world lay before him.

"Oh my sweet Lord," he prayed, "the evil of this world – the suffering." Daniel's stunned mind wandered back to a Bible study course. It was a long time back. "Do you know 65% of all abortions happen on campuses?" his friend Connie was shouting in his face. "No, 70%," Laura countered. "More like 75%, in reality," Sabrina was saying.

"Was it true?" he wondered. "Nice location, hooded man – lots of students to fill your bags of evil," he swore.

After a long time, he came to the bottom of the tall box. A single, final bag lay crumpled. Someone had not bothered to stuff it up. Too shocked to worry, Daniel peered closely. A tiny little fetus, nearly complete, stared at him. "Oh little Angel," he sighed and fell away as a breath of hot air gushed in his face and snapped. The deadly jaws nearly tore away his face. Daniel had barely missed the deadly bite. A giant Rottweiler stared in his face, desperately trying to bite off a chunk of him. Daniel wondered what was keeping it – "A leash of course, you fool!" he told himself and quickly rolled on to his feet, shaken up. The silence of the dog surprised him – but then nothing shocked him anymore that day. The dog had been well trained to kill silently. It lunged desperately.

The Rottweiler was furiously trying to break away – the scraping of its paws on the stones, intensified. Daniel was sure the dog had killed before. He had to move fast. He turned the first, small bin over. It would be the perfect step on to the larger one against the window. Daniel raised himself up wondering if he would ever make it up with his one working hand. The smaller, plastic bin squeaked and nearly crumpled under his weight. Resting his left elbow on the larger bin, and pushing with his right, Daniel pulled himself up. On his third attempt, he made it up coming to rest in fetal position on the bin. A little maneuvering had him standing up, just a step away from the ledge. Daniel turned slowly. His weight would shift precariously to the outer edge if he wanted to step forward.

Down below the Rottweiler seemed silent. Relaxing a little Daniel turned over to look. The metal chain attached to the collar was as strong as ever. The dog was not giving up, even though its furious attempts to break free caused it to choke and gasp on its collar. Daniel was about to turn back, when a multitude of sounds told him his luck had run out. The pressure treated, 6x6, wooden plank kennel to which the metal chain was attached, snapped with a loud cracking sound.

Daniel's turning action on the top of the bin caused it to tilt forward, and land back with a thud, against the wall. Unfortunately for him, whoever had put the large bin there, had left the single set of wheels on the outer side. The bin slammed into the wall and bounced right back. With Daniel's unbalanced sway on it, the bin rocked back and forth. On the other side, the wood cracked further with an ear piercing sound. On the 4th bounce, the bin finally toppled over just as the Rottweiler broke free.

Daniel landed on his right shoulder and head – too stunned to react quickly. The Rottweiler was thrown forward with the sudden snapping of the wood. Both stood on opposite sides from where they had started. Daniel was sure it was the end when he noticed a thick, metal beam sticking out of the low, winter dried hedge. Moving a little he stared in amazement – it was a regular, metal fire escape. He charged for it as the dog stood up to attack. On his third step, Daniel froze in pain as he reached out with this left hand to grasp a step and the Rottweiler's fierce jaws locked onto his boot. Daniel could feel the force of the powerful jaws, as the dog yanked its head from side to side in anger. For all his self-confidence, Daniel realized that the dog was winning. His foot slipped, and he ended up hanging upside down with his left hand hanging limply over. The dog was on it in a flash – and then it stopped. Daniel was sure his hand would be crunched up in a second. Instead, the warm, wet breath became a comfortable feel. The fierce growling turned to a quiet whimper.

Daniel stared blankly – puzzled. "Oh darn – stupid me!" he exclaimed, as he saw the dog settle on the ground quietly at the foot of the hedge. "Thank you, Jesus," he exclaimed, as his heart refused to stop its furious thumping.

"The steps – hmm!" he exclaimed, idiotically. There was only one way to go – up the fire escape. Daniel started climbing cautiously. The second landing was the same. At the third landing, he tried the door, half built into the sloping roof. Someone had expertly converted the attic into a wonderful office. Daniel peeped through the little glass window. He looked for people – there were none. It was white everywhere.

Another little precarious step later, he was sitting on the ledge. He swung in, head bent low; he realized he had chosen the wrong side. His left hand reached up instinctively for support, convulsed in pain and then fell away.

Devoid of support, Daniel fell through the window. About to swear, he controlled himself – "it's Good Friday," he reminded himself. Silently, he thanked whoever had forgotten to lock the window. The office was empty, utterly modern and chic. Neat little, white cupboards built into the walls, covered every inch of the office. The desk, the computer…. everything was white. The computer got his attention – it was a Mac. "Bloody Apple," he swore silently under his breath with half a grin.

A distant thud got his attention. Had someone heard him crashing through? Would he, the brave religious warrior out to the smash evil, end up in the back of a police cruiser, charged with a break-in, he mocked himself. He

stood still listening to the beating of his heart. No other
sound was heard. Daniel crept silently to the door and put
his ear against it. There was no sound. On a hunch, he went
back to the cupboards and opened one gently. The filing
was meticulous. He pulled out one of the indexed binders.
A pretty face stared out at him – Mackie Tillerson – the
name below it read. "Sad, pretty girl – but of course – how
could you have been happy?" he told the picture. He
wondered why, and how, they got the picture, before they
sent the young woman onto the operating table to suck a
little life out of her womb. He closed the file sadly and slid it
back as melancholic thoughts of the girl's experience
clouded his mind.

　　　The inner door opened on to a narrow landing that
led to three other similar sized rooms, identically furnished.
He wondered if the hooded man administered his evil from
up here, in the white aproned garb, insulting one of the
noblest of professions. The steps had thick, plush carpeting
and Daniel began to descend slowly – sticking to the wall.
To his utter surprise, there was a glass door on bright steel
hinges, at the end of the steps. The third floor was restricted
– made sense he thought. He peeped through the glass
panes. Once again, the whiteness surprised him. "Evil loves
a new color," he thought, wondering what his next move
would be. He thought he detected a faint movement at the
end of the passage, as if someone had just entered one of
the rooms. He shivered, shoved his right hand under his left
arm to keep it still. He waited as the thought of Ezekiel,
probably a prisoner in there, and Yokatherine, at the mercy
of the cats and the poncho man, flashed past him.

　　　He peeped again – there was no one, but again a
series of movements seemed to have caught his attention.
"Bloody hell – there is no one there," he swore, wondering
if his mind was playing tricks on him. Frustrated, he opened
the door and stormed into the hallway. It could have been

the neatest, hospital floor he had ever walked on to. Each door had a sign above it. Theatres 1 to 4, supplies, preparation rooms – each room had a white aluminum door with a little, glass window. Little medical trolleys with all sorts of equipment laden on them, were pushed against the sides. Daniel stared at one – bandages, tapes, sealed instruments, masks, plastic gloves – "nice hospital," he swore in his mind, "if only if it was for the right reasons."

"Bad thing to say here – right in our midst," a voice quipped in his ear. Startled, he jumped around in fright – there was no one. Confused, he stood still for a minute sure that he had not imagined that voice in his ear. He closed his eyes, feeling his surrounding, and knew he was not alone. A million figures were reaching out to choke him – unable to grasp him. He lifted his thorn hand. It looked like an ordinary, badly bandaged hand, except that in his mind it shone like a pillar of fire. "Oh my Jesus," he prayed in gratitude, and took a step towards the next flight of steps, hesitantly, expecting whatever was there, to block off his exit.

"Oh you of little faith, why do you doubt?" his mind remembered Jesus telling Peter as he tried to walk on the water. Daniel closed his eyes and prayed, "Lord, help my feeble faith." His eyes were still closed when an ear-shattering scream, once again filled the building. Daniel ran blindly, leaping down the steps. His left hand was on the side of the railings – useless to give him support. Two leaps later, he landed on the half way landing and gasped. A black, leather jacket lay in the middle. Part of it still lay folded up, above the floor, as it had fallen. The collar stood up as if someone on the way up had reluctantly let go of it. Someone, he dared not think of, had been taken upstairs, forcefully.

He reached down for it and his body reacted as if it was on fire. The delicate perfume engulfed him in a storm of emotions. He was back outside the convenience store, wrapped in the arms of a bewitchingly, beautiful woman whom he had never known. Despite his best effort to resist it, his hands grasped the black jacket and held it close feeling the warm, sensuous body that had taken him on a wild emotional ride. He looked up as he felt a million pairs of eyes looking down at him with piercing evil eyes. "But where was she, or the other kid whom the hooded man had kidnapped?" The locked rooms, were they being held there, gagged and bound? Suddenly, the thought of the pregnant teen hit him like a fatal punch. Was he too late?

The scream was back from somewhere below and Daniel bolted, holding the jacket as if it was the last sign of something precious he had lost. "Lead us not into temptation," his mind inadvertently prayed. Yokatherine's admonishing face flashed past him and he threw down the jacket as if it was bewitched. He reached the main floor and was sure he could hear the wind outside. The door was somewhere close by. He started moving towards what appeared to be the main door, when his mind once again picked up a presence. He whirled around and this time it was real. The white coat that vanished down the steps was no figment of his imagination.

Daniel ran towards the steps and took one final leap on to a landing, lost his balance and went rolling down a set of steps. The bright, white glow of modern architecture from the upper floors was gone. Dull steps replaced the bright, linoleum ones on the upper floors. The steps were soft – Daniel felt them – velvet – red. A hand reached out, pulled him up and steadied him. Daniel almost screamed in fright. He looked at the white coat in the faint light. The African face smiled. It didn't lash out, or threaten him for trespassing, or cast an evil spell.

"Easy, brother, the chapel is not running away you know."

"The chapel? But I thought --,"

"Never mind what you thought," the smile was eerily wider, "The master is --,"

"Ok, sorry I thought since the place was closed there would be no…."

Daniel mumbled quickly hoping to buy himself some time. The mention of the chapel had him all confused.

"Well you know the master doesn't really like to be kept waiting, and then, hopefully you don't end up becoming the sacrifice. Anyway, do you have a sacrifice to offer?" the man said pointing to the large shut wooden door.

"The master here? Sorry, I mean what sacrifice – ah yes," Daniel hesitated as he saw the wooden door move a bit. He had to think fast before the deadly chill sweeping through his body engulfed him. Was it the wind he wondered, or just a loose latch, or a faulty hinge? It was neither, as he saw the faint outline of a white fingertip appear to push it for the briefest of instants, and disappear. Trisha – was she hiding in there? Trisha – a light bulb clicked in his head.

"The girls this morning," he said with a wink, hoping the unspoken reference would work. It seemed to, for the man broke off into a massive grin.

"But of course, brother, thank you for assisting the master. We needed one just like that for a day like this. He's been waiting for a long time for this particular damned day – said it was the one time, he would break the jinx and conquer the shame forever."

"You mean the one from 2000 years ago?" The man glared. The smile vanished. The face that replaced it was evil and angry.

"Yes, that one, though I'd be careful with my words. You did well, I am sure the master will reward you."

Daniel breathed a sigh of relief as the man turned to open the door. "You seem to be entering the chapel for the first time, so remember, you must be quick and strong and sure of yourself in there." The partially open door surprised him for an instant. Daniel saw the body go tense. Daniel stood with his heart in his mouth. The door was being opened slowly, from the inside.

Daniel was sure the man knew something was amiss. It was his one chance to escape – but how far would he get? The door opened a little more. The man turned – there was anger written across his face. He glared into Daniel's face.

"You have some explaining to do, my man --," the man was half way through his sentence, when a large club emerged through the door and landed smack on the man's head. Daniel jumped away in fear, ready to escape up the steps but the door swung wide open. The club-bearing figure emerged – club raised, ready to have another go at the man on the floor.

"Daniel! Heard your voice – you made it in."

"Ezekiel – you're ok," Daniel exhaled in relief, "I hope you've not killed the man."

"Doesn't matter, Daniel – this place is evil."

"How do you know, and how did you get in there?"

"The screams, did you hear them?"

"Yes, I thought they were Trisha – captured."

"Oh, I thought so too. They are recorded, seem to emerge from all over the place, the walls, whatever. Never mind – the girls are not in here."

"Did you check properly? Let's take another look. This man isn't coming around soon."

They tiptoed in, quietly and cautiously. The room seemed like a large hexagon. The walls were bare. They seemed to flow down seamlessly into the floor. The faint light came from little lamps embedded into a ceiling that was a copy of the floor. There were six lamps in all. A horrible feeling of despair and doom engulfed them. Ezekiel moved close to Daniel and unabashedly took his hand.

"I know what you're feeling – it happened to me too."

"It's as if something is in here."

"Death, evil death."

"Yes that's it," Daniel whispered back, "the man outside, asked me if I had brought a sacrifice?"

"And what do you reckon that is," Ezekiel asked with a knowing stare.

"Human sacrifices – little human foetuses."

"The lights' fading," Daniel whispered as the lamps slowly dimmed out. In a matter of seconds, the darkness engulfed them completely. A click made them jump in fright. It was the sound of the door closing.

"Oh darn – we're locked in. You think we might be next?"

Daniel did not answer; instead, he dashed in the direction where the door had been. It was hard to tell. Inside, it was just a continuation of the seamless, red, velvet walls; not even the faintest ray of light, made it through.

"Let's kick it down, Daniel," Ezekiel shouted terrified, charging to where Daniel was. He fell with the most horrid sound of bone cracking.

"Yieee," he yelled in pain, "just shattered my knee." Daniel fell on his knees, trying to crawl over to help him. Ezekiel was writhing around in pain. Gently, Daniel held him firm and soothed him down.

"What is it?" he asked, and reached out with this left hand, only to have it jerk back in the most violent way. Shocked, he tucked in his thorn arm and reached out with this right. "It's feels like a tree trunk – bark – a short tree stump with a sticky top – and a massive blade that is rammed in." The handle was long – Daniel's hand slid along it endlessly.

"This is an ancient executioner's axe. Oh my good Lord, Ezekiel – when I was growing up the butchers' used short tree stumps to cut meat and chop apart the goat's legs and to make mince and to...." he fell silent realizing he had been rambling, as the realization of what the tree stump was.

"Would it be safe to conclude that someone is on their way here to butcher us?"

"No Ezekiel – it's this precious thorn that pierced the head of our savior – that's what he wants."

"Well, kill the bearer and get to the thorn," Ezekiel concluded.

Daniel sighed, "What a great comfort you are!"

"Sorry – just being logical. Wouldn't that be his strategy?"

Daniel did not answer. They were silent for a minute. It was completely dark now. Instinctively, they reached out for each other, preparing for the worst, when they heard their names being called.

"Daniel, Ezekiel."

"In here," Daniel yelled back, running to the door and kicking it. "It's that angel – Yokatherine," he shouted as the door swung open. They shielded their eyes as the bright light outside struck their eyes.

"I thought this was the end," Ezekiel sobbed, still bending over and clutching his knee.

"The shortest purgatory I hope I'll ever be in," Daniel said with a big, relieved smile. His body still shivered sporadically with the short experience they had been through.

"What is that place?" Yokatherine asked.

"A mini hell. The man here --," Daniel stopped suddenly. The white coated man was gone. "There was a man here – in a doctor's coat, who referred to this as a chapel where apparently folks bring their sacrifices. In there, we felt death. My young friend here has broken his knee on a tree stump that is probably the chopping block for --,"

He stopped as Yokatherine reached and covered his mouth. "Don't say it, Daniel."

"Strange! The apparently knocked-out doctor vanishes mysteriously from here, strategically open doors and windows, we unchallenged so far, you find and free us without any…I don't like this. I think we all just walked into his trap. How did you find us, anyway? We thought we were sure as hell headed for death."

"The thorn – I prayed in my mind. I am sure it guided me here. We need to find the hooded man, quickly."

"No sign of him so far. I checked out the entire building. No sign of him, Trisha or…." Daniel left the sentence unfinished as a wave of guilt swept him.

"Then let's get out of here," Ezekiel urged.

They started climbing the steps cautiously. Ezekiel stumbled instantly as he transferred his weight to the damaged knee. Daniel reached out and held him. "It's no use," Ezekiel groaned in pain.

"The Lord's thorn, sweetie," Yokatherine whispered, "heal it – heal his knee."

"Are you crazy?" Daniel scolded in shock, scandalized at the very thought.

"The Lord chooses the simple to bring about his miracles," she countered, "believe – have faith." Daniel burst out laughing and then fell silent instantly at Yokatherine's stare.

"Good heavens – a Thornbearer in one day, but healing, miracles, seriously?" He fell silent and gulped as Yokatherine's eyes bored through him. Bending down quietly, he touched Ezekiel's knee with the thorn hand.

"Believe – believe it firmly," Yokatherine encouraged, "it's not about you – it will be if the Lord wishes it."

Daniel stared at the ground as his sinful littleness swarmed around him. Then holding Yokatherine's hand with his right, bending his head low and closing his eyes in prayer, he silently prayed, "Amen, Lord – if it be thy will."

"Amen," they answered.

His eyes remained closed, fearing his faith would be too weak to believe. Instead, he felt Ezekiel's leg pull away from his palm. He sensed a set of soft feet dart ahead on the steps.

"Let me go ahead," Ezekiel said, and leaped two steps at a time. Yokatherine followed with a big, beaming smile. Daniel saw her face glow – the earlier fear in her face had vanished. On a whim, she turned back, the joy oozing out of her face, "It is, after all, The day of the Thorn."

"You just made that up," Daniel smiled as a wild energy burst through his body.

"So what – it's true, isn't it, brother? We just worked a miracle."

"The Lord did – Amen," Daniel answered and followed. They were nearly at the top when a voice engulfed them. It was a whisper at first but still seemed to fill the hallway. Then suddenly it was everywhere. It rang out from all around and found its way maddeningly into their souls. Daniel pointed to the white grill of a speaker that seemed flush with the white walls.

"How dare you?" the voice hissed in anger. "How dare you use the power of that thing in my house?" There was a pause. Daniel thought he sensed a bit of hesitation in the voice as it echoed the word power. A glance at Yokatherine's face seemed to confirm his hunch. "That said, it's the end of that thing today, anyway," the voice laughed a hideous angry laugh. "And – my, my – my ingenious friends. You impress me – truly. I raise my hat to you."

"It's the hooded man," Daniel whispered to the others as the hooded man's laughed filling them with dread.

"Of course, it is me. I have been expecting you – especially that boy." Ezekiel flinched, as if the man stood right over him. "While your girlfriend is about to give me the perfect sacrifice here today, you would have been a welcome bonus. Ah – well then, it's not been a perfect day either. I need that thorn so count yourself lucky."

"The power of the one true God is with us. In small steps you've been failing, you evil one. It will always be a failure for you," Yokatherine snorted back. "Don't you see it? We will get you before the day is through. It's your end today."

"Quiet," the voice, roared back. The speakers vibrated with the force of the voice. "I see you. I have you exactly where I need you – how do you think you fools found that open window, or the front door. I have every little detail planned. I need that thorn or none of you are leaving here alive today."

"Dark evil powers or magic – how does he see us?" Ezekiel asked quietly with a shiver.

"Neither," Daniel answered pointing to a camera on the ceiling that peered at them. "I'm sure there's a series of them. Evil uses modern technology huh – funny!"

"Not so funny when we have our final reckoning. Smart of you again, Thornbearer. However, before the day is through, you will finally see the power of evil that has always lived and waited to rule this land. You will come and hand over the thorn to me."

"The Lord's thorn is not mine to give. It was never mine, nor did it ever belong to any of the Thornbearers down the ages – simple, holy souls whoever they've been. It was never ours to take, nor give – simply to bear for the

Lord. The thorn found its home and will pass down the ages as a reminder of how you lost, and how the Lord defeated sin and death. If you want it, come get it."

"And, I will," the voice shouted and went silent. Daniel, Yokatherine, and Ezekiel instinctively reached out for each other and moved in closer. The silence was absolute. A deadly chill seemed to spread through the air. They stood transfixed; backs to each other. Daniel could see the main door in the distance – it was barely 10 to 15 feet away, yet it seemed their capture was complete – they would never cross that door.

"Ezekiel," he whispered, "the address – what is it?"
"666 Lanark Avenue."
"Text it to whoever you can – mark it FOR 9-1-1."
"But --,"
"Just do it."

Quickly, Daniel began to punch in the address on his own BlackBerry. He fumbled, got the wrong letters, repeated them over and over again, but kept on going. Somewhere deep inside, he remembered Fr. Brian's number. He remembered hitting the enter key just as an icy chill enveloped his body.

The silence began to turn into darkness. The brightness of the building began to fade into a silent shade of grey that turned darker by the minute. Daniel pictured choosing a shade in Excel as he retired one of his servers. It was always a dilemma – how dark could he go? It was always a struggle until he reached black, and then went back to a lighter shade, enough to see the contents of the cell. He knew they were on that darkest cell. He heard Ezekiel sob and Yokatherine prayed silently. Their arms were locked tightly to each other. Something else was crowding in – something else was gripping them. There was only one thing to do – he dialled 911 and hit send just as someone or something yanked the BlackBerry out of his hand. He heard an operator on the other end.

"Fire --,"

"Hooded man – captured – gunman," Daniel yelled as he heard the instrument ground into a million pieces. He could not see anyone – the darkness around them was complete. Daniel could feel the forces around them clearly now.

"The Thorn, Daniel," Yokatherine called, "it's your guard, your angel, your sword, use it." Her voice was fading.

"Yokatherine," he called but there was no answer. Her body was slumped against him. Behind him, he could feel Ezekiel's body droop, yet neither of the two seemed to slide away to the floor. He felt a million pairs of hands bearing them away – a mysterious, dark force. Daniel remembered Yokatherine's last words. He remembered the killer dog that had backed away, the miracle on Ezekiel's knee, "My Lord," he gasped and held his hand out. It was as if he had swung out an invisible sword that slashed away at the invisible attackers. He swung out his left hand again, and the air was filled with a million screams. His hand hit someone real who fell away as if struck with a powerful karate chop.

The reprieve lasted but a minute, and this time the hands, like millions of tentacles, wrapped around them again. They were being borne away – upwards. He felt as light as a feather. At times, the forces around them felt real – like real people, easily bearing them away. Daniel pictured the dark force bearing away a reluctant teen having a change of heart and wanting to back out from an impending abortion. The arms that held her, too powerful. "Easy, Honey. It will be over before you know it and no lifetime of a load to bear." He heard the words echoed in the darkness of the building.

Ezekiel's head rested against Daniel's back awkwardly. Yokatherine was still passed out, but her lips seemed to continue in a soft chant of prayer. Daniel fought hard. The screams got louder with each swing of his hand. The forces came back stronger, slamming into them. He couldn't tell whether it was the chills that swept his body, or a searing pain, as the tentacles lashed him with greater force. He could make out the steps beneath him. They were being borne up the steps.

He felt his right foot sweep something – a coat of sorts. Despite the extreme pain, a warm glow spread through him. A last-ditch swing of his hand had slowed them a bit. Daniel reached below with both his suspended feet and hooked the coat as visions of a black, leather jacket flooded his body again. There was no place for love in this evil kingdom. It was love that caused the Son of Man to lay down his life for humanity. Daniel knew, somewhere in the grand scheme of things, that black leather jacket, and the person who had worn it, had a role to play.

XXIV

At Hell's Door

The big, angry mass of the police commissioner paced the room. The brief moments of silence in between echoed his footsteps. The windowless, neon-lit basement room was cold, steely and desolate. It had been designed that way to instill a sense of fear in the suspect being interrogated there. The distance to it – just two floors below the ground level, was short. Yet, the elevator, more of a cage ride, had been timed with misleading numbers such that a suspect thought he had descended deep into the bowels of the earth.

"Where are the others?" the commissioner whispered, "you know, there is no way out of this mess, you could be gone – put away for life. A ton of people saw you there, gun in hand. You shot a cop, a kid, a crowd – multiple life sentences, my friend."

"Dream on," the voice suddenly awoke.

"Kid – we have the weapon – with your prints on it. Just give us the names – we'll work out a deal."

"Go for it," the voice challenged back.

Those were the first bold words from the subject who had thus far sat in fear. The defiance in the words stunned the room. The two regular interrogators, big suited men, with cold stares, loose ties and stained coffee mugs, conveyed the picture of this being a regular chore. They intentionally sat on either end of the table, dwarfing the suspect on the low chair behind the table. The larger of the two very large men, with steel-grey eyes that matched his steel-grey hair, cropped close to the skin, chopped on the wood as if he missed a scalpel or some other torture instrument.

"Bring my gun – or rather the hooded man's gun. Shove it in my throat and shoot all you want – it won't even spit air," the emboldened suspect defied them further.

"Then where is the real gun?" the smaller of the two, big interrogators yelled, slamming his hand on the table. Dylan did not flinch. Instead, he decided to take the battle to his interrogators.

"I like your accent. Jamaican or Trini?" he toyed with the second one hoping to get under his skin. After the 2 hours of constant torture, he had suddenly found a ray of hope deep within. They were setting him up – trying to break him – not today.

"I may have been caught – wrong place – the wrong action – but I never as much harmed a fly."

"So where did you hide the real gun, boy? What gang are you?" the man screamed – his steel-grey eyes inches from Dylan.

Dylan smiled – he would play them back some more. "Ask the real gunman – if you can find him!" The sarcasm was heavy – he expected a wild onslaught from the interrogators – he prayed – "Please Lord, help me."

A sudden jingle on the wooden table answered his prayer – it broke the flow. It was back again. His Samsung shrieked with an urgency. His bandana above it reflected the bright screen below. It rang again – A RAP SONG. The commissioner walked over and picked up the S7.

"Ah – new message, boy – perhaps your accomplices congratulating you on a job well done."

Dylan smirked, but it did not seem to affect the commissioner. He handed over the phone to Dylan with a soft, caring look. "On your guard," Dylan warned himself. He zigzagged across the number pad to unlock his phone.

"Ezekiel!" He looked up surprised. "It's a friend," he continued, "captured – hooded man – call 911 – 666 Lanark."

Dylan read the words – surprised at first, and then slowly realized the significance of the message as a silent chill swept his body. Dylan dialled back quickly. The phone rang once and instantly went silent.

"This is it," Dylan jumped with a new conviction in his voice holding out the open face of the phone to the cops, "dammit, this is it," he screamed in wild joy. "You can grill me all you want, but look at the words – that's where you'll find the architect of today's mayhem – that's where you'll find the killer as well – there is an address."

The phone was snatched out of his hands. "Hooded," the commissioner, mused over the words, "not coached by the priest are you?" On an impulse, he turned to the long, glass window behind him. It was a one-way glass – he did not need to see.

"Pull up 911 records – emergency – search – trace all mentions of hooded since this morning. And on the double, Walker." There were hurried keystrokes as an officer on the other side of the window punched away. "This is it," Dylan prayed silently in his mind, "Thank you, My Lord Jesus."

* * *

Back at the sacristy, Fr. Brian limped back in after the Italian service. He felt strangely guilty – his mind had wandered during the service. A premonition, more like one of his mystic visions, had been intruding his thoughts. Was the Lord trying to warn him about something? Luckily, it had been a quiet affair. The shock of the morning's events reflected in the faces of the seniors that filled the pews. He looked at the younger generations, regal and gorgeous – he had no heart to go after them for the one time of the year they showed up. Instead, he ripped off his vestments, gratefully took Jojo's supporting arms as he nearly tripped over the single step through the glass door, and crashed into his chair. His eyes were about to close when the table shuddered. Shaken he sat up, "What now, my Lord?" His blank mind searched for a clue. The table shuddered again — his old pen stand made the few pens inside dance like puppets. It was gone before he could trace the source. "Uncle Luigi, my evil uncle, are you here?" he asked looking around.

"Ah, Father Brian," Jojo laughed, "when this week is over — I am calling the bishop to pack you off for a good holiday."

"That still does not explain the shudder."

"How about this?" Jojo said, pulling out the charging BlackBerry from under a pile of papers. He gaped, annoyed for an eternity before he smiled sheepishly.

"That cursed phone has been nothing but a source of embarrassment all morning." Jojo stared with half a smile and hands on her hips. They both laughed.

"Ok, I know, it's just me," he said, looking into the blinking, red LED of the BlackBerry.

"All the more reason for that holiday."

"And, where am I going?" he said, punching in the password and watching the message jump out at him.

"A few days at your dad's farm, and you should be fresh."

"My dad's farm? Seriously Jojo!" Fr. Brian read the text as he muttered the words — something painful was beginning to hammer away in his head. The words, 'hooded' and 'farm', conjured up a deeply, buried fear as the word in his ear, and the text of the message, found a match — an image of a shapeless, green mass flowing over the white picket fence. That was the vision that had intruded his

Italian service, except that it was live and current – a dark vision of something terrible that had just occurred.

"What does it say?" Jojo prompted him back to reality. He had drifted or had he – his blank look made Jojo laugh again. "The text or the message, Father, whatever it is?"

"Ah that," he muttered, absent-mindedly, and realized it was the text that had sent him into a shocked silence as it confirmed his sense of doom. His head ached.

"It's Daniel," he said, ever so silently, "captured by hooded man, 911, 666 Lanark Ave."

"Does he mean call 911?"

"I presume, and there is an address too, Jojo." She saw the shock on his face. "What shall I do?" he asked in a low voice, as if the word said aloud would alert the hooded one.

"Call the police commissioner, Father – this is serious." Her answer was crisp, clear and firm.

"Women – God bless you all," he said, and reached absent-mindedly in his shirt pocket for the commissioner's card that he had slipped in. "What makes you think he will answer my call?"

"Read the reports, Father. The press is going wild. Eglinton is still swarming with news crews, with a million unanswered questions. This city is flooded with rumours – it's on the brink of panic. There are conspiracy theories, galore. So many shootings, dead people, burnt cars, dead cop, clueless cops and just a single arrest. There have been no updates or any clear assurances from anyone. The government has already made a statement after the big van that came out – denying any external, terrorist activity. The mayor is having a field day, exaggerating his role while unsuccessfully trying to soothe nerves – and the poor commissioner is nowhere to be found. Your call might be just the thing he needs."

He nodded. Still staring at the message, he hit the speakerphone on his desk, and dialed the number, as Jojo stormed out to keep a chorus of approaching voices, away.

"Altar servers," she turned, and winked at him, "I'm sure looking for some treats." He was about to get up and point to the kitchen, when a low, powerful voice answered.

"It's Commissioner Ford." It was barely the 3rd ring.

He stared at the phone and then jumped forward, "Oh, er, hello commissioner, it's me, Father Brian from --,"

"I know. I hear an echo – are you on speaker?"

"I am. Just dialled out of --,"

"I suggest you pick up the handset, Father."

"Right," he said, grabbing the phone with fumbling hands.

"What can I do for you, Father Brian?" the tone was impatient; oddly personal, yet frightful.

"Daniel – I mean one of the guys that was with me all morning. Good guy, clean, I mean a parishioner --,"

"I get it – go on."

"Just got a text from him, commissioner – says he's been captured by the hooded man – obviously you know the evil one I mentioned. He's at --,"

"666 Lanark?"

"Yes – that one. How did --,"

"Thank you – please keep me posted if you hear anything further." Fr. Brian had barely asked the question but the commissioner was gone.

"They know the place already – I guess they are on their way there. Should I also --,"

"Seriously, Father Brian," Jojo exclaimed, throwing up her hands in frustration, "unless, you can be in 2 places, the main English service begins in an hour and playing cop at the same time…." She left her sentence hanging and walked out.

"God help me!" he blurted, to the empty air and laughed at his naivety. He was about to joke aloud, when a few faces appeared at his unguarded door. Trying desperately to wipe the embarrassing smile from his face, he bent low, pretending to dig into a drawer. "Please come in – will be up in a minute, I mean --,"

A moment later, he recoiled, not sure what hit him. Was it the smell of the cappuccino in the little cup that Jojo was slipping under his nose, or was it the words from the lady in front of him?

"Hello, Father, my name is Gloria – help me – save my son." The woman was pale. A helpless gloom seemed to descend on the room. Her face had bruises and a nasty black bump on her right temple. She shivered as she spoke.

"Sure Gloria – what happened, you seem to have taken a nasty --,"

"It's not about me, Father, and we don't have time."

"Absolutely, but right now I can't? The main Good Friday service --,"

"You will if I told you I am Dylan's mother," and with that she collapsed into the chair on the other side of his table. He stared from the coffee to the little biscotti next to it, to the woman whom Jojo was helping into the chair, to the lawyer who seemed to have appeared out of thin air.

"Hello, Father Brian, I'm Juanito!"

"Give him a minute to eat and drink, will you?" Jojo commanded, "or else we'll have no priest for the rest of the day."

"I'm fine for now, besides --,"

"Eat it, Father Brian – now." Like a little schoolboy, he gratefully reached for the little cup and downed it in one go. The coffee, like a magic potion, started to do all sorts of things inside his head and his body. Jojo had already taken the cup for a refill.

"Please, keep talking – there's too much happening but I promise you, I'm listening."

"They've arrested Dylan. It's on the news."

"I know," Fr. Brian answered, lost as to what he would say further.

"My son could never ever do such a thing, Father, you must help him."

"Oh, I will Glo – Gloria correct?" She nodded between sobs. "Except that at this moment I must put on my vestments, walk out, and lead about 1000 people through the Passion service of Our Lord."

"We know, Father, but if we don't do something soon, Dylan could be locked in until Tuesday morning."

"What would you like me to do, Glory, oops, sorry Gloria – what can a priest do at this stage?"

"You sat with the commissioner; you did a press conference with him this morning, Father. I am sure you can talk to him – there must be some horrible mistake."

"Oh – that I am sure of, but realistically why would the commissioner even listen to me. With a city on the edge..." His own reluctance to help, shocked him. He wanted to stop, correct it, but something just blocked his correction. Did he find the commissioner intimidating?

"We know you will find a way, Father," the lawyer finally spoke. "We will wait outside for you – we surely don't want to keep an entire congregation waiting, especially on Good Friday."

"Ok – I promise to do my best," he said, as Gloria stared into his face. He felt like a liar – an accomplice to the arrest. If only he could get to 666 Lanark.

* * *

A little further south, not too far from 666 Lanark, Terri groped around for the coffee cup in the holder next to him, keeping his eyes on the treacherous road, and the vanished black Honda. Perhaps Clare was in one of her idle, naughty moods hiding his cup.

"You know, it's unlawful to distract a cop at the helm of a cruiser, Blondie2," he chided, mischievously before realizing she was not there. She would never again occupy that seat. The thought hit him like a sucker punch in the stomach, making him double over and screech to a halt. It was a long time before he pulled aside after a nervous honk from a small fiat behind him.

"I will get you, you stinking, scheming, conjuring *sonofabitch*," he swore, before pulling out again.

Terri's fury increased with each passing signal. It was his third pass on the slope of Bathurst as it crossed Davenport. He knew the Indian had deftly given him the slip, infuriating him further. His first search had taken him all the way down to Queen Street, even though he knew they had given him the slip much earlier. Furious at a construction truck that lazily backed out of a construction site, Terri hit the full range of sirens and shot his way back up north. The terrified construction worker with the stop sign had barely dived out of his path.

"Bad cop," he told himself, as he apologized mentally to the terrified worker, now staring in shock at the speeding cruiser. It was only at the next signal, when he saw the flashing lights of an ambulance headed south, did he realize that his own beacons were creating an almighty racket.

"Think, Terri – think – it's not always about the action cop," he pushed himself. Driving back slowly down Vaughan for a fourth time, he crossed St. Clair. He was sure the black car had headed down further. Driving calmly, he scanned both sides of the road, looking for a clue. On a sudden impulse, he swung off the slope onto Austin Terrace, wondering if they had pulled over to the little hidden hill to shake him off. The snow covered houses seemed frigid and asleep. He saw a middle-aged, bathrobe clad man, run out. Curious, he watched the man dump a bag of recycling into a bin. The man stared at the cop glaring at him, and ran back in from the bitter cold. Embarrassed, he drove on, scanning the cars parked bumper to bumper and came to a dead end. The grand view of Casa Loma loomed ahead. He stepped out. The chill air would help. Looking far into the distance from the top of the hill, he scanned the city below. It was dead – whatever happened on Dufferin and Eglinton that morning, he wondered, as the thought of his Clare stabbed him again. Overcome with grief, he fell to his knees.

"Not fair, please, Dear Lord, turn back time, do something, this just can't be – just once I failed and she's dead."

The icy terrain seemed a relief as it shocked him back to reality. Sorrow turned once more to rage. He stood up and was about to enter the cruiser, when a dark glow filled up the sky, just beyond the slope. Davenport, Dupont and beyond, his cop instinct told him. Blinking, he looked again. Had he imagined it? It was there for an instant, and then was gone. Terri stared hard without blinking and saw it again. This time it seemed to connect with the grief and anger in his heart. Where had he seen it last – "Dufferin and Eglinton of course!" he swore, remembering the doomsday scene that had taken his Clare away from him. Like a clue, it beckoned. Jumping into the cruiser Terri slammed on the accelerator.

"Target at 12 O Clock – Blondie2 – armed and ready, Officer Cl --?" he asked the vacant seat, slammed the steering wheel with both fists, cursed one more time for her absence and swore, "Today, you're going to pay, you *bastard*."

The din from the ever-busy radio filled his ears. He had cut it out mentally. It barged through his defences again. And then, he heard it loud and clear. The directive could not have been clearer. The broadcast was coming on a high emergency level. "666 Lanark – Killer – Dufferin – Eglinton – Kidnapped – hooded. Repeat --," the words began to form a pattern in his ear. Hitting the display on his monitor, he punched in the address and stared – why did it feel like the end – as if the dark cloud had beckoned him in a special way. The broadcast only made it clearer. Hitting the sirens once more, Terri sped, "For my Clare – for Blondie2 – one last time," he said, and released the safety of Clare's gun lying on the empty seat.

Sirens flashing, horns blaring, he turned left onto Bathurst, skidding all the way to the other side. The winter tires found a grip and sent him hurtling down the icy slope, and then left onto Davenport. The cruiser swung from side to side, desperately fighting for a grip on the icy road, but Terri did not take his foot off the accelerator.

He hit DuPont and there it was again, the dark cloud. He was about to swing right, when the radio swung into life again, "Do not approach Lanark Avenue – repeat – do not approach." Terri slammed his brakes in frustration, skid headlong into a snow-covered bush, and watched the street before him. He could not remember if he had ever driven down Lanark Avenue or answered a call there. It seemed like a long dark tunnel. There was no sign of life.

"Come, dark cloud," he beckoned, fearing what evil awaited him. The dark cloud was there, drifting on the ground, alive this time.

"Cats!" he swore. "Damn cats, millions of them," he shouted. Tails raised like long sticks, they wandered about, revealing the white, snow-covered ground, occasionally. He tried to poke a way through the melee wondering what he could do, when a large tomcat leaped on the bonnet, scowling angrily. It was not long before Terri could see nothing. Hundreds of cats leapt on and simply sprawled about on his front and rear screen. "So be it," Terri swore, and stepped on the accelerator. There was nothing much to live for – death or revenge – if he was lucky. The wheels spun on the ice but the cruiser stayed put. Stuck in the bush, he radioed.

"Lanark Avenue swarming with hundreds of rogue cats – repeat – cats – call animal control – and yes – lots of them." Grabbing his gun, he jumped out but his feet never made it to the ground as he tripped over the cats.

"You stinking felines – I've handled bigger stuff," he shouted, but realized he simply kept on sinking to the ground. Memories from some doomsday movie flooded him as the cats buried him with their sheer numbers. He felt a scratch, a paw then realized the pain had been too severe for him to even notice it. Like a soul, separated from the body in the instance of death, realizing a second later that death was nearly complete.

Terri tried one last time but darkness engulfed him. He figured he was buried under a few hundred cats, simply suffocating him off. He saw the last bit of daylight and felt the gun slip out of his hands as a million fangs clamped onto this hands and throat. In his panic and pain, he failed to fire off even a single round. Thoughts of Clare suddenly filled his mind. Maybe he could join her on the other side – his soul suddenly longed to be with her in death.

"So long, Officer Terri, so long," he bid himself farewell and surrendered to the mass of fur, fangs, and claws engulfing him. He imagined there would be a bright light, just as he had heard from those with a near death experience. Maybe Clare would be there to welcome him – in an angel's garb – with real wings maybe.

Instead, he felt the darkness begin to fade away, it was turning gray, and the massive load on his body was lightening up, until it was gone. Was he dead or alive – on the other side? Terri stretched his hand and felt the cold metal of his gun – the most reassuring feeling. Uncertain, he stood, he was alive.

His face and arms were covered with bruises, scratches, and bites. His fists ached from the fierce grasp of the cats. They knew what they were about, he thought. He was very much alive and on Lanark Avenue. Something or someone had scattered away from the cats. He saw a massive, yellow hued man in a strange tunic, walking away. With each swing of the man's staff, the cats disappeared. Suddenly the man was gone too. A yellow cloud that remained slowly dissipated away.

At the end of the road, freed from the presence of the stranger, he saw the black car. Terri swore it had been the weirdest day of his life or just the evillest one. The blood rushed to his head once more and his anger returned.

"I owe you one, stranger," he blew a kiss in the direction the stranger had vanished. He punched his radio, "At hell's door!" and ran ahead.

XXV

The Sacrifice

Trisha's eyes popped open like a doll that had suddenly been propped up – except that she seemed immobile, and on her back. A massive, white abyss blanketed here, inside and outside. She felt no sensation, no consciousness nor any recollection of where she was. A sense of nothingness and helplessness pervaded her entire being. Why had the image of a doll popped into her head she wondered? It came right back against the white nothingness that seemed the only reality around her. The doll was a rag doll – an image of her. Voodoo – her brain prompted. An evil curse chanting voodoo man was inserting pins in her back as he muttered a chant. "No," her mind screamed, terrified, "please don't." It all seemed unreal yet her back could feel the sting of the pain. Her back ached; it seemed to be locked down. Where was she? How long had she been there? Eyes staring wider, she tried to look around, yet her eyes seemed to look just up – locked open just like the rest of her body. Jack Sparrow, the name propped up. Was it Black Beard's voodoo doctor twisting her arm? She tried to feel her arm but it seemed sensationless. Her nose twitched a little itch. It became a desperately irritating one, which she wanted to scrub brutally – she could not. Something held her hands firmly in place. Was she in Davy Jones' locker – on the underside of the world – condemned in a vast, endless, white desert – her ship marooned on an endless white, waterless, sandy ocean?

Ocean – it reminded her of water. "Water," she suddenly screamed, "water, water," she begged. The words barely came forth. Her throat was parched. She imagined a dead, dry cactus growing up her throat, choking off any movement or sound, both inwards and outwards. Trisha tried to lift her head one more time, it was heavy, drugged she thought. She tried her hands once more – they were firmly bound to the side of a narrow bed she was laid out on. Her feet were the same. Her back ached from the rigid position she had been strapped in.

"Water," her mind screamed again, as she became a little more conscious. Slowly it dawned on her that she was bound to a table. Helpless, she gave it one last meaningless tug to break free. She knew it would do nothing. Fully awake now, the room came into view. It seemed like a hospital, an operation theater, with banks of lights overhead. She looked into one bright light and shut her eyes and the darkness felt good. Darkness – it seemed a recent scary feeling. The street, the shootings, and the chaos slowly came back. She remembered being swept up by the dark, hooded man – trapped like a little bird in a dark blanket. Trisha wondered whether to scream or beg for help? She could do neither. Trisha simply closed her eyes and sobbed bitterly – helplessly.

"Oh Dear God of Ezekiel," she prayed for the first time in her life, "if you exist, help me, I don't want to die."

* * *

Down the corridor, Yokatherine fought the darkness swallowing up the building. She had to stay conscious. Every last ray of light that had lit up the deceptively, bright corridors, was consumed by the evil mist. It felt like death was around the corner – a dark, depressing feeling began driving her insane. She played their last

conversation in her head to stay sane as they were being
borne up the corridor.

"I feel so wretched and depressed," Ezekiel had
cried out, "like wanting to just lay down and die."

"Courage, my friend," Daniel reassured him.

"But why?" Ezekiel exclaimed, bursting into tears.

"Because this is hell – be strong," Yokatherine and
Daniel responded in unison. Yokatherine pressed back and
felt with relief the bodies of the other two as the three of
them were being carried away. Daniel's touch filled her with
a renewed strength. This was the battle they had to face –
there were no shortcuts. Would this finally be the day they
would destroy the hooded man, and the evil he had
dispensed down the centuries? She prayed harder, "Protect
us – help us – be our strength, Lord," chanting louder as the
many tentacle-like hands gripped her harder.

"Just do it, send it out quick," she remembered
Daniel urge Ezekiel, frantically. She sensed what they were
up against. The front door had slammed shut all of its own
and Yokatherine knew the house of evil was ready for its
final grab. The elusive thorn – the powerful one from the
head of the Son of Man – the one that had bled for the sins
of the world, and had conquered sin and death, was now in
the den of the evil one. "This is your end – this is where it
all ends for you – this is where the reign of my Lord will
vanquish the last of you," she shouted defiantly, as a million,
invisible arms slapped her.

She felt the two warriors behind her. "Warriors,"
she liked the term, "I am a warrior too for you, my Lord
Jesus," she prayed, "use me as you wish today – even if it is
my life that is needed. Oh, how I long to be with you this
day." Ezekiel had already been overpowered. She felt his
body slumped against her at the back. "Brave lad," she
prayed, "be strong, the final hour is here."

Daniel, on the other hand, amazed her. She felt his body move in vigorous bursts of energy and knew he had found a way to take the battle to the forces of evil. With each swing of his arm, she heard a million, terrifying shrieks. Sadly, it only delayed the enemy, which came back at them with renewed vigor. She felt the sudden surge of a wild, platonic energy sweep through Daniel's body, as his feet brushed the coat left behind. It wasn't a coincidence; the black, leather coat had been left there intentionally.

And then, it struck her. "Daniel, you still have to face your biggest test yet. It won't be a blazing battle with the fires of hell spewing over – rather it will come in the form of --,"

"A woman, I know. The photographer. Amanda."

"Oh the evil one," she swore and panicked. "Be strong, Daniel. The lust of the flesh, the longing of a worldly heart, and a weak soul distracted by the pleasures of this world, will be tough tests for the Thornbearer."

Not feeling so good suddenly she closed her eyes, prayed, and then passed out as a particularly nasty set of arms angrily grabbed her by the neck and smashed her head into the back of Ezekiel's head. The smashing of the two skulls ached – she tried to reach up with her hands to soothe the pain – but they were already bound.

* * *

Daniel gently drifted out of the most beautiful sleep he could remember. He seemed to be wrapped in the softest satin sheets. He stirred gently and felt the sheets slide over him. He felt their soft touch against his body. He knew he was naked and erect, wildly erect. The warm glow swept him once more. Sunshine? Was he on a beach in Punta Cana – being massaged by a team of masseurs as the sun set? He gently opened his eyes expecting someone to slip a sweet

Coco Loco into his hands, "A little extra coconut and rum —
especially for you, sir," he seemed to hear a voice say.

He knew he was smiling broadly — it seemed like
paradise. Gently, he turned over to his side expecting the
massive expanse of a turquoise green ocean to fill his vision.
It didn't. Instead, he smelt a wildly, sensual fragrance. It
excited his body even more. Half sleepy, he reached out for
the one who would satiate him. "Oh let it be a wild,
passionate ride," he corrected himself. His hands felt the
empty air.

Surprised, Daniel opened his bleary eyes knowing
that no one other than Michelle could ever answer that call.
About to dismiss the fantasy, he looked through hazy eyes —
she was there, curled up on a couch, seemingly naked. Her
slender, white body curled up in a black, velvet love seat.
She was staring at him, longingly. Seeing him awake she
turned fully towards him as Daniel nearly erupted. His gaze
traveled up the long, white legs. Her right leg was gently
bent over to cover her nakedness. Her long, black hair fell
all over her breasts, covering them. Her head rested on its
side, over her curled left hand, above her shoulder. She
stared back at him with the softest of looks before reaching
out to him with her right hand, still too far away.

Daniel's heart raced wildly as he saw her long black
hair fall away — yet his eyes remained glued to hers.
"Honey," he was about to call her, when the shock set in. It
wasn't Michelle. "You must be a dream — my wildest
fantasy," he whispered hoarsely, as his body began to
recognize the woman who had captured his soul. Confused,
he looked around, slowly taking in his surroundings.

She sensed it too and immediately jumped up to
walk across to him. His hands fell away and despite the wild
lust that gripped him, he pleaded, "No, please stay away."
Where was he? Punta Cana, Cuba, Goa - a dream, a fantasy
come true - was he dead - in another life? The warmth

seemed real – his body told him. The refreshing feel was genuine – his mind told him he should be utterly tired. He put his left hand down to push himself up for a better look. He expected it to sink into the sand, instead, a wild bolt of lightning swept his body. Daniel froze, immobilized – a million, needle like, pain barbs jolted his body. Somewhere deep in his dizzy head, he felt an intense ache and he collapsed back onto the bed – his left hand awkwardly crushed underneath. This time the pain nearly caused him to topple out of the bed. The warm, comfy feeling was gone as his body burned and then broke into a million rivulets of sweat, drenching him. The left hand would not give up – immobilized under him. An intensely, painful scream wanted to burst out. Daniel knew he had never screamed, nor would he now.

He was about to pass out when he felt the soft touch of her hand. He looked up and saw her stand over him. She had drawn back her hair and stood over him, defiantly naked. Daniel looked into the hauntingly beautiful face that had mesmerized him. His body screamed to grab her – his wildest fantasy come true – his hands moved a fraction to grab the teasing breasts before his soul screamed, "NO," one more time. His shout was real – a blast that tore through the room. The palm that flashed out of the soft satin sheets struck out like a ram, sending the woman crashing back into the love seat. She sat dazed.

The woman looked at him again from the love seat. There was no pain, or hatred or loathing despite his violent rejection. Instead, he looked into her eyes and loved her one more time – she was in a daze. Her eyes stared blankly into the space above him. "I'm sorry, angel," he spoke soothingly, "I know some magnetic attraction draws us – but that is as far as it will go – I don't know why? My body, my being, longs for you. It's as if I want to lose myself in your arms – melt away in your body – yet my very soul screams no."

Daniel paused. She did not respond. She lay fallen on the seat, naked, spread-eagled, hardly bothering to cover her rejected body. He looked into her face and knew she was in a daze – hypnotized – blank. Something seemed to trap her attention. She continued to stare in the space above him. Daniel slowly let himself down flat on the bed, aware of a fierce pain somewhere in his body. Each movement chastising him for the massive pain shooting through his body. Like a dead rock somewhere inside, his body felt the pain and death of a part of him locked up. He lowered his eyes on to the hand, still partially trapped below him. His mind rose to the object of her stare, knowing that something behind him held her attention. Something behind him had appeared and controlled her.

Daniel closed his eyes as a powerful surge of energy, and anxiety, and fear, burst through his body. He looked down at his left hand and knew the source of his strength. "Lead us not into temptation," he prayed. He would have stopped but the years of prayer made him continue, "but deliver us from all evil. Amen."

He paused again and knew whom the woman was staring at. He looked up at the windows behind the woman. It was still there, the clear sky, the one he had imagined as the glorious sky above an endless, stretching ocean. It turned dark as he watched it – as if it had been invaded by a massive swarm of bees. Suddenly, he was back at the church – in the chaos as people had screamed and run about like panicked, headless chickens. Daniel closed his eyes and prayed for strength – he tried to move his left hand gently under the sheets and felt his left fist like a massive stone – dead. "Help me, Lord," he prayed, and felt the dark clouds clear. The woman on the couch sobbed. He saw her right hand frantically look for something to cover her nakedness

– while covering her breasts with the left. Had the hold of the evil one broken over her – he doubted it. The sky turned dark again. The bright, sunny window became a dark mirror and in that moment, Daniel saw the reflection of the hooded man standing right over him. The fiery, blood red eyes stood out in the full reflection. Daniel knew it was time to look fearlessly into the face of evil standing right over him.

He distracted himself – tried to remember where he had passed out. He remembered Yokatherine and Ezekiel – wondering where they were, or how they were being held? He remembered the black, leather jacket that had swept his feet. And now here he was, after what seemed an eternity, at the mercy of the hooded man. There had to be a way. Daniel thought of rolling over and landing on his feet ready to attack with his thorn hand. "Foolish!" he told himself, before he had even given the idea any thought. This was no place for a violent stand. He remembered his struggles as he was carried up the steps and the wild swinging arms.

"My thorn arm," he thought, trying to come up with an action plan still. Then in a flash, as if some trigger device had fired up, he swung his thorn hand wondering why the hooded man had not taken away the thorn, as he lay knocked out. It swung in thin air as a hideous laugh filled the room.

Daniel leaped onto his feet as the satin sheets fell away. "Clothes – I need my clothes," he shouted as a chill gripped his naked body. A hand held out his clothes. She was naked as well. "They are too powerful," she said in a soft voice. It was still a caring voice. He cursed himself for still trying to reach out to her. She sensed it. In a flash, their bodies reached out and enveloped each other. They were back in the riot, just the 2 of them, holding each other in a timeless embrace; two bodies wrapped as one. Daniel knew how close he was to losing it all.

"I know how you feel – it's strange," she said as he pulled away from her. "My life was lonely, bitter, empty, broke, penniless…" – she paused – snickered at herself and continued, "then came a flood of everything good – money, challenge, an assignment, equipment and you – above all, you, and for the first time, my heart simply surrendered."

"As did mine, angel. I'm sorry, I should have controlled myself. I belong to someone else – forever." He saw the pain in her face as he said the words. "I'm naked, Amanda," he said to fill the strange situation. "Me too," she replied quietly, "I like angel though, the way you addressed me first." Embarrassed and blushing, he quickly drew on his trousers and pulled on his shirt.

"I like what I saw – I could die for it," she said with a laugh.

"As would I – you are the stuff my wildest fantasies are made of." She blushed. He gently took her clothes and dressed her, "it's as if I've done this – cared for you all my life." The sun was shining again in his mind and for a second, everything else was forgotten.

"I know we would be so happy together," she said as her tears flowed once again.

"And you can be," another deep resonating voice filled the room. The joy was gone. She shivered at its sound and Daniel swung around protectively, shielding her behind himself. "She is made for you, down to the last cell, physically and emotionally – nothing stops you. Take her and leave."

"And, who would you be to give her away?" Daniel questioned, suddenly encouraged to engage the hooded man, yet recoiling at his nearness. The hood still remained in place, and the face was a strange mix. Somewhere deep within, Daniel sensed a terrifying darkness waiting to envelop the world.

"Words well chosen, my friend. Traditionally, I would, in fact, be the one to give her away."

"Her father – no way."

Daniel felt her shudder at the words in revulsion. "Not much she can do about that," the man continued, "though she does not understand the power she possesses. Take her and leave if you must. Save your angel before I introduce her to her true, evil power and destiny." Daniel knew the price that would be asked.

"Sure," he said, reaching out his right hand to her. She responded quickly. "I'd like to take my friends too," Daniel teased.

"But of course," the man responded. Turning around, he grabbed a remote and a bank of monitors sprang to life. Daniel stared horrified. Trisha lay stretched on an operating table. A man in a doctor's coat yanked the sheet off her. She was strapped to a stark metal stretcher. White bands crisscrossed her body now covered in an apron. An array of medical instruments lay on little white tables, ready for a surgery. "You can take her if you like – intact. We won't cut her open, nor take her little fetus, nor her life. Both rather priceless and juicy, I might add, though valueless in comparison to what I seek today."

"What does he seek?" Amanda asked quietly from the back.

"This," Daniel said holding out his left hand. His fist was shut tight. Daniel struggled to open it. With his right hand, he yanked open the fist, one finger at a time. It was a hideous sight. The hand was blue – puffed up to 3 times its original size. The thorn stuck out of it like a distinct, little black arrow. She gasped at the sight, nearly throwing up. On the other side of the room, the hooded man recoiled. Deep fear filled his face, as he shielded his eyes and cowered.

"You can't even look at it, and yet you seek it?" Daniel challenged as the man shivered.

"Leave it there and go, take your friends, it will only bring you suffering," a quivering voice answered.

"And that I will gladly accept just as my savior."

"Want to play God?" the hooded man teased.

"No, just his most humble servant."

"What is it?" Amanda asked from the back, holding him by the waist with both her hands and peeping over.

"In simple words, an actual thorn, from the actual crown of thorns, that was thrust brutally on my Lord's head." She gasped. "It can't be! Why does he need it – why does the man want it so badly?"

"This man is your father," the hooded man thundered as the house shook under a violent tremor. "We were born to serve the Prince of Darkness. Great are our powers, great will be his reign, but first, we must take this thorn – a literal thorn that stands in our way."

"Take it if you dare," Daniel teased, and stepped forward. He expected the man to cower further, fight maybe; instead, he reached for the remote and stabbed it hurriedly. The picture changed – it was dark – in a few moments the picture adjusted and in the faint light, Daniel saw Yokatherine on her knees. Her long white hair was pulled away and held like a leash. Her head was held down on a tree stump by a dark-robed woman. Daniel had been there – Satan's chapel in the basement. A man stood with a heavy axe over her head.

"My master would like that as well – she's old and near death but a long-awaited trophy."

Yokatherine stirred at the words. "Daniel," she shouted, trying to lift her head. It was slammed back ruthlessly. "I hear you, and I know you can hear me too," she groaned painfully, "don't give in – my life would be crowned if it were taken for my Lord."

"Quiet," the hooded man roared.

"Daniel," Yokatherine groaned again, as the woman holding her reached down to cover her mouth, "the Lord's thorn cannot be taken away – it has to be given away willingly, by surrendering your soul, be strong --,"

The hooded man jabbed the remote once again and the picture was gone. Daniel had expected the picture to swing to Ezekiel, but it did not. He was puzzled yet happy. Perhaps Ezekiel didn't matter – they would just let him go. Maybe Ezekiel would get help. He wondered if Fr. Brian would understand his message and send help quickly. He looked down at his thorn hand and realized it had folded up into a locked fist once again. Somehow, he knew the Lord's thorn would save them and destroy this evil man as it had done down the ages.

Daniel prayed in his heart. "Help me, Lord – show me the way," he begged. He thought he heard the distant wail of a siren, then another. Had there been more shootings? Had his message reached Fr. Brian, and from him the police commissioner? He listened again and the silence of the desolate city was back.

He was about to give up when a tiny spark rose deep within. He was a little boy once again. The monsoons were rampaging across India. His memories recreated the faint whiff of the damp, flooded earth on a rainy day. For little boys like him, there was water everywhere to play in. A warm glow filled his heart. He was looking down at a million streams. Tiny little fish were trying to swim upstream, but a large boulder blocked their path. Bending down into the ankle deep water, Daniel lifted the rock. The waters gushed to fill in the void as the fish found their way through. The simple happiness of his childhood flooded him. Daniel knew instantly, he didn't have to wait for the cops. "The Lord is my help. I will be his servant to rescue my friends and destroy this evil."

He saw Amanda staring at him. "Goodbye, Angel!" he whispered softly, boldly holding her in a deep embrace as if he owned her completely. She heard and understood it, yet clawed him desperately one last time. He kissed her deeply on her forehead as her tears welled up. "We have no future."

He saw a final look of rejection turn to hurt, then anger, and then to revenge. She was the one sought after, not one who took rejection from men. She had given her mind, her heart and her soul – completely – it had been rejected. The hooded man smiled, his daughter was ready to take up her mantle. Revenge was a perfect start.

The three stared at each other and then with a flick of the hooded man's wrist, darkness flooded the room and the building.

XXVI

The final battle

Little Amanda felt herself float on the gentle breeze on the farm. The smell of manure tickled her nose. Green fields stretched endlessly into the distance. Scattered patches of forests interrupted the green at various angles. Corrals with high fences stuck out like sore spots on the otherwise immaculate landscape. She turned to the hedge covered, wooden railing next to her. The enclosed cows grazed lazily as their young one frolicked about.

The sudden, angry mooing of a bull made her draw back. She barely stepped back in time from being gored by it through the fence. Her shock turned to rage. In a wild outburst, she flung out her little hands. Something invisible slammed the cows. Some fell and others were thrown about. The herd fled in wild panic causing a minor stampede. Amanda wriggled her hands and smashed the cows like little puppets. Aghast, at what she had done and unable to understand it, she fled indoors into the warm bosom of her grandmother.

It was a long time ago. This time Amanda let the memory play out in its entirety. She gazed around it was dark. She saw Daniel open the door and crawl out of the room under the cover of the darkness. She saw him clear as daylight and in anger flung out her arms again. He barely slipped out before the doors slammed behind him with a mighty thud. "Filthy worm, run while you can," she growled, enjoying the feeling of power. The growl startled her. From somewhere deep within a real animal surfaced, a bear or a wolf, she did not know. It had been awakened – its time had come.

The thud of the slammed door took her back to another time and place, not too long back. On a lonely mountaintop, in the dead of the night, on a bright moon lit night, she had walked out defiantly into the symphony of the howling wolves. Unable to bear her incarceration any longer – waiting for the moment the wolves would break through and tear her to pieces. Her arrival outside the cabin had caught them unawares.

In a blind rage, she had waved her arms through the air like a scythe and slaughtered half a dozen of them. Their shrieking yelps in the pangs of death had brought her back to reality, making her flee back into the darkness of the cabin before sleep overtook her, tucked deep within the depths of the warm, animal fur that was her bed.

The bear? Had she shot it? With her Nikon or with the Lee? She was not sure. From deep within, she had drawn out a strange power, just like the little Amanda on the farm, and then hidden it away, scared at its realization. The hooded man had sent her there to find more than just the perfect shot.

*   *   *

"You cannot hide from it, my little one," the hooded man spoke softly in her ear from behind, as his fingers drummed on her shoulders. "Nay, you must accept it, master it and then use it," he sang softly as his arms danced, weaving a deadly web of evil. "For too long have you suppressed it," he sang, "delay any longer and it will destroy you from within." She sensed the power of evil and inhaled it deeply as their spirits finally united.

"One more time – who are you and from where do I get this power?"

"Call me father – or Papa – as you did in the few times your wretched mother let me come close to you. That's why you spent all those years at your grandmother's – protected from me."

"Then what stopped your powers, or mine, from reaching out to each other?"

"The stigmata – your wretched grandmother's stigmata. Those cursed wounds each year, surfacing every single Good Friday. She guarded you with it and left you under its protection for a long, long time. If not, you my daughter, destined to be more powerful than all the past ones in our line, would have served the master well a lot earlier."

"And the master is?"

"The Prince of Darkness, Lord of all evil, Lucifer."

"Since when have we served him?" she asked – a violent shiver of anticipation racking her body.

"Since the time that wretched man from Galilee walked this earth. Since the time the first of our forefathers personally wove that crown of thorns for the Son of Man, the Christ. In different forms, clans, and places, our family, our ancestors have been his soldiers. You are the last of that line. You must bear a child for our line to continue."

"And who --," Amanda stopped, sensing the answer.

"The Thornbearer will provide that great seed as you have already sensed. Destiny brought about this day and your instant attraction for a reason. The thorn and the seed tonight – then our purpose will have been served."

"What do I do?" Amanda asked, "Father?" she added hesitantly.

"Just feel the power," he bellowed, stretching his arms out. The room trembled; shriek's and cries of the damned filled the room. "Go on a rampage. The old whore in the chapel, sacrifice her. The purer they are the greater the strength you derive. A human sacrifice is long overdue; the master needs one – from you." His evil face was inches from hers and this time she felt no fear.

"And Daniel – the Thornbearer," she quickly corrected herself.

"He turned out to be a lot more resolute than I imagined. I thought he would fall for your charms but I have a feeling he has crossed that line. We must draw it out from him some other way," the hooded man whispered, softly enjoying the slow conversation with his daughter – many a man would he conquer with her vile charms.

"The old lady," Amanda gasped in delight, "she said it must be given willingly. I saw them; they seem to like each other."

"Then go, daughter, go and do what must be done," the hooded man clapped with delight, "hurry, it is already past the 6th hour. At midnight, the thorn will vanish, deep into the bearer, only to surface this day next year. We must not fail our master this year, we have never been closer."

The hooded man closed his eyes and pondered. Another failure, and that night he would be brutally destroyed, cast home in the raging fires – especially now that his daughter was ready to assume her mantle. Only success would guarantee him living beyond to see her glory. He saw her pore deep within him – sensing what he feared.

"I will not fail you, father," she whispered softly, with a bow. A gentle push of her hands in the air, and she found the doors swinging open. Daniel's trail blazed in the dark, she could smell it. "But of course," she laughed, he was headed down to the chapel, to the old whore. Her nose caught his Yves St. Laurent Poure Homme Sport and lit her body into a rapturous delight once more. "He's still my man, you white haired *bitch*," she cursed, feeling her eyes spew fire, "even if I slaughter him at the end." Despite her words, her longing for him only grew into a wilder obsession. "This time I will take you as I please, my Daniel," she swore, "and you will pleasure me."

* * *

Daniel felt the darkness engulf him as he slipped out of the door. A deadly, fierce, evil shadow followed him. He knew it came from her – puzzled, he ran. He sensed he had been in one of the operation theaters – the steps lay just beyond. The darkness was more than just the absence of light – he felt the gloom and the depression. He knew the place had been cast and sealed in an evil shell. A blast of angry voices greeted him. He sensed they reached out to him but were unable to hold him.

Gripping the banister, he started to leap down the stairs. His right palm burned from the friction of the tight grip, yet, it was his only connection to reality. The first landing came and then the second. Daniel knew he had reached the main floor. There was no sign of the main door or the bright daylight that had shone in from there. Nor was there any sign of the white coated African man. He turned right sharply, knowing the steps to Satan's chapel lay at the end of that short, circular corridor.

A wild screeching of voices greeted him. "Kill him, kill him, kill the Thornbearer," a shrill voice blasted its high pitch cry in his right ear. Deafened and in pain, Daniel covered his right ear but put his hand out again instantly to keep his bearing. The wall was icy cold.

"Fools, has hell lost its fire?" he taunted the voices.

"Ha," they hissed back in anger, "it will burn tonight, cursed one. It will burn with the wretched thorn and the blood of all you mongrels that so willingly wandered in."

The little exchange raised his spirits. Daniel knew the voices were not of the living. He felt no fear. "The Lord

is my Shepherd, there is nothing I shall want," he prayed as
he sensed the end of the wall. A little towards the center was
the start of the red-carpeted steps.

"Here I come," he whispered, as the smell of a
queer smoke filled his nostrils. The feeling of dread and
gloom filled him once more. Fear, like a real person,
enveloped him in a giant embrace and loud booms shattered
his eardrums. "Is this hell?" he wondered shivering
violently.

From somewhere within, Yokatherine's face filled
him with grace and he continued the psalm, "Even though I
walk through the valley of darkness, no evil will I fear, for
you are there with your crook and your staff --," he prayed
hesitatingly. "What would you have done, my Lord Jesus?"
he prayed.

The first step under his feet materialized too early.
The little fumble sent him tumbling down yet again. He
reached out desperately to grab something. He felt
something fleshy. A human, he was sure. The human
reached back and grabbed him, clawed him. Daniel tumbled
a bit more and then fell headlong as shoulder after shoulder
violently hit the steps. The other human was tumbling too.
They reached the bottom.

Daniel's body ached sharply, as if it had taken a
hundred blows. His thorn hand quivered with pain. "Is this
what you felt, my Lord Jesus, with each fall on the way to
Calvary?" he prayed, as a heavy blow landed on his chin.
Daniel's head banged on the wall behind him and bounced
off. A weird taste filled his mouth.

"Blood," he was sure. His entire face felt splattered
with it. "Thank God for drywall," Daniel muttered, stunned
and dazed. "A brick wall and it would have been the end of
me."

Daniel heard the other one panting – preparing to
attack again. Would the punch come again with the right

hand or the left hand? Should he fight back or should he offer the other cheek, nay chin? The martyr thoughts vanished instantly as the figure rushed him flat into the wall. Daniel felt the rage from the other. Its left elbow pinned his neck into the wall. He was sure the right fist was preparing to swing into his stomach.

"Fight," he told himself, "fight, you are the last hope for so many here." There was only one thing to do. Daniel arched back as best as he could and slammed his right knee into his attacker's groin.

"Uuuuhh - Evil Bastar…." the attacker swore, falling away, howling in pain – choking on the rest of his words. It was enough to light up Daniel's spirits. "The voice," he gasped, from his choked and aching throat, "Oh my God, the voice," he groaned in delight as the name failed him as always. "Speak, speak," his mind urged, "speak before the attacker recovers and attacks again."

"It's me, Daniel, for God's sake, stop, it's --,"

"Daniel?" the voice groaned in pain, and Daniel knew his knee had done serious damage.

"Ezekiel," the name popped on Daniel's lips and mind simultaneously.

"Oh my God, I am so sorry, Daniel," Ezekiel groaned. Daniel sensed the voice coming from below him and knelt. Expectant arms reached out to him and he hugged Ezekiel, half-weeping with joy. "My brother – we nearly killed each other."

"How, where, what --," the half questions flew from Daniel's mouth, "never mind, we are in --,"

"Grave danger," Ezekiel finished the sentence. Daniel felt Ezekiel's face, it was sticky as well. He was almost about to recoil when it struck him, blood? Just like his own.

"You're badly injured."

"Yes, but never mind, let's focus. I was tied up but the poncho man freed me. They have armed men and women spreading out on the top floors. Trisha is strapped to an operation table. Whatever is here is desperate. They will slaughter her along with the baby."

"What drew you down here?"

"Just fleeing. I was powerless against whatever was guarding Trisha. It's scary, evil – I fled down here as something wild chased me."

There was no time to continue as every cell in their bodies quivered with an eerie chill. Something was approaching. Even in the dark, they felt its presence. Like helpless little sheep, they felt a fierce dragon hover over them. In a flash, Daniel knew what it was.

"Quick into the chapel – that's where it will all end."

"But that's where they may be the most powerful."

"Well, then that's where we'll strike the head of the serpent – finish it all."

They felt their way into darkened room holding on to each other.

"We just walked into the Lion's den, more like put our heads in its mouth," Ezekiel whispered, with a faltering voice. "Oh my Lord, take me quickly. Don't let this Satan…," he stuttered.

Instead, Daniel prayed a psalm for him, "Save me from the traps that are set for me, the snares of evildoers. That is Psalm 141, Ezekiel. Do you know why we are still alive?" Daniel said, with a sudden, quiet, confident voice. "And for that matter," he suddenly shouted, "as you all just heard – do you know why today, on this holy day, when our Lord conquered you with his Crucifixion – why on this day – why here and now you are powerless against us? It's because in this left hand I bear the one, true, original thorn that pierced my Lord's head – a testimony to the fact that his extreme suffering vanquished you evil relics a long time back."

"Well spoken," a chilling voice spoke from the door with a slow, mocking applause. "Well spoken, Thornbearer, but alas the time has come for us insignificant humans to change the course of history." Daniel knew the voice.

"I would like some light for our human friends to witness their end," Amanda spoke in a voice that Daniel knew had nothing to do with the woman who loved him.

A match flared, it hissed angrily as someone held it to a torch that burst into life with a deafening roar. The chapel looked changed. The wooden walls were lined with dark, robed figures that held pitchforks in their hands. Daniel and Ezekiel covered their eyes as the sudden light from the roaring torch fire jabbed at their darkened eyes. More torches were lit from the burning one.

"So, let's cut short this drama, Daniel," the now sweet, female voice enticed, "a thorn is all we seek."

"We? Oh beautiful Amanda," Daniel laughed hoping to mock her, "do you seriously believe I will do that – put the fate of humanity in your hands?"

"You will if you can bear to see the fate of one other," Amanda challenged. She seemed to direct their eyes magnetically to the center of the room where a brilliant white spot had been vying for his attention.

"But of course," Daniel sighed painfully, trying to reach out to Yokatherine. Her regal, white hair lay spread-eagled on the floor behind her head that lay flattened on the chopping block under a pair of powerful hands. A black robed figure stood over her. The axe they had seen earlier, suddenly seemed massive, its handle – long, its half-moon blade glistening in the firelight.

"The blade thirsty. The master angry. No offering long time," the executioner bellowed in a deep guttural voice that echoed. He could have been a giant or an animal or a demon thought Daniel.

"Then strike," Amanda's cold evil voice spurted out, almost relishing the savage act that was to follow. The axe swung as Daniel and Ezekiel stood immobilized. They heard the thud as the axe struck the wooden block, but a presence had already yanked Yokatherine away.

"Not so fast. I have not waited a lifetime just to see my daughter slaughtered before my very eyes."

The poncho man stood gripping Yokatherine protectively in his embrace like a little doll. Daniel was sure the poncho man wasn't human. His skin was yellowed, and a pale, deathly appearance emanated from him.

"Oh, you half dead relic," one of the acolytes chided and moved forward with a pitchfork but Amanda's hand stopped it. She hissed in anger at Yokatherine's father.

"How dare you – how dare you obstruct my sacrifice?" Raising her hands in worship she chanted, "Oh Prince of Darkness, accept my sacrifice and grant me the privilege of being in your service." She turned towards Yokatherine's father and punched the air angrily. Daniel and Ezekiel felt its blast as they were slammed into the robed figures, but father and daughter stood unmoved.

"I have been dead a long time, stupid girl. Slaughtered and brought back into your father's service. I have been evil in his service for too long, but today, my daughter's grace has saved me."

He turned to Daniel, "A long time ago, many poor desperate men like me sold our souls to the devil. The reward – to find the vast gold buried in the mountain and free our families from the evil of poverty. It was a mistake. We became the living dead – enslaved in his evil service. I followed my daughter here, to this land, with a vow to my evil master that one day, I would bring this pure daughter of mine to him – a trophy he has long desired. Instead, she has saved me from eternal damnation."

"And the cats. There was something about them, and you?" Daniel asked.

Yokatherine spoke, "My father, a prisoner of the hooded man, has waited for a long time for this day to win his freedom. The entire street is filled with souls that the hooded man and his ancestors have enslaved over the years. The cats, they are his army. Today, the thorn will free their souls from the evil spell that binds them."

"Stupid woman," Amanda shouted and flung her arms but once more but the pale figure enveloped his daughter. "The purity of my daughter will not be tainted by you." Turning to Daniel he said, "Leave, while I hold these evil ones here. Take my daughter with you to safety."

Daniel looked at the door, it was shut. Amanda stood before it, the robed figures behind her. Daniel noticed one of them whisper something to her and hand over a spear. It was long with a razor sharp, glistening, diamond shaped head. Daniel could have sworn it was one of the roman spears that had pierced the side of Christ.

"How about this, my dead friend?" Amanda asked with an evil grin. "You know this, don't you?" All eyes turned to Yokatherine's father. It was a resigned look – the inevitability in it, obvious.

"I cherish it, so that it may set me free from my bondage, but until that spear finds me, I entreat the rest of you robed ones to leave. Leave while you still have life or choose my fate."

There was silence. Suddenly, two of the robed figures pulled off their hoods and fled. They were young men. Three steps later, their headless bodies walked another step before crumbling down to the floor where their heads had fallen. A man with a long, glistening sword laughed and threw off his long garb, splattered with the blood of the men.

"Stupid sword – always hated it," he muttered, as a matter of fact, before smoothing out his pinstriped suit. He reached over his back and pulled on his fedora.

"Uncle Luigi," Daniel balked, nearly throwing up at the sight of writhing bodies on the floor, "you survived the commandoes!"

Uncle Luigi glared. Turning to Amanda he muttered, "If I were you, I would be over and done with the sacrifice. The master is impatient, as is your father."

Amanda lifted the spear and walked towards Yokatherine and her father. Daniel looked on helplessly. What was he to do? He looked at his palm in frustration. "Just one time, my Lord – just one time," he prayed, "give me some power through this thorn to save these souls." He pushed out his hands as Amanda had done – no magical power erupted.

In a moment of divine inspiration, it struck him. Closing his eyes, he knelt. This was the Lord's way. This is what the Lord would have done, as he did like a meek lamb on Calvary. Daniel bent his head low and prayed. His mind was filled with visions of the ones that had gone before him, their vivid struggles, just like his now, playing out violently. Each in their own way had battled this evil. The preaching man, the monk, the friar, and the many that had carried the heavy mantle.

He pressed his hand to his chest and felt the Lord's thorn pierce him deeply. Pain shot through his body like a tsunami. He was in a courtyard. This time he knew the place instantly. The chief priests, the scribes, the Pharisees and the Romans, they were all there. The Son of Man looked in his direction. Just as he had humbly knelt and accepted his fate, so would Daniel. The scourge of the thorns absorbing the pain of evil and destroying it.

Daniel smelt the sweet fragrance of flowers. In the midst of the evil, it spread like a mystical charm. He pressed the Lord's thorn deeper into his chest, and felt the pain surge like a pulsating drill, bouncing from bone to bone with violent thuds. From deep within his pain, he heard the cries and shrieks of the evil ones around him.

He saw the suited man draw his gun and aim it in his direction as he yelled to Amanda. "The Spear, girl, the spear – finish that old whore and her father. Through and through one thrust – quickly." Daniel knew Yokatherine's prayers were doing exactly what his suffering was doing.

Uncle Luigi and Amanda moved simultaneously towards their targets as the hooded and garbed figures closed in with their pitchforks. The spear and the trigger were an instant away from their final attack when Ezekiel leaped. His sudden move caught Uncle Luigi and Amanda by surprise. His swinging right heel slammed deep into Amanda's stomach with a fierce Kiai. In the same motion, his head slammed into Uncle Luigi's chest sending him crashing into the wall. The gun fell. Before anyone could recover, Ezekiel grabbed the axe from the block. Yokatherine's father had already enveloped and brought down half the circle in shrieks of pain – all smothered with his gelatinous, yellow mess as Ezekiel's swinging axe did to the rest. Blood splattered everywhere as horrendous screams filled the air. Some of the hoods fell off and Daniel saw the men and women in the throes of death. Fixated eyes that stared into nothingness.

Daniel pierced the Lord's thorn harder into his chest. It seemed to get longer. He pictured the centurion standing over him with a laugh pushing the thorn deeper onto the Lord's head. He smiled in his excruciating pain wondering where the strength came from. He saw one of the heads roll off from the swing of the axe and fall at his feet. It was a woman. The pale white skin of her face was slashed. The axe had missed once before severing the head from the body. Her eyes stared in shock – wide open in death. This was not the way it was to be. This was not the way the Lord would have wanted it.

"Stop," Daniel begged, "stop, this is not how we must fight back."

Another deep voice thundered angrily as well, "Enough." It was the hooded man. His blazing red eyes stared in fury. His presence brought the room to a standstill. Yokatherine's father jumped and enveloped her in his arm as he noticed the hooded man's gaze follow her. Instead, the blazing eyes came to rest on Ezekiel. "You will make a fine soldier, lad. The ones you have slaughtered were dispensable."

"And so am I," Ezekiel yelled back, angrily.

"That's your choice, young man. You can walk free with this girl of yours, or choose death for both of you." The hooded man laughed, yanking Trisha from under his gown. Her bright blonde hair was tied back tightly. Her face was a mask of deathly fear. Her crying was done – resigned to the horror that completely controlled her. She still wore the medical gown. Her feet were bare below the knees. Daniel looked at her and felt the baby still safe inside.

Daniel saw another large figure sneak in behind the door, staying in the shadows. The hooded man noticed it as well but Trisha suddenly struggled to free herself distracting the hooded man in the process. He yanked her down painfully into submission.

"She carries something precious that my master relishes. Alas, today everything pales in comparison to something more precious than all the souls on earth. Let us make this quick, Thornbearer. How many of your friends will you sacrifice here today for that thorn?"

"All of them," Daniel answered instantly, sinking back from his kneeling position on his aching knees.

Unknown to those around him, he used the motion to stab himself deeper with the Lord's thorn and felt the shiver of pain strike the evil around. The hooded man stumbled back with a grimace, as a suddenly free Trisha ran to Ezekiel. They stared at each other before gripping each other fiercely in a tight embrace.

"If we live through this day, Ezekiel," Trisha spoke bravely, "I will bear our child for you, your God and for everything that is good in this world."

"And I will be the greatest father any child has ever known, Trisha," he answered her.

"Daniel," Ezekiel spoke loudly, "Trisha and I have discovered something greater than anything that we could have in a lifetime. Me, a scared funk, I found my courage here in the depths of evil. We will die here, sacrificed for God's glory rather than be the cause of your failure."

"Enough," the hooded man yelled, knowing what Daniel was on to, "damn all you Thornbearers."

"It's always been this way, hasn't it?" Daniel spoke softly, "we Thornbearers discovering the way, quietly and surely."

"Not today, my friend," the hooded man answered, "today we all burn here, and with us, the thorn."

"And yet, that would not be the end of it," Yokatherine's voice suddenly emerged. "You know, you and your ancestors have been through that. The Thornbearer, me, all of us," she swayed her hand, "all of us have seen the grace of the Lord – even these two kids," she said pointing to Ezekiel and Trisha. "We will die – blessed to be chosen as martyrs' for the Lord, and his thorn will find a new home."

"Then you shall be the first, you whore," the hooded man yelled, grabbing the spear from Amanda. Daniel knew he had to act fast or buy time to delay the charge. The hooded man was getting desperate. Daniel repeatedly stabbed himself in the chest as the blood poured and the evil around groaned. Uncle Luigi seemed to feel the worst of it. He coughed and began to sweat profusely.

The distraction was just what Daniel needed to rise and begin moving towards the hooded man. His plan, though crazy and suicidal, was the only way he figured this evil menace would end. The hooded man was still distracted. Uncle Luigi slammed his fedora down as sweat poured out from his head. He peeled off his coat as his body erupted in agony. The empty leather holster under the jacket was distinct. It caught everyone's attention including Uncle Luigi's, reminding him of the deadly weapon that had wrecked so much havoc that day. He was on the floor in an instant, suddenly erupting into life on finding it.

"Master," he called proudly, holding up his gun, "the only sure thing I know today is this. You know the damage it has done today. That stupid jumping kid, the blonde cop, the zombie crowd, the lustful cabbie – all fell by this today – let me finish it now." Daniel felt the pain of all the death the gun had caused. He sensed the hidden figure in the shadows react to the words as well. Uncle Luigi nearly fired off a shot at another fleeing acolyte but the hooded man swatted him down with a wave of his hand.

"Fool, are you dumb? We are this close to the thorn. That sound is all that is needed to bring those dozens of cops I sense outside, swarming in." He paused at the brief delight in Daniel's face.

"Oh I wouldn't celebrate so early, Thornbearer, they will all die, gunned down, as soon as I have taken that thing from you."

He threw the spear to Amanda, "Take down that good for nothing father and daughter and prove to me you are ready to take over my mantle." Daniel wondered how Amanda would react but her steely eyes looked on Yokatherine and her father with relish. She raised the spear

as Uncle Luigi aimed his gun towards him. Daniel raised his
arms and felt the figure by the door angrily raise something
as well.

"It's your call now, Daniel," the hooded man
suddenly addressed Daniel by name. "Come, shake my hand
willingly and the thorn will be mine. No one else has to die.
Nothing will change for now. You can all leave alive. You
may see nothing change in your lifetime, or the next. By the
time my master takes over you will be long gone, having
lived a life beyond any you can imagine. Luxuries, wealth,
power – anything. Take this daughter of mine – a slave for
your lifetime, bound to your service and I will give you a
thousand more like her. Why be foolish now?"

Daniel saw Uncle Luigi and Amanda desperate to
avenge them. Could he let Yokatherine, Ezekiel, Trisha and
her baby die so that the world be saved? It did not make
sense. Their death was exactly what evil would gloat over.
He prayed hard in his mind and in his soul.

He looked to Yokatherine for some inspiration and
found the same peaceful smile, as she remained wrapped
protectively in the arms of her father. He sensed each of
their struggles to sacrifice themselves to save the other. He
looked to Ezekiel and Trisha and saw a calm, confident
smile light their faces as they held each other tight – their
faces turned sideways pressed against each other, looking at
him. "Beautiful," he muttered, "but not the answer I'm
looking for."

He wondered how the Lord's thorn would survive if
they all sacrificed themselves that day. How would it find its
way to a new bearer? The preaching man came to his mind.
How had that angel lived and fought through his own
struggles with this hooded man? He remembered the
bleeding head and felt his own hand and chest bleeding
profusely now.

He looked to his right and gasped. A white glow was forming. His predecessor, the preaching man stood with a big, angelic smile. He held his left hand out and Daniel grabbed it with his right. They stood shoulder to shoulder and looked further right.

Daniel saw a smiling, bleeding friar take the preaching man's hand. Slowly, one by one, the line extended and Daniel knew he had the answer. This was not his fight alone. This was the day they would take down this evil one, together. Smiling and beaming, his right hand firmly grasping the one to his right, his left hand stabbing his chest furiously and openly with the thorn, he stepped forward towards the hooded man.

He was conscious of the whole line stepping forward and encircling the hooded man. The hooded man winced in pain from the stabbing of the thorn. Daniel noticed fear in the hooded face for the first time. The line was one step away from the hooded man. Daniel knew this was his to complete. Holding out both his hands in a brotherly embrace, he reached for the hooded man.

The mesmerized, hooded man barely broke out of the spell of love and peace that bound him, yelling, "Fools, now!" Daniel knew that fateful order. The spear flew out of Amanda's hand like a powerful thunderbolt. He felt it strike father and daughter in a single strike, piercing two souls simultaneously. Daniel cried knowing it was over.

He saw Uncle Luigi raise his gun to fire at him, at Ezekiel and Trisha. He heard the loud thuds of the bullets. He expected to see the two kids and himself go down in a pool of blood; instead, the blood spurted from Uncle Luigi's white shirt, as he crumbled to the floor. There was one shot, then another, and then another, as Daniel saw the bright flashes of the bullets leave the gun of the hidden figure by the door.

He heard the stranger's cry, "For my Clare – for Blondie2 – for my love."

Daniel felt his own body engulfed in a roaring blaze as he enveloped the hooded man in a tight embrace. He felt the sting of burning hair as it melted in the flames. He wondered for a minute if the hooded man had dragged him down into the burning fires of hell.

"What's that stink, Mummy?" he was asking as a little boy, remembering the smell of burning hair as they passed an open crematorium. The funeral pyre was blazing furiously as the flames leaped and danced. The memory of the body ablaze in a fire came roaring back from his childhood. This time he was the one in it.

He felt something grip his shirt at the back once, and then again, and rip it off as the blood flowed, or was it rivers of lava flowing down the sides of an erupting volcano. The blazing hands of the hooded man reached down, again and again, trying to tear away the body of the Thornbearer as it hugged him. Daniel wanted to scream in agony but a heavenly grace and strength began to fill him.

"There is peace and redemption for you too, my brother," Daniel whispered into the fierce evil that lit the space of where the stranger's face had been.

From deep within the chasm where the face had been, came the hideous answer, "Never, we all burn here today. Come, my daughter, we go together," the hooded man called but Daniel had seen Amanda escape. The stranger by the door had aimed at her too late having vented all of the fury of his gun at Uncle Luigi.

Somewhere in the distance, he heard a volley of bullets strike the building. It shuddered from the impact. There were cries as the bullets found their mark. He heard the heavy trampling of boots and knew the cops had stormed in – was it too late? Had they walked in to their own death?

"Welcome to Hell!" the hooded man screamed one last time, before erupting into a massive ball of fire. Daniel clasped his hands together behind the hooded man's back and felt the thorn pierce his right wrist as well. He heard an amen escape his own lips in answer to the hooded man's curse and then he felt nothing more.

XXVII

Amanda, the Evil Angel

Fr. Brian glanced up briefly. He could not understand the emotions overtaking him. It was a long gospel but his congregation stood strong through the afternoon, Good Friday Liturgy of the Word. He felt their eyes glued to him. He glanced at the other readers around the altar. They had all practiced their parts well. He loved the Gospel of Luke – its finer details about the crucifixion touched him deeply. He looked down at his finger following the reading, even though his mind had wandered away. Something had intruded into his thoughts and then vanished quickly – almost as if in reverence to the solemnity and significance of the moment he was in. The narrator continued and then it was his turn. His voice seemed to fail; he choked but managed to carry on.

"Amen, I say to you, today you will be with me in Paradise." The narrator continued on. "It was now about noon and darkness came over the whole land until three in the afternoon because of an eclipse of the sun. Then the veil of the temple was torn down the middle. Jesus cried out in a loud voice."

"Father, into your hands I commend my spirit."

They paused, sensing the cracking in Fr. Brian's voice as he spoke Jesus' final words before his death. The surprised narrator stared as well, before remembering to finish off, "And when he had said this he breathed his last."

"Please kneel," Fr. Brian heard the words leave him as if from a distance. The silence was absolute; he heard his own heavy breath and then a sob. For the first time ever, Fr. Brian wept with grief. He could not understand why. There was a sense of elation as Jesus conquered sin, yet it seemed real and closer. The grief felt deeply personal – a death – where? He begged the Lord to forgive him for his distraction and to help him. Closing his eyes Fr. Brian reached deep within and prayed. An evil, dark chamber zoomed by. A battle – his memory dug up that word from somewhere. His vision cast him three spirits in trouble and then there were just two. Daniel, Yokatherine and Ezekiel – he remembered and begged the Lord to be with them as a wave of helplessness swept over him.

* * *

The short radio burst from Officer Terri was a ramble. "Danger – am inside the house – recon report – armoured sentries moving into windows facing Lanark. Do not enter – repeat – do not enter – will provide further reports."

The arrival of the SWAT team was quick. The commissioner, glad at their arrival and in awe of Lynx, had instantly yielded control. His own cops, armed with their regular pistols, had backed away letting the heavily, armoured commandoes with their military grade weapons take control. Their fascinating array of electronic devices had him spellbound. By the time, he uttered his first word; each weapon inside the house had been marked out and covered by the unit.

"Suckers," he muttered, looking into the live handheld screen that Lynx showed him. The infrared dots lit up their intended targets. "How about those?" he pointed to a particular set of dots, "they seem to be behind the wall."

"Quick learning, commissioner – good – these weapons will take out a truck at a mile – the ammo – DU – depleted Uranium – will pass through a tank."

"Like the ones from a massive 30 mm GAU-8 Avenger Multi barrel Cannon on an A-10 Warthog?"

Lynx turned around in surprise with half a salute, "Right on, commissioner."

"I love that brute of a plane," the commissioner blushed, "wish I could fly one."

The volley of shots from Terri's gun from within the house caught the commissioner's and Lynx's ears distinctly. "Charge," the commissioner's voice erupted into the megaphone nearly at the same instant as Lynx's steady, steely, professional voice hissed, "Go," into his mouthpiece. The first blast of shots was over before the commissioner had recovered from his 'charge' command. He entered the building barely a minute after the attack but the commandoes had already taken control. Bright, white beams from their helmets pierced the darkness, moving about quickly. Their short, quick communication was orderly.

"Down here – this way," a hand grasped him. He followed Lynx quickly as a dark figure stumbled into them and fell. The female sigh was distinct.

"Sorry, that was my boot," the commissioner apologized, gasping at the stunning, disheveled young woman in black at his feet. She stared back, angry at having been brought down. A strange, violent and furious stare, that had the 2 powerful men gasp and take a rare step back.

"I'm fine, officers," she said rising quickly and forcing a smile, "the people down there need you badly, many dead and injured, a gunman too, down that way," she choked as heavy smoke and an acrid smell began to fill the air.

"Let me help," a commando stepped in extending a hand but she was up already and running to the door. The commissioner stared after the bewitchingly, beautiful woman as she stumbled through the door.

"Strange one, that. Exuded some kind of power, like a force that..." he left the sentence unfinished as Lynx tugged him on. They ran forward as more white beams lit the way. After the chaos above, a chilly silence greeted them below. A fire burned fiercely in the center with an unbearable stench.

"Commissioner, here." He recognized the desperate voice, "Kick that fireball – kick it." They stared blankly. "Just do it dammit," the voice yelled again, cracking in desperation. One of the commandoes stepped forward and punched the blaze with his heel. A fiery figure fell out of the blaze. They rolled him on the floor to douse the flames. "The second one for the day," the commando whispered under his breath.

"There should be another – watch out – that's Satan himself." They stopped for the briefest of seconds before Lynx drew a canister from his thigh pocket and sprayed the fire. It simply blazed on. "That's a fire straight from hell," they heard Terri splutter and collapse as the smoke spread.

The commissioner looked around. Bloodied bodies lay everywhere. Some were headless. A young boy and girl knelt, weeping and holding each other. The commandoes were huddled on the floor in one instant and then stepped away instantly. Before them stood the strangest sight. A woman seemed hung in mid-air, arched backward like a statue. Her arms spread-eagled – her long, white hair hanging limp. A long, black, shaft stuck out of her chest – a slimy, yellow gel dripped all over her.

"Sorry, couldn't save her, but I got our culprit for the day," Terri said with a sad voice. One of the commandoes stepped behind her and threw up and was helped outside.

"What evil is this?" another muttered, as the commissioner felt his feet wobble as the sight became clearer with all the lights focussed there. "She's been speared – its half way through – dead, do we…." Even the battle-hardened commandoes grappled for an answer.

"Draw it out for god's sake, towards the back, and here take this dead one out too – he's dead but we need him intact," Terri's voice rasped. He held one gun in his right hand and another with a kerchief in his left. Two commandoes ran out with the boy and the girl in their powerful arms just as the entire place erupted in a massive ball of fire. Lynx knelt as his men crawled towards the figure that had fallen out of the fire. A quick rub of the blackened face and he knew. "From the convenience store – we've got to save him." They got to the main floor as Lynx shouted into his mouthpiece.

"Evacuate – repeat, evacuate immediately."

Some of the commandoes were already on their way out, dragging strangely clothed men and women, their long black garbs torn and tattered.

"Report," Lynx asked, grabbing one of his men on the way out.

"Too many rooms above to secure – the fire is dense above – we've got to get out, this place will cave in anytime."

"Control – advice on evacuation status," Lynx ordered, as he reached the door. He had to ensure all his men were out. The radio crackled. A voice began to speak and was instantly drowned out by a thunderous roar next to him as the wooden stairwell collapsed in a massive heap. He breathed deeply into his mask, still reluctant to leave before a hand grabbed him and leaped out. Lynx and the commissioner rolled out into the small, ivy covered passage as burning debris rained down. He was up first dragging the commissioner this time as the façade came down in a massive crash. They did not stop running until they hit the MRAP.

"All men accounted for – safe and sound," the voice burst in.

"Survivors? Evacuation status?"

"One boy and girl – unhurt. One badly burnt man. One armed cop – smoke inhalation. And one woman – white – clad – dead – possibly stabbed. One dead male – possibly a killer as notified to the team. 15 others, males and females – arrested by the team. A dozen or more corpses left behind." The voice stopped as loud booms echoed from the building; each of them with an equally, violent flame that leaped higher into the air.

"The woman in black," Terri's choked voice spurted out, "a young, white woman in black – accomplice of the gang – a killer – what of her?"

Lynx and the commissioner looked at each other guiltily. They knew the woman had deceived them well.

"Terri, get into a cruiser, my man, and send out a description – she couldn't have gotten far away. She has no coat, no shoes; she will be easy to pick up. And, order follow-up teams to seal off all the streets around, don't want those pesky reporters in here, yet – and get the hazmat team in as well. Looks like a whole lot of chemicals or something blasting off," he finished, wrinkling his nose at the stench.

Another massive boom made them duck instinctively, as the first of the fire trucks pulled up. "What was this place?" Lynx asked, shocked at his own surprise, "here, in the middle of the city."

"An evil cult," the commissioner answered quickly as a possible, victorious story for the press began to form in his head.

"Evil cult, that's mild," Terri's voice reappeared, "that was a direct messenger of Satan, if not the *SOB* himself. Apparently the brown man – I mean – the guy that fell out of the fire has something from — never mind — he has something religious that the evil world has been after for 2000 years." He saw the sceptical looks of the two men and stopped. "I know, I know, sounds like a whole lot of bull, but are you surprised after what you saw?"

"What of the dead gunman?"

"He was their executioner, commissioner. Boasted about having taken down my Cla --, Officer Clare, the black kid and possibly everyone that fell this morning. Should be an easy match from forensics since we have the weapon."

"That means an innocent young man sits in our cells."

"Possibly — I heard enough to know that every single bullet came from the one gun..." Terri left the words hanging, suddenly realizing the finality of the situation.

*   *   *

It had been an easy escape for Amanda despite the flood of police and emergency vehicles that surrounded the house. How had they zeroed in so quickly? "Daniel," her mind answered and she gritted her teeth in anger. The smell from the poncho man's house, the cats, and her own newfound instinct had brought her quickly to the house just across. It had an evil desolation to it as if it stood on another dark planet. Death and pain hung in the air. There was no furniture, just mold-covered walls. No human had walked in there for a long time. The few that trespassed lay in the basement below — just skeletons.

She followed the yellow trail up the steps as the smell grew. The poncho man — she shivered with delight as the feel of power from the spear still lingered in her hand. The old woman had died instantly. The zombie father had been reduced to pulp. She remembered reaching out for the sword, grasping it as it responded to her call but the

shooting officer had denied her the final pleasure of
chopping off the white haired woman's head, smiling
blissfully in victory, as she died a martyr. The sight of the
speared woman, suspended in death gave her an exhilarating
thrill. A power she had never felt before had erupted
through her body as if she had just emerged successful from
a deadly ritual. She peeped into a faded old mirror, on a
landing, which stank of urine. Hideous eyes flashed once
and then paled as her original face appeared.

"Hello, Gorgeous," she growled and the mirror
crumbled. The blasts from across the street were getting
louder. With each explosion, she felt her power grow and
then there was a sudden silence as she entered the room
overlooking the street.

A long, dark, hooded gown floated in midair, in the
center of the room. It called to her. Stripping off her
clothes, naked, head bowed reverently, she fell on her knees
below it. It slipped over her raised hands onto her. She
closed her eyes and felt a powerful, evil presence slip over
her, possessing her completely.

"Daniel," she screamed in lust – for his body, his
soul, but above all, for the thorn that had been so
tantalizingly close.

"I will bring it to you, master," she swore, moving
to the little window smeared with the yellow stuff. It stank
of the poncho man as if he had just left the spot. She looked
at the chaos below. They were evacuating hurriedly from the
burning house. A limp, burnt body covered in soot was
brought out.

"Daniel," she licked her lips recognizing him
instantly. She saw him being laid out on a stretcher. She
sensed him alive and her body squirmed in delight, her
senses hungry, hands clawing the wall before her. She felt
her newfound power push her to storm out and steal him
away – for herself. A fleeting thought of the two of them,

hidden away from the world, happy in her little den, nearly made her leap out. He was surrounded by a ton of emergency personnel. "I will have you soon, darling, soon."

She wondered why he attracted her so — so very deeply. Was it just a plain romance — a love at first sight? She knew it was something more, for even from a distance, at the very first sight, her whole being had been drawn to him.

Was it their destinies — horribly entwined by some divine mistake? Her father's words echoed in her mind, "She is made for you, down to the last cell." Maybe she would win him over in time — him and the thorn — destroy it. Their offspring to be the most powerful, evil entity to ever walk this earth. Or, maybe it was simply because he was the man who had stolen her heart. In a single day, she had gone from a relatively innocent, helpless, broke, nervous wreck to being wildly in love; discovering and losing an evil father she had never known, and finally taking possession of a deadly power that she could not even begin to fathom. Her tiny, forsaken den now felt like a beautiful and peaceful paradise.

"We could have been so happy together, Daniel," a tiny voice mumbled somewhere deep within as they wheeled the stretcher towards an ambulance just below her window. She felt his spirit and knew the powers of evil had failed against him. His simple faith and sacrifice had crushed the evil that her father represented.

Anger, revenge and finally defeat engulfed her as she saw him open his eyes. Lying flat on the stretcher, she saw him look directly into her eyes, 3-storeys above him — two bright brown spots on a blackened face, lit up by the flashing lights all around. Despite the evil overtaking her, her heart leaped as their eyes met. His eyes danced mischievously, his soul pure, purified by the thorn, the fire, and the victory.

"I will save thee yet, my Angel," he laughed with a tease from inside the burnt body bathed in pure happiness. She slammed the wall in fury and disgust. Her anger exploded and in a final thrust, she hurled it out as a massive, black menacing cloud.

*   *   *

Down below, Lynx spoke quietly, "Have your men secure the site for the fire crews – time for my team to hand over control, commissioner." Commissioner Ford turned and saluted. He knew he would have lost a lot of men and women, had it not been for the commandoes. "In fact --," Lynx continued, but his sentence was drowned out by a massive blast as a massive, black cloud with a mighty gust of wind blew in from behind, knocking them down. The dark cloud hovered for an instant before the fire in the house leaped, fanned by the evil wind. The house erupted in a massive ball of fire that lit the sky. With a final ear-shattering boom it crumbled down – a column of pure ash and smoke was all that remained.

*   *   *

Deep within the destroyed house, Amanda felt the hooded man, her father, no more; sucked away, crushed in the eternal flame. She felt his power – a massive force finding its way to her. Looking down hungrily on the world she felt in command – her mission had begun.

Easter

XXVIII

Daniel, anew

The gentle breeze caressed Daniel's face, as it floated past. Sweet mists of fragrances tickled his nostrils with gentle bursts. Each flower had a turn to send their greetings along to him. Daniel stared lazily at the garden. It was green as far as the eye could see. From the lawn below to the tall sequoias that seemed to reach the sky, bright patches of colourful blooms, decorated the flow of the green.

Little streams flowed all over and their gentle, gurgling sounds seemed like a beat for the many birds that danced merrily in the branches around. He tried to move towards one of the streams but found himself rooted to the spot where he was. He found himself laid out on a soft, white bed. His own clothes were pristine white.

"Is this heaven?" he wondered. Someone held a large, cloth umbrella over his head. The sunshine was bright. He wanted some of its warmth. Before he could call out, someone sensed his need and moved the umbrella.

The sunshine felt good – warm and comforting. The warmth reminded him of something hot – burning – a fire? Something told him he had been in it. Was he burnt? Someone else seemed to have sensed that thought as well.

"It's unbelievable how someone could be enveloped by a blazing fire and come out unscathed," a burly voice remarked.

"Remember Isaiah chapter 43 verse 2," another answered, "when you pass through the waters, I will be with you; and when you pass through the rivers, they will not sweep over you. When you walk through the fire, you will not be burned; the flames will not set you ablaze." The voice sounded biblical – familiar.

A busy chirping nearby caught his attention. A flock of brightly colored little birds had been disturbed from their bush. "The garden of Eden?" he wondered as a bright light struck his eyes.

"He's awake, he's awake," a happy, little murmur went around. Where were these voices? Daniel tried to cover his eyes from the bright light but felt his hands unable to move.

And then for the first time, the light was real. He was not dead – nor in heaven but on a real bed. There was a window next to him. The sparrows that nested under the ledge of the roof had been rudely scared away – by a raven.

Daniel stared as the giant raven swooped onto the windowsill. Strange he thought, it seemed to look at him – with piercing, blazing red eyes.

There was another wild flutter of wings as a dove swooped down on the raven, knocking it off its perch. The whiteness of the dove was serene – powerful. It too seemed to look at Daniel – lovingly. It raised its wings, and with a mighty flutter and rose into the air – hovering long enough for Daniel to notice a dark black mark on its breast. White – dark mark – pierced – a spear crossed his mind suddenly.

"Yokatherine – oh my dear sweet, Jesus," he jumped, nearly sitting upright. A soft hand calmed him down.

"Careful, honey, you'll rip out the needles for the drip."

"She's ok – she's home with the Lord, in paradise," the same biblical voice answered.

"Father Brian!" he exclaimed.

"Daniel! We are so thrilled to see you awake and safe. You were so right when you mentioned the word battle. I saw some of the aerial coverage of the, err – battlefield, hard to believe all of you got out of there alive."

"I hope you got a complete account of what happened inside, Father."

"I got the whole story from Ezekiel, and Trisha too. They're right here," he said pointing to the two huddled in a corner with big shy smiles.

"What about Yokatherine?"

"Despite that horrible – well never mind, she had an ecstatic look on her face. It was as if the Lord himself came down to take her. Strangely, there was a bright red colored garment that --,"

"A poncho."

"A poncho! Never mind. As I was saying, a bright colored garment seemed inseparable from her. We buried her with it – yesterday."

"Thank you, Fr. Brian."

"You'll be happy to know that we buried your predecessor, the Thornbearer, with her as well. Like two angels, already with the Lord, they simply seemed asleep. We thought it was the best way to honour them so that they would truly rise with the Lord today."

"Even in death, Yokatherine saved a soul, her father. That means her father has been saved too and that also means its Easter today?"

"Sure is," Fr. Brian answered with a big laugh, walking around the bed to Daniel's left. He pulled up a stool and gently held Daniel's left hand. It did not feel painful anymore. Daniel looked down and noticed the tubes from the drip injected into his right hand. The left hand was still closed in a tight fist. "The doctors tried a lot but that fist of yours seems permanently closed."

"Dear Lord. I guess I didn't burn up with the --,"

"No, you didn't. In fact, you look all radiant and I wonder why?" Fr. Brian teased. "You will let me worship the thorn of my Lord won't you, Daniel?" he added quietly under his breath.

"Anytime, Father – though I have a feeling it might be a year away. By the way, was it hard to believe Ezekiel's account? A zombie father and a loving daughter, both brutally speared, Satan's chapel, human sacrifices – even a fire from hell!"

"Ezekiel? Gosh no," Fr. Brian laughed, but continued quickly seeing the puzzled look on Daniel's face. "It was this big gentleman here – Officer Terri – who filled me in on a ton of other details, including, sadly the evil dispensed by my own Uncle Luigi. In fact, Ezekiel tells me that it if wasn't for Officer Terri, you, Trisha and he would have been a part of the long list of victims that fell to my uncle's evil weapon."

Daniel stared at the massive hulk that stepped out of shadows and stood by his bed. "My sincere apologies for suspecting you, Daniel."

"And, my gratitude for saving my life and the lives of my friends here. Thank you, officer." Daniel answered. "What about my little trigger-happy friend Dylan?"

"He's home now. The commissioner had him released the same evening, though he needs a good talking to!"

"My responsibility. These cops, I tell you, great people," Fr. Brian jumped in with a mixture of relief and gratitude written all over his face.

"I am so sorry about your colleague, officer," Daniel added gently taking the cop's hand. He sensed the cop's pain. He was on the verge of tears, "She is home with the Lord now."

"As is Dylan – home with his mother now," the cop added, quickly changing the subject.

"I'm so glad for his mother," Daniel said.

"You should be!" Fr. Brian excitedly interrupted, "the woman is so excited. She has promised us the biggest Filipino banquet ever. I hear you played a big part in helping him surrender safely and peacefully as well."

"Just like you said, Father Brian – that's how the Lord works. Oh, what of my car?"

"Don't worry it's all taken care of. With the commissioner and Officer Terri here, as our new allies, there is nothing to worry about. I still have those cameras that your, err, your lady friend left behind."

Daniel burst out laughing. "I'll make sure I get them over to her."

"You're not going to go and --,"

Daniel laughed again, rather hard, and choked, "Don't worry, Father Brian – just think it was a bad dream. In fact --," he tried to continue but burst into a bout of coughing.

"Folks, I think it's time for everyone to leave," scolded the nurse who had been busy with the stethoscope, pressure gauge, charts and a ton of other medical chores by his bedside.

"I think that's a great idea!" Fr. Brian said, though the disappointment in his voice gave him away as he bent down and kissed Daniel's left fist. Ezekiel left with a sheepish grin and a wave, but Trisha walked right over and kissed him hard.

"Ezekiel and I are going to have our baby and I am going to be counting on your help in a big way."

"Brave girl," he smiled choking up a bit, "count on it, always."

The giant frame of Officer Terri half saluted, tapped his toes and left.

"You must sleep," the nurse, chided.

"What's wrong with me – definitely not burnt."

"True now, but when they brought you in, you were charred black. None of us have seen anything like it, even though we've treated thousands in this burns unit. The burns simply fell away like dried scabs. We do need to observe you though. The doctor thinks you've inhaled a lot of acidic fumes."

"Toxic?"

"Quite possibly, young man," she said holding a spoon of some reddish liquid to his lips. It felt soothing on his parched throat.

"Where am I?"

"St. Gabriel's Hospital – Burns Unit. Now sleep," she said with a smile. She was halfway out of the door but turned and walked right back to him.

"Just between you and me – I kind of followed the conversation that group had as they waited by your bedside. Not too impossible to believe after all those crazy events that happened in our city last Friday. It's scary with so many dead."

"You can relax now, it's over."

"I know, but for some reason, I keep coming back here to your bedside. There is calm, peaceful presence here – blows away all my tensions."

"Come back anytime you want, doc," he teased. Daniel waited for the door to close before looking out to the window again. The dove was gone.

"Oh Yokatherine – Rest in Peace with the Lord," he prayed, blowing a kiss to the beautiful sunshine outside. A gust of wind picked up the snow piled over the roof ledge and sent it crashing over.

"As if I need a reminder of that," he muttered to himself. The room was silent and he felt lonely. He knew he was longing to open his left fist and venerate the little weapon the Lord had left behind. His feelings told him the Lord's thorn would be gone – buried deep within.

The loneliness overpowered him even more. He lifted his hand to his face and opened his palm gently. It opened easily. The swollen, bluish-scarred hand was gone. Instead, his palm seemed pinker than it had ever been. He looked at the center and noticed the little black dot.

"My Lord and My God – let me suffer with thee," he exclaimed, missing the Lord's thorn already even though it was so close to him.

Daniel closed his eyes and drifted off to sleep. It was a long while before his eyes opened again. A dull grey sky had replaced the brightness of the morning. The winds blew harder and his ears caught their fierce whooshing outside. The loneliness still lingered. He tried to close his eyes; instead, a little squeak startled him. Someone was pushing open the door, inch by inch so as not to disturb him. Instead, the slow pushing created, even more, squeaks.

"Darn it – what the hell," the pretty voice exclaimed and marched in. Daniel stared and stared, and burst out laughing and crying at the same time.

"Where is she?" she screamed – hands on her hips. She glared a while longer and then ran over to his bed.

"Oh my God – you're in a hospital and look at me screaming," Michelle suddenly whispered before burying him under her in the biggest hug ever.

"I don't understand anything, babes. First; Father Brian calls long distance, to India that too, and tells me I'd better be here if I don't want to lose you. Then, he answers your phone and picks me up from the airport – says nothing on the way. Strangest of all he directs me to the Burns-Unit. I almost died. And instead look at you here, looking all fresh and rosy, like a Johnson's Baby."

Daniel stared at her for a long time and felt sick at how easily he had risked their love and many years of marriage. Voices approached in the passage outside. Michelle sat gripping his hands tightly.

"You know; you've not said a word since I walked in."

"I love thee. Now take me home, my beautiful," he finally whispered.